Classic Crime Stories

13 TALES FROM EDGAR ALLAN POE TO LAWRENCE BLOCK

Edited by
James Daley

DOVER PUBLICATIONS, INC.
Mineola, New York

Copyright

Bibliographical Note

This Dover edition, first published in 2007, is a new collection of thirteen stories reprinted from standard texts. Please see the Acknowledgments for additional bibliographical information.

Library of Congress Cataloging-in-Publication Data

Classic crime stories: 13 tales from Edgar Allan Poe to Lawrence Block / edited by James Daley.
    p. cm.
ISBN-13: 978-0-486-45682-9 (pbk.)
ISBN-10: 0-486-45682-X (pbk.)
    1. Detective and mystery stories, American. 2. Detective and mystery stories, English. I. Daley, James, 1979–

PS648.D4C53 2007
823'.087208—dc22

                                2007012780

Manufactured in the United States by LSC Communications
45682X04   2018
www.doverpublications.com

Acknowledgments

"The Gutting of Couffignal" from *The Big Knockover* by Dashiell Hammett, copyright © 1966 by Lillian Hellman. Reprinted by permission of Random House, Inc.

"Pastorale" by James M. Cain. First published in *The American Mercury*. Copyright © 1928 by The American Mercury, Inc. Copyright © renewed 1955 by James M. Cain. Reprinted by permission of Harold Ober Associates, Incorporated.

"I'll be Waiting" from *The Simple Art of Murder* by Raymond Chandler. Copyright © 1950 by Raymond Chandler. Copyright © renewed 1978 by Helga Greene. Reprinted by permission of Houghton Mifflin Company. All rights reserved.

"Slowly, Slowly in the Wind" from *Slowly, Slowly in the Wind* by Patricia Highsmith. Copyright © 1972, 1973, 1974, 1976, 1977, and 1979 by Patricia Highsmith. Copyright © 1993 by Diogenes Verlag AG, Zurich. Reprinted by permission of W.W. Norton & Company, Inc.

"By the Dawn's Early Light" from *Some Days You Get the Bear* by Lawrence Block, copyright © 1994 by Lawrence Block. Reprinted by permission of HarperCollins, Publishers.

Introduction

When Edgar Allan Poe first published "The Murders in the Rue Morgue" in *Graham's Magazine* in 1841, he unknowingly ushered in what would become one of literature's greatest and most beloved of genres: the crime story. A beautiful and grisly tale of how Parisian *Chevalier* C. Auguste Dupin solves the mystery of a brutal double homicide, "The Murders at the Rue Morgue" provided the impetus and the model for every story in this collection—from Doyle's Sherlock Holmes to Block's Matthew Scudder—and indeed, the entire canon of crime and detective fiction, as well.

The class of crime fiction that owes its emergence and popularity most directly to Poe is the Whodunit. Nearly every example of a Whodunit is a structural imitation of "The Murders in the Rue Morgue," down to each turn of the plot: First, a crime (usually a murder) is committed, and the usual authorities are powerless to solve it. Then, a great sleuth is brought into the case. He or she inspects the scene, makes inquiries, deduces, and, inevitably, reveals the solution to the crime, often coupled with an ingenious device for catching the culprit. Sir Arthur Conan Doyle was the most famous purveyor of this brand of crime story, but Orczy, Chesterton, Freeman, Green, and countless others rode quite successfully on Doyle and Poe's coattails for decades since.

The second class of crime fiction represented in this collection is that of the Private Eye story—a class that, although certainly a later incarnation, nonetheless traces its heritage back to Poe and his *Monsieur Dupin*. The Private Eye story retains a good deal of

Poe's original structure (there is a crime, or mystery, which a brilliant detective has been brought in to solve); however, the focus is more on action than deduction, and the heroes are lauded more for their common-man cunning and two-fisted street-smarts than their erudite intelligence or keen powers of observation. Furthermore, being an almost wholly American class of crime fiction, the Private Eye story espouses a cold, capitalistic nihilism, which is quite contrary to the idealistic Victorian nature of its mostly British predecessors. This is evident from the early twentieth-century work of Dashiell Hammett and Raymond Chandler to the much later work of Lawrence Block.

Finally, there is the class of crime fiction known as the Pure Crime story, which traces its heritage back to Poe more through its fascination with the criminal act than through any reliance on a brilliant sleuth. Reaching the height of its popularity during the *noir* era, this type of story features no prominent detective whatsoever; rather, these are tales of crime for crime's sake. Often dark, violent, and even more nihilistic than the Private Eye story, these tales feature the criminal as an anti-hero, glorifying the crimes he perpetrates, supported by a cast of characters even less admirable than he. One of the first authors to explore this type of crime story was British author E. W. Hornung (ironically, a brother-in-law of Arthur Conan Doyle). Although Hornung's protagonist, A. J. Raffles, was less grim and violent than his successors (he refers to himself as a "gentleman thief"), he nonetheless laid the groundwork for the criminal-as-hero role that was taken up with such success in the fiction of James M. Cain, Cornell Woolrich, and, even later, Patricia Highsmith.

All in all, what we have in this collection is not so much a representative history of the crime story, as a small sampling of its major authors and movements. From the deductive detectives of Doyle and Poe to the hardened private eyes of Chandler and Hammett to the cold criminals of Highsmith and Cain, this anthology aims first and foremost to engross, enthrall, intrigue, and entertain.

JAMES DALEY, Editor
December 2006

Contents

The Murders in the Rue Morgue
(1841)
Edgar Allan Poe

What song the Syrens sang, or what name Achilles assumed when he hid himself among women, although puzzling questions are not beyond all conjecture.

—Sir Thomas Browne, "Urn-Burial"

The mental features discoursed of as the analytical, are, in themselves, but little susceptible of analysis. We appreciate them only in their effects. We know of them, among other things, that they are always to their possessor, when inordinately possessed, a source of the liveliest enjoyment. As the strong man exults in his physical ability, delighting in such exercises as call his muscles into action, so glories the analyst in that moral activity which *disentangles*. He derives pleasure from even the most trivial occupations bringing his talents into play. He is fond of enigmas, of conundrums, of hieroglyphics; exhibiting in his solutions of each a degree of *acumen* which appears to the ordinary apprehension preternatural. His results, brought about by the very soul and essence of method, have, in truth, the whole air of intuition. The faculty of re-solution is possibly much invigorated by mathematical study, and especially by that highest branch of it which, unjustly, and merely on account of its retrograde operations, has been called, as if *par excellence*, analysis. Yet to calculate is not in itself to analyze. A chess-player, for example, does the one without effort at the other. It follows that the game of chess, in its effects upon mental character, is greatly misunderstood. I am not now writing a treatise, but simply prefacing a somewhat peculiar narrative by observations very much at random; I will, therefore, take occasion to assert that the higher powers of the reflective intellect are more decidedly and more usefully tasked by the unostentatious game of draughts than by all the elaborate frivolity of chess. In this latter, where the pieces have different and *bizarre* motions, with various and variable values, what is only complex is mistaken (a not unusual error) for what is profound. The *attention* is here called powerfully into play. If it flag for an instant, an oversight is committed, resulting in injury or defeat. The possible moves being not only manifold but involute, the chances of such oversights are multiplied; and in nine cases out of ten it is the more concentrative rather than the more acute player who conquers. In draughts, on the contrary, where the moves are *unique* and have but little variation, the probabilities of inadvertence are diminished, and the mere attention being left comparatively unemployed, what advantages are obtained by either party are obtained by superior *acumen*. To be less abstract—Let us suppose a game of draughts where the pieces are reduced to four kings, and where, of course, no oversight is to be expected. It is obvious that here the victory can be decided (the players being at all equal) only by some *recherché* movement, the result of some strong exertion of the intellect. Deprived of ordinary resources, the analyst throws himself into the spirit of his opponent, identifies himself therewith, and not unfrequently sees thus, at a glance, the sole methods (sometimes indeed absurdly simple ones) by which he may seduce into error or hurry into miscalculation.

Whist has long been noted for its influence upon what is termed calculating power; and men of the highest order of intellect have been known to take an apparently unaccountable delight in it, while eschewing chess as frivolous. Beyond doubt there is nothing of a similar nature so greatly tasking the faculty of analysis. The best chess-player in Christendom *may* be little more than the best player of chess; but proficiency in whist implies capacity for success in all these more important undertakings where mind struggles with mind. When I say proficiency, I mean that perfection in the game which includes a comprehension of *all* the sources whence legitimate advantage may be derived. These are not only manifold but multiform, and lie frequently among recesses of thought altogether inaccessible to the ordinary understanding. To observe attentively is to remember distinctly; and, so far, the concentrative chess-player will do very well at whist; while the rules of Hoyle (themselves based upon the mere mechanism of the game) are sufficiently and generally comprehensible. Thus to have a retentive memory, and to proceed by "the book," are points commonly regarded as the sum total of good playing. But it is in matters beyond the limits of mere rule that the skill of the analyst is evinced. He makes, in silence, a host of observations and inferences. So, perhaps, do his companions; and the difference in the extent of the information obtained, lies not so much in the validity of the inference as in the quality of the observation. The necessary knowledge is that of *what* to observe. Our player confines himself not at all; nor, because the game is the object, does he reject deductions from things external to the game. He examines the countenance of his partner, comparing it carefully with that of each of his opponents. He considers the mode of assorting the cards in each hand; often counting trump by trump, and honor by honor, through the glances bestowed by their holders upon each. He notes every variation of face as the play progresses, gathering a fund of thought from the differences in the expression of certainty, of surprise, of triumph, or chagrin. From the manner of gathering up a trick he judges whether the person taking it can make another in the suit. He recognizes what is played through feint, by the air with which it is thrown upon the table. A casual or inadvertent word; the accidental dropping or turning of a card, with the accompanying anxiety or carelessness in regard to its concealment; the counting of the tricks, with the order of their arrangement; embarrassment, hesitation, eagerness or trepidation—all afford, to his apparently intuitive perception, indications of the true state of affairs. The first two or three rounds having been played, he is in full possession of the contents of each hand, and thenceforward puts down his cards with as absolute a precision of purpose as if the rest of the party had turned outward the faces of their own.

The analytical power should not be confounded with simple

ingenuity; for while the analyst is necessarily ingenious, the ingenious man is often remarkably incapable of analysis. The consecutive or combining power, by which ingenuity is usually manifested, and to which the phrenologists (I believe erroneously) have assigned a separate organ, supposing it a primitive faculty, has been so frequently seen in those whose intellect bordered otherwise upon idiocy, as to have attracted general observation among writers on morals. Between ingenuity and the analytic ability there exists a difference far greater, indeed, than that between the fancy and the imagination, but of a character very strictly analogous. It will be found, in fact, that the ingenious are always fanciful, and the *truly* imaginative never otherwise than analytic.

The narrative which follows will appear to the reader somewhat in the light of a commentary upon the propositions just advanced.

Residing in Paris during the spring and part of the summer of 18—, I there became acquainted with a Monsieur C. Auguste Dupin. This young gentleman was of an excellent—indeed of an illustrious family, but, by a variety of untoward events, had been reduced to such poverty that the energy of his character succumbed beneath it, and he ceased to bestir himself in the world, or to care for the retrieval of his fortunes. By courtesy of his creditors, there still remained in his possession a small remnant of his patrimony; and, upon the income arising from this, he managed, by means of rigorous economy, to procure the necessaries of life, without troubling himself about its superfluities. Books, indeed, were his sole luxuries, and in Paris these are easily obtained.

Our first meeting was at an obscure library in the Rue Montmartre, where the accident of our both being in search of the same very rare and very remarkable volume, brought us into closer communion. We saw each other again and again. I was deeply interested in the little family history which he detailed to me with all that candor which a Frenchman indulges whenever mere self is the theme. I was astonished, too, at the vast extent of his reading; and, above all, I felt my soul enkindled within me by the wild fervor, and the vivid freshness of his imagination. Seeking in Paris the objects I then sought, I felt that the society of such a man would be to me a treasure beyond price; and this feeling I frankly confided to him. It was at length arranged that we should live together during my stay in the city; and as my worldly circumstances were somewhat less embarrassed than his own, I was permitted to be at the expense of renting, and furnishing in a style which suited the rather fantastic gloom of our common temper, a time-eaten and grotesque mansion, long deserted through superstitions into which we did not inquire, and tottering to its fall in a retired and desolate portion of the Faubourg St. Germain.

Had the routine of our life at this place been known to the world, we should have been regarded as madmen—although, perhaps, as madmen of a harmless nature. Our seclusion was perfect. We admitted no visitors. Indeed the locality of our retirement had been carefully kept a secret from my own former associates; and it had been many years since Dupin had ceased to know or be known in Paris. We existed within ourselves alone.

It was a freak of fancy in my friend (for what else shall I call it?) to be enamored of the Night for her own sake; and into this *bizarrerie*, as into all his others, I quietly fell; giving myself up to his wild whims with a perfect *abandon*. The sable divinity would not herself dwell with us always; but we could counterfeit her presence. At the first dawn of the morning we closed all the massy shutters of our old building; lighted a couple of tapers which, strongly perfumed, threw out only the ghastliest and feeblest of rays. By the aid of these we then busied our souls in dreams—reading, writing, or conversing, until warned by the clock of the advent of the true Darkness. Then we sallied forth into the streets, arm in arm, continuing the topics of the day, or roaming far and wide until a late hour, seeking, amid the wild lights and shadows of the populous city, that infinity of mental excitement which quiet observation can afford.

At such times I could not help remarking and admiring (although from his rich ideality I had been prepared to expect it) a peculiar analytic ability in Dupin. He seemed, too, to take an eager delight in its exercise—if not exactly in its display—and did not hesitate to confess the pleasure thus derived. He boasted to me, with a low chuckling laugh, that most men, in respect to himself, wore windows in their bosoms, and was wont to follow up such assertions by direct and very startling proofs of his intimate knowledge of my own. His manner at these moments was frigid and abstract; his eyes were vacant in expression; while his voice, usually a rich tenor, rose into a treble which would have sounded petulantly but for the deliberateness and entire distinctness of the enunciation. Observing him in these moods, I often dwelt meditatively upon the old philosophy of the Bi-Part Soul, and amused myself with the fancy of a double Dupin—the creative and the resolvent.

Let it not be supposed, from what I have just said, that I am detailing any mystery, or penning any romance. What I have described in the Frenchman was merely the result of an excited, or perhaps of a diseased intelligence. But of the character of his remarks at the periods in question an example will best convey the idea.

We were strolling one night down a long dirty street, in the vicinity of the Palais Royal. Being both, apparently, occupied with thought, neither of us had spoken a syllable for fifteen minutes at least. All at once Dupin broke forth with these words:

"He is a very little fellow, that's true, and would do better for the *Théâtre des Variétés.*"

"There can be no doubt of that," I replied unwittingly, and not at first observing (so much had I been absorbed in reflection) the extraordinary manner in which the speaker had chimed in with my meditations. In an instant afterward I recollected myself, and my astonishment was profound.

"Dupin," said I, gravely, "this is beyond my comprehension. I do not hesitate to say that I am amazed, and can scarcely credit my senses. How was it possible you should know I was thinking of—?" Here I paused, to ascertain beyond a doubt whether he really knew of whom I thought.

"—of Chantilly," said he, "why do you pause? You were remarking to yourself that his diminutive figure unfitted him for tragedy."

This was precisely what had formed the subject of my reflections. Chantilly was a *quondam* cobbler of the Rue St. Denis, who, becoming stage-mad, had attempted the *rôle* of Xerxes, in Crébillon's tragedy so called, and been notoriously Pasquinaded for his pains.

"Tell me, for Heaven's sake," I exclaimed, "the method—if method there is—by which you have been enabled to fathom my soul in this matter." In fact I was even more startled than I would have been willing to express.

"It was the fruiterer," replied my friend, "who brought you to the conclusion that the mender of soles was not of sufficient height for Xerxes *et id genus omne.*"

"The fruiterer!—you astonish me—I know no fruiterer whomsoever."

"The man who ran up against you as we entered the street—it may have been fifteen minutes ago."

I now remembered that, in fact, a fruiterer, carrying upon his head a large basket of apples, had nearly thrown me down, by accident, as we passed from the Rue C—— into the thoroughfare where we stood; but what this had to do with Chantilly I could not possibly understand.

There was not a particle of *charlatanerie* about Dupin. "I will explain," he said, "and that you may comprehend all clearly, we will first retrace the course of your meditations, from the moment in which I spoke to you until that of the *rencontre* with the fruiterer in question. The larger links of the chain run thus—Chantilly, Orion, Dr. Nicholas, Epicurus, Stereotomy, the street stones, the fruiterer."

There are few persons who have not, at some period of their lives, amused themselves in retracing the steps by which particular conclusions of their own minds have been attained. The occupation is often full of interest; and he who attempts it for the first time is astonished by the apparently illimitable distance and incoherence between the starting-point and the goal. What, then, must have been my amazement when I heard the Frenchman speak what he had just spoken? And when I could not help acknowledging that he had spoken the truth. He continued:

"We had been talking of horses, if I remember aright, just before leaving the Rue C——. This was the last subject we discussed. As we crossed into this street, a fruiterer, with a large basket upon his head, brushing quickly past us, thrust you upon a pile of paving-stones collected at a spot where the causeway is undergoing repair. You stepped upon one of the loose fragments, slipped, slightly strained your ankle, appeared vexed or sulky, muttered a few words, turned to look at the pile, and then proceeded in silence. I was not particularly attentive to what you did; but observation has become with me, of late, a species of necessity.

"You kept your eyes upon the ground—glancing, with a petulant expression, at the holes and ruts in the pavement (so that I saw you were still thinking of the stones), until we reached the little alley called Lamartine, which has been paved, by way of experiment, with the overlapping and riveted blocks. Here your countenance brightened up, and, perceiving your lips move, I could not doubt that you murmured the word 'stereotomy,' a term very affectedly applied to this species of pavement. I knew that you could not say to yourself 'stereotomy' without being brought to think of atomies, and thus of the theories of Epicurus; and since, when we discussed this subject not very long ago, I mentioned to you how singularly, yet with how little notice, the vague guesses of that noble Greek had met with confirmation in the late nebular cosmogony, I felt that you could not avoid casting your eyes upward to the great *nebula* in Orion, and I certainly expected that you would do so. You did look up; and I was now assured that I had correctly followed your steps. But in that bitter *tirade* upon Chantilly, which appeared in yesterday's '*Musée*,' the satirist, making some disgraceful allusions to the cobbler's change of name upon assuming the buskin, quoted a Latin line about which we have often conversed. I mean the line

Perdidit antiquum litera prima sonum.

I had told you that this was in reference to Orion, formerly written Urion; and, from certain pungencies connected with this explanation, I was aware that you could not have forgotten it. It was clear, therefore, that you would not fail to combine the two ideas of Orion and Chantilly. That you did combine them I saw by the character of the smile which passed over your lips. You thought of the poor cobbler's immolation. So far, you had been stooping in your gait; but now I saw you draw yourself up to your full height. I was then sure that you reflected upon the diminutive figure of Chantilly. At this point I interrupted your meditations to remark that as, in fact, he *was* a very little fellow—that Chantilly—he would do better at the *Théâtre des Variétés*."

Not long after this, we were looking over an evening edition of the "Gazette des Tribunaux," when the following paragraphs arrested our attention.

"EXTRAORDINARY MURDERS.—This morning, about three o'clock, the inhabitants of the Quartier St. Roch were aroused from sleep by a succession of terrific shrieks, issuing, apparently, from the fourth story of a house in the Rue Morgue, known to be in the sole occupancy of one Madame L'Espanaye, and her daughter, Mademoiselle Camille L'Espanaye. After some delay, occasioned by a fruitless attempt to procure admission in the usual manner, the gateway was broken in with a crowbar, and eight or ten of the neighbors entered, accompanied by two *gendarmes*. By this time the cries had ceased; but, as the party rushed up the first flight of stairs, two or more rough voices, in angry contention, were distinguished, and seemed to proceed from the upper part of the house. As the second landing was reached, these sounds, also, had ceased, and everything remained perfectly quiet. The party spread themselves, and hurried from room to room. Upon arriving at a large back chamber in the fourth story (the door of which, being found locked, with the key inside, was forced open), a spectacle presented itself which struck every one present not less with horror than with astonishment.

"The apartment was in the wildest disorder—the furniture broken and thrown about in all directions. There was only one bedstead; and from this the bed had been removed, and thrown into the middle of the floor. On a chair lay a razor, besmeared with blood. On the hearth were two or three long and thick tresses of grey human hair, also dabbled in blood, and seeming to have been pulled out by the roots. Upon the floor were found four Napoleons, an ear-ring of topaz, three large silver spoons, three smaller of *métal d'Alger*, and two bags containing nearly four thousand francs in gold. The drawers of a *bureau*, which stood in one corner, were open, and had been, apparently, rifled, although many articles still remained in them. A small iron safe was discovered under the *bed* (not under the bedstead). It was open, with the key still in the door. It had no contents beyond a few old letters, and other papers of little consequence.

"Of Madame L'Espanaye no traces were here seen; but an

unusual quantity of soot being observed in the fireplace, a search was made in the chimney and (horrible to relate!) the corpse of the daughter, head downward, was dragged therefrom; it having been thus forced up the narrow aperture for a considerable distance. The body was quite warm. Upon examining it, many excoriations were perceived, no doubt occasioned by the violence with which it had been thrust up and disengaged. Upon the face were many severe scratches, and, upon the throat, dark bruises, and deep indentations of finger nails, as if the deceased had been throttled to death.

"After a thorough investigation of every portion of the house, without farther discovery, the party made its way into a small paved yard in the rear of the building, where lay the corpse of the old lady, with her throat so entirely cut that, upon an attempt to raise her, the head fell off. The body, as well as the head, was fearfully mutilated—the former so much so as scarcely to retain any semblance of humanity.

"To this horrible mystery there is not as yet, we believe, the slightest clew."

The next day's paper had these additional particulars.

"*The Tragedy in the Rue Morgue.* Many individuals have been examined in relation to this most extraordinary and frightful affair." [The word '*affaire*' has not yet, in France, that levity of import which it conveys with us,] "but nothing whatever has transpired to throw light upon it. We give below all the material testimony elicited.

"*Pauline Dubourg*, laundress, deposes that she has known both the deceased for three years, having washed for them during that period. The old lady and her daughter seemed on good terms—very affectionate toward each other. They were excellent pay. Could not speak in regard to their mode or means of living. Believed that Madame L. told fortunes for a living. Was reputed to have money put by. Never met any persons in the house when she called for the clothes or took them home. Was sure that they had no servant in employ. There appeared to be no furniture in any part of the building except in the fourth story.

"*Pierre Moreau*, tobacconist, deposes that he has been in the habit of selling small quantities of tobacco and snuff to Madame L'Espanaye for nearly four years. Was born in the neighborhood, and has always resided there. The deceased and her daughter had occupied the house in which the corpses were found, for more than six years. It was formerly occupied by a jeweller, who under-let the upper rooms to various persons. The house was the property of Madame L. She became dissatisfied with the abuse of the premises by her tenant, and moved into them herself, refusing to let any portion. The old lady was childish. Witness had seen the daughter some five or six times during the six years. The two lived an exceedingly retired life—were reputed to have money. Had heard it said among the neighbors that Madame L. told fortunes—did not believe it. Had never seen any person enter the door except the old lady and her daughter, a porter once or twice, and a physician some eight or ten times.

"Many other persons, neighbors, gave evidence to the same effect. No one was spoken of as frequenting the house. It was not known whether there were any living connexions of Madame L. and her daughter. The shutters of the front windows were seldom opened. Those in the rear were always closed, with the exception of the large back room, fourth story. The house was a good house—not very old.

"*Isidore Muset, gendarme,* deposes that he was called to the house about three o'clock in the morning, and found some twenty or thirty persons at the gateway, endeavoring to gain admittance. Forced it open, at length, with a bayonet—not with a crowbar. Had but little difficulty in getting it open, on account of its being a double or folding gate, and bolted neither at bottom nor top. The shrieks were continued until the gate was forced—and then suddenly ceased. They seemed to be screams of some person (or persons) in great agony—were loud and drawn out, not short and quick. Witness led the way upstairs. Upon reaching the first landing, heard two voices in loud and angry contention—the one a gruff voice, the other much shriller—a very strange voice. Could distinguish some words of the former, which was that of a Frenchman. Was positive that it was not a woman's voice. Could distinguish the words 'sacré' and 'diable.' The shrill voice was that of a foreigner. Could not be sure whether it was the voice of a man or of a woman. Could not make out what was said, but believed the language to be Spanish. The state of the room and of the bodies was described by this witness as we described them yesterday.

"*Henri Duval,* a neighbor, and by trade a silversmith, deposes that he was one of the party who first entered the house. Corroborates the testimony of Muset in general. As soon as they forced an entrance, they reclosed the door, to keep out the crowd, which collected very fast, notwithstanding the lateness of the hour. The shrill voice, the witness thinks, was that of an Italian. Was certain it was not French. Could not be sure that it was a man's voice. It might have been a woman's. Was not acquainted with the Italian language. Could not distinguish the words, but was convinced by the intonation that the speaker was an Italian. Knew Madame L. and her daughter. Had conversed with both frequently. Was sure that the shrill voice was not that of either of the deceased.

"—*Odenheimer, restaurateur.* This witness volunteered his testimony. Not speaking French, was examined through an interpreter. Is a native of Amsterdam. Was passing the house at the time of the shrieks. They lasted for several minutes—probably ten. They were long and loud—very awful and distressing. Was one of those who entered the building. Corroborated the previous evidence in every respect but one. Was sure the shrill voice was that of a man—of a Frenchman. Could not distinguish the words uttered. They were loud and quick—unequal—spoken apparently in fear as well as in anger. The voice was harsh—not so much shrill as harsh. Could not call it a shrill voice. The gruff voice said repeatedly 'sacré,' 'diable,' and once 'mon Dieu.'

"*Jules Mignaud,* banker, of the firm of Mignaud et Fils, Rue Deloraine. Is the elder Mignaud. Madame L'Espanaye had some property. Had opened an account with his banking house in the spring of the year———(eight years previously). Made frequent deposits in small sums. Had checked for nothing until the third day before her death, when she took out in person the sum of 4000 francs. This sum was paid in gold, and a clerk sent home with the money.

"*Adolphe Le Bon,* clerk to Mignaud et Fils, deposes that on the day in question, about noon, he accompanied Madame L'Espanaye to her residence with the 4000 francs, put up in two bags. Upon the door being opened, Mademoiselle L. appeared and took from his hands one of the bags, while the old lady relieved him of the other. He then bowed and departed. Did not see any person in the street at the time. It is a bye-street—very lonely.

"*William Bird,* tailor, deposes that he was one of the party who entered the house. Is an Englishman. Has lived in Paris two years. Was one of the first to ascend the stairs. Heard the voices in contention. The gruff voice was that of a Frenchman. Could make out several words, but cannot now remember all. Heard distinctly '*sacré*' and '*mon Dieu.*' There was a sound at the moment as if of several persons struggling—a scraping and scuffling sound. The shrill voice was very loud—louder than the gruff one. Is sure that it was not the voice of an Englishman. Appeared to be that of a German. Might have been a woman's voice. Does not understand German.

"Four of the above-named witnesses, being recalled, deposed that the door of the chamber in which was found the body of Mademoiselle L. was locked on the inside when the party reached it. Every thing was perfectly silent—no groans or noises of any kind. Upon forcing the door no person was seen. The windows, both of the back and front room, were down and firmly fastened from within. A door between the two rooms was closed, but not locked. The door leading from the front room into the passage was locked, with the key on the inside. A small room in the front of the house, on the fourth story, at the head of the passage, was open, the door being ajar. This room was crowded with old beds, boxes, and so forth. These were carefully removed and searched. There was not an inch of any portion of the house which was not carefully searched. Sweeps were sent up and down the chimneys. The house was a four-story one, with garrets *(mansardes).* A trap-door on the roof was nailed down very securely—did not appear to have been opened for years. The time elapsing between the hearing of the voices in contention and the breaking open of the room door, was variously stated by the witnesses. Some made it as short as three minutes—some as long as five. The door was opened with difficulty.

"*Alfonzo Garcio,* undertaker, deposes that he resides in the Rue Morgue. Is a native of Spain. Was one of the party who entered the house. Did not proceed upstairs. Is nervous, and was apprehensive of the consequences of agitation. Heard the voices in contention. The gruff voice was that of a Frenchman. Could not distinguish what was said. The shrill voice was that of an Englishman—is sure of this. Does not understand the English language, but judges by the intonation.

"*Alberto Montani,* confectioner, deposes that he was among the first to ascend the stairs. Heard the voices in question. The gruff voice was that of a Frenchman. Distinguished several words. The speaker appeared to be expostulating. Could not make out the words of the shrill voice. Spoke quick and unevenly. Thinks it the voice of a Russian. Corroborates the general testimony. Is an Italian. Never conversed with a native of Russia.

"Several witnesses, recalled, here testified that the chimneys of all the rooms on the fourth story were too narrow to admit the passage of a human being. By 'sweeps' were meant cylindrical sweeping-brushes, such as are employed by those who clean chimneys. These brushes were passed up and down every flue in the house. There is no back passage by which any one could have descended while the party proceeded upstairs. The body of Mademoiselle L'Espanaye was so firmly wedged in the chimney that it could not be got down until four or five of the party united their strength.

"*Paul Dumas,* physician, deposes that he was called to view the bodies about day-break. They were both then lying on the sacking of the bedstead in the chamber where Mademoiselle L. was found. The corpse of the young lady was much bruised and excoriated. The fact that it had been thrust up the chimney would sufficiently account for these appearances. The throat was greatly chafed. There were several deep scratches just below the chin, together with a series of livid spots which were evidently the impression of fingers. The face was fearfully discolored, and the eye-balls protruded. The tongue had been partially bitten through. A large bruise was discovered upon the pit of the stomach, produced, apparently, by the pressure of a knee. In the opinion of M. Dumas, Mademoiselle L'Espanaye had been throttled to death by some person or persons unknown. The corpse of the mother was horribly mutilated. All the bones of the right leg and arm were more or less shattered. The left *tibia* much splintered, as well as all the ribs of the left side. Whole body dreadfully bruised and discolored. It was not possible to say how the injuries had been inflicted. A heavy club of wood, or a broad bar of iron—a chair—any large, heavy, and obtuse weapon would have produced such results, if wielded by the hands of a very powerful man. No woman could have inflicted the blows with any weapon. The head of the deceased, when seen by witness, was entirely separated from the body, and was also greatly shattered. The throat had evidently been cut with some very sharp instrument—probably with a razor.

"*Alexandre Etienne,* surgeon, was called with M. Dumas to view the bodies. Corroborated the testimony, and the opinions of M. Dumas.

"Nothing farther of importance was elicited, although several other persons were examined. A murder so mysterious, and so perplexing in all its particulars, was never before committed in Paris—if indeed a murder has been committed at all. The police are entirely at fault—an unusual occurrence in affairs of this nature. There is not, however, the shadow of a clew apparent."

The evening edition of the paper stated that the greatest excitement still continued in the Quartier St. Roch—that the premises in question had been carefully re-searched, and fresh examinations of witnesses instituted, but all to no purpose. A postscript, however, mentioned that Adolphe Le Bon had been arrested and imprisoned—although nothing appeared to criminate him, beyond the facts already detailed.

Dupin seemed singularly interested in the progress of this affair—at least so I judged from his manner, for he made no comments. It was only after the announcement that Le Bon had been imprisoned that he asked me my opinion respecting the murders.

I could merely agree with all Paris in considering them an insoluble mystery. I saw no means by which it would be possible to trace the murderer.

"We must not judge of the means," said Dupin, "by this shell of an examination. The Parisian police, so much extolled for *acumen*, are cunning, but no more. There is no method in their proceedings, beyond the method of the moment. They make a vast parade of measures; but, not unfrequently, these are so ill adapted to the objects proposed, as to put us in mind of Monsieur Jourdain's calling for his *robe-de-chambre—pour mieux entendre la musique.* The results attained by them are not infrequently surprising, but, for the most part, are brought about by simple diligence and activity. When these qualities are unavailing, their schemes fail. Vidocq, for example, was a good guesser, and a persevering man. But, without educated thought, he erred continually by the very intensity of his investigations. He impaired his vision by holding the object too close. He might see, perhaps, one or two points with unusual clearness, but in so doing he, necessarily, lost sight of the matter as a whole. Thus there is such a thing as being too profound. Truth is not always in a well. In fact, as regards the more important knowledge, I do believe that she is invariably superficial. The depth lies in the valleys where we seek her, and not upon the mountain-tops where she is found. The modes and sources of this kind of error are well typified in the contemplation of the heavenly bodies. To look at a star by glances—to view it in a sidelong way, by turning toward it the exterior portions of the *retina* (more susceptible of feeble impressions of light than the interior), is to behold the star distinctly—is to have the best appreciation of its lustre—a lustre which grows dim just in proportion as we turn our vision *fully* upon it. A greater number of rays actually fall upon the eye in the latter case, but, in the former, there is the more refined capacity for comprehension. By undue profundity we perplex and enfeeble thought; and it is possible to make even Venus herself vanish from the firmament by a scrutiny too sustained, too concentrated, or too direct.

"As for these murders, let us enter into some examinations for ourselves, before we make up an opinion respecting them. An inquiry will afford us amusement" (I thought this an odd term, so applied, but said nothing), "and, besides, Le Bon once rendered me a service for which I am not ungrateful. We will go and see the premises with our own eyes. I know G——, the Prefect of Police, and shall have no difficulty in obtaining the necessary permission."

The permission was obtained, and we proceeded at once to the Rue Morgue. This is one of those miserable thoroughfares which intervene between the Rue Richelieu and the Rue St. Roch. It was late in the afternoon when we reached it; as this quarter is at a great distance from that in which we resided. The house was readily found; for there were still many persons gazing up at the closed shutters, with an objectless curiosity, from the opposite side of the way. It was an ordinary Parisian house, with a gateway, on one side of which was a glazed watch-box, with a sliding panel in the window, indicating a *loge de concierge*. Before going in we walked up the street, turned down an alley, and then, again turning, passed in the rear of the building—Dupin, meanwhile, examining the whole neighborhood, as well as the house, with a minuteness of attention for which I could see no possible object.

Retracing our steps, we came again to the front of the dwelling, rang, and, having shown our credentials, were admitted by the agents in charge. We went upstairs—into the chamber where the body of Mademoiselle L'Espanaye had been found, and where both the deceased still lay. The disorders of the room had, as usual, been suffered to exist. I saw nothing beyond what had been stated in the "Gazette des Tribunaux." Dupin scrutinized everything—not excepting the bodies of the victims. We then went into the other rooms, and into the yard; a *gendarme* accompanying us throughout. The examination occupied us until dark, when we took our departure. On our way home my companion stopped in for a moment at the office of one of the daily papers.

I have said that the whims of my friend were manifold, and that *je les ménageais:*—for this phrase there is no English equivalent. It was his humor, now, to decline all conversation on the subject of the murder, until about noon the next day. He then asked me, suddenly, if I had observed anything *peculiar* at the scene of the atrocity.

There was something in his manner of emphasizing the word "peculiar," which caused me to shudder, without knowing why.

"No, nothing *peculiar*," I said; "nothing more, at least, than we both saw stated in the paper."

"The 'Gazette,'" he replied, "has not entered, I fear, into the unusual horror of the thing. But dismiss the idle opinions of this print. It appears to me that this mystery is considered insoluble, for the very reason which should cause it to be regarded as easy of solution—I mean for the *outré* character of its features. The police are confounded by the seeming absence of motive—not for the murder itself—but for the atrocity of the murder. They are puzzled, too, by the seeming impossibility of reconciling the voices heard in contention with the facts that no one was discovered upstairs but the assassinated Mademoiselle L'Espanaye, and that there were no means of egress without the notice of the party ascending. The wild disorder of the room; the corpse thrust, with the head downward, up the chimney; the frightful mutilation of the body of the old lady; these considerations, with those just mentioned, and others which I need not mention, have sufficed to paralyze the powers, by putting completely at fault the boasted *acumen,* of the government agents. They have fallen into the gross but common error of confounding the unusual with the abstruse. But it is by these deviations from the plane of the ordinary that reason feels its way, if at all, in its search for the true. In investigations such as we are now pursuing, it should not be so much asked 'what has occurred,' as 'what has occurred that has never occurred before.' In fact, the facility with which I shall arrive, or have arrived, at the solution of this mystery is in the direct ratio of its apparent insolubility in the eyes of the police."

I stared at the speaker in mute astonishment.

"I am now awaiting," continued he, looking toward the door of our apartment—"I am now awaiting a person who, although perhaps not the perpetrator of these butcheries, must have been in some measure implicated in their perpetration. Of the worst portion of the crimes committed, it is probable that he is innocent. I hope that I am right in this supposition; for upon it I build my expectation of reading the entire riddle. I look for the man here—in this room—every moment. It is true that he may not arrive; but the probability is that he will. Should he come, it will be necessary to detain him. Here are pistols; and we both know how to use them when occasion demands their use."

I took the pistols, scarcely knowing what I did, or believing what I heard, while Dupin went on, very much as if in a soliloquy. I have already spoken of his abstract manner at such times. His discourse was addressed to myself; but his voice, although by no means loud, had that intonation which is commonly employed in speaking to some one at a great distance. His eyes, vacant in expression, regarded only the wall.

"That the voices heard in contention," he said, "by the party upon the stairs, were not the voices of the women themselves, was fully proved by the evidence. This relieves us of all doubt upon the question whether the old lady could have first destroyed the daughter, and afterward have committed suicide. I speak of this point chiefly for the sake of method; for the strength of Madame L'Espanaye would have been utterly unequal to the task of thrusting her daughter's corpse up the chimney as it was found; and the nature of the wounds upon her own person entirely preclude the idea of self-destruction. Murder, then, has been committed by some third party; and the voices of this third party were those heard in contention. Let me now advert—not to the whole testimony respecting these voices—but to what was *peculiar* in that testimony. Did you observe anything peculiar about it?"

I remarked that, while all the witnesses agreed in supposing the gruff voice to be that of a Frenchman, there was much disagreement in regard to the shrill, or, as one individual termed it, the harsh voice.

"That was the evidence itself," said Dupin, "but it was not the peculiarity of the evidence. You have observed nothing distinctive. Yet there *was* something to be observed. The witnesses, as you remark, agreed about the gruff voice; they were here unanimous. But in regard to the shrill voice, the peculiarity is—not that they disagreed—but that, while an Italian, an Englishman, a Spaniard, a Hollander, and a Frenchman attempted to describe it, each one spoke of it as that *of a foreigner*. Each is sure that it was not the voice of one of his own countrymen. Each likens it—not to the voice of an individual of any nation with whose language he is conversant—but the converse. The Frenchman supposes it the voice of a Spaniard, and 'might have distinguished some words *had he been acquainted with the Spanish.*' The Dutchman maintains it to have been that of a Frenchman; but we find it stated that '*not understanding French this witness was examined through an interpreter.*' The Englishman thinks it the voice of a German, and '*does not understand German.*' The Spaniard 'is sure' that it was that of an Englishman, but 'judges by the intonation' altogether, '*as he has no knowledge of the English.*' The Italian believes it the voice of a Russian, but '*has never conversed with a native of Russia.*' A second Frenchman differs, moreover, with the first, and is positive that the voice is that of an Italian; but, *not being cognizant of that tongue*, is, like the Spaniard, 'convinced by the intonation.' Now, how strangely unusual must that voice have really been, about which such testimony as this *could* have been elicited!—in whose *tones*, even, denizens of the five great divisions of Europe could recognize nothing familiar! You will say that it might have been the voice of an Asiatic—of an African. Neither Asiatics nor Africans abound in Paris; but, without denying the inference, I will now merely call your attention to three points. The voice is termed by one witness 'harsh rather than shrill.' It is represented by two others to have been 'quick and *unequal.*' No words—no sounds resembling words—were by any witness mentioned as distinguishable.

"I know not," continued Dupin, "what impression I may have made, so far, upon your own understanding; but I do not hesitate to say that legitimate deductions even from this portion of the testimony—the portion respecting the gruff and shrill voices— are in themselves sufficient to engender a suspicion which should give direction to all farther progress in the investigation of the mystery. I said 'legitimate deductions': but my meaning is not thus fully expressed. I designed to imply that the deductions are the *sole* proper ones, and that the suspicion arises *inevitably* from them as the single result. What the suspicion is, however, I will not say just yet. I merely wish you to bear in mind that, with myself, it was sufficiently forcible to give a definite form—a cer- tain tendency—to my inquiries in the chamber.

"Let us now transport ourselves, in fancy, to this chamber. What shall we first seek here? The means of egress employed by the murderers. It is not too much to say that neither of us believe in præternatural events. Madame and Mademoiselle L'Espanaye were not destroyed by spirits. The doers of the deed were material and escaped materially. Then how? Fortunately, there is but one mode of reasoning upon the point, and that mode *must* lead us to a definite decision. Let us examine, each by each, the possible means of egress. It is clear that the assas- sins were in the room where Mademoiselle L'Espanaye was found, or at least in the room adjoining, when the party ascended the stairs. It is then only from these two apartments that we have to seek issues. The police have laid bare the floors, the ceilings, and the masonry of the walls, in every direction. No *secret* issues could have escaped their vigilance. But, not trust- ing to *their* eyes, I examined with my own. There were, then, *no* secret issues. Both doors leading from the rooms into the pas- sage were securely locked, with the keys inside. Let us turn to the chimneys. These, although of ordinary width for some eight or ten feet above the hearths, will not admit, throughout their extent, the body of a large cat. The impossibility of egress, by means already stated, being thus absolute, we are reduced to the windows. Through those of the front room no one could have escaped without notice from the crowd in the street. The murderers *must* have passed, then, through those of the back room. Now, brought to this conclusion in so unequivocal a manner as we are, it is not our part, as reasoners, to reject it on account of apparent impossibilities. It is only left for us to prove that these apparent 'impossibilities' are, in reality, not such.

"There are two windows in the chamber. One of them is unobstructed by furniture, and is wholly visible. The lower portion of the other is hidden from view by the head of the unwieldy bedstead which is thrust close up against it. The former was found securely fastened from within. It resisted the utmost force of those who endeavored to raise it. A large gimlet-hole had been pierced in its frame to the left, and a very stout nail was found fitted therein, nearly to the head. Upon examining the other window, a similar nail was seen similarly fitted in it; and a vigorous attempt to raise this sash, failed also. The police were now entirely satisfied that egress had not been in these directions. And, therefore, it was thought a matter of supererogation to withdraw the nails and open the windows.

"My own examination was somewhat more particular, and was so for the reason I have just given—because here it was, I knew, that all apparent impossibilities *must* be proved to be not such in reality.

"I proceeded to think thus—*à posteriori*. The murderers *did* escape from one of these windows. This being so, they could not have re-fastened the sashes from the inside, as they were found fastened;—the consideration which put a stop, through its obviousness, to the scrutiny of the police in this quarter. Yet the sashes *were* fastened. They *must*, then, have the power of fastening themselves. There was no escape from this conclusion. I stepped to the unobstructed casement, withdrew the nail with some difficulty, and attempted to raise the sash. It resisted all my efforts, as I had anticipated. A concealed spring must, I now knew, exist; and this corroboration of my idea convinced me that my premises, at least, were correct, however mysterious still appeared the circumstances attending the nails. A careful search soon brought to light the hidden spring. I pressed it, and, satisfied with the discovery, forebore to upraise the sash.

"I now replaced the nail and regarded it attentively. A person passing out through this window might have reclosed it, and the spring would have caught—but the nail could not have been replaced. The conclusion was plain, and again narrowed in the field of my investigations. The assassins *must* have escaped through the other window. Supposing, then, the springs upon each sash to be the same, as was probable, there *must* be found a difference between the nails, or at least between the modes of their fixture. Getting upon the sacking of the bedstead, I looked over the head-board minutely at the second casement. Passing my hand down behind the board, I readily discovered and pressed the spring, which was, as I had supposed, identical in character with its neighbor. I now looked at the nail. It was as stout as the other, and apparently fitted in the same manner— driven in nearly up to the head.

"You will say that I was puzzled; but, if you think so, you must have misunderstood the nature of the inductions. To use a sporting phrase, I had not been once 'at fault.' The scent had never for an instant been lost. There was no flaw in any link of the chain. I had traced the secret to its ultimate result,—and that result was the *nail*. It had, I say, in every respect, the appearance of its fellow in the other window; but this fact was an absolute nullity (conclusive as it might seem to be) when compared with the consideration that here, at this point, terminated the clew. 'There *must* be something wrong,' I said, 'about the nail.' I touched it; and the head, with about a quarter of an inch of the shank, came off in my fingers. The rest of the shank was in the gimlet-hole, where it had been broken off. The fracture was an old one (for its edges were incrusted with rust), and had apparently been accomplished by the blow of a hammer, which had partially imbedded, in the top of the bottom sash, the head portion of the nail. I now carefully replaced this head portion in the indentation whence I had taken it, and the resemblance to a perfect nail was complete—the fissure was invisible. Pressing the spring, I gently raised the sash for a few inches; the head went up with it, remaining firm in its bed. I closed the window, and the semblance of the whole nail was again perfect.

"The riddle, so far, was now unriddled. The assassin had escaped through the window which looked upon the bed. Dropping of its own accord upon his exit (or perhaps purposely closed), it had become fastened by the spring; and it was the retention of this spring which had been mistaken by the police for that of the nail,—farther inquiry being thus considered unnecessary.

"The next question is that of the mode of descent. Upon this point I had been satisfied in my walk with you around the building. About five feet and a half from the casement in question there runs a lightning-rod. From this rod it would have been impossible for any one to reach the window itself, to say nothing of entering it. I observed, however, that the shutters of the fourth story were of the peculiar kind called by Parisian carpenters *ferrades*—a kind rarely employed at the present day, but frequently seen upon very old mansions at Lyons and Bordeaux. They are in the form of an ordinary door (a single, not a folding door), except that the upper half is latticed or worked in open trellis—thus affording an excellent hold for the hands. In the present instance these shutters are fully three feet and a half broad. When we saw them from the rear of the house, they were both about half open—that is to say, they stood off at right angles from the wall. It is probable that the police, as well as myself, examined the back of the tenement; but, if so, in looking at these *ferrades* in the line of their breadth (as they must have done), they did not perceive this great breadth itself, or, at all events, failed to take it into due consideration. In fact, having once satisfied themselves that no egress could have been made in this quarter, they would naturally bestow here a very cursory examination. It was clear to me, however, that the shutter belonging to the window at the head of the bed, would, if swung fully back to the wall, reach to within two feet of the lightning-rod. It was also evident that, by exertion of a very unusual degree of activity and courage, an entrance into the window, from the rod, might have been thus effected.—By reaching to the distance of two feet and a half (we now suppose the shutter open to its whole extent) a robber might have taken a firm grasp upon the trellis-work. Letting go, then, his hold upon the rod, placing his feet securely against the wall, and springing boldly from it, he might have swung the shutter so as to close it, and, if we imagine the window open at the time, might even have swung himself into the room.

"I wish you to bear especially in mind that I have spoken of a *very* unusual degree of activity as requisite to success in so hazardous and so difficult a feat. It is my design to show you, first, that the thing might possibly have been accomplished:—but, secondly and *chiefly,* I wish to impress upon your understanding the *very extraordinary*—the almost præternatural character of that agility which could have accomplished it.

"You will say, no doubt, using the language of the law, that 'to make out my case' I should rather undervalue, than insist upon a full estimation of the activity required in this matter. This may be the practice in law, but it is not the usage of reason. My ultimate object is only the truth. My immediate purpose is to lead you to place in juxta-position that *very unusual* activity of which I have just spoken, with that *very peculiar* shrill (or harsh) and *unequal* voice, about whose nationality no two persons could be found to agree, and in whose utterances no syllabification could be detected."

At these words a vague and half-formed conception of the meaning of Dupin flitted over my mind. I seemed to be upon the verge of comprehension, without power to comprehend—as men, at times, find themselves upon the brink of remembrance, without being able, in the end, to remember. My friend went on with his discourse.

"You will see," he said, "that I have shifted the question from the mode of egress to that of ingress. It was my design to suggest that both were effected in the same manner, at the same point. Let us now revert to the interior of the room. Let us survey the appearances here. The drawers of the bureau, it is said, had been rifled, although many articles of apparel still remained within them. The conclusion here is absurd. It is a mere guess— a very silly one—and no more. How are we to know that the articles found in the drawers were not all these drawers had originally contained? Madame L'Espanaye and her daughter lived an exceedingly retired life—saw no company—seldom went out— had little use for numerous changes of habiliment. Those found were at least of as good quality as any likely to be possessed by these ladies. If a thief had taken any, why did he not take the best—why did he not take all? In a word, why did he abandon four thousand francs in gold to encumber himself with a bundle of linen? The gold *was* abandoned. Nearly the whole sum mentioned by Monsieur Mignaud, the banker, was discovered, in bags, upon the floor. I wish you, therefore, to discard from your thoughts the blundering idea of *motive*, engendered in the brains of the police by that portion of the evidence which speaks of money delivered at the door of the house. Coincidences ten times as remarkable as this (the delivery of the money, and murder committed within three days upon the party receiving it), happen to all of us every hour of our lives, without attracting even momentary notice. Coincidences, in general, are great stumbling-blocks in the way of that class of thinkers who have been educated to know nothing of the theory of probabilities— that theory to which the most glorious objects of human research are indebted for the most glorious of illustration. In the present instance, had the gold been gone, the fact of its delivery three days before would have formed something more than a coincidence. It would have been corroborative of this idea of motive. But, under the real circumstances of the case, if we are to suppose gold the motive of this outrage, we must also imagine the perpetrator so vacillating an idiot as to have abandoned his gold and his motive together.

"Keeping now steadily in mind the points to which I have drawn your attention—that peculiar voice, that unusual agility, and that startling absence of motive in a murder so singularly atrocious as this—let us glance at the butchery itself. Here is a woman strangled to death by manual strength, and thrust up a chimney, head downward. Ordinary assassins employ no such modes of murder as this. Least of all, do they thus dispose of the murdered. In the manner of thrusting the corpse up the chimney, you will admit that there was something *excessively outré*— something altogether irreconcilable with our common notions of human action, even when we suppose the actors the most depraved of men. Think, too, how great must have been that strength which could have thrust the body *up* such an aperture so forcibly that the united vigor of several persons was found barely sufficient to drag it *down*!

"Turn, now, to other indications of the employment of a vigor most marvellous. On the hearth were thick tresses—very thick tresses—of grey human hair. These had been torn out by the roots. You are aware of the great force necessary in tearing thus from the head even twenty or thirty hairs together. You saw the locks in question as well as myself. Their roots (a hideous sight!) were clotted with fragments of the flesh of the scalp—sure token of the prodigious power which had been exerted in uprooting perhaps half a million of hairs at a time. The throat of the old lady was not merely cut, but the head absolutely severed from the body: the instrument was a mere razor. I wish you also to look at the *brutal* ferocity of these deeds. Of the bruises upon the body of Madame L'Espanaye I do not speak. Monsieur Dumas, and his worthy coadjutor Monsieur Etienne, have pronounced that they were inflicted by some obtuse instrument; and so far these gentlemen are very correct. The obtuse instrument was clearly the stone pavement in the yard, upon which the victim had fallen from the window which looked in upon the bed. This idea, however simple it may now seem, escaped the police for the same reason that the breadth of the shutters escaped them—because, by the affair of the nails, their perceptions had been hermetically sealed against the possibility of the windows having ever been opened at all.

"If now, in addition to all these things, you have properly reflected upon the odd disorder of the chamber, we have gone so far as to combine the ideas of an agility astounding, a strength superhuman, a ferocity brutal, a butchery without motive, a *grotesquerie* in horror absolutely alien from humanity, and a voice foreign in tone to the ears of men of many nations, and devoid of all distinct or intelligible syllabification. What result, then, has ensued? What impression have I made upon your fancy?"

I felt a creeping of the flesh as Dupin asked me the question. "A madman," I said, "has done this deed—some raving maniac, escaped from a neighboring *Maison de Santé*."

"In some respects," he replied, "your idea is not irrelevant. But the voices of madmen, even in their wildest paroxysms, are never found to tally with that peculiar voice heard upon the stairs. Madmen are of some nation, and their language, however incoherent in its words, has always the coherence of syllabification.

Besides, the hair of a madman is not such as I now hold in my hand. I disentangled this little tuft from the rigidly clutched fingers of Madame L'Espanaye. Tell me what you can make of it."

"Dupin!" I said, completely unnerved; "this hair is most unusual—this is no *human* hair."

"I have not asserted that it is," said he, "but, before we decide this point, I wish you to glance at the little sketch I have here traced upon the paper. It is a *fac-simile* drawing of what has been described in one portion of the testimony as 'dark bruises, and deep indentations of fingernails,' upon the throat of Mademoiselle L'Espanaye, and in another (by Messrs. Dumas and Etienne), as a 'series of livid spots, evidently the impression of fingers.'

"You will perceive," continued my friend, spreading out the paper upon the table before us, "that this drawing gives the idea of a firm and fixed hold. There is no *slipping* apparent. Each finger has retained—possibly until the death of the victim—the fearful grasp by which it originally imbedded itself. Attempt, now, to place all your fingers, at the same time, in the respective impressions as you see them."

I made the attempt in vain.

"We are possibly not giving this matter a fair trial," he said. "The paper is spread out upon a plane surface; but the human throat is cylindrical. Here is a billet of wood, the circumference of which is about that of the throat. Wrap the drawing around it, and try the experiment again."

I did so; but the difficulty was even more obvious than before. "This," I said, "is the mark of no human hand."

"Read now," replied Dupin, "this passage from Cuvier."

It was a minute anatomical and generally descriptive account of the large fulvous Ourang-Outang of the East Indian Islands. The gigantic stature, the prodigious strength and activity, the wild ferocity, and the imitative propensities of these mammalia are sufficiently well known to all. I understood the full horrors of the murder at once.

"The description of the digits," said I, as I made an end of reading, "is in exact accordance with this drawing. I see that no animal but an Ourang-Outang, of the species here mentioned, could have impressed the indentations as you have traced them.

This tuft of tawny hair, too, is identical in character with that of the beast of Cuvier. But I cannot possibly comprehend the particulars of this frightful mystery. Besides, there were *two* voices heard in contention, and one of them was unquestionably the voice of a Frenchman."

"True; and you will remember an expression attributed almost unanimously, by the evidence, to this voice,—the expression, *'mon Dieu!'* This, under the circumstances, has been justly characterized by one of the witnesses (Montani, the confectioner), as an expression of remonstrance or expostulation. Upon these two words, therefore, I have mainly built my hopes of a full solution of the riddle. A Frenchman was cognizant of the murder. It is possible—indeed it is far more than probable—that he was innocent of all participation in the bloody transactions which took place. The Ourang-Outang may have escaped from him. He may have traced it to the chamber; but, under the agitating circumstances which ensued, he could never have re-captured it. It is still at large. I will not pursue these guesses—for I have no right to call them more—since the shades of reflection upon which they are based are scarcely of sufficient depth to be appreciable by my own intellect, and since I could not pretend to make them intelligible to the understanding of another. We will call them guesses then, and speak of them as such. If the Frenchman in question is indeed, as I suppose, innocent of this atrocity, this advertisement, which I left last night, upon our return home, at the office of 'Le Monde' (a paper devoted to the shipping interest, and much sought by sailors), will bring him to our residence."

He handed me a paper, and I read thus:

CAUGHT—*In the Bois de Boulogne, early in the morning of the—inst. (the morning of the murder), a very large, tawny Ourang-Outang of the Bornese species. The owner (who is ascertained to be a sailor, belonging to a Maltese vessel), may have the animal again, upon identifying it satisfactorily and paying a few charges arising from its capture and keeping. Call at No.——, Rue——, Faubourg St. Germain—au troisième.*

"How was it possible," I asked, "that you should know the man to be a sailor, and belonging to a Maltese vessel?"

"I do *not* know it," said Dupin. "I am not *sure* of it. Here, however, is a small piece of ribbon, which from its form, and from its greasy appearance, has evidently been used in tying the hair in one of those long *queues* of which sailors are so fond. Moreover, this knot is one which few besides sailors can tie, and is peculiar to the Maltese. I picked the ribbon up at the foot of the lightning-rod. It could not have belonged to either of the deceased. Now if, after all, I am wrong in my induction from this ribbon, that the Frenchman was a sailor belonging to a Maltese vessel, still I can have done no harm in saying what I did in the advertisement. If I am in error, he will merely suppose that I have been misled by some circumstance into which he will not take the trouble to inquire. But if I am right, a great point is gained. Cognizant although innocent of the murder, the Frenchman will naturally hesitate about replying to the advertisement—about demanding the Ourang-Outang. He will reason thus:—'I am innocent; I am poor; my Ourang-Outang is of great value—to one in my circumstances a fortune of itself—why should I lose it through idle apprehensions of danger? Here it is, within my grasp. It was found in the Bois de Boulogne—at a vast distance from the scene of that butchery. How can it ever be suspected that a brute beast should have done the deed? The police are at fault—they have failed to procure the slightest clew. Should they even trace the animal, it would be impossible to prove me cognizant of the murder, or to implicate me in guilt on account of that cognizance. Above all, *I am known*. The advertiser designates me as the possessor of the beast. I am not sure to what limit his knowledge may extend. Should I avoid claiming a property of so great value, which it is known that I possess, I will render the animal, at least, liable to suspicion. It is not my policy to attract attention either to myself or to the beast. I will answer the advertisement, get the Ourang-Outang, and keep it close until this matter has blown over.'"

At this moment we heard a step upon the stairs.

"Be ready," said Dupin, "with your pistols, but neither use them nor show them until at a signal from myself."

The front door of the house had been left open, and the visitor had entered, without ringing, and advanced several steps upon the staircase. Now, however, he seemed to hesitate. Presently we heard him descending. Dupin was moving quickly to the door, when we again heard him coming up. He did not turn back a second time, but stepped up with decision and rapped at the door of our chamber.

"Come in," said Dupin, in a cheerful and hearty tone.

A man entered. He was a sailor, evidently,—a tall, stout, and muscular-looking person, with a certain dare-devil expression of countenance, not altogether unprepossessing. His face, greatly sunburnt, was more than half hidden by whisker and *mustachio.* He had with him a huge oaken cudgel, but appeared to be otherwise unarmed. He bowed awkwardly, and bade us "good evening," in French accents, which, although somewhat Neufchatelish, were still sufficiently indicative of a Parisian origin.

"Sit down, my friend," said Dupin. "I suppose you have called about the Ourang-Outang. Upon my word, I almost envy you the possession of him; a remarkably fine, and no doubt a very valuable animal. How old do you suppose him to be?"

The sailor drew a long breath, with the air of a man relieved of some intolerable burden, and then replied, in an assured tone:

"I have no way of telling—but he can't be more than four or five years old. Have you got him here?"

"Oh, no; we had no conveniences for keeping him here. He is at a livery stable in the Rue Dubourg, just by. You can get him in the morning. Of course you are prepared to identify the property?"

"To be sure I am, sir."

"I shall be sorry to part with him," said Dupin.

"I don't mean that you should be at all this trouble for nothing, sir," said the man. "Couldn't expect it. Am very willing to pay a reward for the finding of the animal—that is to say, any thing in reason."

"Well," replied my friend, "that is all very fair, to be sure. Let me think!—what should I have? Oh! I will tell you. My reward shall be this. You shall give me all the information in your power about these murders in the Rue Morgue."

Dupin said the last words in a very low tone, and very quietly. Just as quietly, too, he walked toward the door, locked it, and put the key in his pocket. He then drew a pistol from his bosom and placed it, without the least flurry, upon the table.

The sailor's face flushed up as if he were struggling with

suffocation. He started to his feet and grasped his cudgel; but the next moment he fell back into his seat, trembling violently, and with the countenance of death itself. He spoke not a word. I pitied him from the bottom of my heart.

"My friend," said Dupin, in a kind tone, "you are alarming yourself unnecessarily—you are indeed. We mean you no harm whatever. I pledge you the honor of a gentleman, and of a Frenchman, that we intend you no injury. I perfectly well know that you are innocent of the atrocities in the Rue Morgue. It will not do, however, to deny that you are in some measure implicated in them. From what I have already said, you must know that I have had means of information about this matter—means of which you could never have dreamed. Now the thing stands thus. You have done nothing which you could have avoided—nothing, certainly, which renders you culpable. You were not even guilty of robbery, when you might have robbed with impunity. You have nothing to conceal. You have no reason for concealment. On the other hand, you are bound by every principle of honor to confess all you know. An innocent man is now imprisoned, charged with that crime of which you can point out the perpetrator."

The sailor had recovered his presence of mind, in a great measure, while Dupin uttered these words; but his original boldness of bearing was all gone.

"So help me God," said he, after a brief pause, "I *will* tell you all I know about this affair;—but I do not expect you to believe one half I say—I would be a fool indeed if I did. Still, I *am* innocent, and I will make a clean breast if I die for it."

What he stated was, in substance, this. He had lately made a voyage to the Indian Archipelago. A party, of which he formed one, landed at Borneo, and passed into the interior on an excursion of pleasure. Himself and a companion had captured the Ourang-Outang. This companion dying, the animal fell into his own exclusive possession. After great trouble, occasioned by the intractable ferocity of his captive during the home voyage, he at length succeeded in lodging it safely at his own residence in Paris, where, not to attract toward himself the unpleasant curiosity of his neighbors, he kept it carefully secluded, until such time as it should recover from a wound in the foot, received from a splinter on board ship. His ultimate design was to sell it.

Returning home from some sailors' frolic on the night, or rather in the morning of the murder, he found the beast occupying his own bed-room, into which it had broken from a closet adjoining, where it had been, as was thought, securely confined. Razor in hand, and fully lathered, it was sitting before a looking-glass, attempting the operation of shaving, in which it had no doubt previously watched its master through the keyhole of the closet. Terrified at the sight of so dangerous a weapon in the possession of an animal so ferocious, and so well able to use it, the man, for some moments, was at a loss what to do. He had been accustomed, however, to quiet the creature, even in its fiercest moods, by the use of a whip, and to this he now resorted. Upon sight of it, the Ourang-Outang sprang at once through the door of the chamber, down the stairs, and thence, through a window, unfortunately open, into the street.

The Frenchman followed in despair; the ape, razor still in hand, occasionally stopping to look back and gesticulate at its pursuer, until the latter had nearly come up with it. It then again made off. In this manner the chase continued for a long time. The streets were profoundly quiet, as it was nearly three o'clock in the morning. In passing down an alley in the rear of the Rue Morgue, the fugitive's attention was arrested by a light gleaming from the open window of Madame L'Espanaye's chamber, in the fourth story of her house. Rushing to the building, it perceived the lightning-rod, clambered up with inconceivable agility, grasped the shutter, which was thrown fully back against the wall, and, by its means, swung itself directly upon the head-board of the bed. The whole feat did not occupy a minute. The shutter was kicked open again by the Ourang-Outang as it entered the room.

The sailor, in the meantime, was both rejoiced and perplexed. He had strong hopes of now recapturing the brute, as it could scarcely escape from the trap into which it had ventured, except by the rod, where it might be intercepted as it came down. On the other hand, there was much cause for anxiety as to what it might do in the house. This latter reflection urged the man still to follow the fugitive. A lightning-rod is ascended without difficulty, especially by a sailor; but, when he had arrived as high as the window, which lay far to his left, his career was stopped; the most that he could accomplish was to reach over so as to obtain a glimpse of the interior of the room. At this glimpse he nearly fell from his hold through excess of horror. Now it was that those hideous shrieks arose upon the night, which had startled from slumber the inmates of the Rue Morgue. Madame L'Espanaye and her daughter, habited in their night clothes, had apparently been arranging some papers in the iron chest already mentioned, which had been wheeled into the middle of the room. It was open, and its contents lay beside it on the bed. The victims must have been sitting with their backs toward the window; and, from the time elapsing between the ingress of the beast and the screams, it seems probable that it was not immediately perceived. The flapping-to of the shutter would naturally have been attributed to the wind.

As the sailor looked in, the gigantic animal had seized Madame L'Espanaye by the hair (which was loose, as she had been combing it), and was florishing the razor about her face, in imitation of the motions of a barber. The daughter lay prostrate and motionless; she had swooned. The screams and struggles of the old lady (during which the hair was torn from her head) had the effect of changing the probably pacific purposes of the Ourang-Outang into those of wrath. With one determined sweep of its muscular arm it nearly severed her head from her body. The sight of blood inflamed its anger into frenzy. Gnashing its teeth, and flashing fire from its eyes, it flew upon the body of the girl, and imbedded its fearful talons in her throat, retaining its grasp until she expired. Its wandering and wild glances fell at this moment upon the head of the bed, over which the face of its master, rigid with horror, was just discernible. The fury of the beast, who no doubt bore still in mind the dreaded whip, was instantly converted into fear. Conscious of having deserved punishment, it seemed desirous of concealing its bloody deeds, and skipped about the chamber in an agony of nervous agitation; throwing down and breaking the furniture as it moved, and dragging the bed from the bedstead. In conclusion, it seized first the corpse of the daughter, and thrust it up the chimney, as it was found; then that of the old lady, which it immediately hurled through the window headlong.

As the ape approached the casement with its mutilated burden, the sailor shrank aghast to the rod, and, rather gliding than clambering down it, hurried at once home—dreading the consequences of the butchery, and gladly abandoning, in his terror, all solicitude about the fate of the Ourang-Outang. The words heard by the party upon the staircase were the Frenchman's exclamations of horror and affright, commingled with the fiendish jabberings of the brute.

I have scarcely anything to add. The Ourang-Outang must have escaped from the chamber, by the rod, just before the breaking of the door. It must have closed the window as it passed through it. It was subsequently caught by the owner himself, who obtained for it a very large sum at the *Jardin des Plantes*. Le Bon was instantly released, upon our narration of the circumstances (with some comments from Dupin) at the *bureau* of the Prefect of Police. This functionary, however well disposed to my friend, could not altogether conceal his chagrin at the turn which affairs had taken, and was fain to indulge in a sarcasm or two, about the propriety of every person minding his own business.

"Let them talk," said Dupin, who had not thought it necessary to reply. "Let him discourse; it will ease his conscience. I am satisfied with having defeated him in his own castle. Nevertheless, that he failed in the solution of this mystery, is by no means that matter for wonder which he supposes it; for, in truth, our friend the Prefect is somewhat too cunning to be profound. In his wisdom is no *stamen*. It is all head and no body, like the pictures of the Goddess Laverna,—or, at best, all head and shoulders, like a codfish. But he is a good creature after all. I like him especially for one master stroke of cant, by which he has attained his reputation for ingenuity. I mean the way he has '*de nier ce qui est, et d'expliquer ce qui n'est pas*.'" ("To deny what exists, and to explain what doesn't.")

A Scandal in Bohemia
(1891)
Sir Arthur Conan Doyle

To Sherlock Holmes she is always *the* woman. I have seldom heard him mention her under any other name. In his eyes she eclipses and predominates the whole of her sex. It was not that he felt any emotion akin to love for Irene Adler. All emotions, and that one particularly, were abhorrent to his cold, precise but admirably balanced mind. He was, I take it, the most perfect reasoning and observing machine that the world has seen, but as a lover he would have placed himself in a false position. He never spoke of the softer passions, save with a gibe and a sneer. They were admirable things for the observer—excellent for drawing the veil from men's motives and actions. But for the trained reasoner to admit such intrusions into his own delicate and finely adjusted temperament was to introduce a distracting factor which might throw a doubt upon all his mental results. Grit in a sensitive instrument, or a crack in one of his own high-power lenses, would not be more disturbing than a strong emotion in a nature such as his. And yet there was but one woman to him, and that woman was the late Irene Adler, of dubious and questionable memory.

I had seen little of Holmes lately. My marriage had drifted us away from each other. My own complete happiness, and the home-centred interests which rise up around the man who first finds himself master of his own establishment, were sufficient to absorb all my attention, while Holmes, who loathed every form of society with his whole Bohemian soul, remained in our lodgings in Baker Street, buried among his old books, and alternating from week to week between cocaine and ambition, the drowsiness of the drug, and the fierce energy of his own keen nature. He was still, as ever, deeply attracted by the study of crime, and occupied his immense faculties and extraordinary powers of observation in following out those clues, and clearing up those mysteries which had been abandoned as hopeless by the official police. From time to time I heard some vague account of his doings: of his summons to Odessa in the case of the Trepoff murder, of his clearing up of the singular tragedy of the Atkinson brothers at Trincomalee, and finally of the mission which he had accomplished so delicately and successfully for the reigning family of Holland. Beyond these signs of his activity, however, which I merely shared with all the readers of the daily press, I knew little of my former friend and companion.

One night—it was on the twentieth of March, 1888—I was returning from a journey to a patient (for I had now returned to civil practice), when my way led me through Baker Street. As I passed the well-remembered door, which must always be associated in my mind with my wooing, and with the dark incidents of the *Study in Scarlet,* I was seized with a keen desire to see Holmes again, and to know how he was employing his extraordinary powers. His rooms were brilliantly lit, and, even as I looked up, I saw his tall, spare figure pass twice in a dark silhouette against the blind. He was pacing the room swiftly, eagerly, with his head sunk upon his chest and his hands clasped behind him. To me, who knew his every mood and habit, his attitude and manner told their own story. He was at work again. He had risen out of his drug-created dreams and was hot upon the scent of some new problem. I rang the bell and was shown up to the chamber which had formerly been in part my own.

His manner was not effusive. It seldom was; but he was glad, I think, to see me. With hardly a word spoken, but with a kindly eye, he waved me to an armchair, threw across his case of cigars, and indicated a spirit case and a gasogene in the corner. Then he stood before the fire and looked me over in his singular introspective fashion.

"Wedlock suits you," he remarked. "I think, Watson, that you have put on seven and a half pounds since I saw you."

"Seven!" I answered.

"Indeed, I should have thought a little more. Just a trifle more, I fancy, Watson. And in practice again, I observe. You did not tell me that you intended to go into harness."

"Then, how do you know?"

"I see it, I deduce it. How do I know that you have been getting yourself very wet lately, and that you have a most clumsy and careless servant girl?"

"My dear Holmes," said I, "this is too much. You would certainly have been burned, had you lived a few centuries ago. It is true that I had a country walk on Thursday and came home in a dreadful mess, but as I have changed my clothes I can't imagine how you deduce it. As to Mary Jane, she is incorrigible, and my wife has given her notice; but there, again, I fail to see how you work it out."

He chuckled to himself and rubbed his long, nervous hands together.

"It is simplicity itself," said he; "my eyes tell me that on the inside of your left shoe, just where the firelight strikes it, the leather is scored by six almost parallel cuts. Obviously they have been caused by someone who has very carelessly scraped round the edges of the sole in order to remove crusted mud from it. Hence, you see, my double deduction that you had been out in vile weather, and that you had a particularly malignant boot-slitting specimen of the London slavey. As to your practice, if a gentleman walks into my rooms smelling of iodoform, with a black mark of nitrate of silver upon his right forefinger, and a bulge on the right side of his top-hat to show where he has secreted his stethoscope, I must be dull, indeed, if I do not pronounce him to be an active member of the medical profession."

I could not help laughing at the ease with which he explained his process of deduction. "When I hear you give your reasons," I remarked, "the thing always appears to me to be so ridiculously simple that I could easily do it myself, though at each successive instance of your reasoning I am baffled until you explain your process. And yet I believe that my eyes are as good as yours."

"Quite so," he answered, lighting a cigarette, and throwing himself down into an armchair. "You see, but you do not observe. The distinction is clear. For example, you have frequently seen the steps which lead up from the hall to this room."

"Frequently."

"How often?"

"Well, some hundreds of times."

"Then how many are there?"

"How many? I don't know."

"Quite so! You have not observed. And yet you have seen. That is just my point. Now, I know that there are seventeen steps, because I have both seen and observed. By the way, since you are interested in these little problems, and since you are good enough to chronicle one or two of my trifling experiences, you may be interested in this." He threw over a sheet of thick, pink-tinted note-paper which had been lying open upon the table. "It came by the last post," said he. "Read it aloud."

The note was undated, and without either signature or address.

"There will call upon you to-night, at a quarter to eight o'clock [it said], a gentleman who desires to consult you upon a matter of the very deepest moment. Your recent services to one of the royal houses of Europe have shown that you are one who may safely be trusted with matters which are of an importance which can hardly be exaggerated. This account of you we have from all quarters received. Be in your chamber then at that hour, and do not take it amiss if your visit or wear a mask."

"This is indeed a mystery," I remarked. "What do you imagine that it means?"

"I have no data yet. It is a capital mistake to theorize before one has data. Insensibly one begins to twist facts to suit theories, instead of theories to suit facts. But the note itself. What do you deduce from it?"

I carefully examined the writing, and the paper upon which it was written.

"The man who wrote it was presumably well to do," I remarked, endeavoring to imitate my companion's processes.

"Such paper could not be bought under half a crown a packet. It is peculiarly strong and stiff."

"Peculiar—that is the very word," said Holmes. "It is not an English paper at all. Hold it up to the light."

I did so, and saw a large "*E*" with a small "*g*," a "*P,*" and a large "*G*" with a small "*t*" woven into the texture of the paper.

"What do you make of that?" asked Holmes.

"The name of the maker, no doubt; or his monogram, rather."

"Not at all. The '*G*' with the small '*t*' stands for 'Gesellschaft,' which is the German for 'Company.' It is a customary contraction like our 'Co.' '*P,*' of course, stands for 'Papier.' Now for the '*Eg.*' Let us glance at our Continental Gazetteer." He took down a heavy brown volume from his shelves. "Eglow, Eglonitz—here we are, Egria. It is in a German-speaking country—in Bohemia, not far from Carlsbad. 'Remarkable as being the scene of the death of Wallenstein, and for its numerous glass-factories and paper-mills.' Ha, ha, my boy, what do you make of that?" His eyes sparkled, and he sent up a great blue triumphant cloud from his cigarette.

"The paper was made in Bohemia," I said.

"Precisely. And the man who wrote the note is a German. Do you note the peculiar construction of the sentence—'This account of you we have from all quarters received.' A Frenchman or Russian could not have written that. It is the German who is so uncourteous to his verbs. It only remains, therefore, to discover what is wanted by this German who writes upon Bohemian paper and prefers wearing a mask to showing his face. And here he comes, if I am not mistaken, to resolve all our doubts."

As he spoke there was the sharp sound of horses' hoofs and grating wheels against the curb, followed by a sharp pull at the bell. Holmes whistled.

"A pair, by the sound," said he. "Yes," he continued, glancing out of the window. "A nice little brougham and a pair of beauties. A hundred and fifty guineas apiece. There's money in this case, Watson, if there is nothing else."

"I think that I had better go, Holmes."

"Not a bit, Doctor. Stay where you are. I am lost without my

Boswell. And this promises to be interesting. It would be a pity to miss it."

"But your client—"

"Never mind him. I may want your help, and so may he. Here he comes. Sit down in that armchair, Doctor, and give us your best attention."

A slow and heavy step, which had been heard upon the stairs and in the passage, paused immediately outside the door. Then there was a loud and authoritative tap.

"Come in!" said Holmes.

A man entered who could hardly have been less than six feet six inches in height, with the chest and limbs of a Hercules. His dress was rich with a richness which would, in England, be looked upon as akin to bad taste. Heavy bands of astrakhan were slashed across the sleeves and fronts of his double-breasted coat, while the deep blue cloak which was thrown over his shoulders was lined with flame-colored silk and secured at the neck with a brooch which consisted of a single flaming beryl. Boots which extended halfway up his calves, and which were trimmed at the tops with rich brown fur, completed the impression of barbaric opulence which was suggested by his whole appearance. He carried a broad-brimmed hat in his hand, while he wore across the upper part of his face, extending down past the cheekbones, a black vizard mask, which he had apparently adjusted that very moment, for his hand was still raised to it as he entered. From the lower part of the face he appeared to be a man of strong character, with a thick, hanging lip, and a long, straight chin suggestive of resolution pushed to the length of obstinacy.

"You had my note?" he asked with a deep harsh voice and a strongly marked German accent. "I told you that I would call." He looked from one to the other of us, as if uncertain which to address.

"Pray take a seat," said Holmes. "This is my friend and colleague, Dr. Watson, who is occasionally good enough to help me in my cases. Whom have I the honor to address?"

"You may address me as the Count Von Kramm, a Bohemian nobleman. I understand that this gentleman, your friend, is a man of honor and discretion, whom I may trust with a matter of the most extreme importance. If not, I should much prefer to communicate with you alone."

I rose to go, but Holmes caught me by the wrist and pushed me back into my chair. "It is both, or none," said he. "You may say before this gentleman anything which you may say to me."

The Count shrugged his broad shoulders. "Then I must begin," said he, "by binding you both to absolute secrecy for two years; at the end of that time the matter will be of no importance. At present it is not too much to say that it is of such weight it may have an influence upon European history."

"I promise," said Holmes.

"And I."

"You will excuse this mask," continued our strange visitor. "The august person who employs me wishes his agent to be unknown to you, and I may confess at once that the title by which I have just called myself is not exactly my own."

"I was aware of it," said Holmes drily.

"The circumstances are of great delicacy, and every precaution has to be taken to quench what might grow to be an immense scandal and seriously compromise one of the reigning families of Europe. To speak plainly, the matter implicates the great House of Ormstein, hereditary kings of Bohemia."

"I was also aware of that," murmured Holmes, settling himself down in his armchair and closing his eyes.

Our visitor glanced with some apparent surprise at the languid, lounging figure of the man who had been no doubt depicted to him as the most incisive reasoner and most energetic agent in Europe. Holmes slowly reopened his eyes and looked impatiently at his gigantic client.

"If your Majesty would condescend to state your case," he remarked, "I should be better able to advise you."

The man sprang from his chair and paced up and down the room in uncontrollable agitation. Then, with a gesture of desperation, he tore the mask from his face and hurled it upon the ground. "You are right," he cried; "I am the King. Why should I attempt to conceal it?"

"Why, indeed?" murmured Holmes. "Your Majesty had not spoken before I was aware that I was addressing Wilhelm

Gottsreich Sigismond von Ormstein, Grand Duke of Cassel-Felstein, the hereditary King of Bohemia."

"But you can understand," said our strange visitor, sitting down once more and passing his hand over his high white forehead, "you can understand that I am not accustomed to doing such business in my own person. Yet the matter was so delicate that I could not confide it to an agent without putting myself in his power. I have come incognito from Prague for the purpose of consulting you."

"Then, pray consult," said Holmes, shutting his eyes once more.

"The facts are briefly these: Some five years ago, during a lengthy visit to Warsaw, I made the acquaintance of the well-known adventuress, Irene Adler. The name is no doubt familiar to you."

"Kindly look her up in my index, Doctor," murmured Holmes without opening his eyes. For many years he had adopted a system of docketing all paragraphs concerning men and things, so that it was difficult to name a subject or a person on which he could not at once furnish information. In this case I found her biography sandwiched in between that of a Hebrew rabbi and that of a staff-commander who had written a monograph upon the deep-sea fishes.

"Let me see!" said Holmes. "Hum! Born in New Jersey in the year 1858. Contralto—hum! La Scala, hum! Prima donna Imperial Opera of Warsaw—yes! Retired from operatic stage—ha! Living in London—quite so! Your Majesty, as I understand, became entangled with this young person, wrote her some compromising letters, and is now desirous of getting those letters back."

"Precisely so. But how—"

"Was there a secret marriage?"

"None."

"No legal papers or certificates?"

"None."

"Then I fail to follow your Majesty. If this young person should produce her letters for blackmailing or other purposes, how is she to prove their authenticity?"

"There is the writing."

"Pooh, pooh! Forgery."

"My private note-paper."

"Stolen."

"My own seal."

"Imitated."

"My photograph."

"Bought."

"We were both in the photograph."

"Oh, dear! That is very bad! Your Majesty has indeed committed an indiscretion."

"I was mad—insane."

"You have compromised yourself seriously."

"I was only Crown Prince then. I was young. I am but thirty now."

"It must be recovered."

"We have tried and failed."

"Your Majesty must pay. It must be bought."

"She will not sell."

"Stolen, then."

"Five attempts have been made. Twice burglars in my pay ransacked her house. Once we diverted her luggage when she travelled. Twice she has been waylaid. There has been no result."

"No sign of it?"

"Absolutely none."

Holmes laughed. "It is quite a pretty little problem," said he.

"But a very serious one to me," returned the King reproachfully.

"Very, indeed. And what does she propose to do with the photograph?"

"To ruin me."

"But how?"

"I am about to be married."

"So I have heard."

"To Clotilde Lothman von Saxe-Meningen, second daughter of the King of Scandinavia. You may know the strict principles of her family. She is herself the very soul of delicacy. A shadow of a doubt as to my conduct would bring the matter to an end."

"And Irene Adler?"

"Threatens to send them the photograph. And she will do it. I know that she will do it. You do not know her, but she has a soul of steel. She has the face of the most beautiful of women, and the mind of the most resolute of men. Rather than I should marry another woman, there are no lengths to which she would not go—none."

"You are sure that she has not sent it yet?"

"I am sure."

"And why?"

"Because she has said that she would send it on the day when the betrothal was publicly proclaimed. That will be next Monday."

"Oh, then we have three days yet," said Holmes with a yawn. "That is very fortunate, as I have one or two matters of importance to look into just at present. Your Majesty will, of course, stay in London for the present?"

"Certainly. You will find me at the Langham under the name of the Count Von Kramm."

"Then I shall drop you a line to let you know how we progress."

"Pray do so. I shall be all anxiety."

"Then, as to money?"

"You have carte blanche."

"Absolutely?"

"I tell you that I would give one of the provinces of my kingdom to have that photograph."

"And for present expenses?"

The King took a heavy chamois leather bag from under his cloak and laid it on the table.

"There are three hundred pounds in gold and seven hundred in notes," he said.

Holmes scribbled a receipt upon a sheet of his note-book and handed it to him.

"And Mademoiselle's address?" he asked.

"Is Briony Lodge, Serpentine Avenue, St. John's Wood."

Holmes took a note of it. "One other question," said he. "Was the photograph a cabinet?"

"It was."

"Then, good-night, your Majesty, and I trust that we shall soon have some good news for you. And good-night, Watson," he added, as the wheels of the royal brougham rolled down the street. "If you will be good enough to call to-morrow afternoon at three o'clock I should like to chat this little matter over with you."

2

At three o'clock precisely I was at Baker Street, but Holmes had not yet returned. The landlady informed me that he had left the house shortly after eight o'clock in the morning. I sat down beside the fire, however, with the intention of awaiting him, however long he might be. I was already deeply interested in his inquiry, for, though it was surrounded by none of the grim and strange features which were associated with the two crimes which I have already recorded, still, the nature of the case and the exalted station of his client gave it a character of its own. Indeed, apart from the nature of the investigation which my friend had on hand, there was something in his masterly grasp of a situation, and his keen, incisive reasoning, which made it a pleasure to me to study his system of work, and to follow the quick, subtle methods by which he disentangled the most inextricable mysteries. So accustomed was I to his invariable success that the very possibility of his failing had ceased to enter into my head.

It was close upon four before the door opened, and a drunken-looking groom, ill-kempt and side-whiskered, with an inflamed face and disreputable clothes, walked into the room. Accustomed as I was to my friend's amazing powers in the use of disguises, I had to look three times before I was certain that it was indeed he. With a nod he vanished into the bedroom, whence he emerged in five minutes tweed-suited and respectable, as of old. Putting his hands into his pockets, he stretched out his legs in front of the fire and laughed heartily for some minutes.

"Well, really!" he cried, and then he choked and laughed again until he was obliged to lie back, limp and helpless, in the chair.

"What is it?"

"It's quite too funny. I am sure you could never guess how I employed my morning, or what I ended by doing."

"I can't imagine. I suppose that you have been watching the habits, and perhaps the house, of Miss Irene Adler."

"Quite so; but the sequel was rather unusual. I will tell you, however. I left the house a little after eight o'clock this morning in the character of a groom out of work. There is a wonderful sympathy and freemasonry among horsy men. Be one of them, and you will know all that there is to know. I soon found Briony Lodge. It is a *bijou* villa, with a garden at the back, but built out in front right up to the road, two stories. Chubb lock to the door. Large sitting-room on the right side, well furnished, with long windows almost to the floor, and those preposterous English window fasteners which a child could open. Behind there was nothing remarkable, save that the passage window could be reached from the top of the coach-house. I walked round it and examined it closely from every point of view, but without noting anything else of interest.

"I then lounged down the street and found, as I expected, that there was a mews in a lane which runs down by one wall of the garden. I lent the ostlers a hand in rubbing down their horses, and received in exchange twopence, a glass of half and half, two fills of shag tobacco, and as much information as I could desire about Miss Adler, to say nothing of half a dozen other people in the neighborhood in whom I was not in the least interested, but whose biographies I was compelled to listen to."

"And what of Irene Adler?" I asked.

"Oh, she has turned all the men's heads down in that part. She is the daintiest thing under a bonnet on this planet. So say the Serpentine-mews, to a man. She lives quietly, sings at concerts, drives out at five every day, and returns at seven sharp for dinner. Seldom goes out at other times, except when she sings. Has only one male visitor, but a good deal of him. He is dark, handsome, and dashing, never calls less than once a day, and often twice. He is a Mr. Godfrey Norton, of the Inner Temple. See the advantages of a cabman as a confidant. They had driven him home a dozen times from Serpentine-mews, and knew all about him. When I had listened to all they had to tell, I began to walk up and down near Briony Lodge once more, and to think over my plan of campaign.

"This Godfrey Norton was evidently an important factor in the matter. He was a lawyer. That sounded ominous. What was the relation between them, and what the object of his repeated visits? Was she his client, his friend, or his mistress? If the former, she had probably transferred the photograph to his keeping. If the latter, it was less likely. On the issue of this question depended whether I should continue my work at Briony Lodge, or turn my attention to the gentleman's chambers in the Temple. It was a delicate point, and it widened the field of my inquiry. I fear that I bore you with these details, but I have to let you see my little difficulties, if you are to understand the situation."

"I am following you closely," I answered.

"I was still balancing the matter in my mind when a hansom cab drove up to Briony Lodge, and a gentleman sprang out. He was a remarkably handsome man, dark, aquiline, and moustached—evidently the man of whom I had heard. He appeared to be in a great hurry, shouted to the cabman to wait, and brushed past the maid who opened the door with the air of a man who was thoroughly at home.

"He was in the house about half an hour, and I could catch glimpses of him in the windows of the sitting-room, pacing up and down, talking excitedly, and waving his arms. Of her I could see nothing. Presently he emerged, looking even more flurried than before. As he stepped up to the cab, he pulled a gold watch from his pocket and looked at it earnestly, 'Drive like the devil,' he shouted, 'first to Gross & Hankey's in Regent Street, and then to the Church of St. Monica in the Edgeware Road. Half a guinea if you do it in twenty minutes!'

"Away they went, and I was just wondering whether I should not do well to follow them when up the lane came a neat little landau, the coachman with his coat only half-buttoned, and his tie under his ear, while all the tags of his harness were sticking out of the buckles. It hadn't pulled up before she shot out of the hall door and into it. I only caught a glimpse of her at the moment, but she was a lovely woman, with a face that a man might die for.

"'The Church of St. Monica, John,' she cried, 'and half a sovereign if you reach it in twenty minutes.'

"This was quite too good to lose, Watson. I was just balancing whether I should run for it, or whether I should perch behind her landau when a cab came through the street. The driver looked twice at such a shabby fare, but I jumped in before he could object. 'The Church of St. Monica,' said I, 'and half a sovereign if you reach it in twenty minutes.' It was twenty-five minutes to twelve, and of course it was clear enough what was in the wind.

"My cabby drove fast. I don't think I ever drove faster, but the others were there before us. The cab and the landau with their steaming horses were in front of the door when I arrived. I paid the man and hurried into the church. There was not a soul there save the two whom I had followed and a surpliced clergyman, who seemed to be expostulating with them. They were all three standing in a knot in front of the altar. I lounged up the side aisle like any other idler who has dropped into a church. Suddenly, to my surprise, the three at the altar faced round to me, and Godfrey Norton came running as hard as he could towards me.

"'Thank God,' he cried. 'You'll do. Come! Come!'"

"'What then?' I asked.

"'Come, man, come, only three minutes, or it won't be legal.'

"I was half-dragged up to the altar, and before I knew where I was I found myself mumbling responses which were whispered in my ear, and vouching for things of which I knew nothing, and generally assisting in the secure tying up of Irene Adler, spinster, to Godfrey Norton, bachelor. It was all done in an instant, and there was the gentleman thanking me on the one side and the lady on the other, while the clergyman beamed on me in front. It was the most preposterous position in which I ever found myself in my life, and it was the thought of it that started me laughing just now. It seems that there had been some informality about their license, that the clergyman absolutely refused to marry them without a witness of some sort, and that my lucky appearance saved the bridegroom from having to sally out into the streets in search of a best man. The bride gave me a sovereign, and I mean to wear it on my watch-chain in memory of the occasion."

"This is a very unexpected turn of affairs," said I; "and what then?"

"Well, I found my plans very seriously menaced. It looked as if the pair might take an immediate departure, and so necessitate very prompt and energetic measures on my part. At the church door, however, they separated, he driving back to the Temple, and she to her own house. 'I shall drive out in the park at five as usual,' she said as she left him. I heard no more. They drove away in different directions, and I went off to make my own arrangements."

"Which are?"

"Some cold beef and a glass of beer," he answered, ringing the bell. "I have been too busy to think of food, and I am likely to be busier still this evening. By the way, Doctor, I shall want your coöperation."

"I shall be delighted."

"You don't mind breaking the law?"

"Not in the least."

"Nor running a chance of arrest?"

"Not in a good cause."

"Oh, the cause is excellent!"

"Then I am your man."

"I was sure that I might rely on you."

"But what is it you wish?"

"When Mrs. Turner has brought in the tray I will make it clear to you. Now," he said as he turned hungrily on the simple fare that our landlady had provided, "I must discuss it while I eat, for I have not much time. It is nearly five now. In two hours we must be on the scene of action. Miss Irene, or Madame, rather, returns from her drive at seven. We must be at Briony Lodge to meet her."

"And what then?"

"You must leave that to me. I have already arranged what is to occur. There is only one point on which I must insist. You must not interfere, come what may. You understand?"

"I am to be neutral?"

"To do nothing whatever. There will probably be some small unpleasantness. Do not join in it. It will end in my being conveyed into the house. Four or five minutes afterwards the sitting-room window will open. You are to station yourself close to that open window."

"Yes."

"You are to watch me, for I will be visible to you."

"Yes."

"And when I raise my hand—so—you will throw into the room what I give you to throw, and will, at the same time, raise the cry of fire. You quite follow me?"

"Entirely."

"It is nothing very formidable," he said, taking a long cigar-shaped roll from his pocket. "It is an ordinary plumber's smoke-rocket, fitted with a cap at either end to make it self-lighting. Your task is confined to that. When you raise your cry of fire, it will be taken up by quite a number of people. You may then walk to the end of the street, and I will rejoin you in ten minutes. I hope that I have made myself clear?"

"I am to remain neutral, to get near the window, to watch you, and at the signal to throw in this object, then to raise the cry of fire, and to wait you at the corner of the street."

"Precisely."

"Then you may entirely rely on me."

"That is excellent. I think, perhaps, it is almost time that I prepare for the new rôle I have to play."

He disappeared into his bedroom and returned in a few minutes in the character of an amiable and simple-minded Nonconformist clergyman. His broad black hat, his baggy trousers, his white tie, his sympathetic smile, and general look of peering and benevolent curiosity were such as Mr. John Hare alone could have equalled. It was not merely that Holmes changed his costume. His expression, his manner, his very soul seemed to vary with each fresh part that he assumed. The stage lost a fine actor, even as science lost an acute reasoner, when he became a specialist in crime.

It was a quarter past six when we left Baker Street, and it still wanted ten minutes to the hour when we found ourselves in Serpentine Avenue. It was already dusk, and the lamps were just being lighted as we paced up and down in front of Briony Lodge, waiting for the coming of its occupant. The house was just such as I had pictured it from Sherlock Holmes's succinct description, but the locality appeared to be less private than I expected. On the contrary, for a small street in a quiet neighborhood, it was remarkably animated. There was a group of shabbily dressed men smoking and laughing in a corner, a scissors-grinder with his wheel, two guardsmen who were flirt-ing with a nurse-girl, and several well-dressed young men who were lounging up and down with cigars in their mouths.

"You see," remarked Holmes, as we paced to and fro in front of the house, "this marriage rather simplifies matters. The pho-tograph becomes a double-edged weapon now. The chances are that she would be as averse to its being seen by Mr. Godfrey Norton, as our client is to its coming to the eyes of his princess. Now the question is, Where are we to find the photograph?"

"Where, indeed?"

"It is most unlikely that she carries it about with her. It is cab-inet size. Too large for easy concealment about a woman's dress. She knows that the King is capable of having her waylaid and searched. Two attempts of the sort have already been made. We may take it, then, that she does not carry it about with her."

"Where, then?"

"Her banker or her lawyer. There is that double possibility. But I am inclined to think neither. Women are naturally secre-tive, and they like to do their own secreting. Why should she hand it over to anyone else? She could trust her own guardian-ship, but she could not tell what indirect or political influence might be brought to bear upon a business man. Besides, remember that she had resolved to use it within a few days. It must be where she can lay her hands upon it. It must be in her own house."

"But it has twice been burgled."

"Pshaw! They did not know how to look."

"But how will you look?"

"I will not look."

"What then?"

"I will get her to show me."

"But she will refuse."

"She will not be able to. But I hear the rumble of wheels. It is her carriage. Now carry out my orders to the letter."

As he spoke the gleam of the side-lights of a carriage came round the curve of the avenue. It was a smart little landau which rattled up to the door of Briony Lodge. As it pulled up, one of the loafing men at the corner dashed forward to open the door in the hope of earning a copper, but was elbowed away by another loafer, who had rushed up with the same intention. A fierce quarrel broke out, which was increased by the two guardsmen, who took sides with one of the loungers, and by the scissors-grinder, who was equally hot upon the other side. A blow was struck, and in an instant the lady, who had stepped from her carriage, was the centre of a little knot of flushed and struggling men, who struck savagely at each other with their fists and sticks. Holmes dashed into the crowd to protect the lady; but just as he reached her he gave a cry and dropped to the ground, with the blood running freely down his face. At his fall the guardsmen took to their heels in one direction and the loungers in the other, while a number of better-dressed people, who had watched the scuffle without taking part in it, crowded in to help the lady and to attend to the injured man. Irene Adler, as I will still call her, had hurried up the steps; but she stood at the top with her superb figure outlined against the lights of the hall, looking back into the street.

"Is the poor gentleman much hurt?" she asked.

"He is dead," cried several voices.

"No, no, there's life in him!' shouted another. "But he'll be gone before you can get him to hospital."

"He's a brave fellow," said a woman. "They would have had the lady's purse and watch if it hadn't been for him. They were a gang, and a rough one, too. Ah, he's breathing now."

"He can't lie in the street. May we bring him in, marm?"

"Surely. Bring him into the sitting-room. There is a comfortable sofa. This way, please!"

Slowly and solemnly he was borne into Briony Lodge and laid out in the principal room, while I still observed the proceedings from my post by the window. The lamps had been lit, but the blinds had not been drawn, so that I could see Holmes as he lay upon the couch. I do not know whether he was seized with compunction at that moment for the part he was playing, but I know that I never felt more heartily ashamed of myself in my life than when I saw the beautiful creature against whom I was conspiring, or the grace and kindliness with which she waited upon the injured man. And yet it would be the blackest treachery to Holmes to draw back now from the part which he had intrusted to me. I hardened my heart, and took the smoke-rocket from under my ulster. After all, I thought, we are not injuring her. We are but preventing her from injuring another.

Holmes had sat up upon the couch, and I saw him motion like a man who is in need of air. A maid rushed across and threw open the window. At the same instant I saw him raise his hand, and at the signal I tossed my rocket into the room with a cry of "Fire!" The word was no sooner out of my mouth than the whole crowd of spectators, well dressed and ill—gentlemen, ostlers, and servant-maids—joined in a general shriek of "Fire!" Thick clouds of smoke curled through the room and out at the open window. I caught a glimpse of rushing figures, and a moment later the voice of Holmes from within assuring them that it was a false alarm. Slipping through the shouting crowd I made my way to the corner of the street, and in ten minutes was rejoiced to find my friend's arm in mine, and to get away from the scene of the uproar. He walked swiftly and in silence for some few minutes until we had turned down one of the quiet streets which lead towards the Edgeware Road.

"You did it very nicely, Doctor," he remarked. "Nothing could have been better. It is all right."

"You have the photograph?"

"I know where it is."

"And how did you find out?"

"She showed me, as I told you she would."

"I am still in the dark."

"I do not wish to make a mystery," said he, laughing. "The matter was perfectly simple. You, of course, saw that everyone in the street was an accomplice. They were all engaged for the evening."

"I guessed as much."

"Then, when the row broke out, I had a little moist red paint in the palm of my hand. I rushed forward, fell down, clapped my hand to my face, and became a piteous spectacle. It is an old trick."

"That also I could fathom."

"Then they carried me in. She was bound to have me in. What else could she do? And into her sitting-room, which was the very room which I suspected. It lay between that and her bedroom, and I was determined to see which. They laid me on a couch, I motioned for air, they were compelled to open the window, and you had your chance."

"How did that help you?"

"It was all-important. When a woman thinks that her house is on fire, her instinct is at once to rush to the thing which she values most. It is a perfectly overpowering impulse, and I have more than once taken advantage of it. In the case of the Darlington substitution scandal it was of use to me, and also in the Arnsworth Castle business. A married woman grabs at her baby; an unmarried one reaches for her jewel-box. Now it was clear to me that our lady of to-day had nothing in the house more precious to her than what we are in quest of. She would rush to secure it. The alarm of fire was admirably done. The smoke and shouting were enough to shake nerves of steel. She responded beautifully. The photograph is in a recess behind a sliding panel just above the right bell-pull. She was there in an instant, and I caught a glimpse of it as she half-drew it out. When I cried out that it was a false alarm, she replaced it, glanced at the rocket, rushed from the room, and I have not seen her since. I rose, and, making my excuses, escaped from the house. I hesitated whether to attempt to secure the photograph at once; but the coachman had come in, and as he was watching me narrowly it seemed safer to wait. A little over-precipitance may ruin all."

"And now?" I asked.

"Our quest is practically finished. I shall call with the King to-morrow, and with you, if you care to come with us. We will be shown into the sitting-room to wait for the lady, but it is probable that when she comes she may find neither us nor the photograph. It might be a satisfaction to his Majesty to regain it with his own hands."

"And when will you call?"

"At eight in the morning. She will not be up, so that we shall have a clear field. Besides, we must be prompt, for this marriage may mean a complete change in her life and habits. I must wire to the King without delay."

We had reached Baker Street and had stopped at the door.

He was searching his pockets for the key when someone passing said:

"Good-night, Mister Sherlock Holmes."

There were several people on the pavement at the time, but the greeting appeared to come from a slim youth in an ulster who had hurried by.

"I've heard that voice before," said Holmes, staring down the dimly lit street. "Now, I wonder who the deuce that could have been."

3

I slept at Baker Street that night, and we were engaged upon our toast and coffee in the morning when the King of Bohemia rushed into the room.

"You have really got it!" he cried, grasping Sherlock Holmes by either shoulder and looking eagerly into his face.

"Not yet."

"But you have hopes?"

"I have hopes."

"Then, come. I am all impatience to be gone."

"We must have a cab."

"No, my brougham is waiting."

"Then that will simplify matters." We descended and started off once more for Briony Lodge.

"Irene Adler is married," remarked Holmes.

"Married! When?"

"Yesterday."

"But to whom?"

"To an English lawyer named Norton."

"But she could not love him."

"I am in hopes that she does."

"And why in hopes?"

"Because it would spare your Majesty all fear of future annoyance. If the lady loves her husband, she does not love your Majesty. If she does not love your Majesty, there is no reason why she should interfere with your Majesty's plan."

"It is true. And yet—Well! I wish she had been of my own sta-

tion! What a queen she would have made!" He relapsed into a
moody silence, which was not broken until we drew up in
Serpentine Avenue.

The door of Briony Lodge was open, and an elderly woman
stood upon the steps. She watched us with a sardonic eye as we
stepped from the brougham.

"Mr. Sherlock Holmes, I believe?" said she.

"I am Mr. Holmes," answered my companion, looking at her
with a questioning and rather startled gaze.

"Indeed! My mistress told me that you were likely to call. She
left this morning with her husband by the 5:15 train from
Charing Cross for the Continent."

"What!" Sherlock Holmes staggered back, white with chagrin
and surprise. "Do you mean that she has left England?"

"Never to return."

"And the papers?" asked the King hoarsely. "All is lost."

"We shall see." He pushed past the servant and rushed into
the drawing-room, followed by the King and myself. The furniture was scattered about in every direction, with dismantled
shelves and open drawers, as if the lady had hurriedly ransacked
them before her flight. Holmes rushed at the bell-pull, tore
back a small sliding shutter, and, plunging in his hand, pulled
out a photograph and a letter. The photograph was of Irene
Adler herself in evening dress, the letter was superscribed to
"Sherlock Holmes, Esq. To be left till called for." My friend tore
it open, and we all three read it together. It was dated at midnight of the preceding night and ran in this way:

MY DEAR MR. SHERLOCK HOLMES:

You really did it very well. You took me in completely. Until
after the alarm of fire, I had not a suspicion. But then, when I
found how I had betrayed himself, I began to think. I had been
warned against you months ago. I had been told that if the King
employed an agent it would certainly be you. And your address
had been given me. Yet, with all this, you made me reveal what
you wanted to know. Even after I became suspicious, I found it
hard to think evil of such a dear, kind old clergyman. But, you
know, I have been trained as an actress myself. Male costume is
nothing new to me. I often take advantage of the freedom which

it gives. I sent John, the coachman, to watch you, ran upstairs, got into my walking-clothes, as I call them, and came down just as you departed.

Well, I followed you to your door, and so made sure that I was really an object of interest to the celebrated Mr. Sherlock Holmes. Then I, rather imprudently, wished you good-night, and started for the Temple to see my husband.

We both thought the best resource was flight, when pursued by so formidable an antagonist; so you will find the nest empty when you call to-morrow. As to the photograph, your client may rest in peace. I love and am loved by a better man than he. The King may do what he will without hindrance from one whom he has cruelly wronged. I keep it only to safeguard myself, and to preserve a weapon which will always secure me from any steps which he might take in the future. I have a photograph which he might care to possess; and I remain, dear Mr. Sherlock Holmes,

Very truly yours,

IRENE NORTON, *née* ADLER.

"What a woman—oh, what a woman!" cried the King of Bohemia, when we had all three read this epistle. "Did I not tell you how quick and resolute she was? Would she not have made an admirable queen? Is it not a pity that she was not on my level?"

"From what I have seen of the lady she seems indeed to be on a very different level to your Majesty," said Holmes coldly. "I am sorry that I have not been able to bring your Majesty's business to a more successful conclusion."

"On the contrary, my dear sir," cried the King; "nothing could be more successful. I know that her word is inviolate. The photograph is now as safe as if it were in the fire."

"I am glad to hear your Majesty say so."

"I am immensely indebted to you. Pray tell me in what way I can reward you. This ring—" He slipped an emerald snake ring from his finger and held it out upon the palm of his hand.

"Your Majesty has something which I should value even more highly," said Holmes.

"You have but to name it."

"This photograph!"

The King stared at him in amazement.

"Irene's photograph!" he cried. "Certainly, if you wish it."

"I thank your Majesty. Then there is no more to be done in the matter. I have the honour to wish you a very good-morning." He bowed, and, turning away without observing the hand which the King had stretched out to him, he set off in my company for his chambers.

And that was how a great scandal threatened to affect the kingdom of Bohemia, and how the best plans of Mr. Sherlock Holmes were beaten by a woman's wit. He used to make merry over the cleverness of women, but I have not heard him do it of late. And when he speaks of Irene Adler, or when he refers to her photograph, it is always under the honorable title of *the* woman.

A Costume Piece

(1899)

E. W. Hornung

Londono was just then talking of one whose name is already a name and nothing more. Reuben Rosenthall had made his millions on the diamond fields of South Africa, and had come home to enjoy them according to his lights; how he went to work will scarcely be forgotten by any reader of the halfpenny evening papers, which revelled in endless anecdotes of his original indigence and present prodigality, varied with interesting particulars of the extraordinary establishment which the millionaire set up in St. John's Wood. Here he kept a retinue of Kaffirs, who were literally his slaves; and hence he would sally with enormous diamonds in his shirt and on his finger, in the convoy of a prize-fighter of heinous repute, who was not, however, by any means the worst element in the Rosenthall menage. So said common gossip; but the fact was sufficiently established by the interference of the police on at least one occasion, followed by certain magisterial proceedings which were reported with justifiable gusto and huge headlines in the newspapers aforesaid. And this was all one knew of Reuben Rosenthall up to the time when the Old Bohemian Club, having fallen on evil days, found it worth its while to organize a great dinner in honour of so wealthy an exponent of the club's principles. I was not at the banquet myself, but a member took Raffles, who told me all about it that very night.

"Most extraordinary show I ever went to in my life," said he. "As for the man himself—well, I was prepared for something grotesque, but the fellow fairly took my breath away. To begin with, he's the most astounding brute to look at, well over six feet, with a chest like a barrel and a great hook-nose, and the reddest hair and whiskers you ever saw. Drank like a fire-engine, but only got drunk enough to make us a speech that I wouldn't have missed for ten pounds. I'm only sorry you weren't there, too, Bunny, old chap."

I began to be sorry myself, for Raffles was anything but an excitable person, and never had I seen him so excited before. Had he been following Rosenthall's example? His coming to my rooms at midnight, merely to tell me about his dinner, was in itself enough to excuse a suspicion which was certainly at variance with my knowledge of A. J. Raffles.

"What did he say?" I inquired mechanically, divining some subtler explanation of this visit, and wondering what on earth it could be.

"Say?" cried Raffles. "What did he not say! He boasted of his vice, he bragged of his riches, and he blackguarded society for taking him up for his money and dropping him out of sheer pique and jealousy because he had so much. He mentioned names, too, with the most charming freedom, and swore he was as good a man as the Old Country had to show—*pace* the Old Bohemians. To prove it he pointed to a great diamond in the middle of his shirt-front with a little finger loaded with another just like it: which of our bloated princes could show a pair like that? As a matter of fact, they seemed quite wonderful stones, with a curious purple gleam to them that must mean a pot of money. But old Rosenthall swore he wouldn't take fifty thousand pounds for the two, and wanted to know where the other man was who went about with twenty-five thousand in his shirt-front, and the other twenty-five on his little finger. He didn't exist. If he did, he wouldn't have the pluck to wear them. But he had—he'd tell us why. And before you could say Jack Robinson he had whipped out a whacking great revolver!"

"Not at the table?"

"At the table! In the middle of his speech! But it was nothing to what he wanted to do. He actually wanted us to let him write his name in bullets on the opposite wall to show us why he wasn't afraid to go about in all his diamonds! That brute Purvis, the prize-fighter, who is his paid bully, had to bully his master before he could be persuaded out of it. There was quite a panic for the moment; one fellow was saying his prayers under the table, and the waiters bolted to a man."

"What a grotesque scene!"

"Grotesque enough, but I rather wish they had let him go the whole hog and blaze away. He was as keen as knives to show us how he could take care of his purple diamonds; and, do you know, Bunny, I was as keen as knives to see."

And Raffles leant towards me with a sly, slow smile that made the hidden meaning of his visit only too plain to me at last.

"So you think of having a try for his diamonds yourself?"

He shrugged his shoulders.

"It is horribly obvious, I admit. But—yes, I have set my heart upon them! To be quite frank, I have had them on my conscience for some time; one couldn't hear so much of the man, and his prize-fighter, and his diamonds, without feeling it a kind of duty to have a go for them; but when it comes to brandishing a revolver and practically challenging the world, the thing becomes inevitable. It is simply thrust upon one. I was fated to hear that challenge, Bunny, and I, for one, must take it up. I was only sorry I couldn't get on my hind legs and say so then and there."

"Well," I said, "I don't see the necessity as things are with us; but, of course, I'm your man."

My tone may have been half-hearted. I did my best to make it otherwise. But it was barely a month since our Bond Street exploit, and we certainly could have afforded to behave ourselves for some time to come. We had been getting along so nicely: by his advice I had scribbled a thing or two; inspired by Raffles, I had even done an article on our own jewel robbery; and for the moment I was quite satisfied with this sort of adventure. I thought we ought to know when we were well off, and could see no point in our running fresh risks before we were obliged. On the other hand, I was anxious not to show the least disposition to break the pledge that I had given a month ago. But it was not on my manifest disinclination that Raffles fastened.

"Necessity, my dear Bunny? Does the writer only write when the wolf is at the door? Does the painter paint for bread alone? Must you and I be driven to crime like Tom of Bow and Dick of Whitechapel? You pain me, my dear chap; you needn't laugh, because you do. Art for art's sake is a vile catchword, but I confess it appeals to me. In this case my motives are absolutely pure, for I doubt if we shall ever be able to dispose of such peculiar stones. But if I don't have a try for them—after to-night,— I shall never be able to hold up my head again."

His eye twinkled, but it glittered too.

"We shall have our work cut out," was all I said.

"And do you suppose I should be keen on it if we hadn't?" cried Raffles. "My dear fellow, I would rob St. Paul's Cathedral if I could, but I could no more scoop a till when the shopwalker wasn't looking than I could bag apples out of an old woman's basket. Even that little business last month was a sordid affair, but it was necessary, and I think its strategy redeemed it to some extent. Now there's some credit, and more sport, in going where they boast they're on their guard against you. The Bank of England, for example, is the ideal crib; but that would need half a dozen of us with years to give to the job; and meanwhile Reuben Rosenthall is high enough game for you and me. We know he's armed. We know how Billy Purvis can fight. It'll be no soft thing, I grant you. But what of that, my good Bunny—what of that? A man's reach must exceed his grasp, dear boy, or what the dickens is a heaven for?"

"I would rather we didn't exceed ours just yet," I answered, laughing, for his spirit was irresistible, and the plan was growing upon me, despite my qualms.

"Trust me for that," was his reply; "I'll see you through. After all, I expect to find that the difficulties are nearly all on the surface. These fellows both drink like the devil, and that should simplify matters considerably. But we shall see, and we must take our time. There will probably turn out to be a dozen different ways in which the thing might be done, and we shall have to choose between them. It will mean watching the house for at least a week in any case; it may mean lots of other things that will take much longer; but give me a week, and I will tell you more. That's to say if you're really on?"

"Of course I am," I replied indignantly. "But why should I give you a week? Why shouldn't we watch the house together?" "Because two eyes are as good as four, and take up less room. Never hunt in couples unless you're obliged. But don't you look offended, Bunny; there'll be plenty for you to do when the time comes, that I promise you. You shall have your share of the fun, never fear, and a purple diamond all to yourself—if we're lucky."

On the whole, however, this conversation left me less than lukewarm, and I still remember the depression which came over me when Raffles was gone. I saw the folly of the enterprise to which I had committed myself—the sheer, gratuitous, unnecessary folly of it. And the paradoxes in which Raffles revelled, and the frivolous casuistry which was nevertheless half sincere, and which his mere personality rendered wholly plausible at the moment of utterance, appealed very little to me when recalled in cold blood. I admired the spirit of pure mischief in which he seemed prepared to risk his liberty and his life, but I did not find it an infectious spirit on calm reflection. Yet the thought of withdrawal was not to be entertained for a moment. On the contrary, I was impatient of the delay ordained by Raffles; and, perhaps, no small part of my secret disaffection came of his galling determination to do without me until the last moment.

It made it no better that this was characteristic of the man and of his attitude towards me. For a month we had been, I suppose, the thickest thieves in all London, and yet our intimacy was curiously incomplete. With all his charming frankness, there was in Raffles a vein of capricious reserve which was perceptible enough to be very irritating. He had the instinctive secretiveness of the inveterate criminal. He would make mysteries of matters of common concern; for example, I never knew how or where he disposed of the Bond Street jewels, on the proceeds of which we were both still leading the outward lives of hundreds of other young fellows about town. He was consistently mysterious about that and other details, of which it seemed to me that I had already earned the right to know everything. I could not but remember how he had led me into my first felony, by means of a trick, while yet uncertain whether he could trust me or not. That I could no longer afford to resent, but I did resent his want of confidence in me now. I said nothing about it, but it rankled every day, and never more than in the week that succeeded the Rosenthall dinner. When I met Raffles at the club he would tell me nothing; when I went to his rooms he was out, or pretended to be. One day he told me he was getting on well, but slowly; it was a more ticklish game than he had thought; but when I began to ask questions he would say no more. Then and there, in my annoyance, I took my own decision. Since he would tell me nothing of the result of his vigils, I determined to keep one on my own account, and that very evening found my way to the millionaire's front gates.

The house he was occupying is, I believe, quite the largest in the St. John's Wood district. It stands in the angle formed by two broad thoroughfares, neither of which, as it happens, is a 'bus route, and I doubt if many quieter spots exist within the four-mile radius. Quiet also was the great square house, in its garden of grass-plots and shrubs; the lights were low, the millionaire and his friends obviously spending their evening elsewhere. The garden walls were only a few feet high. In one there was a side door opening into a glass passage; in the other two five-barred grained-and-varnished gates, one at either end of the little semi-circular drive, and both wide open. So still was the place that I had a great mind to walk boldly in and learn something of the premises; in fact, I was on the point of doing so, when I heard a quick, shuffling step on the pavement behind me. I turned round and faced the dark scowl and the dirty clenched fists of a dilapidated tramp.

"You fool!" said he. "You utter idiot!"

"Raffles!"

"That's it," he whispered savagely; "tell all the neighbourhood—give me away at the top of your voice!"

With that he turned his back upon me, and shambled down the road, shrugging his shoulders and muttering to himself as though I had refused him alms. A few moments I stood astounded, indignant, at a loss; then I followed him. His feet trailed, his knees gave, his back was bowed, his head kept nodding; it was the gait of a man eighty years of age. Presently he waited for me midway between two lamp-posts. As I came up he was lighting rank tobacco, in a cutty pipe, with an evil-smelling match, and the flame showed me the suspicion of a smile.

"You must forgive my heat, Bunny, but it really was very foolish of you. Here am I trying every dodge—begging at the door one night—hiding in the shrubs the next—doing every mortal thing but stand and stare at the house as you went and did. It's a costume piece, and in you rush in your ordinary clothes. I tell you they're on the look-out for us night and day. It's the toughest nut I ever tackled!"

"Well," said I, "if you had told me so before I shouldn't have come. You told me nothing."

He looked hard at me from under the broken brim of a battered billycock.

"You're right," he said at length. "I've been too close. It's become second nature with me, when I've anything on. But here's an end of it, Bunny, so far as you're concerned. I'm going home now, and I want you to follow me; but for heaven's sake keep your distance, and don't speak to me again till I speak to you. There—give me a start." And he was off again, a decrepit vagabond, with his hands in his pockets, his elbows squared, and frayed coat-tails swinging raggedly from side to side.

I followed him to the Finchley Road. There he took an omnibus, and I sat some rows behind him on the top, but not far enough to escape the pest of his vile tobacco. That he could carry his character-sketch to such a pitch—he who would only smoke one brand of cigarettes! It was the last, least touch of the insatiable artist, and it charmed away what mortification there still remained in me. Once more I felt the fascination of a comrade who was for ever dazzling one with a fresh and unsuspected facet of his character.

As we neared Piccadilly I wondered what he would do. Surely he was not going into the Albany like that? No, he took another omnibus to Sloane Street, I sitting behind him as before. At Sloane Street we changed again, and were presently in the long lean artery of the King's Road. I was now all agog to know our destination, nor was I kept many more minutes in doubt. Raffles got down. I followed. He crossed the road and disappeared up a dark turning. I pressed after him, and was in time to see his coat-tails as he plunged into a still darker flagged alley to the right. He was holding himself up and stepping out like a young man once more; also, in some subtle way, he already looked less disreputable. But I alone was there to see him, the alley was absolutely deserted, and desperately dark. At the farther end he opened a door with a latchkey, and it was darker yet within.

Instinctively I drew back and heard him chuckle. We could no longer see each other.

"All right, Bunny! There's no hanky-panky this time. These are studios, my friend, and I'm one of the lawful tenants."

Indeed, in another minute we were in a lofty room with sky-light, easels, dressing-cupboard, platform, and every other adjunct save the signs of actual labor. The first thing I saw, as Raffles lit the gas, was its reflection in his silk hat on the pegs beside the rest of his normal garments.

"Looking for the works of art?" continued Raffles, lighting a cigarette and beginning to divest himself of his rags. "I'm afraid you won't find any, but there's the canvas I'm always going to make a start upon. I tell them I'm looking high and low for my ideal model. I have the stove lit on principle twice a week, and look in and leave a newspaper and a smell of Sullivans—how good they are after shag! Meanwhile I pay my rent and am a good tenant in every way; and it's a very useful little *pied-à-terre*—there's no saying how useful it might be at a pinch. As it is, the billycock comes in and the topper goes out, and nobody takes the slightest notice of either; at this time of night the chances are that there's not a soul in the building except ourselves."

"You never told me you went in for disguises," said I, watching him as he cleansed the grime from his face and hands.

"No, Bunny, I've treated you very shabbily all round. There was really no reason why I shouldn't have shown you this place a month ago, and yet there was no point in my doing so, and circumstances are just conceivable in which it would have suited us both for you to be in genuine ignorance of my whereabouts. I have something to sleep on, as you perceive, in case of need, and, of course, my name is not Raffles in the King's Road. So you will see that one might bolt farther and fare worse."

"Meanwhile you use the place as a dressing-room?"

"It's my private pavilion," said Raffles. "Disguises? In some cases they're half the battle, and it's always pleasant to feel that, if the worst comes to the worst, you needn't necessarily be convicted under your own name. Then they're indispensable in dealing with the fences. I drive all my bargains in the tongue

and raiment of Shoreditch. If I didn't there'd be the very devil
to pay in blackmail. Now, this cupboard's full of all sorts of tog-
gery. I tell the woman who cleans the room that it's for my mod-
els when I find 'em. By the way, I only hope I've got something
that'll fit you, for you'll want a rig for to-morrow night."

"To-morrow night!" I exclaimed. "Why, what do you mean
to do?"

"The trick," said Raffles. "I intended writing to you as soon as
I got back to my rooms, to ask you to look me up to-morrow
afternoon; then I was going to unfold my plan of campaign, and
take you straight into action then and there. There's nothing like
putting the nervous players in first; it's the sitting with their pads
on that upsets their applecart; that was another of my reasons
for being so confoundedly close. You must try to forgive me. I
couldn't help remembering how well you played up last trip,
without any time to weaken on it beforehand. All I want is for
you to be as cool and smart to-morrow night as you were then;
though, by Jove, there's no comparison between the two cases!"

"I thought you would find it so."

"You were right. I have. Mind you, I don't say this will be the
tougher job all round; we shall probably get in without any difficulty at all; it's the getting out again that may flummux us.
That's the worst of an irregular household!" cried Raffles, with
quite a burst of virtuous indignation. "I assure you, Bunny, I
spent the whole of Monday night in the shrubbery of the garden
next door, looking over the wall, and, if you'll believe me, somebody was about all night long! I don't mean the Kaffirs. I don't
believe they ever get to bed at all, poor devils! No, I mean
Rosenthall himself, and that pasty-faced beast Purvis. They
were up and drinking from midnight, when they came in, to
broad daylight, when I cleared out. Even then I left them sober
enough to slang each other. By the way, they very nearly came
to blows in the garden, within a few yards of me, and I heard
something that might come in useful and make Rosenthall shoot
crooked at a critical moment. You know what an I. D. B. is?"

"Illicit Diamond Buyer?"

"Exactly. Well, it seems that Rosenthall was one. He must
have let it out to Purvis in his cups. Anyhow, I heard Purvis
taunting him with it, and threatening him with the breakwater

at Capetown; and I begin to think our friends are friend and foe. But about to-morrow night: there's nothing subtle in my plan. It's simply to get in while these fellows are out on the loose, and to lie low till they come back, and longer. If possible, we must doctor the whisky. That would simplify the whole thing, though it's not a very sporting game to play; still, we must remember Rosenthall's revolver; we don't want him to sign his name on us. With all those Kaffirs about, however, it's ten to one on the whisky, and a hundred to one against us if we go looking for it. A brush with the heathen would spoil everything, if it did no more. Besides, there are the ladies—"

"The deuce there are!"

"Ladies with an 'i', and the very voices for raising Cain. I fear, I fear the clamour! It would be fatal to us. *Au contraire*, if we can manage to stow ourselves away unbeknowns, half the battle will be won. If Rosenthall turns in drunk, it's a purple diamond apiece. If he sits up sober, it may be a bullet instead. We will hope not, Bunny; and all the firing wouldn't be on one side; but it's on the knees of the gods."

And so we left it when we shook hands in Piccadilly—not by any means as much later as I could have wished. Raffles would not ask me to his rooms that night. He said he made it a rule to have a long night before playing cricket and—other games. His final word to me was framed on the same principle.

"Mind, only one drink to-night, Bunny. Two at the outside— as you value your life—and mine!"

I remember my abject obedience, and the endless, sleepless night it gave me; and the roofs of the houses opposite standing out at last against the blue-grey London dawn. I wondered whether I should ever see another, and was very hard on myself for that little expedition which I had made on my own wilful account.

It was between eight and nine o'clock in the evening when we took up our position in the garden adjoining that of Reuben Rosenthall; the house itself was shut up, thanks to the outrageous libertine next door, who, by driving away the neighbours, had gone far towards delivering himself into our hands. Practically secure from surprise on that side, we could watch our house under cover of a wall just high enough to see over, while a fair margin of shrubs in either garden afforded us additional protection. Thus entrenched we had stood an hour, watching a pair of lighted bow-windows with vague shadows flitting continually across the blinds, and listening to the drawing of corks, the clink of glasses, and a gradual crescendo of coarse voices within. Our luck seemed to have deserted us: the owner of the purple diamonds was dining at home and dining at undue length. I thought it was a dinner-party. Raffles differed; in the end he proved right. Wheels grated in the drive, a carriage and pair stood at the steps; there was a stampede from the dining-room, and the loud voices died away, to burst forth presently from the porch.

Let me make our position perfectly clear. We were over the wall, at the side of the house, but a few feet from the dining-room windows. On our right, one angle of the building cut the back lawn in two diagonally; on our left another angle just permitted us to see the jutting steps and the waiting carriage. We saw Rosenthall come out—saw the glimmer of his diamonds before anything. Then came the pugilist; then a lady with a head of hair like a bath sponge; then another, and the party was complete.

Raffles ducked and pulled me down in great excitement.

"The ladies are going with them," he whispered. "This is great!"

"That's better still."

"The Gardenia!" the millionaire had bawled.

"And that's best of all," said Raffles, standing upright as hoofs and wheels crunched through the gates and rattled off at a fine speed.

"Now what?" I whispered, trembling with excitement.

"They'll be clearing away. Yes, here come their shadows. The drawing-room windows open on the lawn. Bunny, it's the psychological moment. Where's that mask?"

I produced it with a hand whose trembling I tried in vain to still, and could have died for Raffles when he made no comment on what he could not fail to notice. His own hands were firm and cool as he adjusted my mask for me, and then his own.

"By Jove, old boy," he whispered cheerily, "you look about the greatest ruffian I ever saw! These masks alone will down a nigger, if we meet one. But I'm glad I remembered to tell you not to shave. You'll pass for Whitechapel if the worst comes to the

worst and you don't forget to talk the lingo. Better sulk like a
mule if you're not sure of it, and leave the dialogue to me; but,
please our stars, there will be no need. Now, are you ready?"

"Quite."

"Got your gag?"

"Yes."

"Shooter?"

"Yes."

"Then follow me."

In an instant we were over the wall, in another on the lawn
behind the house. There was no moon. The very stars in their
courses had veiled themselves for our benefit. I crept at my
leader's heels to some French windows opening upon a shallow
verandah. He pushed. They yielded.

"Luck again," he whispered; "nothing but luck! Now for a
light."

And the light came!

A good score of electric burners glowed red for the fraction
of a second, then rained merciless white beams into our blinded
eyes. When we found our sight, four revolvers covered us, and
between two of them the colossal frame of Reuben Rosenthall
shook with a wheezy laughter from head to foot.

"Good-evening, boys," he hiccoughed. "Glad to see ye at last.
Shift foot or finger, you on the left, though, and you're a dead
boy. I mean you, you greaser!" he roared out at Raffles. "I know
you. I've been waitin' for you. I've been watchin' you all this
week! Plucky smart you thought yerself, didn't you? One day
beggin', next time shammin' tight, and next one o' them old pals
from Kimberley what never come when I'm in. But you left the
same tracks every day, you buggins, an' the same tracks every
night, all round the blessed premises."

"All right, guv'nor," drawled Raffles; "don't excite. It's a fair
cop. We don't sweat to know 'ow you brung it orf. On'y don't you
go for to shoot, 'cos we 'aint awmed, s'help me Gord!"

"Ah, you're a knowin' one," said Rosenthall, fingering his trig-
gers. "But you've struck a knowin'er."

"Ho, yuss, we know all abaht thet! Set a thief to catch a
thief—ho, yuss."

My eyes had torn themselves from the round black muzzles, from the accursed diamonds that had been our snare, the pasty pig-face of the over-fed pugilist, and the flaming cheeks and hook nose of Rosenthall himself. I was looking beyond them at the doorway filled with quivering silk and plush, black faces, white eye-balls, woolly pates. But a sudden silence recalled my attention to the millionaire. And only his nose retained its colour.

"What d'ye mean?" he whispered with a hoarse oath. "Spit it out, or, by Christmas, I'll drill you!"

"Whort price thet brikewater?" drawled Raffles, coolly.

"Eh?"

Rosenthall's revolvers were describing widening orbits.

"Whort price thet brikewater—old I. D. B.?"

"Where in hell did you get hold o' that?" asked Rosenthall, with a rattle in his thick neck meant for mirth.

"You may well arst," says Raffles. "It's all over the plice w'ere I come from."

"Who can have spread such rot?"

"I dunno," says Raffles; "arst the gen'leman on yer left; p'raps 'e knows."

The gentleman on his left had turned livid with emotion. Guilty conscience never declared itself in plainer terms. For a moment his small eyes bulged like currants in the suet of his face; the next, he had pocketed his pistols on a professional instinct, and was upon us with his fists.

"Out o' the light—out o' the light!" yelled Rosenthall in a frenzy.

He was too late. No sooner had the burly pugilist obstructed his fire than Raffles was through the window at a bound; while I, for standing still and saying nothing, was scientifically felled to the floor.

I cannot have been many moments without my senses. When I recovered them there was a great to-do in the garden, but I had the drawing-room to myself. I sat up. Rosenthall and Purvis were rushing about outside, cursing the Kaffirs and nagging at each other.

"Over that wall, I tell yer!"

"I tell you it was this one. Can't you whistle for the police?"

"Police be damned! I've had enough of the blessed police."

"Then we'd better get back and make sure of the other rotter."

"Oh, make sure o' yer skin. That's what you'd better do. Jala, you black hog, if I catch you skulkin'. . ."

I never heard the threat. I was creeping from the drawing-room on my hands and knees, my own revolver swinging by its steel ring from my teeth.

For an instant I thought that the hall also was deserted. I was wrong, and I crept upon a Kaffir on all fours. Poor devil, I could not bring myself to deal him a base blow, but I threatened him most hideously with my revolver, and left the white teeth chattering in his black head as I took the stairs three at a time. Why I went upstairs in that decisive fashion, as though it were my only course, I cannot explain. But garden and ground floor seemed alive with men and I might have done worse.

I turned into the first room I came to. It was a bedroom—empty, though lit up; and never shall I forget how I started as I entered, on encountering the awful villain that was myself at full length in a pier-glass! Masked, armed, and ragged, I was indeed fit carrion for a bullet or the hangman, and to one or the other I made up my mind. Nevertheless, I hid myself in the wardrobe behind the mirror; and there I stood shivering and cursing my fate, my folly, and Raffles most of all—Raffles first and last—for I daresay half an hour. Then the wardrobe door was flung suddenly open; they had stolen into the room without a sound; and I was hauled downstairs, an ignominious captive.

Gross scenes followed in the hall. The ladies were now upon the stage, and at sight of the desperate criminal they screamed with one accord. In truth I must have given them fair cause, though my mask was now torn away and hid nothing but my left ear. Rosenthall answered their shrieks with a roar for silence; the woman with the bath-sponge hair swore at him shrilly in return; the place became a Babel impossible to describe. I remember wondering how long it would be before the police appeared. Purvis and the ladies were for calling them in and giving me in charge without delay. Rosenthall would not hear of it. He swore that he would shoot man or woman who left his sight. He had had enough of the police. He was not going to have them coming there to spoil sport; he was going to deal with me in his own way. With that he dragged me from all other hands, flung me against a door, and sent a bullet crashing through the wood within an inch of my ear.

"You drunken fool! It'll be murder!" shouted Purvis, getting in the way a second time.

"Wha' do I care? He's armed, isn't he? I shot him in self-defence. It'll be a warning to others. Will you stand aside, or d'ye want it yourself?"

"You're drunk," said Purvis, still between us. "I saw you take a neat tumblerful since you came in, and it's made you drunk as a fool. Pull yourself together, old man. You ain't a-going to do what you'll be sorry for."

"Then I won't shoot at him, I'll only shoot roun' an' roun' the beggar. You're quite right, ole feller. Wouldn't hurt him. Great mishtake. Roun' an' roun'. There—like that!"

His freckled paw shot up over Purvis's shoulder, mauve light-ning came from his ring, a red flash from his revolver, and shrieks from the women as the reverberations died away. Some splinters lodged in my hair.

Next instant the prize-fighter disarmed him; and I was safe from the devil, but finally doomed to the deep sea. A policeman was in our midst. He had entered through the drawing-room win-dow; he was an officer of few words and creditable promptitude. In a twinkling he had the handcuffs on my wrist, while the pugilist explained the situation, and his patron reviled the force and its representative with impotent malignity. A fine watch they kept; a lot of good they did; coming in when all was over and the whole household might have been murdered in their sleep. The officer only deigned to notice him as he marched me off.

"We know all about you, sir," said he contemptuously, and he refused the sovereign Purvis proffered. "You will be seeing me again, sir, at Marylebone."

"Shall I come now?"

"As you please, sir. I rather think the other gentleman requires you more, and I don't fancy this young man means to give much trouble."

"Oh, I'm coming quietly," I said.

And I went.

In silence we traversed perhaps a hundred yards. It must have been midnight. We did not meet a soul. At last I whispered:

"How on earth did you manage it?"

"Purely by luck," said Raffles. "I had the luck to get clear away through knowing every brick of those back-garden walls, and the double luck to have these togs with the rest over at Chelsea. The helmet is one of a collection I made up at Oxford; here it goes over this wall, and we'd better carry the coat and belt before we meet a real officer. I got them once for a fancy ball—ostensibly—and thereby hangs a yarn. I always thought they might come in useful a second time. My chief crux to-night was getting rid of the cab that brought me back. I sent him off to Scotland Yard with ten bob and a special message to good old Mackenzie. The whole detective department will be at Rosenthall's in about half an hour. Of course, I speculated on our gentleman's hatred of the police—another huge slice of luck. If you'd got away, well and good; if not, I felt he was the man to play with his mouse as long as possible. Yes, Bunny, it's been more of a costume piece than I intended, and we've come out of it, with a good deal less credit. But, by Jove, we're jolly lucky to have come out of it at all!"

Midnight in Beauchamp Row
(1900)
Anna Katharine Green

It was the last house in Beauchamp Row, and it stood several rods away from its nearest neighbor. It was a pretty house in the daytime, but owing to its deep, sloping roof and small bediamonded windows it had a lonesome look at night, notwithstanding the crimson hall-light which shone through the leaves of its vine-covered doorway.

Ned Chivers lived in it with his six months' married bride, and as he was both a busy fellow and a gay one there were many evenings when pretty Letty Chivers sat alone until near midnight.

She was of an uncomplaining spirit, however, and said little, though there were times when both the day and evening seemed very long and married life not altogether the paradise she had expected.

On this evening—a memorable evening for her, the twenty-fourth of December, 1894—she had expected her husband to remain with her, for it was not only Christmas eve, but the night when, as manager of a large manufacturing concern, he brought up from New York the money with which to pay off the men on the next working day, and he never left her when there was any unusual amount of money in the house. But from the first glimpse she had of him coming up the road she knew she was to be disappointed in this hope, and, indignant, alarmed almost, at the prospect of a lonesome evening under these circumstances, she ran hastily down to the gate to meet him, crying:

"Oh, Ned, you look so troubled I know you have only come home for a hurried supper. But you cannot leave me to-night. Tennie" (their only maid) "has gone for a holiday, and I never can stay in this house alone with all that." She pointed to the small bag he carried, which, as she knew, was filled to bursting with bank notes.

He certainly looked troubled. It is hard to resist the entreaty in a young bride's uplifted face. But this time he could not help himself, and he said:

"I am dreadful sorry, but I must ride over to Fairbanks tonight. Mr. Pierson has given me an imperative order to conclude a matter of business there, and it is very important that it should be done. I should lose my position if I neglected the matter, and no one but Hasbrouck and Suffren knows that we keep the money in the house. I have always given out that I intrusted it to Hale's safe over night."

"But I cannot stand it," she persisted. "You have never left me on these nights. That is why I let Tennie go. I will spend the evening at The Larches, or, better still, call in Mr. and Mrs. Talcott to keep me company."

But her husband did not approve of her going out or of her having company. The Larches was too far away, and as for Mr. and Mrs. Talcott, they were meddlesome people, whom he had never liked; besides, Mrs. Talcott was delicate, and the night threatened storm. It seemed hard to subject her to this ordeal, and he showed that he thought so by his manner, but, as circumstances were, she would have to stay alone, and he only hoped she would be brave and go to bed like a good girl, and think nothing about the money, which he would take care to put away in a very safe place.

"Or," said he, kissing her downcast face, "perhaps you would rather hide it yourself; women always have curious ideas about such things."

"Yes, let me hide it," she murmured. "The money, I mean, not the bag. Every one knows the bag. I should never dare to leave it in that." And begging him to unlock it, she began to empty it with a feverish haste that rather alarmed him, for he surveyed her anxiously and shook his head as if he dreaded the effects of this excitement upon her.

But as he saw no way of averting it he confined himself to using such soothing words as were at his command, and then, humoring her weakness, helped her to arrange the bills in the place she had chosen, and restuffing the bag with old receipts till it acquired its former dimensions, he put a few bills on top to make the whole look natural, and, laughing at her white face, relocked the bag and put the key back in his pocket.

"There, dear; a notable scheme and one that should relieve your mind entirely!" he cried. "If any one should attempt burglary in my absence and should succeed in getting into a house as safely locked as this will be when I leave it, then trust to their being satisfied when they see this booty, which I shall hide where I always hide it—in the cupboard over my desk."

"And when will you be back?" she murmured, trembling in spite of herself at these preparations.

"By one o'clock if possible. Certainly by two."

"And our neighbors go to bed at ten," she murmured. But the words were low, and she was glad he did not hear them, for if it was his duty to obey the orders he had received, then it was her duty to meet the position in which it left her as bravely as she could.

At supper she was so natural that his face rapidly brightened, and it was with quite an air of cheerfulness that he rose at last to lock up the house and make such preparations as were necessary for his dismal ride over the mountains to Fairbanks. She had the supper dishes to wash up in Tennie's absence, and as she was a busy little housewife she found herself singing a snatch of song as she passed back and forth from dining-room to kitchen. He heard it, too, and smiled to himself as he bolted the windows on the ground floor and examined the locks of the three lower doors, and when he finally came into the kitchen with his great-coat on to give her his final kiss, he had but one parting injunction to urge, and that was that she should lock the front door after him and then forget the whole matter till she heard his double knock at midnight.

She smiled and held up her ingenuous face.

"Be careful of yourself," she murmured. "I hate this dark ride for you, and on such a night too." And she ran with him to the door to look out.

"It is certainly very dark," he responded, "but I'm to have one of Brown's safest horses. Do not worry about me. I shall do well enough, and so will you, too, or you are not the plucky little woman I have always thought you."

She laughed, but there was a choking sound in her voice that made him look at her again. But at sight of his anxiety she recovered herself, and pointing to the clouds said earnestly:

"It is going to snow. Be careful as you ride by the gorge, Ned; it is very deceptive there in a snowstorm."

But he vowed that it would not snow before morning, and giving her one final embrace he dashed down the path toward Brown's livery stable. "Oh, what is the matter with me?" she murmured to herself as his steps died out in the distance. "I never knew I was such a coward." And she paused for a moment, looking up and down the road, as if in despite of her husband's command she had the desperate idea of running away to some neighbor.

But she was too loyal for that, and smothering a sigh she retreated into the house. As she did so the first flakes fell of the storm that was not to have come till morning.

It took her an hour to get her kitchen in order, and nine o'clock struck before she was ready to sit down. She had been so busy she had not noticed how the wind had increased or how rapidly the snow was falling. But when she went to the front door for another glance up and down the road she started back, appalled at the fierceness of the gale and at the great pile of snow that had already accumulated on the doorstep.

Too delicate to breast such a wind, she saw herself robbed of her last hope of any companionship, and sighing heavily she locked and bolted the door for the night and went back into her little sitting-room, where a great fire was burning. Here she sat down, and determined, now that she must pass the evening alone, to do it as cheerfully as possible, and so began to sew. "Oh, what a Christmas eve!" she thought, and a picture of other homes rose before her eyes, homes in which husbands sat by wives and brothers by sisters, and a great wave of regret poured over her and a longing for something, she hardly dared say what, lest her unhappiness should acquire a sting that would leave traces beyond the passing moment.

The room in which she sat was the only one on the ground floor except the dining-room and kitchen. It therefore was used both as parlor and sitting-room, and held not only her piano, but her husband's desk.

Communicating with it was the tiny dining-room. Between the two, however, was an entry leading to a side entrance. A lamp was in this entry, and she had left it burning, as well as the one in the kitchen, that the house might look cheerful and as if all the family were at home.

She was looking toward this entry and wondering whether it was the mist made by her tears that made it look so dismally dark to her when there came a faint sound from the door at its further end.

Knowing that her husband must have taken peculiar pains with the fastenings of this door, as it was the one toward the woods and therefore most accessible to wayfarers, she sat where she was, with all her faculties strained to listen. But no further sound came from that direction, and after a few minutes of silent terror she was allowing herself to believe that she had been deceived by her fears when she suddenly heard the same sound at the kitchen door, followed by a muffled knock.

Frightened now in good earnest, but still alive to the fact that the intruder was as likely to be a friend as a foe, she stepped to the door, and with her hand on the lock stooped and asked boldly enough who was there. But she received no answer, and more affected by this unexpected silence than by the knock she had heard she recoiled farther and farther till not only the width of the kitchen, but the dining-room also, lay between her and the scene of her alarm, when to her utter confusion the noise shifted again to the side of the house, and the door she thought so securely fastened, swung violently open as if blown in by a fierce gust, and she saw precipitated into the entry the burly figure of a man covered with snow and shaking with the violence of the storm that seemed at once to fill the house.

Her first thought was that it was her husband come back, but before she could clear her eyes from the cloud of snow which had entered with him he had thrown off his outer covering and she found herself face to face with a man in whose powerful frame and cynical visage she saw little to comfort her and much to surprise and alarm.

"Ugh!" was his coarse and rather familiar greeting. "A hard night, missus! Enough to drive any man indoors. Pardon the liberty, but I couldn't wait for you to lift the latch; the wind drove me right in."

"Was—was not the door locked?" she feebly asked, thinking he must have staved it in with his foot, that looked only too well fitted for such a task.

"Not much," he chuckled. "I s'pose you're too hospitable for that." And his eyes passed from her face to the comfortable fire-light shining through the sitting-room.

"Is it refuge you want?" she demanded, suppressing as much as possible all signs of fear.

"Sure, missus—what else! A man can't live in a gale like that, specially after a tramp of twenty miles or more. Shall I shut the door for you?" he asked, with a mixture of bravado and good nature that frightened her more and more.

"I will shut it," she replied, with a half notion of escaping this sinister stranger by a flight through the night.

But one glance into the swirling snow-storm deterred her, and making the best of the alarming situation, she closed the door, but did not lock it, being more afraid now of what was inside the house than of anything left to threaten her from without.

The man, whose clothes were dripping with water, watched her with a cynical smile, and then, without any invitation, entered the dining-room, crossed it and moved toward the kitchen fire.

"Ugh! ugh! But it is warm here!" he cried, his nostrils dilating with an animal-like enjoyment that in itself was repugnant to her womanly delicacy. "Do you know, missus, I shall have to stay here all night? Can't go out in that gale again; not such a fool." Then with a sly look at her trembling form and white face he insinuat-ingly added, "All alone, missus?"

The suddenness with which this was put, together with the leer that accompanied it, made her start. Alone? Yes, but should she acknowledge it? Would it not be better to say that her husband was up-stairs. The man evidently saw the struggle going on in her mind, for he chuckled to himself and called out quite boldly:

"Never mind, missus; it's all right. Just give me a bit of cold meat and a cup of tea or something, and we'll be very comfortable together. You're a slender slip of a woman to be minding a house like this. I'll keep you company if you don't mind, leastwise until the storm lets up a bit, which ain't likely for some hours to come. Rough night, missus, rough night."

"I expect my husband home at any time," she hastened to say. And thinking she saw a change in the man's countenance at this she put on quite an air of sudden satisfaction and bounded toward the front of the house. "There! I think I hear him now," she cried.

Her motive was to gain time, and if possible to obtain the opportunity of shifting the money from the place where she had first put it into another and safer one. "I want to be able," she thought, "of swearing that I have no money with me in this house. If I can only get it into my apron I will drop it outside the door into the snowbank. It will be as safe there as in the bank it came from." And dashing into the sitting-room she made a feint of dragging down a shawl from a screen, while she secretly filled her skirt with the bills which had been put between some old pamphlets on the bookshelves.

She could hear the man grumbling in the kitchen, but he did not follow her front, and taking advantage of the moment's respite from his none too encouraging presence she unbarred the door and cheerfully called out her husband's name.

The ruse was successful. She was enabled to fling the notes where the falling flakes would soon cover them from sight, and feeling more courageous, now that the money was out of the house, she went slowly back, saying she had made a mistake, and that it was the wind she had heard.

The man gave a gruff but knowing guffaw and then resumed his watch over her, following her steps as she proceeded to set him out a meal, with a persistency that reminded her of a tiger just on the point of springing. But the inviting look of the viands with which she was rapidly setting the table soon distracted his attention, and allowing himself one grunt of satisfaction, he drew up a chair and set himself down to what to him was evidently a most savory repast.

"No beer? No ale? Nothing o' that sort, eh? Don't keep a bar?" he growled, as his teeth closed on a huge hunk of bread.

She shook her head, wishing she had a little cold poison bottled up in a tight-looking jug.

"Nothing but tea," she smiled, astonished at her own ease of manner in the presence of this alarming guest.

"Then let's have that," he grumbled, taking the bowl she handed him, with an odd look that made her glad to retreat to the other side of the room.

"Jest listen to the howling wind," he went on between the huge mouthfuls of bread and cheese with which he was gorging himself. "But we're very comfortable, we two! We don't mind the storm, do we?"

Shocked by his familiarity and still more moved by the look of mingled inquiry and curiosity with which his eyes now began to wander over the walls and cupboards, she took an anxious step toward the side of the house looking toward her neighbors, and lifting one of the shades, which had all been religiously pulled down, she looked out. A swirl of snowflakes alone confronted her. She could neither see her neighbors, nor could she be seen by them. A shout from her to them would not be heard. She was as completely isolated as if the house stood in the center of a desolate western plain.

"I have no trust but in God," she murmured as she came from the window. And, nerved to meet her fate, she crossed to the kitchen.

It was now half-past ten. Two hours and a half must elapse before her husband could possibly arrive.

She set her teeth at the thought and walked resolutely into the room.

"Are you done?" she asked.

"I am, ma'am," he leered. "Do you want me to wash the dishes? I kin, and I will." And he actually carried his plate and cup to the sink, where he turned the water upon them with another loud guffaw.

"If only his fancy would take him into the pantry," she thought, "I could shut and lock the door upon him and hold him prisoner till Ned gets back."

But his fancy ended its flight at the sink, and before her hopes had fully subsided he was standing on the threshold of the sitting-room door.

"It's pretty here," he exclaimed, allowing his eye to rove again over every hiding-place within sight. "I wonder now"— He stopped. His glance had fallen on the cupboard over her husband's desk.

"Well?" she asked, anxious to break the thread of his thought, which was only too plainly mirrored in his eager countenance.

He started, dropped his eyes, and turning looked at her with a momentary fierceness. But, as she did not let her own glance quail, but continued to look at him with what she meant for a smile on her pale lips, he subdued this outward manifestation of passion, and, chuckling to hide his embarrassment, began backing into the entry, leering in evident enjoyment of the fears he caused, with what she felt was a most horrible smile. Once in the hall, he hesitated, however, for a long time; then he slowly went toward the garment he had dropped on entering and stooping, drew from underneath its folds a wicked-looking stick. Giving a kick to the coat, which sent it into a remote corner, he bestowed upon her another smile, and still carrying the stick went slowly and reluctantly away into the kitchen.

"Oh, God Almighty, help me!" was her prayer.

There was nothing for her to do now but endure, so throwing herself into a chair, she tried to calm the beating of her heart and summon up courage for the struggle which she felt was before her. That he had come to rob and only waited to take her off her guard she now felt certain, and rapidly running over in her mind all the expedients of self-defense possible to one in her situation, she suddenly remembered the pistol which Ned kept in his desk. Oh, why had she not thought of it before! Why had she let herself grow mad with terror when here, within reach of her hand, lay such a means of self-defense? With a feeling of joy (she had always hated pistols before and scolded Ned when he bought this one) she started to her feet and slid her hand into the drawer. But it came back empty. Ned had taken the weapon away with him.

For a moment, a surge of the bitterest feeling she had ever experienced passed over her; then she called reason to her aid and was obliged to acknowledge that the act was but natural, and that from his standpoint he was much more likely to need it than herself. But the disappointment, coming so soon after hope, unnerved her, and she sank back in her chair, giving herself up for lost.

How long she sat there with her eyes on the door, through which she momentarily expected her assailant to reappear, she never knew. She was conscious only of a sort of apathy that made movement difficult and even breathing a task. In vain she tried to change her thoughts. In vain she tried to follow her husband in fancy over the snow-covered roads and into the gorge of the mountains. Imagination failed her at this point. Do what she would, all was misty in her mind's eye, and she could not see that wandering image. There was blankness between his form and her, and no life or movement anywhere but here in the scene of her terror.

Her eyes were on a strip of rug that covered the entry floor, and so strange was the condition of her mind that she found herself mechanically counting the tassels that finished its edge, growing wroth over one that was worn, till she hated that sixth tassel and mentally determined that if she ever outlived this night she would strip them all off and be done with them.

The wind had lessened, but the air had grown cooler and the snow made a sharp sound where it struck the panes. She felt it falling, though she had cut off all view of it. It seemed to her that a pall was settling over the world and that she would soon be smothered under its folds. Meanwhile no sound came from the kitchen, only that dreadful sense of a doom creeping upon her—a sense that grew in intensity till she found herself watching for the shadow of that lifted stick on the wall of the entry, and almost imagined she saw the tip of it appearing, when without any premonition, that fatal side door again blew in and admitted another man of so threatening an aspect that she succumbed instantly before him and forgot all her former fears in this new terror.

The second intruder was a negro of powerful frame and glowering aspect, and as he came forward and stood in the doorway there was observable in his fierce and desperate countenance no attempt at the insinuation of the other, only a fearful resolution that made her feel like a puppet before him, and drove her, almost without her volition, to her knees.

"Money? Is it money you want?" was her desperate greeting. "If so, here's my purse and here are my rings and watch. Take them and go."

But the stolid wretch did not even stretch out his hands. His eyes went beyond her, and the mingled anxiety and resolve which he displayed would have cowed a stouter heart than that of this poor woman.

"Keep de trash," he growled. "I want de company's money. You've got it—two thousand dollars. Show me where it is, that's all, and I won't trouble you long after I close on it."

"But it's not in the house," she cried. "I swear it is not in the house. Do you think Mr. Chivers would leave me here alone with two thousand dollars to guard?"

But the negro, swearing that she lied, leaped into the room, and tearing open the cupboard above her husband's desk, seized the bag from the corner where they had put it.

"He brought it in this," he muttered, and tried to force the bag open, but finding this impossible he took out a heavy knife and cut a big hole in its side. Instantly there fell out the pile of old receipts with which they had stuffed it, and seeing these he stamped with rage, and flinging them in one great handful at her rushed to the drawers below, emptied them, and, finding nothing, attacked the bookcase.

"The money is somewhere here. You can't fool me," he yelled. "I saw the spot your eyes lit on when I first came into the room. Is it behind these books?" he growled, pulling them out and throwing them helter-skelter over the floor. "Women is smart in the hiding business. Is it behind these books, I say?"

They had been, or rather had been placed between the books, but she had taken them away, as we know, and he soon began to realize that his search was bringing him nothing, for leaving the bookcase he gave the books one kick, and seizing her by the arm, shook her with a murderous glare on his strange and distorted features.

"Where's the money?" he hissed. "Tell me, or you are a goner."

He raised his heavy fist. She crouched and all seemed over, when, with a rush and a cry, a figure dashed between them and he fell, struck down by the very stick she had so long been expecting to see fall upon her own head. The man who had been her terror for hours had at the moment of need acted as her protector.

She must have fainted, but if so, her unconscious was but momentary, for when she again recognized her surroundings she found the tramp still standing over her adversary.

"I hope you don't mind, ma'am," he said, with an air of humbleness she certainly had not seen in him before, "but I think the man's dead." And he stirred with his foot the heavy figure before him.

"Oh, no, no, no!" she cried. "That would be too fearful. He's shocked, stunned; you cannot have killed him."

But the tramp was persistent. "I'm 'fraid I have," he said. "I done it before, and it's been the same every time. But I couldn't see a man of that color frighten a lady like you. My supper was too warm in me, ma'am. Shall I throw him outside the house?"

"Yes," she said, and then, "No; let us first be sure there is no life in him." And, hardly knowing what she did, she stooped down and peered into the glassy eyes of the prostrate man.

Suddenly she turned pale—no, not pale, but ghastly, and cowering back, shook so that the tramp, into whose features a certain refinement had passed since he had acted as her protector, thought she had discovered life in those set orbs, and was stooping down to make sure that this was so, when he saw her suddenly lean forward and, impetuously plunging her hand into the negro's throat, tear open the shirt and give one look at his bared breast.

It was white.

"O God! O God!" she moaned, and lifting the head in her two hands she gave the motionless features a long and searching look. "Water!" she cried. "Bring water." But before the now obedient tramp could respond, she had torn off the woolly wig disfiguring the dead man's head, and seeing the blond curls beneath had uttered such a shriek that it rose above the gale and was heard by her distant neighbors.

It was the head and hair of her husband.

They found out afterwards that he had contemplated this theft for months, that each and every precaution possible to a successful issue to this most daring undertaking had been made use of and that but for the unexpected presence in the house of the tramp, he would doubtless have not only extorted the money from his wife, but have so covered up the deed by a plausible *alibi* as to have retained her confidence and that of his employers.

Whether the tramp killed him out of sympathy for the defenseless woman or in rage at being disappointed in his own plans has never been determined. Mrs. Chivers herself thinks he was actuated by a rude sort of gratitude.

The Case of Miss Elliott
(1905)
Baroness Orczy

DRAMATIS PERSONAE

THE OLD MAN IN THE CORNER
who relates the story to
THE LADY JOURNALIST

MISS ELLIOTT
(matron of the Convalescent Home)

DR. KINNAIRD
(president of the Convalescent Home)

DR. STAPYLTON
(hon. sec. and treasurer of the Convalescent Home)

MARY DAWSON
(nurse of the Convalescent Home)

MR. JAMES ELLIOTT
(brother of the matron)

DR. EARNSHAW
(a consultant of the Convalescent Home)

CONSTABLE FISKE

1

The man in the corner was watching me over the top of his great bone-rimmed spectacles.

"Well?" he asked after a little while.

"Well," I repeated with some acerbity. I had been wondering

for the last ten minutes how many more knots he would manage to make in that same bit of string, before he actually started undoing them again.

"Do I fidget you?" he asked apologetically, whilst his long bony fingers buried themselves, string, knots, and all, into the capacious pockets of his magnificent tweed ulster.

"Yes, that is another awful tragedy," he said quietly after a while. "Lady doctors are having a pretty bad time of it just now."

This was only his usual habit of speaking in response to my thoughts. There was no doubt that at the present moment my mind was filled with that extraordinary mystery which was setting all Scotland Yard by the ears and had completely thrown into the shade the sad story of Miss Hickman's tragic fate.

The *Daily Telegraph* had printed two columns headed "Murder or Suicide?" on the subject of the mysterious death of Miss Elliott, matron of the Convalescent Home, in Suffolk Avenue—and I must confess that a more profound and bewildering mystery had never been set before our able detective department.

"It has puzzled them this time, and no mistake," said the man in the corner, with one of his most gruesome chuckles, "but I dare say the public is quite satisfied that there is no solution to be found, since the police have found none."

"Can you find one?" I retorted with withering sarcasm.

"Oh, my solution would only be sneered at," he replied. "It is far too simple—and yet how logical! There was Miss Elliott, a good-looking, youngish, ladylike woman, fully qualified in the medical profession and in charge of the Convalescent Home in Suffolk Avenue, which is a private institution largely patronised by the benevolent.

"For sometime, already, there had appeared vague comments and rumors in various papers, that the extensive charitable contributions did not all go towards the upkeep of the Home. But, as is usual in institutions of that sort, the public was not allowed to know anything very definite, and contributions continued to flow in, whilst the Honorary Treasurer of the great Convalescent Home kept up his beautiful house in Hamilton Terrace, in a style which would not have shamed a peer of the realm.

"That is how matters stood, when on November 2nd last the morning papers contained the brief announcement that at a quarter past midnight two workmen walking along Blomfield Road, Maida Vale, suddenly came across the body of a young lady, lying on her face, close to the wooden steps of the narrow footbridge which at this point crosses the canal.

"This part of Maida Vale is, as you know, very lonely at all times, but at night it is usually quite deserted. Blomfield Road, with its row of small houses and bits of front gardens, faces the canal, and beyond the footbridge is continued in a series of small riverside wharves, which is practically unknown ground to the average Londoner. The footbridge itself, with steps at right angles and high wooden parapet, would offer excellent shelter at all hours of the night for any nefarious deed.

"It was within its shadows that the men had found the body, and to their credit be it said, they behaved like good and dutiful citizens—one of them went off in search of the police, whilst the other remained beside the corpse.

"From papers and books found upon her person, it was soon ascertained that the deceased was Miss Elliott, the young matron of the Suffolk Avenue Convalescent Home; and as she was very popular in her profession and had a great many friends, the terrible tragedy caused a sensation, all the more acute as very quickly the rumor gained ground that the unfortunate young woman had taken her own life in a most gruesome and mysterious manner.

"Preliminary medical and police investigation had revealed the fact that Miss Elliott had died through a deep and scientifically administered gash in the throat, whilst the surgical knife with which the deadly wound was inflicted still lay tightly grasped in her clenched hand."

2

The man in the corner, ever conscious of any effect he produced upon my excited imagination, had paused for a while, giving me time, as it were, to coordinate in my mind the few simple facts he had put before me. I had no wish to make a remark, knowing of old that my one chance of getting the whole of his interesting argument was to offer neither comment nor contradiction.

"When a young, good-looking woman in the heyday of her success in an interesting profession," he began at last, "is alleged to have committed suicide, the outside public immediately want to know the reason why she did such a thing, and a kind of freemasonic, amateur detective works goes on, which generally brings a few important truths to light. Thus, in the case of Miss Elliott, certain facts had begun to leak out, even before the inquest, with its many sensational developments. Rumors concerning the internal administration, or rather maladministration of the Home began to take more definite form.

"That its finances had been in a very shaky condition for some time was known to all those who were interested in its welfare. What was not so universally known was that few hospitals had had more munificent donations and subscriptions showered upon them in recent years, and yet it was openly spoke of by all the nurses that Miss Elliott had on more than one occasion petitioned for actual necessities for the patients—necessities which were denied to her on the plea of necessary economy.

"The Convalescent Home was, as sometimes happens in institutions of this sort, under the control of a committee of benevolent and fashionable people who understood nothing about business, and less still about the management of a hospital. Dr. Kinnaird, president of the institution, was a young, eminently successful consultant; he had recently married the daughter of a peer, who had boundless ambitions for herself and her husband.

"Dr. Kinnaird, by adding the prestige of his name to the Home, no doubt felt that he had done enough for its welfare. Against that, Dr. Stapylton, hon. sec. and treasurer of the Home, threw himself heart and soul into the work connected with it, and gave a great deal of his time to it. All subscriptions and donations went, of course, through his hands, the benevolent and fashionable committee being only too willing to shift all their financial responsibilities onto his willing shoulders. He was a very popular man in society—a bachelor with a magnificent house in Hamilton Terrace, where he entertained the more eminent and fashionable clique in his own profession.

"It was the evening papers, however, which contained the most sensational development of this tragic case. It appears that on the

Saturday afternoon Mary Dawson, one of the nurses in the Home, was going to the house surgeon's office with a message from the head nurse, when her attention was suddenly arrested in one of the passages by the sound of loud voices proceeding from one of the rooms. She paused to listen for a moment and at once recognised the voices of Miss Elliott and of Dr. Stapylton, the honorary treasurer and chairman of the Committee.

"The subject of conversation was evidently that of the eternal question of finance. Miss Elliott spoke very indignantly and Nurse Dawson caught the words:

"'Surely you must agree with me that Dr. Kinnaird ought to be informed at once.'

"Dr. Stapylton's voice in reply seems to have been at first bitingly sarcastic, then threatening. Dawson heard nothing more after that and went on to deliver her message. On her way back she stopped in the passage again, and tried to listen. This time it seemed to her as if she could hear the sound of someone crying bitterly, and Dr. Stapleton's voice speaking very gently.

"'You may be right, Nellie,' he was saying. 'At any rate wait a few days, before telling Kinnaird. You know what he is—he'll make a frightful fuss and—'

"Whereupon Miss Elliott interrupted him.

"'It isn't fair on Dr. Kinnaird to keep him in ignorance any longer. Whoever the thief may be it is your duty or mine to expose him, and if necessary bring him to justice.'

"There was a good deal of discussion at the time, if you remember, as to whether Nurse Dawson had overheard and repeated this speech accurately: whether, in point of fact, Miss Elliott had used the words 'or mine' or 'and mine.' You see the neat little point, don't you?" continued the man in the corner. "The little word 'and' would imply that she considered herself at one with Dr. Stapylton in the matter, but 'or' would mean that she was resolved to act alone if he refused to join her in unmasking the thief.

"All these facts, as I remarked before, had leaked out, as such facts have a way of doing. No wonder, therefore, that on the day fixed for the inquest the coroner's court was filled to overflowing, both with the public—ever eager for new sensations—and with the many friends of the deceased lady, among whom young medical students of both sexes and nurses in uniform were most conspicuous.

"I was there early, and therefore had a good seat, from which I could comfortably watch the various actors in the drama about to be performed. People who seemed to be in the know pointed out various personages to one another, and it was a matter of note that, in spite of professional engagements, the members of the staff of the Convalescent Home were present in full force and stayed on almost the whole time. The personages who chiefly arrested my attention were, firstly, Dr. Kinnaird, a good-looking Irishman of about forty, and president of the institution; also Dr. Earnshaw, a rising young consultant, with boundless belief in himself written all over his pleasant, rubicund countenance.

"The expert medical evidence was once again thoroughly gone into. There was absolutely no doubt that Miss Elliott had died from having her throat cut with the surgical knife which was found grasped in her right hand. There were absolutely no signs of a personal struggle in the immediate vicinity of the body, and rigid examination proved that there was no other mark of violence upon the body; there was nothing, therefore, to prove that the poor girl had not committed suicide in a moment of mental aberration or of great personal grief.

"Of course, it was strange that she should have chosen this curious mode of taking her own life. She had access to all kinds of poisons, amongst which her medical knowledge could prompt her to choose the least painful and most efficacious ones. Therefore, to have walked out on a Sunday night to a wretched and unfrequented spot and there committed suicide in that grim fashion seemed almost the work of a madwoman. And yet the evidence of her family and friends all tended to prove that Miss Elliott was a peculiarly sane, large-minded, and happy individual.

"However, the suicide theory was at this stage of the proceedings taken as being absolutely established, and when Police-Constable Fiske came forward to give his evidence no one in the court was prepared for a statement which suddenly revealed this case to be as mysterious as it was magic.

"Fiske's story was this: close upon midnight on that memo-

rable Sunday night he was walking down Blomfield Road along
the side of the canal and towards the footbridge, when he overtook a lady and gentleman who were walking in the same direction as himself. He turned to look at them, and noticed that the
gentleman was in evening dress and wore a high hat, and that
the lady was crying.

"Blomfield Road is at best very badly lighted, especially on
the side next to the canal, where there are no lamps at all. Fiske,
however, was prepared to swear positively that the lady was the
deceased. As for the gentleman, he might know him again or he
might not.

"Fiske then crossed the footbridge, and walked on towards
the Harrow Road. As he did so, he heard St. Mary Magdalen's
church clock chime the hour of midnight. It was a quarter of an
hour after that, that the body of the unfortunate girl was found,
and clasping in her hand the knife with which that awful deed
had been done. By whom? Was it really by her own self? But if
so, why did not that man in evening dress who had last seen her
alive come forward and throw some light upon this fast thicken-
ing veil of mystery?

"It was Mr. James Elliott, brother of the deceased, however,
who first mentioned a name then in open court, which has ever
since in the minds of everyone been associated with Miss
Elliott's tragic fate.

"He was speaking in answer to a question of the coroner's
anent his sister's disposition and recent frame of mind.

"She was always extremely cheerful," he said, "but recently
had been peculiarly bright and happy. I understood from her
that this was because she believed that a man for whom she had
a great regard was also very much attached to her, and meant to
ask her to be his wife."

"'And do you know who this man was?' asked the coroner.

"'Oh, yes,' replied Mr. Elliott, 'it was Dr. Stapylton.'

"Everyone had expected that name, of course, for everyone
remembered Nurse Dawson's story, yet when it came, there
crept over all those present an indescribable feeling that something terrible was impending.

"'Is Dr. Stapylton here?'

"But Dr. Stapylton had sent an excuse. A professional case of the utmost urgency had kept him at a patient's bedside. But Dr. Kinnaird, the president of the institution, came forward.

"Questioned by the coroner, Dr. Kinnaird, however, who evidently had a great regard for his colleague, repudiated any idea that the funds of the institution had ever been tampered with by the treasurer.

"'The very suggestion of such a thing,' he said, 'was an outrage upon one of the most brilliant men in the profession.'

"He further added that, although he knew that Dr. Stapylton thought very highly of Miss Elliott, he did not think that there was any actual engagement, and most decidedly he (Dr. Kinnaird) had heard nothing of any disagreement between them.

"'Then did Dr. Stapylton never tell you that Miss Elliott had often chafed under the extraordinary economy practised in the richly-endowed Home?' asked the coroner again.

"'No,' replied Dr. Kinnaird.

"'Was not that rather strange reticence?'

"'Certainly not. I am only the honorary president of the institution—Stapylton has chief control of its finances.'

"'Ah!' remarked the coroner blandly.

"However, it was clearly no business of his at this moment to enter into the financial affairs of the Home. His duty at this point was to try and find out if Dr. Stapylton and the man in evening dress were one and the same person.

"The men who found the body testified to the hour: a quarter past midnight. As Fiske had seen the unfortunate girl alive a little before twelve, she must have been murdered or had committed suicide between midnight and a quarter past. But there was something more to come.

"How strange and dramatic it all was," continued the man in the corner, with a bland smile, altogether out of keeping with the poignancy of his narrative; "all these people in that crowded court trying to reconstruct the last chapter of that bright young matron's life and then—but I must not anticipate.

"One more witness was to be heard—one whom the police, with a totally unconscious sense of what is dramatic, had reserved for the last. This was Dr. Earnshaw, one of the staff of the Convalescent Home. His evidence was very short, but of deeply momentous import. He explained that he had consulting rooms in Weymouth Street, but resided in Westbourne Square. On Sunday, November 1st, he had been dining out in Maida Vale, and returning home a little before midnight saw a woman standing close by the steps of the footbridge in the Blomfield Road.

"'I had been coming down Formosa Street and had not specially taken notice of her, when just as I reached the corner of Blomfield Road she was joined by a man in evening dress and high hat. Then I crossed the road, and recognised both Miss Elliott and—'

"The young doctor paused, almost as if hesitating before the enormity of what he was about to say, whilst the excitement in court became almost painful.

"'And—?' urged the coroner.

"'And Dr. Stapylton,' said Dr. Earnshaw at last, almost under his breath.

"'You are quite sure?' asked the coroner.

"'Absolutely positive. I spoke to them both and they spoke to me.'

"'What did you say?'

"'Oh, the usual, "Hello, Stapylton!" to which he replied, "Hello!" I then said "Goodnight" to them both, and Miss Elliott also said "Goodnight." I saw her face more clearly then, and thought that she looked very tearful and unhappy, and Stapylton looked ill-tempered. I wondered why they had chosen that unhallowed spot for a midnight walk.'

"'And you say the hour was—?' asked the coroner.

"'Ten minutes to twelve. I looked at my watch as I crossed the footbridge, and had heard a quarter to twelve strike five minutes before.'

"Then it was that the coroner adjourned the inquest. Dr. Stapylton's attendance had become absolutely imperative. According to Dr. Earnshaw's testimony, he had been with deceased certainly a quarter of an hour before she met her terrible death. Fiske had seen them together ten minutes later; she was then crying bitterly. There was as yet no actual charge against the fashionable and rich doctor, but already the ghostly bird of suspicion had touched him with its ugly wing."

3

"As for the next day," continued the man in the corner after a slight pause, "I can assure you that there was not a square foot of standing room in the coroner's court for the adjourned inquest. It was timed for eleven A.M., and at six o'clock on that cold winter's morning the pavement outside the court was already crowded. As for me, I always manage to get a front seat, and I did on that occasion, too. I fancy that I was the first among the general public to note Dr. Stapylton, as he entered the room accompanied by his solicitor, and by Dr. Kinnaird, with whom he was chatting very cheerfully and pleasantly.

"Mind you, I am a great admirer of the medical profession, and I think a clever and successful doctor usually has a most delightful air about him—the consciousness of great and good work done with profit to himself—which is quite unique and quite admirable.

"Dr. Stapylton had that air even to a greater extent than his colleague, and from the affectionate way in which Dr. Kinnaird finally shook him by the hand, it was quite clear that the respected chief of the Convalescent Home, at any rate, refused to harbor any suspicion of the integrity of its treasurer.

"Well, I must not weary you by dwelling on the unimportant details of this momentous inquest. Constable Fiske, who was asked to identify the gentleman in evening dress whom he had seen with the deceased at a few minutes before twelve, failed to recognise Dr. Stapylton very positively: pressed very closely, he finally refused to swear either way. Against that, Dr. Earnshaw repeated, clearly and categorically, looking his colleague straight in the face the while, the damnatory evidence he had given the day before.

"'I saw Dr. Stapylton, I spoke to him, and he spoke to me,' he repeated most emphatically.

"Everyone in that court was watching Dr. Stapylton's face, which wore an air of supreme nonchalance, even of contempt, but certainly neither of guilt nor fear.

"Of course, by that time *I* had fully made up my mind as to where the hitch lay in this extraordinary mystery; but no one else had, and everyone held their breath as Dr. Stapylton quietly stepped into the box, and after a few preliminary questions the coroner asked him very abruptly:

"'You were in the company of the deceased a few minutes before she died, Dr. Stapylton?'

"'Pardon me,' replied the latter quietly, 'I last saw Miss Elliott alive on Saturday afternoon, just before I went home from my work.'

"This calm reply, delivered without a tremor, positively made everyone gasp. For the moment coroner and jury were alike staggered.

"'But we have two witnesses here who saw you in the company of the deceased within a few minutes of twelve o'clock on the Sunday night!' the coroner managed to gasp out at last.

"'Pardon me,' again interposed the doctor, 'these witnesses were mistaken.'

"'Mistaken!'

"I think everyone would have shouted out the word in boundless astonishment had they dared to do so.

"'Dr. Earnshaw was mistaken,' reiterated Dr. Stapylton quietly. 'He neither saw me nor did he speak to me.'

"'You can substantiate that, of course?' queried the coroner.

"'Pardon me,' once more said the doctor, with utmost calm; 'it is surely Dr. Earnshaw who should substantiate *his* statement.'

"'There is Constable Fiske's corroborative evidence for that,' retorted the coroner, somewhat nettled.

"'Hardly, I think. You see, the constable states that he saw a gentleman in evening dress, etc., talking to the deceased at a minute or two before twelve o'clock, and that when he heard the clock of St. Mary Magdalen chime the hour of midnight he was just walking away from the footbridge. Now, just as that very church clock was chiming that hour, I was stepping into a cab at the corner of Harrow Road, not a hundred yards *in front* of Constable Fiske.'

"'You swear to that?' queried the coroner in amazement.

"'I can easily prove it,' said Dr. Stapylton. 'The cabman who drove me from there to my club is here and can corroborate my statement.'

"And amidst boundless excitement, John Smith, a hansom cab-driver, stated that he was hailed in the Harrow Road by the last witness, who told him to drive to the Royal Clinical Club, in Mardon Street. Just as he started off, St. Mary Magdalen's church, close by, struck the hour of midnight.

"At that very moment, if you remember, Constable Fiske had just crossed the footbridge, and was walking towards the Harrow Road, and he was quite sure (for he was closely questioned afterwards) that no one overtook him from behind. Now there would be no way of getting from one side of the canal to the other at this point except over that footbridge; the nearest bridge is fully 200 yards further down the Blomfield Road. The girl was alive a minute *before* the constable crossed the footbridge, and it would have been absolutely impossible for anyone to have murdered a girl, placed the knife in her hand, run a couple of hundred yards to the next bridge and another 300 to the corner of Harrow Road, all in the space of three minutes.

"This alibi, therefore, absolutely cleared Dr. Stapylton from any suspicion of having murdered Miss Elliott. And yet, looking on that man as he sat there, calm, cool, and contemptuous, no one could have had the slightest doubt but that he was lying— lying when he said he had not seen Miss Elliott that evening; lying when he denied Dr. Earnshaw's statement; lying when he professed himself ignorant of the poor girl's fate.

"Dr. Earnshaw repeated his statement with the same emphasis, but it was one man's word against another's, and as Dr. Stapylton was so glaringly innocent of the actual murder, there seemed no valid reason at all why he should have denied having seen her that night, and the point was allowed to drop. As for Nurse Dawson's story of his alleged quarrel with Miss Elliott on the Saturday night, Dr. Stapylton again had a simple and logical explanation.

"'People who listen at keyholes,' he said quietly, 'are apt to hear only fragments of conversation, and often mistake ordinary loud voices for quarrels. As a matter of fact, Miss Elliott and I were discussing the dismissal of certain nurses from the Home, whom she deemed incompetent. Nurse Dawson was among the number. She desired their immediate dismissal, and I tried to pacify her. That was the subject of my conversation with the deceased lady. I can swear to every word of it.'"

4

The man in the corner had long ceased speaking, and was placing quietly before me a number of photographs. One by one I saw the series of faces which had been watched so eagerly in the coroner's court that memorable afternoon by an excited crowd.

"So the fate of poor Miss Elliott has remained wrapt in mystery?" I said thoughtfully at last.

"To everyone," rejoined the funny creature, "except to me."

"Ah! What is your theory, then?"

"A simple one, dear lady; so simple that it really amazes me that no one, not even you, my faithful pupil, ever thought of it."

"It may be so simple that it becomes idiotic," I retorted with lofty disdain.

"Well, that may be. Shall I at any rate try to make it clear?"

"If you like."

"For this I think the best way would be, if you were to follow me through what transpired before the inquest. But first tell me, what do you think of Dr. Earnshaw's statement?"

"Well," I replied, "a good many people thought that it was he who murdered Miss Elliott, and that his story of meeting Dr. Stapylton with her was a lie from beginning to end."

"Impossible," he retorted, making an elaborate knot in his bit of string. "Dr. Earnshaw's friends with whom he had been dining that night swore that he was *not* in evening dress, nor wore a high hat. And on that point—the evening dress, and the hat—Constable Fiske was most positive."

"Then Dr. Earnshaw was mistaken, and it was not Dr. Stapylton he met."

"Impossible!" he shrieked, whilst another knot went to join its fellows. "He spoke to Dr. Stapylton, and Dr. Stapylton spoke to him."

"Very well, then," I argued; "why should Dr. Stapylton tell a lie about it? He had such a conclusive alibi that there could be no object in his making a false statement about that."

"No object!" shrieked the excited creature. "Why, don't you *see* that he had to tell the lie in order to set police, coroner, and jury by the ears, because he did not wish it to be even remotely hinted at, that the man whom Dr. Earnshaw saw with Miss Elliott, and the man whom Constable Fiske saw with her ten minutes later were *two different persons.*"

"Two different persons!" I ejaculated.

"Aye! two confederates in this villainy. No one has ever attempted to deny the truth of the shaky finances of the Home; no one has really denied that Miss Elliott suspected certain defalcations and was trying to force the hands of the Honorary Treasurer towards a full inquiry. That the Honorary Treasurer knew where all the money went to was pretty clear all along— his magnificent house in Hamilton Terrace fully testifies to that. That the president of the institution was a party to these defalcations and largely profited by them I for one am equally convinced."

"Dr. Kinnaird?" I ejaculated in amazement.

"Aye, Dr. Kinnaird. Do you mean to tell me that he alone among the entire staff of that Home was ignorant of those defalcations? Impossible! And if he knew of them, and did neither inquire into them nor attempt to stop them, then he *must* have been a party to them. Do you admit that?"

"Yes, I admit that," I replied.

"Very well then. The rest is quite simple; these two men, unworthy to bear the noble appellation of doctor, must for years have quietly stolen the money subscribed by the benevolent for the Home, and converted it to their own use; then, they suddenly find themselves face to face with immediate discovery in the shape of a young girl determined to unmask the systematic frauds of the past few years. That meant exposure, disgrace, ruin for them both, and they determine to be rid of her.

"Under the pretence of an evening walk, her so-called lover entices her to a lonely and suitable spot; his confederate is close by, hidden in the shadows, ready to give him assistance if the girl struggles and screams. But suddenly Dr. Earnshaw appears. He recognises Stapylton and challenges him. For a moment the villains are nonplussed, then Kinnaird—the cleverer of the two—steps forward, greets the two lovers unconcernedly, and after two minutes' conversation casually reminds Stapylton of an appointment the latter is presumed to have at a club in St. James' Street.

"The latter understands and takes the hint, takes a quick farewell of the girl, leaving her in his friend's charge, then, as fast as he can, goes off, presently takes a cab, leaving his friend to do the deed, whilst the alibi he can prove, coupled with Dr. Earnshaw's statement, was sure to bewilder and mislead the police and the public.

"Thus it was that though Dr. Earnshaw saw and recognised Dr. Stapylton, Constable Fiske saw Dr. Kinnaird, whom he did *not* recognise, on whom no suspicion had fallen, and whose name had never been coupled with that of Miss Elliott. When Constable Fiske had turned his back, Kinnaird murdered the girl and went off quietly, whilst Dr. Stapylton, on whom all suspicions were bound to fasten sooner or later, was able to prove the most perfect alibi ever concocted.

"One day I feel certain that the frauds at the Home will be discovered, and then who knows what else may see the light?

"Think of it all quietly when I am gone, and tomorrow when we meet tell me whether if *I* am wrong what is *your* explanation of this extraordinary mystery."

Before I could reply he had gone, and I was left wondering, gazing at the photographs of two good-looking, highly respectable and respected men, whom an animated scarecrow had just boldly accused of committing one of the most dastardly crimes ever recorded in our annals.

The Problem of Cell 13
(1907)
Jacques Futrelle

I

Practically all those letters remaining in the alphabet after
Augustus S. F. X. Van Dusen was named were afterward
acquired by that gentleman in the course of a brilliant scientific
career, and, being honorably acquired, were tacked on to the
other end. His name, therefore, taken with all that belonged to
it, was a wonderfully imposing structure. He was a Ph.D., an
LL.D., an F.R.S., an M.D., and an M.D.S. He was also some
other things—just what he himself couldn't say—through recognition of his ability by various foreign educational and scientific
institutions.

In appearance he was no less striking than in nomenclature.
He was slender with the droop of the student in his thin shoulders and the pallor of a close, sedentary life on his clean-shaven
face. His eyes wore a perpetual, forbidding squint—of a man
who studies little things—and when they could be seen at all
through his thick spectacles, were mere slits of watery blue. But
above his eyes was his most striking feature. This was a tall,
broad brow, almost abnormal in height and width, crowned by a
heavy shock of bushy, yellow hair. All these things conspired to
give him a peculiar, almost grotesque, personality.

Professor Van Dusen was remotely German. For generations

his ancestors had been noted in the sciences; he was the logical result, the master-mind. First and above all he was a logician. At least thirty-five years of the half-century or so of his existence had been devoted exclusively to proving that two and two always equal four, except in unusual cases, where they equal three or five, as the case may be. He stood broadly on the general proposition that all things that start must go somewhere, and was able to bring the concentrated mental force of his forefathers to bear on a given problem. Incidentally it may be remarked that Professor Van Dusen wore a No. 8 hat.

The world at large had heard vaguely of Professor Van Dusen as The Thinking Machine. It was a newspaper catchphrase applied to him at the time of a remarkable exhibition at chess; he had demonstrated then that a stranger to the game might, by the force of inevitable logic, defeat a champion who had devoted a lifetime to its study. The Thinking Machine! Perhaps that more nearly described him than all his honorary initials, for he spent week after week, month after month, in the seclusion of his small laboratory from which had gone forth thoughts that staggered scientific associates and deeply stirred the world at large.

It was only occasionally that The Thinking Machine had visitors, and these were usually men who, themselves high in the sciences, dropped in to argue a point and perhaps convince themselves. Two of these men, Dr. Charles Ransome and Alfred Fielding, called one evening to discuss some theory which is not of consequence here.

"Such a thing is impossible," declared Dr. Ransome emphatically, in the course of the conversation.

"Nothing is impossible," declared The Thinking Machine with equal emphasis. He always spoke petulantly. "The mind is master of all things. When science fully recognizes that fact a great advance will have been made."

"How about the airship?" asked Dr. Ransome.

"That's not impossible at all," asserted The Thinking Machine. "It will be invented some time. I'd do it myself, but I'm busy."

Dr. Ransome laughed tolerantly.

"I've heard you say such things before," he said. "But they mean nothing. Mind may be master of matter, but it hasn't yet found a way to apply itself. There are some things that can't be *thought* out of existence, or rather which would not yield to any amount of thinking."

"What, for instance?" demanded The Thinking Machine.

Dr. Ransome was thoughtful for a moment as he smoked.

"Well, say prison walls," he replied. "No man can *think* himself out of a cell. If he could, there would be no prisoners."

"A man can so apply his brain and ingenuity that he can leave a cell, which is the same thing," snapped The Thinking Machine.

Dr. Ransome was slightly amused.

"Let's suppose a case," he said, after a moment. "Take a cell where prisoners under sentence of death are confined—men who are desperate and, maddened by fear, would take any chance to escape—suppose you were locked in such a cell. Could you escape?"

"Certainly," declared The Thinking Machine.

"Of course," said Mr. Fielding, who entered the conversation for the first time, "you might wreck the cell with an explosive—but inside, a prisoner, you couldn't have that."

"There would be nothing of that kind," said The Thinking Machine. "You might treat me precisely as you treated prisoners under sentence of death, and I would leave the cell."

"Not unless you entered it with tools prepared to get out," said Dr. Ransome.

The Thinking Machine was visibly annoyed and his blue eyes snapped.

"Lock me in any cell in any prison anywhere at any time, wearing only what is necessary, and I'll escape in a week," he declared, sharply.

Dr. Ransome sat up straight in his chair, interested. Mr. Fielding lighted a new cigar.

"You mean you could actually *think* yourself out?" asked Dr. Ransome.

"I would get out," was the response.

"Are you serious?"

"Certainly I am serious."

Dr. Ransome and Mr. Fielding were silent for a long time.

"Would you be willing to try it?" asked Mr. Fielding, finally.

"Certainly," said Professor Van Dusen, and there was a trace of irony in his voice. "I have done more asinine things than that to convince other men of less important truths."

The tone was offensive and there was an undercurrent strongly resembling anger on both sides. Of course it was an absurd thing, but Professor Van Dusen reiterated his willingness to undertake the escape and it was decided upon.

"To begin now," added Dr. Ransome.

"I'd prefer that it begin to-morrow," said The Thinking Machine, "because—"

"No, now," said Mr. Fielding, flatly. "You are arrested, figuratively, of course, without any warning locked in a cell with no chance to communicate with friends, and left there with identically the same care and attention that would be given to a man under sentence of death. Are you willing?"

"All right, now, then," said The Thinking Machine, and he arose.

"Say, the death-cell in Chisholm Prison."

"The death-cell in Chisholm Prison."

"And what will you wear?"

"As little as possible," said The Thinking Machine. "Shoes, stockings, trousers and a shirt."

"You will permit yourself to be searched, of course?"

"I am to be treated precisely as all prisoners are treated," said The Thinking Machine. "No more attention and no less."

There were some preliminaries to be arranged in the matter of obtaining permission for the test, but all three were influential men and everything was done satisfactorily by telephone, albeit the prison commissioners, to whom the experiment was explained on purely scientific grounds, were sadly bewildered. Professor Van Dusen would be the most distinguished prisoner they had ever entertained.

When The Thinking Machine had donned those things which he was to wear during his incarceration he called the little old woman who was his housekeeper, cook and maidservant all in one.

"Martha," he said, "it is now twenty-seven minutes past nine o'clock. I am going away. One week from to-night, at half-past nine, these gentlemen and one, possibly two, others will take supper with me here. Remember Dr. Ransome is very fond of artichokes."

The three men were driven to Chisholm Prison, where the warden was awaiting them, having been informed of the matter by telephone. He understood merely that the eminent Professor Van Dusen was to be his prisoner, if he could keep him, for one week; that he had committed no crime, but that he was to be treated as all other prisoners were treated.

"Search him," instructed Dr. Ransome.

The Thinking Machine was searched. Nothing was found on him; the pockets of the trousers were empty; the white, stiff-bosomed shirt had no pocket. The shoes and stockings were removed, examined, then replaced. As he watched all these preliminaries—the rigid search and the pitiful, childlike physical weakness of the man, the colorless face, and the thin, white hands—Dr. Ransome almost regretted his part in the affair.

"Are you sure you want to do this?" he asked.

"Would you be convinced if I did not?" inquired The Thinking Machine in turn.

"No."

"All right. I'll do it."

What sympathy Dr. Ransome had was dissipated by the tone. It nettled him, and he resolved to see the experiment to the end; it would be a stinging reproof to egotism.

"It will be impossible for him to communicate with anyone outside?" he asked.

"Absolutely impossible," replied the warden. "He will not be permitted writing materials of any sort."

"And your jailers, would they deliver a message from him?"

"Not one word, directly or indirectly," said the warden. "You may rest assured of that. They will report anything he might say or turn over to me anything he might give them."

"That seems entirely satisfactory," said Mr. Fielding, who was frankly interested in the problem.

"Of course, in the event he fails," said Dr. Ransome, "and asks for his liberty, you understand you are to set him free?"

"I understand," replied the warden.

The Thinking Machine stood listening, but had nothing to say until this was all ended, then:

"I should like to make three small requests. You may grant them or not, as you wish."

"No special favors, now," warned Mr. Fielding.

"I am asking none," was the stiff response. "I would like to have some tooth powder—buy it yourself to see that it is tooth powder—and I should like to have one five-dollar and two ten-dollar bills."

Dr. Ransome, Mr. Fielding and the warden exchanged astonished glances. They were not surprised at the request for tooth powder, but were at the request for money.

"Is there any man with whom our friend would come in contact that he could bribe with twenty-five dollars?" asked Dr. Ransome of the warden.

"Not for twenty-five hundred dollars," was the positive reply.

"Well, let him have them," said Mr. Fielding. "I think they are harmless enough."

"And what is the third request?" asked Dr. Ransome.

"I should like to have my shoes polished."

Again the astonished glances were exchanged. This last request was the height of absurdity, so they agreed to it. These things all being attended to, The Thinking Machine was led back into the prison from which he had undertaken to escape.

"Here is Cell 13," said the warden, stopping three doors down the steel corridor. "This is where we keep condemned murderers. No one can leave it without my permission; and no one in it can communicate with the outside. I'll stake my reputation on that. It's only three doors back of my office and I can readily hear any unusual noise."

"Will this cell do, gentlemen?" asked The Thinking Machine. There was a touch of irony in his voice.

"Admirably," was the reply.

The heavy steel door was thrown open, there was a great scurrying and scampering of tiny feet, and The Thinking Machine passed into the gloom of the cell. Then the door was closed and double locked by the warden.

"What is that noise in there?" asked Dr. Ransome, through the bars.

"Rats—dozens of them," replied The Thinking Machine, tersely.

The three men, with final good-nights, were turning away when The Thinking Machine called:

"What time is it exactly, warden?"

"Eleven seventeen," replied the warden.

"Thanks. I will join you gentlemen in your office at half-past eight o'clock one week from to-night," said The Thinking Machine.

"And if you do not?"

"There is no 'if' about it."

II

Chisholm Prison was a great, spreading structure of granite, four stories in all, which stood in the center of acres of open space. It was surrounded by a wall of solid masonry eighteen feet high, and so smoothly finished inside and out as to offer no foothold to a climber, no matter how expert. Atop of this fence, as a further precaution, was a five-foot fence of steel rods, each terminating in a keen point. This fence in itself marked an absolute deadline between freedom and imprisonment, for, even if a man escaped from his cell, it would seem impossible for him to pass the wall.

The yard, which on all sides of the prison building was twenty-five feet wide, that being the distance from the building to the wall, was by day an exercise ground for those prisoners to whom was granted the boon of occasional semi-liberty. But that was not for those in Cell 13.

At all times of the day there were armed guards in the yard, four of them, one patrolling each side of the prison building.

By night the yard was almost as brilliantly lighted as by day. On each of the four sides was a great arc light which rose above the prison wall and gave to the guards a clear sight. The lights, too, brightly illuminated the spiked top of the wall. The wires which fed the arc lights ran up the side of the prison building on insulators and from the top story led out to the poles supporting the arc lights.

All these things were seen and comprehended by The Thinking Machine, who was only enabled to see out his closely barred cell window by standing on his bed. This was on the morning following his incarceration. He gathered, too, that the river lay over there beyond the wall somewhere, because he heard faintly the pulsation of a motor boat and high up in the air saw a river bird. From that same direction came the shouts of boys at play and the occasional crack of a batted ball. He knew then that between the prison wall and the river was an open space, a playground.

Chisholm Prison was regarded as absolutely safe. No man had ever escaped from it. The Thinking Machine, from his perch on the bed, seeing what he saw, could readily understand why. The wall of the cell, though built he judged twenty years before, were perfectly solid, and the window bars of new iron had not a shadow of rust on them. The window itself, even with the bars out, would be a difficult mode of egress because it was small.

Yet, seeing these things, The Thinking Machine was not discouraged. Instead, he thoughtfully squinted at the great arc light—there was bright sunlight now—and traced with his eyes the wire which led from it to the building. That electric wire, he reasoned, must come down the side of the building not a great distance from his cell. That might be worth knowing.

Cell 13 was on the same floor with the offices of the prison— that is, not in the basement, nor yet upstairs. There were only four steps up to the office floor, therefore the level of the floor must be only three or four feet above the ground. He couldn't see the ground directly beneath his window, but he could see it further out toward the wall. It would be an easy drop from the window. Well and good.

Then The Thinking Machine fell to remembering how he had come to the cell. First, there was the outside guard's booth, a part of the wall. There were two heavily barred gates there, both of steel. At this gate was one man always on guard. He admitted persons to the prison after much clanking of keys and locks, and let them out when ordered to do so. The warden's office was in the prison building, and in order to reach that official from the prison yard one had to pass a gate of solid steel with only a peep-hole in it. Then coming from that inner office to Cell 13, where he was now, one must pass a heavy wooden door and two steel doors into the corridors of the prison; and always there was the double-locked door of Cell 13 to reckon with.

There were then, The Thinking Machine recalled, seven doors to be overcome before one could pass from Cell 13 into the outer world, a free man. But against this was the fact that he was rarely interrupted. A jailer appeared at his cell door at six in the morning with a breakfast of prison fare; he would come again at noon, and again at six in the afternoon. At nine o'clock at night would come the inspection tour. That would be all.

"It's admirably arranged, this prison system," was the mental tribute paid by The Thinking Machine. "I'll have to study it a little when I get out. I had no idea there was such great care exercised in the prisons."

There was nothing, positively nothing, in his cell, except his iron bed, so firmly put together that no man could tear it to pieces save with sledges or a file. He had neither of these. There was not even a chair, or a small table, or a bit of tin or crockery. Nothing! The jailer stood by when he ate, then took away the wooden spoon and bowl which he had used.

One by one these things sank into the brain of The Thinking Machine. When the last possibility had been considered he began an examination of his cell. From the roof, down the walls on all sides, he examined the stones and the cement between them. He stamped over the floor carefully time after time, but it was cement, perfectly solid. After the examination he sat on the edge of the iron bed and was lost in thought for a long time. For Professor Augustus S. F. X. Van Dusen, The Thinking Machine, had something to think about.

He was disturbed by a rat, which ran across his foot, then scampered away into a dark corner of the cell, frightened at its own daring. After a while The Thinking Machine, squinting steadily into the darkness of the corner where the rat had gone, was able to make out in the gloom many little beady eyes staring at him. He counted six pair, and there were perhaps others; he didn't see very well.

Then The Thinking Machine, from his seat on the bed, noticed for the first time the bottom of his cell door. There was an opening there of two inches between the steel bar and the floor. Still looking steadily at the opening, The Thinking Machine backed suddenly into the corner where he had seen the beady eyes. There was a great scampering of tiny feet, several squeaks of frightened rodents, and then silence.

None of the rats had gone out the door, yet there were none in the cell. Therefore there must be another way out of the cell, however small. The Thinking Machine, in hands and knees, started a search for this spot, feeling in the darkness with his long, slender fingers.

At last his search was rewarded. He came upon a small opening in the floor, level with the cement. It was perfectly round and somewhat larger than a silver dollar. This was the way the rats had gone. He put his fingers deep into the opening; it seemed to be a disused drainage pipe and was dry and dusty.

Having satisfied himself on this point, he sat on the bed again for an hour, then made another inspection of his surroundings through the small cell window. One of the outside guards stood directly opposite, beside the wall, and happened to be looking at the window of Cell 13 when the head of The Thinking Machine appeared. But the scientist didn't notice the guard.

Noon came and the jailer appeared with the prison dinner of repulsively plain food. At home The Thinking Machine merely ate to live; here he took what was offered without comment. Occasionally he spoke to the jailer who stood outside the door watching him.

"Any improvements made here in the last few years?" he asked.

"Nothing particularly," replied the jailer. "New wall was built four years ago."

"Anything done to the prison proper?"

"Painted the woodwork outside, and I believe about seven years ago a new system of plumbing was put in."

"Ah!" said the prisoner. "How far is the river over there?"

"About three hundred feet. The boys have a baseball ground between the wall and the river."

The Thinking Machine had nothing further to say just then, but when the jailer was ready to go he asked for some water.

"I get very thirsty here," he explained. "Would it be possible for you to leave a little water in a bowl for me?"

"I'll ask the warden," replied the jailer, and he went away.

Half an hour later he returned with water in a small earthen bowl.

"The warden says you may keep this bowl," he informed the prisoner. "But you must show it to me when I ask for it. If it is broken, it will be the last."

"Thank you," said The Thinking Machine. "I shan't break it."

The jailer went on about his duties. For just the fraction of a second it seemed that The Thinking Machine wanted to ask a question, but he didn't.

Two hours later this same jailer, in passing the door of Cell No. 13, heard a noise inside and stopped. The Thinking Machine was down on his hands and knees in a corner of the cell, and from that same corner came several frightened squeaks. The jailer looked on interestedly.

"Ah, I've got you," he heard the prisoner say.

"Got what?" he asked, sharply.

"One of these rats," was the reply. "See?" And between the scientist's long fingers the jailer saw a small gray rat struggling. The prisoner brought it over to the light and looked at it closely. "It's a water rat," he said.

"Ain't you got anything better to do than to catch rats?" asked the jailer.

"It's disgraceful that they should be here at all," was the irritated reply. "Take this one away and kill it. There are dozens more where it came from."

The jailer took the wriggling, squirmy rodent and flung it down on the floor violently. It gave one squeak and lay still. Later he reported the incident to the warden, who only smiled.

Still later that afternoon the outside armed guard on Cell 13 side of the prison looked up again at the window and saw the prisoner looking out. He saw a hand raised to the barred window and then something white fluttered to the ground, directly under the window of Cell 13. It was a little roll of linen, evidently of white shirting material, and tied around it was a five-dollar bill. The guard looked up at the window again, but the face had disappeared.

With a grim smile he took the little linen roll and the five-dollar bill to the warden's office. There together they deciphered something which was written on it with a queer sort of ink, frequently blurred. On the outside was this:

"Finder of this please deliver to Dr. Charles Ransome."

"Ah," said the warden, with a chuckle. "Plan of escape number one has gone wrong." Then, as an afterthought: "But why did he address it to Dr. Ransome?"

"And where did he get the pen and ink to write with?" asked the guard.

The warden looked at the guard and the guard looked at the warden. There was no apparent solution of that mystery. The warden studied the writing carefully, then shook his head.

"Well, let's see what he was going to say to Dr. Ransome," he said at length, still puzzled, and he unrolled the inner piece of linen.

"Well, if that—what—what do you think of that?" he asked, dazed.

The guard took the bit of linen and read this:

"Epa cseot d'net niiy awe htto n'si sih. T."

III

The warden spent an hour wondering what sort of cipher it was, and half an hour wondering why his prisoner should attempt to communicate with Dr. Ransome, who was the cause of him being there. After this the warden devoted some thought to the question of where the prisoner got writing materials, and what sort of writing materials he had. With the idea of illuminating this point, he examined the linen again. It was a torn part of a white shirt and had ragged edges.

Now it was possible to account for the linen, but what the prisoner had used to write with was another matter. The warden knew it would have been impossible for him to have either pen or pencil, and, besides, neither pen nor pencil had been used in this writing. What, then? The warden decided to personally investigate. The Thinking Machine was his prisoner; he had orders to hold his prisoners; if this one sought to escape by sending cipher messages to persons outside, he would stop it, as he would have stopped it in the case of any other prisoner.

The warden went back to Cell 13 and found The Thinking Machine on his hands and knees on the floor, engaged in nothing more alarming than catching rats. The prisoner heard the warden's step and turned to him quickly.

"It's disgraceful," he snapped, "these rats. There are scores of them."

"Other men have been able to stand them," said the warden. "Here is another shirt for you—let me have the one you have on."

"Why?" demanded The Thinking Machine, quickly. His tone was hardly natural, his manner suggested actual perturbation.

"You have attempted to communicate with Dr. Ransome," said the warden severely. "As my prisoner, it is my duty to put a stop to it."

The Thinking Machine was silent for a moment.

"All right," he said, finally. "Do your duty."

The warden smiled grimly. The prisoner arose from the floor and removed the white shirt, putting on instead a striped convict shirt the warden had brought. The warden took the white shirt eagerly, and then and there compared the pieces of linen on which was written the cipher with certain torn places in the shirt. The Thinking Machine looked on curiously.

"The guard brought *you* those, then?" he asked.

"He certainly did," replied the warden triumphantly. "And that ends your first attempt to escape."

The Thinking Machine watched the warden as he, by comparison, established to his own satisfaction that only two pieces of linen had been torn from the white shirt.

"What did you write this with?" demanded the warden.

"I should think it part of your duty to find out," said The Thinking Machine, irritably.

The warden started to say some harsh things, then restrained himself and made a minute search of the cell and of the prisoner instead. He found absolutely nothing; not even a match or toothpick which might have been used for a pen. The same mystery surrounded the fluid with which the cipher had been written. Although the warden left Cell 13 visibly annoyed, he took the torn shirt in triumph.

"Well, writing notes on a shirt won't get him out, that's certain," he told himself with some complacency. He put the linen scraps into his desk to await developments. "If that man escapes from that cell I'll—hang it—I'll resign."

On the third day of his incarceration The Thinking Machine openly attempted to bribe his way out. The jailer had brought his dinner and was leaning against the barred door, waiting, when The Thinking Machine began the conversation.

"The drainage pipes of the prison lead to the river, don't they?" he asked.

"Yes," said the jailer.

"I suppose they are very small?"

"Too small to crawl through, if that's what you're thinking about," was the grinning response.

There was silence until The Thinking Machine finished his meal. Then:

"You know I'm not a criminal, don't you?"

"Yes."

"And that I've a perfect right to be freed if I demand it?"

"Yes."

"Well, I came here believing that I could make my escape," said the prisoner, and his squint eyes studied the face of the jailer. "Would you consider a financial reward for aiding me to escape?"

The jailer, who happened to be an honest man, looked at the slender, weak figure of the prisoner, at the large head with its mass of yellow hair, and was almost sorry.

"I guess prisons like these were not built for the likes of you to get out of," he said, at last.

"But would you consider a proposition to help me get out?" the prisoner insisted, almost beseechingly.

"No," said the jailer, shortly.

"Five hundred dollars," urged The Thinking Machine. "I am not a criminal."

"No," said the jailer.

"A thousand?"

"No," again said the jailer, and he started away hurriedly to escape further temptation. Then he turned back. "If you should give me ten thousand dollars I couldn't get you out. You'd have to pass through seven doors, and I only have the keys to two."

Then he told the warden all about it.

"Plan number two fails," said the warden, smiling grimly. "First a cipher, then bribery."

When the jailer was on his way to Cell 13 at six o'clock, again bearing food to The Thinking Machine, he paused, startled by the unmistakable scrape, scrape of steel against steel. It stopped at the sound of his steps, then craftily the jailer, who was beyond the prisoner's range of vision, resumed his tramping, the sound being apparently that of a man going away from Cell 13. As a matter of fact he was in the same spot.

After a moment there came again the steady scrape, scrape, and the jailer crept cautiously on tiptoes to the door and peered between the bars. The Thinking Machine was standing on the iron bed working at the bars of the little window. He was using a file, judging from the backward and forward swing of his arms.

Cautiously the jailer crept back to the office, summoned the warden in person, and they returned to Cell 13 on tiptoes. The steady scrape was still audible. The warden listened to satisfy himself and then suddenly appeared at the door.

"Well?" he demanded, and there was a smile on his face.

The Thinking Machine glanced back from his perch on the bed and leaped suddenly to the floor, making frantic efforts to hide something. The warden went in, with hand extended.

"Give it up," he said.

"No," said the prisoner, sharply.

"Come, give it up," urged the warden. "I don't want to have to search you again."

"No," repeated the prisoner.

"What was it, a file?" asked the warden.

The Thinking Machine was silent and stood squinting at the warden with something very nearly approaching disappointment on his face—nearly, but not quite. The warden was almost sympathetic.

"Plan number three fails, eh?" he asked, good-naturedly. "Too bad, isn't it?"

The prisoner didn't say.

"Search him," instructed the warden.

The jailer searched the prisoner carefully. At last, artfully concealed in the waist band of the trousers, he found a piece of steel about two inches long, with one side curved like a half moon.

"Ah," said the warden, as he received it from the jailer. "From your shoe heel," and he smiled pleasantly.

The jailer continued his search and on the other side of the trousers waist band found another piece of steel identical with the first. The edges showed where they had been worn against the bars of the window.

"You couldn't saw through those bars with these," said the warden.

"I could have," said The Thinking Machine firmly.

"In six months, perhaps," said the warden, good-naturedly.

The warden shook his head slowly as he gazed into the slightly flushed face of his prisoner.

"Ready to give up?" he asked.

"I haven't started yet," was the prompt reply.

Then came another exhaustive search of the cell. Carefully the two men went over it, finally turning out the bed and searching that. Nothing. The warden in person climbed upon the bed and examined the bars of the window where the prisoner had been sawing. When he looked he was amused.

"Just made it a little bright by hard rubbing," he said to the prisoner, who stood looking on with a somewhat crestfallen air. The warden grasped the iron bars in his strong hands and tried to shake them. They were immovable, set firmly in the solid granite. He examined each in turn and found them all satisfactory. Finally he climbed down from the bed.

"Give it up, professor," he advised.

The Thinking Machine shook his head and the warden and jailer passed on again. As they disappeared down the corridor The Thinking Machine sat on the edge of the bed with his head in his hands.

"He's crazy to try to get out of that cell," commented the jailer.

"Of course he can't get out," said the warden. "But he's clever. I would like to know what he wrote that cipher with."

.   .   .   .

It was four o'clock next morning when an awful, heart-racking shriek of terror resounded through the great prison. It came from a cell, somewhere about the center, and its tone told a tale of horror, agony, terrible fear. The warden heard and with three of his men rushed into the long corridor leading to Cell 13.

IV

As they ran there came again that awful cry. It died away in a sort of wail. The white faces of prisoners appeared at cell doors upstairs and down, staring out wonderingly, frightened.

"It's that fool in Cell 13," grumbled the warden.

He stopped and stared in as one of the jailers flashed a lantern. "That fool in Cell 13" lay comfortably on his cot, flat on his back with his mouth open, snoring. Even as they looked there came again the piercing cry, from somewhere above. The warden's face blanched a little as he started up the stairs. There on the top floor he found a man in Cell 43, directly above Cell 13, but two floors higher, cowering in the corner of his cell.

"What's the matter?" demanded the warden.

"Thank God you've come," exclaimed the prisoner, and he cast himself against the bars of his cell.

"What is it?" demanded the warden again.

He threw open the door and went in. The prisoner dropped on his knees and clasped the warden about the body. His face was white with terror, his eyes were widely distended, and he was shuddering. His hands, icy cold, clutched at the warden's.

"Take me out of this cell, please take me out," he pleaded.

"What's the matter with you, anyhow?" insisted the warden, impatiently.

"I've heard something—something," said the prisoner, and his eyes roved nervously around the cell.

"What did you hear?"

"I—I can't tell you," stammered the prisoner. Then, in a sudden burst of terror: "Take me out of this cell—put me anywhere—but take me out of here."

The warden and the three jailers exchanged glances.

"Who is this fellow? What's he accused of?" asked the warden.

"Joseph Ballard," said one of the jailers. "He's accused of throwing acid in a woman's face. She died from it."

"But they can't prove it," gasped the prisoner. "They can't prove it. Please put me in some other cell."

He was still clinging to the warden, and that official threw his arms off roughly. Then for a time he stood looking at the cowering wretch, who seemed possessed of all the wild, unreasoning terror of a child.

"Look here, Ballard," said the warden, finally, "if you heard anything, I want to know what it was. Now tell me."

"I can't, I can't," was the reply. He was sobbing.

"Where did it come from?"

"I don't know. Everywhere—nowhere. I just heard it."

"What was it—a voice?"

"Please don't make me answer," pleaded the prisoner.

"You must answer," said the warden, sharply.

"It was a voice—but—but it wasn't human," was the sobbing reply.

"Voice, but not human?" repeated the warden, puzzled.

"It sounded muffled and—and far away—and ghostly," explained the man.

"Did it come from inside or outside the prison?"

"It didn't seem to come from anywhere—it was just here, here, everywhere. I heard it. I heard it."

For an hour the warden tried to get the story, but Ballard had become suddenly obstinate and would say nothing—only pleaded to be placed in another cell, or to have one of the jailers remain near him until daylight. These requests were gruffly refused.

"And see here," said the warden, in conclusion, "if there's any more of this screaming I'll put you in the padded cell."

Then the warden went his way, a sadly puzzled man. Ballard sat at his cell door until daylight, his face, drawn and white with terror, pressed against the bars, and looked out into the prison with wide, staring eyes.

That day, the fourth since the incarceration of The Thinking Machine, was enlivened considerably by the volunteer prisoner, who spent most of his time at the little window of his cell. He began proceedings by throwing another piece of linen down to the guard, who picked it up dutifully and took it to the warden. On it was written:

"Only three days more."

The warden was in no way surprised at what he read; he understood that The Thinking Machine meant only three days more of his imprisonment, and he regarded the note as a boast. But how was the thing written? Where had The Thinking Machine found the new piece of linen? Where? How? He carefully examined the linen. It was white, of fine texture, shirting material. He took the shirt which he had taken and carefully fitted the two original pieces of the linen to the torn places. The third piece was entirely superfluous; it didn't fit anywhere, and yet it was unmistakably the same goods.

"And where—where does he get anything to write with?" demanded the warden of the world at large.

Still later on the fourth day The Thinking Machine, through the window of his cell, spoke to the armed guard outside.

"What day of the month is it?" he asked.

"The fifteenth," was the answer.

The Thinking Machine made a mental astronomical calculation and satisfied himself that the moon would not rise until after nine o'clock that night. Then he asked another question:

"Who attends to those arc lights?"

"Man from the company."

"You have no electricians in the building?"

"No."

"I should think you could save money if you had your own man."

"None of my business," replied the guard.

The guard noticed The Thinking Machine at the cell window frequently during that day, but always the face seemed listless and there was a certain wistfulness in the squint eyes behind the glasses. After a while he accepted the presence of the leonine head as a matter of course. He had seen other prisoners do the same thing; it was the longing for the outside world.

That afternoon, just before the day guard was relieved, the head appeared at the window again, and The Thinking Machine's hand held something out between the bars. It fluttered to the ground and the guard picked it up. It was a five-dollar bill.

"That's for you," called the prisoner.

As usual, the guard took it to the warden. That gentleman looked at it suspiciously; he looked at everything that came from Cell 13 with suspicion.

"He said it was for me," explained the guard.

"It's a sort of a tip, I suppose," said the warden. "I see no particular reason why you shouldn't accept—"

Suddenly he stopped. He had remembered that The Thinking Machine had gone into Cell 13 with one five-dollar bill and two ten-dollar bills; twenty-five dollars in all. Now a five-dollar bill had been tied around the first pieces of linen that came from the cell. The warden still had it, and to convince himself he took it out and looked at it. It was five dollars; yet here was another five dollars, and The Thinking Machine had only had ten-dollar bills.

"Perhaps somebody changed one of the bills for him," he thought at last, with a sigh of relief.

But then and there he made up his mind. He would search Cell 13 as a cell was never before searched in this world. When a man could write at will, and change money, and do other wholly inexplicable things, there was something radically wrong with his prison. He planned to enter the cell at night—three o'clock would be an excellent time. The Thinking Machine must do all the weird things he did sometime. Night seemed the most reasonable.

Thus it happened that the warden stealthily descended upon Cell 13 that night at three o'clock. He paused at the door and listened. There was no sound save the steady, regular breathing of the prisoner. The keys unfastened the double locks with scarcely a clank, and the warden entered, locking the door behind him. Suddenly he flashed his dark lantern in the face of the recumbent figure.

If the warden had planned to startle The Thinking Machine he was mistaken, for that individual merely opened his eyes quietly, reached for his glasses and inquired, in a most matter-of-fact tone:

"Who is it?"

It would be useless to describe the search that the warden made. It was minute. Not one inch of the cell or the bed was overlooked. He found the round hole in the floor, and with a flash of inspiration thrust his fingers into it. After a moment of fumbling there he drew up something and looked at it in the light of his lantern.

"Ugh!" he exclaimed.

The thing he had taken out was a rat—a dead rat. His inspiration fled as a mist before the sun. But he continued the search.

The Thinking Machine, without a word, arose and kicked the rat out of the cell into the corridor.

The warden climbed on the bed and tried the steel bars in the tiny window. They were perfectly rigid; every bar of the door was the same.

Then the warden searched the prisoner's clothing, beginning at the shoes. Nothing hidden in them! Then the trousers waist band. Still nothing! Then the pockets of the trousers. From one side he drew out some paper money and examined it.

"Five one-dollar bills," he gasped.

"That's right," said the prisoner.

"But the—you had two tens and a five—what the—how do you do it?"

"That's my business," said The Thinking Machine.

"Did any of my men change this money for you—on your word of honor?"

The Thinking Machine paused just a fraction of a second.

"No," he said.

"Well, do you make it?" asked the warden. He was prepared to believe anything.

"That's my business," again said the prisoner.

The warden glared at the eminent scientist fiercely. He felt—he knew—that this man was making a fool out of him, yet he didn't know how. If he were a real prisoner he would get the truth—but, then, perhaps, these inexplicable things which had happened would not have been brought before him so sharply. Neither of the men spoke for a long time, then suddenly the warden turned fiercely and left the cell, slamming the door behind him. He didn't dare to speak, then.

He glanced at the clock. It was ten minutes to four. He had hardly settled himself in bed when again came the heart-breaking shriek through the prison. With a few muttered words, which, while not elegant, were highly expressive, he relighted his lantern and rushed through the prison again to the cell on the upper floor.

Again Ballard was crushing himself against the steel door,

shrieking, shrieking at the top of his voice. He stopped only when the warden flashed his lamp in the cell.

"Take me out, take me out," he screamed. "I did it, I did it, I killed her. Take it away."

"Take what away?" asked the warden.

"I threw the acid in her face—I did it—I confess. Take me out of here."

Ballard's condition was pitiable; it was only an act of mercy to let him out into the corridor. There he crouched in a corner, like an animal at bay, and clasped his hands to his ears. It took half an hour to calm him sufficiently to speak. Then he told incoherently what had happened. On the night before at four o'clock he had heard a voice—a sepulchral voice, muffled and wailing in tone.

"What did it say?" asked the warden, curiously.

"Acid—acid—acid!" gasped the prisoner. "It accused me. Acid! I threw the acid, and the woman died. Oh!" It was a long, shuddering wail of terror.

"Acid?" echoed the warden, puzzled. The case was beyond him.

"Acid. That's all I heard—that one word, repeated several times. There were other things, too, but I didn't hear them."

"That was last night, eh?" asked the warden. "What happened to-night—what frightened you just now?"

"It was the same thing," gasped the prisoner. "Acid—acid—acid!" He covered his face with his hands and sat shivering. "It was acid I used on her, but I didn't mean to kill her. I just heard the words. It was something accusing me—accusing me." He mumbled, and was silent.

"Did you hear anything else?"

"Yes—but I couldn't understand—only a little bit—just a word or two."

"Well, what was it?"

"I heard 'acid' three times, then I heard a long, moaning sound, then—then—I heard 'No. 8 hat.' I heard that voice."

"No. 8 hat," repeated the warden. "What the devil—No. 8 hat? Accusing voices of conscience have never talked about No. 8 hats, so far as I ever heard."

"He's insane," said one of the jailers, with an air of finality.

"I believe you," said the warden. "He must be. He probably heard something and got frightened. He's trembling now. No. 8 hat! What the—"

V

When the fifth day of The Thinking Machine's imprisonment rolled around the warden was wearing a hunted look. He was anxious for the end of the thing. He could not help but feel that his distinguished prisoner had been amusing himself. And if this were so, The Thinking Machine had lost none of his sense of humor. For on this fifth day he flung down another linen note to the outside guard, bearing the words: "Only two days more." Also he flung down half a dollar.

Now the warden knew—he *knew*—that the man in Cell 13 didn't have any half dollars—he *couldn't* have any half dollars, no more than he could have pen and ink and linen, and yet he did have them. It was a condition, not a theory; that is one reason why the warden was wearing a hunted look.

That ghastly, uncanny thing, too, about "Acid" and "No. 8 hat" clung to him tenaciously. They didn't mean anything, of course, merely the ravings of an insane murderer who had been driven by fear to confess his crime, still there were so many things that "didn't mean anything" happening in the prison now since The Thinking Machine was there.

On the sixth day the warden received a postal stating that Dr. Ransome and Mr. Fielding would be at Chisholm Prison on the following evening, Thursday, and in the event Professor Van Dusen had not yet escaped—and they presumed he had not because they had not heard from him—they would meet him there.

"In the event he had not yet escaped!" The warden smiled grimly. Escaped!

The Thinking Machine enlivened this day for the warden with three notes. They were on the usual linen and bore generally on the appointment at half-past eight o'clock Thursday night, which appointment the scientist had made at the time of his imprisonment.

On the afternoon of the seventh day the warden passed Cell

13 and glanced in. The Thinking Machine was lying on the iron bed, apparently sleeping lightly. The cell appeared precisely as it always did from a casual glance. The warden would swear that no man was going to leave it between that hour— it was then four o'clock—and half-past eight o'clock that evening.

On his way back past the cell the warden heard the steady breathing again, and coming close to the door looked in. He wouldn't have done so if The Thinking Machine had been looking, but now—well, it was different.

A ray of light came through the high window and fell on the face of the sleeping man. It occurred to the warden for the first time that his prisoner appeared haggard and weary. Just then The Thinking Machine stirred slightly and the warden hurried on up the corridor guiltily. That evening after six o'clock he saw the jailer.

"Everything all right in Cell 13?" he asked.

"Yes, sir," replied the jailer. "He didn't eat much, though."

It was with a feeling of having done his duty that the warden received Dr. Ransome and Mr. Fielding shortly after seven o'clock. He intended to show them the linen notes and lay before them the full story of his woes, which was a long one. But before this came to pass the guard from the river side of the prison yard entered the office.

"The arc light in my side of the yard won't light," he informed the warden.

"Confound it, that man's a hoodoo," thundered the official. "Everything has happened since he's been here."

The guard went back to his post in the darkness, and the warden 'phoned to the electric light company.

"This is Chisholm Prison," he said through the 'phone. "Send three or four men down here quick, to fix an arc light."

The reply was evidently satisfactory, for the warden hung up the receiver and passed out into the yard. While Dr. Ransome and Mr. Fielding sat waiting the guard at the outer gate came in with a special delivery letter. Dr. Ransome happened to notice the address, and, when the guard went out, looked at the letter more closely.

"By George!" he exclaimed.

"What is it?" asked Mr. Fielding.

Silently the doctor offered the letter. Mr. Fielding examined it closely.

"Coincidence," he said. "It must be."

It was nearly eight o'clock when the warden returned to his office. The electricians had arrived in a wagon, and were now at work. The warden pressed the buzz-button communicating with the man at the outer gate in the wall.

"How many electricians came in?" he asked, over the short 'phone. "Four? Three workmen in jumpers and overalls and the manager? Frock coat and silk hat? All right. Be certain that only four go out. That's all."

He turned to Dr. Ransome and Mr. Fielding.

"We have to be careful here—particularly," and there was broad sarcasm in his tone, "since we have scientists locked up."

The warden picked up the special delivery letter carelessly, and then began to open it.

"When I read this I want to tell you gentlemen something about how—Great Cæsar!" he ended, suddenly, as he glanced at the letter. He sat with mouth open, motionless, from astonishment.

"What is it?" asked Mr. Fielding.

"A special delivery letter from Cell 13," gasped the warden. "An invitation to supper."

"What?" and the two others arose, unanimously.

The warden sat dazed, staring at the letter for a moment, then called sharply to a guard outside in the corridor.

"Run down to Cell 13 and see if that man's in there."

The guard went as directed, while Dr. Ransome and Mr. Fielding examined the letter.

"It's Van Dusen's handwriting; there's no question of that," said Dr. Ransome. "I've seen too much of it."

Just then the buzz on the telephone from the outer gate sounded, and the warden, in a semi-trance, picked up the receiver.

"Hello! Two reporters, eh? Let 'em come in." He turned suddenly to the doctor and Mr. Fielding. "Why; the man *can't* be out. He must be in his cell."

Just at that moment the guard returned.

"He's still in his cell, sir," he reported. "I saw him. He's lying down."

"There, I told you so," said the warden, and he breathed freely again. "But how did he mail that letter?"

There was a rap on the steel door which led from the jail yard into the warden's office.

"It's the reporters," said the warden. "Let them in," he instructed the guard; then to the other two gentlemen: "Don't say anything about this before them, because I'd never hear the last of it."

The door opened, and the two men from the front gate entered.

"Good-evening, gentlemen," said one. That was Hutchinson Hatch; the warden knew him well.

"Well?" demanded the other, irritably. "I'm here."

That was The Thinking Machine.

He squinted belligerently at the warden, who sat with mouth agape. For the moment that official had nothing to say. Dr. Ransome and Mr. Fielding were amazed, but they didn't know what the warden knew. They were only amazed; he was paralyzed. Hutchinson Hatch, the reporter, took in the scene with greedy eyes.

"How—how—how did you do it?" gasped the warden, finally.

"Come back to the cell," said The Thinking Machine, in the irritated voice which his scientific associates knew so well.

The warden, still in a condition bordering on trance, led the way.

"Flash your light in there," directed The Thinking Machine.

The warden did so. There was nothing unusual in the appearance of the cell, and there—there on the bed lay the figure of The Thinking Machine. Certainly! There was the yellow hair! Again the warden looked at the man beside him and wondered at the strangeness of his own dreams.

With trembling hands he unlocked the cell door and The Thinking Machine passed inside.

"See here," he said.

He kicked at the steel bars in the bottom of the cell door and three of them were pushed out of place. A fourth broke off and rolled away in the corridor.

"And here, too," directed the erstwhile prisoner as he stood on the bed to reach the small window. He swept his hand across the opening and every bar came out.

"What's this in the bed?" demanded the warden, who was slowly recovering.

"A wig," was the reply. "Turn down the cover."

The warden did so. Beneath it lay a large coil of strong rope, thirty feet or more, a dagger, three files, ten feet of electric wire, a thin, powerful pair of steel pliers, a small tack hammer with its handle, and—and a Derringer pistol.

"How did you do it?" demanded the warden.

"You gentlemen have an engagement to supper with me at half-past nine o'clock," said The Thinking Machine. "Come on, or we shall be late."

"But how did you do it?" insisted the warden.

"Don't ever think you can hold any man who can use his brain," said The Thinking Machine. "Come on; we shall be late."

VI

It was an impatient supper party in the rooms of Professor Van Dusen and a somewhat silent one. The guests were Dr. Ransome, Alfred Fielding, the warden, and Hutchinson Hatch, reporter. The meal was served to the minute, in accordance with Professor Van Dusen's instructions of one week before; Dr. Ransome found the artichokes delicious. At last the supper was finished and The Thinking Machine turned full on Dr. Ransome and squinted at him fiercely.

"Do you believe it now?" he demanded.

"I do," replied Dr. Ransome.

"Do you admit that it was a fair test?"

"I do."

With the others, particularly the warden, he was waiting anxiously for the explanation.

"Suppose you tell us how—" began Mr. Fielding.

"Yes, tell us how," said the warden.

The Thinking Machine readjusted his glasses, took a couple of preparatory squints at his audience, and began the story. He told it from the beginning logically; and no man ever talked to more interested listeners.

"My agreement was," he began, "to go into a cell, carrying nothing except what was necessary to wear, and to leave that cell within a week. I had never seen Chisholm Prison. When I went into the cell I asked for tooth powder, two ten- and one five-dollar bills, and also to have my shoes blacked. Even if these requests had been refused it would not have mattered seriously. But you agreed to them.

"I knew there would be nothing in the cell which you thought I might use to advantage. So when the warden locked the door on me I was apparently helpless, unless I could turn three seemingly innocent things to use. They were things which would have been permitted any prisoner under sentence of death, were they not, warden?"

"Tooth powder and polished shoes, yes, but not money," replied the warden.

"Anything is dangerous in the hands of a man who knows how to use it," went on The Thinking Machine. "I did nothing that first night but sleep and chase rats." He glared at the warden. "When the matter was broached I knew I could do nothing that night, so suggested next day. You gentlemen thought I wanted time to arrange an escape with outside assistance, but this was not true. I knew I could communicate with whom I pleased, when I pleased."

The warden stared at him a moment, then went on smoking solemnly.

"I was aroused next morning at six o'clock by the jailer with my breakfast," continued the scientist. "He told me dinner was at twelve and supper at six. Between these times, I gathered, I would be pretty much to myself. So immediately after breakfast I examined my outside surroundings from my cell window. One look told me it would be useless to try to scale the wall, even should I decide to leave my cell by the window, for my purpose was to leave not only the cell, but the prison. Of course, I could have gone over the wall, but it would have taken me longer to lay my plans that way. Therefore, for the moment, I dismissed all idea of that.

"From this first observation I knew the river was on that side of the prison, and that there was also a playground there. Subsequently these surmises were verified by a keeper. I knew then one important thing—that anyone might approach the prison wall from that side if necessary without attracting any particular attention. That was well to remember. I remembered it.

"But the outside thing which most attracted my attention was the feed wire to the arc light which ran within a few feet—probably three or four—of my cell window. I knew that would be valuable in the event I found it necessary to cut off that arc light."

"Oh, you shut it off to-night, then?" asked the warden.

"Having learned all I could from that window," resumed The Thinking Machine, without heeding the interruption, "I considered the idea of escaping through the prison proper. I recalled just how I had come into the cell, which I knew would be the only way. Seven doors lay between me and the outside. So, also for the time being, I gave up the idea of escaping that way. And I couldn't go through the solid granite walls of the cell."

The Thinking Machine paused for a moment and Dr. Ransome lighted a new cigar. For several minutes there was silence, then the scientific jail-breaker went on:

"While I was thinking about these things a rat ran across my foot. It suggested a new line of thought. There were at least half a dozen rats in the cell—I could see their beady eyes. Yet I had noticed none come under the cell door. I frightened them purposely and watched the cell door to see if they went out that way. They did not, but they were gone. Obviously they went another way. Another way meant another opening.

"I searched for this opening and found it. It was an old drain pipe, long unused and partly choked with dirt and dust. But this was the way the rats had come. They came from somewhere. Where? Drain pipes usually lead outside prison grounds. This one probably led to the river, or near it. The rats must therefore come from that direction. If they came a part of the way, I reasoned that they came all the way, because it was extremely unlikely that a solid iron or lead pipe would have any hole in it except at the exit.

"When the jailer came with my luncheon he told me two important things, although he didn't know it. One was that a new system of plumbing had been put in the prison seven years before; another that the river was only three hundred feet away. Then I knew positively that the pipe was a part of an old system; I knew, too, that it slanted generally toward the river. But did the pipe end in the water or on land?

"This was the next question to be decided. I decided it by

catching several of the rats in the cell. My jailer was surprised to see me engaged in this work. I examined at least a dozen of them. They were perfectly dry; they had come through the pipe, and, most important of all, they were *not house rats, but field rats*. The other end of the pipe was on land, then, outside the prison walls. So far, so good.

"Then, I knew that if I worked freely from this point I must attract the warden's attention in another direction. You see, by telling the warden that I had come there to escape you made the test more severe, because I had to trick him by false scents."

The warden looked up with a sad expression in his eyes.

"The first thing was to make him think I was trying to communicate with you, Dr. Ransome. So I wrote a note on a piece of linen I tore from my shirt, addressed it to Dr. Ransome, tied a five-dollar bill around it and threw it out the window. I knew the guard would take it to the warden, but I rather hoped the warden would send it as addressed. Have you that first linen note, warden?"

The warden produced the cipher.

"What the deuce does it mean, anyhow?" he asked.

"Read it backward, beginning with the 'T' signature and disregard the division into words," instructed The Thinking Machine.

The warden did so.

"T-h-i-s, this," he spelled, studied it for a moment, then read it off, grinning:

"This is not the way I intend to escape.

"Well, now what do you think o' that?" he demanded, still grinning.

"I knew that would attract your attention, just as it did," said The Thinking Machine, "and if you really found out what it was it would be a sort of gentle rebuke."

"What did you write it with?" asked Dr. Ransome, after he had examined the linen and passed it to Mr. Fielding.

"This," said the erstwhile prisoner, and he extended his foot. On it was the shoe he had worn in prison, though the polish was gone—scraped off clean. "The shoe blacking, moistened with water, was my ink; the metal tip of the shoe lace made a fairly good pen."

The warden looked up and suddenly burst into a laugh, half of relief, half of amusement.

"You're a wonder," he said, admiringly. "Go on."

"That precipitated a search of my cell by the warden, as I had intended," continued The Thinking Machine. "I was anxious to get the warden into the habit of searching my cell, so that finally, constantly finding nothing, he would get disgusted and quit. This at last happened, practically."

The warden blushed.

"He then took my white shirt away and gave me a prison shirt. He was satisfied that those two pieces of the shirt were all that was missing. But while he was searching my cell I had another piece of that same shirt, about nine inches square, rolled into a small ball in my mouth."

"Nine inches of that shirt?" demanded the warden. "Where did it come from?"

"The bosoms of all stiff white shirts are of triple thickness," was the explanation. "I tore out the inside thickness, leaving the bosom only two thicknesses. I knew you wouldn't see it. So much for that."

There was a little pause, and the warden looked from one to another of the men with a sheepish grin.

"Having disposed of the warden for the time being by giving him something else to think about, I took my first serious step toward freedom," said Professor Van Dusen. "I knew, within reason, that the pipe led somewhere to the playground outside; I knew a great many boys played there; I knew that rats came into my cell from out there. Could I communicate with some one outside with these things at hand?

"First was necessary, I saw, a long and fairly reliable thread, so—but here," he pulled up his trousers legs and showed that the tops of both stockings, of fine, strong lisle, were gone. "I unraveled those—after I got them started it wasn't difficult—and I had easily a quarter of a mile of thread that I could depend on.

"Then on half of my remaining linen I wrote, laboriously enough I assure you, a letter explaining my situation to this gentleman here," and he indicated Hutchinson Hatch. "I knew he would assist me—for the value of the newspaper story. I tied firmly to this linen letter a ten-dollar bill—there is no surer way of attracting the eye of anyone—and wrote on the linen: 'Finder of this deliver to Hutchinson Hatch, *Daily American,* who will give another ten dollars for the information.'

"The next thing was to get this note outside on that playground where a boy might find it. There were two ways, but I chose the best. I took one of the rats—I became adept in catching them—tied the linen and money firmly to one leg, fastened my lisle thread to another, and turned him loose in the drain pipe. I reasoned that the natural fright of the rodent would make him run until he was outside the pipe and then out on earth he would probably stop to gnaw off the linen and money.

"From the moment the rat disappeared into that dusty pipe I became anxious. I was taking so many chances. The rat might gnaw the string, of which I held one end; other rats might gnaw it; the rat might run out of the pipe and leave the linen and money where they would never be found; a thousand other things might have happened. So began some nervous hours, but the fact that the rat ran on until only a few feet of the string remained in my cell made me think he was outside the pipe. I had carefully instructed Mr. Hatch what to do in case the note reached him. The question was: Would it reach him?

"This done, I could only wait and make other plans in case this one failed. I openly attempted to bribe my jailer, and learned from him that he held the keys to only two of seven doors between me and freedom. Then I did something else to make the warden nervous. I took the steel supports out of the heels of my shoes and made a pretense of sawing the bars of my cell window. The warden raised a pretty row about that. He developed, too, the habit of shaking the bars of my cell window to see if they were solid. They were—then."

Again the warden grinned. He had ceased being astonished.

"With this one plan I had done all I could and could only wait to see what happened," the scientist went on. "I couldn't know whether my note had been delivered or even found, or whether the mouse had gnawed it up. And I didn't dare to draw back through the pipe that one slender thread which connected me with the outside.

"When I went to bed that night I didn't sleep, for fear there would come the slight signal twitch at the thread which was to tell me that Mr. Hatch had received the note. At half-past three o'clock, I judge, I felt this twitch, and no prisoner actually under sentence of death ever welcomed a thing more heartily."

The Thinking Machine stopped and turned to the reporter.

"You'd better explain just what you did," he said.

"The linen note was brought to me by a small boy who had been playing baseball," said Mr. Hatch. "I immediately saw a big story in it, so I gave the boy another ten dollars, and got several spools of silk, some twine, and a roll of light, pliable wire. The professor's note suggested that I have the finder of the note show me just where it was picked up, and told me to make my search from there, beginning at two o'clock in the morning. If I found the other end of the thread I was to twitch it gently three times, then a fourth.

"I began the search with a small bulb electric light. It was an hour and twenty minutes before I found the end of the drain pipe, half hidden in weeds. The pipe was very large there, say twelve inches across. Then I found the end of the lisle thread, twitched it as directed and immediately I got an answering twitch.

"Then I fastened the silk to this and Professor Van Dusen began to pull it into his cell. I nearly had heart disease for fear the string would break. To the end of the silk I fastened the twine, and when that had been pulled in I tied on the wire. Then that was drawn into the pipe and we had a substantial line, which rats couldn't gnaw, from the mouth of the drain into the cell."

The Thinking Machine raised his hand and Hatch stopped.

"All this was done in absolute silence," said the scientist. "But when the wire reached my hand I could have shouted. Then we tried another experiment, which Mr. Hatch was prepared for. I tested the pipe as a speaking tube. Neither of us could hear very clearly, but I dared not speak loud for fear of attracting attention in the prison. At last I made him understand what I wanted immediately. He seemed to have great difficulty in understanding when I asked for nitric acid, and I repeated the word 'acid' several times.

"Then I heard a shriek from a cell above me. I knew instantly that some one had overheard, and when I heard you coming, Mr. Warden, I feigned sleep. If you had entered my cell at that moment that whole plan of escape would have ended there. But you passed on. That was the nearest I ever came to being caught.

"Having established this improvised trolley it is easy to see how I got things in the cell and made them disappear at will. I merely dropped them back into the pipe. You, Mr. Warden, could not have reached the connecting wire with your fingers; they are too large. My fingers, you see, are longer and more slender. In addition I guarded the top of that pipe with a rat— you remember how."

"I remember," said the warden, with a grimace.

"I thought that if any one were tempted to investigate that hole the rat would dampen his ardor. Mr. Hatch could not send me anything useful through the pipe until next night, although he did send me change for ten dollars as a test, so I proceeded with other parts of my plan. Then I evolved the method of escape, which I finally employed.

"In order to carry this out successfully it was necessary for the guard in the yard to get accustomed to seeing me at the cell window. I arranged this by dropping linen notes to him, boastful in tone, to make the warden believe, if possible, one of his assistants was communicating with the outside for me. I would stand at my window for hours gazing out, so the guard could see, and occasionally I spoke to him. In that way I learned the prison had no electricians of its own, but was dependent upon the lighting company if anything should go wrong.

"That cleared the way to freedom perfectly. Early in the evening of the last day of my imprisonment, when it was dark, I planned to cut the feed wire which was only a few feet from my window, reaching it with an acid-tipped wire I had. That would make that side of the prison perfectly dark while the electricians were searching for the break. That would also bring Mr. Hatch into the prison yard.

"There was only one more thing to do before I actually began the work of setting myself free. This was to arrange final details with Mr. Hatch through our speaking tube. I did this within half an hour after the warden left my cell on the fourth night of my imprisonment. Mr. Hatch again had serious difficulty in understanding me, and I repeated the word 'acid' to him several

times, and later the words: 'Number eight hat'—that's my size—
and these were the things which made a prisoner upstairs confess to murder, so one of the jailers told me the next day. This
prisoner heard our voices, confused of course, through the pipe,
which also went to his cell. The cell directly over me was not
occupied, hence no one else heard.

"Of course the actual work of cutting the steel bars out of the
window and door was comparatively easy with nitric acid, which
I got through the pipe in tin bottles, but it took time. Hour after
hour on the fifth and sixth and seventh days the guard below was
looking at me as I worked on the bars of the window with the
acid on a piece of wire. I used the tooth powder to prevent the
acid spreading. I looked away abstractedly as I worked and each
minute the acid cut deeper into the metal. I noticed that the jailers always tried the door by shaking the upper part, never the
lower bars, therefore I cut the lower bars, leaving them hanging
in place by thin strips of metal. But that was a bit of daredevil-
try. I could not have gone that way so easily."

The Thinking Machine sat silent for several minutes.

"I think that makes everything clear," he went on. "Whatever
points I have not explained were merely to confuse the warden
and jailers. These things in my bed I brought in to please Mr.
Hatch, who wanted to improve the story. Of course, the wig was
necessary in my plan. The special delivery letter I wrote and
directed in my cell with Mr. Hatch's fountain pen, then sent it
out to him and he mailed it. That's all, I think."

"But your actually leaving the prison grounds and then coming in through the outer gate to my office?" asked the warden.

"Perfectly simple," said the scientist. "I cut the electric light
wire with acid, as I said, when the current was off. Therefore
when the current was turned on the arc didn't light. I knew it
would take some time to find out what was the matter and make
repairs. When the guard went to report to you the yard was dark.
I crept out the window—it was a tight fit, too—replaced the bars
by standing on a narrow ledge and remained in a shadow until the
force of electricians arrived. Mr. Hatch was one of them.

"When I saw him I spoke and he handed me a cap, a jumper
and overalls, which I put on within ten feet of you, Mr. Warden,
while you were in the yard. Later Mr. Hatch called me, presum-

ably as a workman, and together we went out the gate to get something out of the wagon. The gate guard let us pass out readily as two workmen who had just passed in. We changed our clothing and reappeared, asking to see you. We saw you. That's all."

There was a silence for several minutes. Dr. Ransome was first to speak.

"Wonderful!" he exclaimed. "Perfectly amazing."

"How did Mr. Hatch happen to come with the electricians?" asked Mr. Fielding.

"His father is manager of the company," replied The Thinking Machine.

"But what if there had been no Mr. Hatch outside to help?"

"Every prisoner has one friend outside who would help him escape if he could."

"Suppose—just suppose—there had been no old plumbing system there?" asked the warden, curiously.

"There were two other ways out," said The Thinking Machine, enigmatically.

Ten minutes later the telephone bell rang. It was a request for the warden.

"Light all right, eh?" the warden asked, through the 'phone. "Good. Wire cut beside Cell 13? Yes, I know. One electrician too many? What's that? Two came out?"

The warden turned to the others with a puzzled expression.

"He only let in four electricians, he has let out two and says there are three left."

"I was the odd one," said The Thinking Machine.

"Oh," said the warden. "I see." Then through the 'phone: "Let the fifth man go. He's all right."

The Blue Cross
(1911)
G. K. Chesterton

Between the silver ribbon of morning and the green glittering ribbon of sea, the boat touched Harwich and let loose a swarm of folk like flies, among whom the man we must follow was by no means conspicuous—nor wished to be. There was nothing notable about him, except a slight contrast between the holiday gaiety of his clothes and the official gravity of his face. His clothes included a slight, pale grey jacket, a white waistcoat, and a silver straw hat with a grey-blue ribbon. His lean face was dark by contrast, and ended in a curt black beard that looked Spanish and suggested an Elizabethan ruff. He was smoking a cigarette with the seriousness of an idler. There was nothing about him to indicate the fact that the grey jacket covered a loaded revolver, that the white waistcoat covered a police card, or that the straw hat covered one of the most powerful intellects in Europe. For this was Valentin himself, the head of the Paris police and the most famous investigator of the world; and he was coming from Brussels to London to make the greatest arrest of the century.

Flambeau was in England. The police of three countries had tracked the great criminal at last from Ghent to Brussels, from Brussels to the Hook of Holland; and it was conjectured that he would take some advantage of the unfamiliarity and confusion of the Eucharistic Congress, then taking place in London.

Probably he would travel as some minor clerk or secretary connected with it; but, of course, Valentin could not be certain; nobody could be certain about Flambeau.

It is many years now since this colossus of crime suddenly ceased keeping the world in a turmoil; and when he ceased, as they said after the death of Roland, there was a great quiet upon the earth. But in his best days (I mean, of course, his worst) Flambeau was a figure as statuesque and international as the Kaiser. Almost every morning the daily paper announced that he had escaped the consequences of one extraordinary crime by committing another. He was a Gascon of gigantic stature and bodily daring; and the wildest tales were told of his outbursts of athletic humour; how he turned the *juge d'instruction* upside down and stood him on his head, "to clear his mind"; how he ran down the Rue de Rivoli with a policeman under each arm. It is due to him to say that his fantastic physical strength was generally employed in such bloodless though undignified scenes; his real crimes were chiefly those of ingenious and wholesale robbery. But each of his thefts was almost a new sin, and would make a story by itself. It was he who ran the great Tyrolean Dairy Company in London, with no dairies, no cows, no carts, no milk, but with some thousand subscribers. These he served by the simple operation of moving the little milk-cans outside people's doors to the doors of his own customers. It was he who had kept up an unaccountable and close correspondence with a young lady whose whole letter-bag was intercepted, by the extraordinary trick of photographing his messages infinitesimally small upon the slides of a microscope. A sweeping simplicity, however, marked many of his experiments. It is said he once repainted all the numbers in a street in the dead of night merely to divert one traveller into a trap. It is quite certain that he invented a portable pillar-box, which he put up at corners in quiet suburbs on the chance of strangers dropping postal orders into it. Lastly he was known to be a startling acrobat; despite his huge figure, he could leap like a grasshopper and melt into the treetops like a monkey. Hence the great Valentin, when he set out to find Flambeau, was perfectly aware that his adventures would not end when he had found him.

But how was he to find him? On this the great Valentin's ideas were still in process of settlement.

There was one thing which Flambeau, with all his dexterity of disguise, could not cover, and that was his singular height. If Valentin's quick eye had caught a tall apple-woman, a tall grenadier, or even a tolerably tall duchess, he might have arrested them on the spot. But all along his train there was nobody that could be a disguised Flambeau, any more than a cat could be a disguised giraffe. About the people on the boat he had already satisfied himself; and the people picked up at Harwich or on the journey limited themselves with certainty to six. There was a short railway official travelling up to the terminus, three fairly short market-gardeners picked up two stations afterwards, one very short widow lady going up from a small Essex town, and a very short Roman Catholic priest going up from a small Essex village. When it came to the last case, Valentin gave it up and almost laughed. The little priest was so much the essence of those Eastern flats: he had a face as round and dull as a Norfolk dumpling; he had eyes as empty as the North Sea; he had several brown-paper parcels which he was quite incapable of collecting. The Eucharistic Congress had doubtless sucked out of their local stagnation many such creatures, blind and helpless, like moles disinterred. Valentin was a sceptic in the severe style of France, and could have no love for priests. But he could have pity for them, and this one might have provoked pity in anybody. He had a large, shabby umbrella, which constantly fell on the floor. He did not seem to know which was the right end of his return ticket. He explained with a moon-calf simplicity to everybody in the carriage that he had to be careful, because he had something made of real silver "with blue stones" in one of his brown-paper parcels. His quaint blending of Essex flatness with saintly simplicity continuously amused the Frenchman till the priest arrived (somehow) at Stratford with all his parcels, and came back for his umbrella. When he did the last, Valentin even had the good nature to warn him not to take care of the silver by telling everybody about it. But to whomever he talked, Valentin kept his eye open for someone else; he looked out steadily for anyone, rich or poor, male or female, who was well up to six feet; for Flambeau was four inches above it.

He alighted at Liverpool Street, however, quite conscientiously secure that he had not missed the criminal so far. He then went to Scotland Yard to regularise his position and arrange for help in case of need; he then lit another cigarette and went for a long stroll in the streets of London. As he was walking in the streets and squares beyond Victoria, he paused suddenly and stood. It was a quaint, quiet square, very typical of London, full of an accidental stillness. The tall, flat houses round looked at once prosperous and uninhabited; the square of shrubbery in the centre looked as deserted as a green Pacific islet. One of the four sides was much higher than the rest, like a dais; and the line of this side was broken by one of London's admirable accidents—a restaurant that looked as if it had strayed from Soho. It was an unreasonably attractive object, with dwarf plants in pots and long, striped blinds of lemon yellow and white. It stood specially high above the street, and in the usual patchwork way of London, a flight of steps from the street ran up to meet the front door almost as a fire-escape might run up to a first-floor window. Valentin stood and smoked in front of the yellow-white blinds and considered them long.

The most incredible thing about miracles is that they happen. A few clouds in heaven do come together into the staring shape of one human eye. A tree does stand up in the landscape of a doubtful journey in the exact and elaborate shape of a note of interrogation. I have seen both these things myself within the last few days. Nelson does die in the instant of victory; and a man named Williams does quite accidentally murder a man named Williamson; it sounds like a sort of infanticide. In short, there is in life an element of elfin coincidence which people reckoning on the prosaic may perpetually miss. As it has been well expressed in the paradox of Poe, wisdom should reckon on the unforeseen.

Aristide Valentin was unfathomably French; and the French intelligence is intelligence specially and solely. He was not "a thinking machine"; for that is a brainless phrase of modern fatalism and materialism. A machine only *is* a machine because it cannot think. But he was a thinking man, and a plain man at the same time. All his wonderful successes, that looked like conjuring, had been gained by plodding logic, by clear and commonplace French thought. The French electrify the world not by starting any paradox, they electrify it by carrying out a truism. They carry a truism so far—as in the French Revolution. But exactly because Valentin understood reason, he understood the limits of reason. Only a man who knows nothing of motors talks of motoring without petrol; only a man who knows nothing of reason talks of reasoning without strong, undisputed first principles. Here he had no strong first principles. Flambeau had been missed at Harwich; and if he was in London at all, he might be anything from a tall tramp on Wimbledon Common to a tall toastmaster at the Hôtel Métropole. In such a naked state of nescience, Valentin had a view and a method of his own.

In such cases he reckoned on the unforeseen. In such cases, when he could not follow the train of the reasonable, he coldly and carefully followed the train of the unreasonable. Instead of going to the right places—banks, police-stations, rendezvous—he systematically went to the wrong places; knocked at every empty house, turned down every *cul de sac,* went up every lane blocked with rubbish, went round every crescent that led him uselessly out of the way. He defended this crazy course quite logically. He said that if one had a clue this was the worst way; but if one had no clue at all it was the best, because there was just the chance that any oddity that caught the eye of the pursuer might be the same that had caught the eye of the pursued. Somewhere a man must begin, and it had better be just where another man might stop. Something about that flight of steps up to the shop, something about the quietude and quaintness of the restaurant, roused all the detective's rare romantic fancy and made him resolve to strike at random. He went up the steps, and sitting down by the window, asked for a cup of black coffee.

It was half-way through the morning, and he had not breakfasted; the slight litter of other breakfasts stood about on the table to remind him of his hunger; and adding a poached egg to his order, he proceeded musingly to shake some white sugar into his coffee, thinking all the time about Flambeau. He remembered how Flambeau had escaped, once by a pair of nail scissors, and once by a house on fire; once by having to pay for an unstamped letter, and once by getting people to look through a telescope at a comet that might destroy the world. He thought his detective brain as good as the criminal's, which was true. But he fully realised the disadvantage. "The criminal is the creative artist; the detective only the critic," he said with a sour smile, and lifted his coffee cup to his lips slowly, and put it down very quickly. He had put salt in it.

He looked at the vessel from which the silvery powder had come; it was certainly a sugar-basin; as unmistakably meant for sugar as a champagne-bottle for champagne. He wondered why they should keep salt in it. He looked to see if there were any more orthodox vessels. Yes, there were two salt-cellars quite full. Perhaps there was some speciality in the condiment in the salt-cellars. He tasted it; it was sugar. Then he looked round at the restaurant with a refreshed air of interest, to see if there were any other traces of that singular artistic taste which puts the sugar in the salt-cellars and the salt in the sugar-basin. Except for an odd splash of some dark fluid on one of the white-papered walls, the whole place appeared neat, cheerful and ordinary. He rang the bell for the waiter.

When that official hurried up, fuzzy-haired and somewhat blear-eyed at that early hour, the detective (who was not without an appreciation of the simpler forms of humor) asked him to taste the sugar and see if it was up to the high reputation of the hotel. The result was that the waiter yawned suddenly and woke up.

"Do you play this delicate joke on your customers every morning?" inquired Valentin. "Does changing the salt and sugar never pall on you as a jest?"

The waiter, when this irony grew clearer, stammeringly assured him that the establishment had certainly no such intention; it must be a most curious mistake. He picked up the sugar-basin and looked at it; he picked up the salt-cellar and looked at that, his face growing more and more bewildered. At last he abruptly excused himself, and hurrying away, returned in a few seconds with the proprietor. The proprietor also examined the sugar-basin and then the salt-cellar; the proprietor also looked bewildered.

Suddenly the waiter seemed to grow inarticulate with a rush of words.

"I zink," he stuttered eagerly, "I zink it is those two clergymen."

"What two clergymen?"

"The two clergymen," said the waiter, "that threw soup at the wall."

"Threw soup at the wall?" repeated Valentin, feeling sure this must be some Italian metaphor.

"Yes, yes," said the attendant excitedly, and pointing at the dark splash on the white paper; "threw it over there on the wall."

Valentin looked his query at the proprietor, who came to his rescue with fuller reports.

"Yes, sir," he said, "it's quite true, though I don't suppose it has anything to do with the sugar and salt. Two clergymen came in and drank soup here very early, as soon as the shutters were taken down. They were both very quiet, respectable people; one of them paid the bill and went out; the other, who seemed a slower coach altogether, was some minutes longer getting his things together. But he went at last. Only, the instant before he stepped into the street he deliberately picked up his cup, which he had only half emptied, and threw the soup slap on the wall. I was in the back room myself, and so was the waiter; so I could only rush out in time to find the wall splashed and the shop empty. It didn't do any particular damage, but it was confounded cheek; and I tried to catch the men in the street. They were too far off though; I only noticed they went round the corner into Carstairs Street."

The detective was on his feet, hat settled and stick in hand. He had already decided that in the universal darkness of his mind he could only follow the first odd finger that pointed; and this finger was odd enough. Paying his bill and clashing the glass doors behind him, he was soon swinging round into the other street.

It was fortunate that even in such fevered moments his eye was cool and quick. Something in a shop-front went by him like a mere flash; yet he went back to look at it. The shop was a popular greengrocer and fruiterer's, an array of goods set out in the open air and plainly ticketed with their names and prices. In the two most prominent compartments were two heaps, of oranges and of nuts respectively. On the heap of nuts lay a scrap of cardboard, on which was written in bold, blue chalk, "Best tangerine oranges, two a penny." On the oranges was the equally clear and exact description, "Finest Brazil nuts, 4d. a lb." M. Valentin looked at these two placards and fancied he had met this highly subtle form of humor before, and that somewhat recently. He drew the attention of the red-faced fruiterer, who was looking rather sullenly up and down the street, to this inaccuracy in his advertisements. The fruiterer said nothing, but sharply put each card into its proper place. The detective, leaning elegantly on his walking-cane, continued to scrutinise the shop. At last he said, "Pray excuse my apparent irrelevance, my good sir, but I should like to ask you a question in experimental psychology and the association of ideas."

The red-faced shopman regarded him with an eye of menace; but he continued gaily, swinging his cane. "Why," he pursued, "why are two tickets wrongly placed in a greengrocer's shop like a shovel hat that has come to London for a holiday? Or, in case I do not make myself clear, what is the mystical association which connects the idea of nuts marked as oranges with the idea of two clergymen, one tall and the other short?"

The eyes of the tradesman stood out of his head like a snail's; he really seemed for an instant likely to fling himself upon the stranger. At last he stammered angrily: "I don't know what you 'ave to do with it, but if you're one of their friends, you can tell 'em from me that I'll knock their silly 'eads off, parsons or no parsons, if they upset my apples again."

"Indeed?" asked the detective, with great sympathy. "Did they upset your apples?"

"One of 'em did," said the heated shopman; "rolled 'em all over the street. I'd 'ave caught the fool but for havin' to pick 'em up."

"Which way did these parsons go?" asked Valentin.

"Up that second road on the left-hand side, and then across the square," said the other promptly.

"Thanks," said Valentin, and vanished like a fairy. On the other side of the second square he found a policeman, and said: "This is urgent, constable; have you seen two clergymen in shovel hats?"

The policeman began to chuckle heavily. "I 'ave, sir; and if you arst me, one of 'em was drunk. He stood in the middle of the road that bewildered that—"

"Which way did they go?" snapped Valentin.

"They took one of them yellow buses over there," answered the man; "them that go to Hampstead."

Valentin produced his official card and said very rapidly: "Call up two of your men to come with me in pursuit," and crossed the road with such contagious energy that the ponderous policeman was moved to almost agile obedience. In a minute and a half the French detective was joined on the opposite pavement by an inspector and a man in plain clothes.

"Well, sir," began the former, with smiling importance, "and what may—?"

Valentin pointed suddenly with his cane. "I'll tell you on the top of that omnibus," he said, and was darting and dodging across the tangle of the traffic. When all three sank panting on the top seats of the yellow vehicle, the inspector said: "We could go four times as quick in a taxi."

"Quite true," replied their leader placidly, "if we only had an idea of where we were going."

"Well, where *are* you going?" asked the other, staring.

Valentin smoked frowningly for a few seconds; then, removing his cigarette, he said: "If you *know* what a man's doing, get in front of him; but if you want to guess what he's doing, keep behind him. Stray when he strays; stop when he stops; travel as slowly as he. Then you may see what he saw and may act as he acted. All we can do is to keep our eyes skinned for a queer thing."

"What sort of a queer thing do you mean?" asked the inspector.

"Any sort of queer thing," answered Valentin, and relapsed into obstinate silence.

The yellow omnibus crawled up the northern roads for what seemed like hours on end; the great detective would not explain further, and perhaps his assistants felt a silent and growing doubt of his errand. Perhaps, also, they felt a silent and growing desire for lunch, for the hours crept long past the normal luncheon hour, and the long roads of the North London suburbs seemed to shoot out into length after length like an infernal telescope. It was one of those journeys on which a man perpetually feels that now at last he must have come to the end of the universe, and then finds he has only come to the beginning of Tufnell Park. London died away in draggled taverns and dreary scrubs, and then was unaccountably born again in blazing high streets and blatant hotels. It was like passing through thirteen separate vulgar cities all just touching each other. But though the winter twilight was already threatening the road ahead of them, the Parisian detective still sat silent and watchful, eyeing the frontage of the streets that slid by on either side. By the time they had left Camden Town behind, the policemen were nearly asleep; at least, they gave something like a jump as Valentin leapt erect, struck a hand on each man's shoulder, and shouted to the driver to stop.

They tumbled down the steps into the road without realising why they had been dislodged; when they looked round for enlightenment they found Valentin triumphantly pointing his finger towards a window on the left side of the road. It was a large window, forming part of the long façade of a gilt and pala-tial public-house; it was the part reserved for respectable dining, and labelled "Restaurant." This window, like all the rest along the frontage of the hotel, was of frosted and figured glass, but in the middle of it was a big, black smash, like a star in the ice.

"Our cue at last," cried Valentin, waving his stick; "the place with the broken window."

"What window? What cue?" asked his principal assistant. "Why, what proof is there that this has anything to do with them?"

Valentin almost broke his bamboo stick with rage.

"Proof!" he cried. "Good God! the man is looking for proof! Why, of course, the chances are twenty to one that it has *nothing* to do with them. But what else can we do? Don't you see we must either follow one wild possibility or else go home to bed?" He banged his way into the restaurant, followed by his compan-ions, and they were soon seated at a late luncheon at a little table, and looking at the star of smashed glass from the inside. Not that it was very informative to them even then.

"Got your window broken, I see," said Valentin to the waiter, as he paid his bill.

"Yes, sir," answered the attendant, bending busily over the change, to which Valentin silently added an enormous tip. The waiter straightened himself with mild but unmistakable animation.

"Ah, yes, sir," he said. "Very odd thing, that, sir."

"Indeed? Tell us about it," said the detective with careless curiosity.

"Well, two gents in black came in," said the waiter; "two of those foreign parsons that are running about. They had a cheap and quiet little lunch, and one of them paid for it and went out. The other was just going out to join him when I looked at my change again and found he'd paid me more than three times too much. 'Here,' I says to the chap who was nearly out of the door, 'you've paid too much.' 'Oh,' he says, very cool, 'have we?' 'Yes,' I says, and picks up the bill to show him. Well, that was a knock-out."

"What do you mean?" asked his interlocutor.

"Well, I'd have sworn on seven Bibles that I'd put 4s. on that bill. But now I saw I'd put 14s., as plain as paint."

"Well?" cried Valentin, moving slowly, but with burning eyes, "and then?"

"The parson at the door he says, all serene, 'Sorry to confuse your accounts, but it'll pay for the window.' 'What window?' I says. 'The one I'm going to break,' he says, and smashed that blessed pane with his umbrella."

All three inquirers made an exclamation; and the inspector said under his breath: "Are we after escaped lunatics?" The waiter went on with some relish for the ridiculous story:

"I was so knocked silly for a second, I couldn't do anything. The man marched out of the place and joined his friend just round the corner. Then they went so quick up Bullock Street that I couldn't catch them, though I ran round the bars to do it."

"Bullock Street," said the detective, and shot up that thoroughfare as quickly as the strange couple he pursued.

Their journey now took them through bare brick ways like tunnels; streets with few lights and even with few windows; streets that seemed built out of the blank backs of everything and everywhere. Dusk was deepening, and it was not easy even for the London policemen to guess in what exact direction they were treading. The inspector, however, was pretty certain that they would eventually strike some part of Hampstead Heath. Abruptly one bulging and gas-lit window broke the blue twilight like a bull's-eye lantern; and Valentin stopped an instant before a little garish sweetstuff shop. After an instant's hesitation he went in; he stood amid the gaudy colors of the confectionery with entire gravity and bought thirteen chocolate cigars with a certain care. He was clearly preparing an opening; but he did not need one.

An angular, elderly young woman in the shop had regarded his elegant appearance with a merely automatic inquiry; but when she saw the door behind him blocked with the blue uniform of the inspector, her eyes seemed to wake up.

"Oh," she said, "if you've come about that parcel, I've sent it off already."

"Parcel?" repeated Valentin; and it was his turn to look inquiring.

"I mean the parcel the gentleman left—the clergyman gentleman."

"For goodness' sake," said Valentin, leaning forward with his first real confession of eagerness, "for Heaven's sake tell us what happened exactly."

"Well," said the woman, a little doubtfully, "the clergymen came in about half an hour ago and bought some peppermints and talked a bit, and then went off towards the Heath. But a second after, one of them runs back into the shop and says, 'Have I left a parcel!' Well, I looked everywhere and couldn't see one; so he says, 'Never mind; but if it should turn up, please post it to this address,' and he left me the address and a shilling for my trouble. And sure enough, though I thought I'd looked everywhere, I found he'd left a brown-paper parcel, so I posted it to the place he said. I can't remember the address now; it was somewhere in Westminster. But as the thing seemed so important, I thought perhaps the police had come about it."

"So they have," said Valentin shortly. "Is Hampstead Heath near here?"

"Straight on for fifteen minutes," said the woman, "and you'll come right out on the open." Valentin sprang out of the shop and began to run. The other detectives followed him at a reluctant trot.

The street they threaded was so narrow and shut in by shadows that when they came out unexpectedly into the void common and vast sky they were startled to find the evening still so light and clear. A perfect dome of peacock-green sank into gold amid the blackening trees and the dark violet distances. The glowing green tint was just deep enough to pick out in points of crystal one or two stars. All that was left of the daylight lay in a golden glitter across the edge of Hampstead and that popular hollow which is called the Vale of Health. The holiday makers who roam this region had not wholly dispersed; a few couples sat shapelessly on benches; and here and there a distant girl still shrieked in one of the swings. The glory of heaven deepened and darkened around the sublime vulgarity of man; and standing on the slope and looking across the valley, Valentin beheld the thing which he sought.

Among the black and breaking groups in that distance was one especially black which did not break—a group of two figures clerically clad. Though they seemed as small as insects, Valentin could see that one of them was much smaller than the other. Though the other had a student's stoop and an inconspicuous manner, he could see that the man was well over six feet high. He shut his teeth and went forward, whirling his stick impatiently. By the time he had substantially diminished the distance and magnified the two black figures as in a vast microscope, he had perceived something else; something which startled him, and yet which he had somehow expected. Whoever was the tall priest, there could be no doubt about the identity of the short one. It was his friend of the Harwich train, the stumpy little *curé* of Essex whom he had warned about his brown-paper parcels.

Now, so far as this went, everything fitted in finally and rationally enough. Valentin had learned by his inquiries that morning that a Father Brown from Essex was bringing up a silver cross with sapphires, a relic of considerable value, to show some of the foreign priests at the congress. This undoubtedly was the "silver with blue stones"; and Father Brown undoubtedly was the little greenhorn in the train. Now there was nothing wonderful about the fact that what Valentin had found out Flambeau had also found out; Flambeau found out everything. Also there was nothing wonderful in the fact that when Flambeau heard of a sapphire cross he should try to steal it; that was the most natural thing in all natural history. And most certainly there was nothing wonderful about the fact that Flambeau should have it all his own way with such a silly sheep

as the man with the umbrella and the parcels. He was the sort
of man whom anybody could lead on a string to the North Pole;
it was not surprising that an actor like Flambeau, dressed as
another priest, could lead him to Hampstead Heath. So far the
crime seemed clear enough; and while the detective pitied the
priest for his helplessness, he almost despised Flambeau for
condescending to so gullible a victim. But when Valentin
thought of all that had happened in between, of all that had led
him to his triumph, he racked his brains for the smallest rhyme
or reason in it. What had the stealing of a blue-and-silver cross
from a priest from Essex to do with chucking soup at wall-paper?
What had it to do with calling nuts oranges, or with paying for
windows first and breaking them afterwards? He had come to
the end of his chase; yet somehow he had missed the middle of
it. When he failed (which was seldom), he had usually grasped
the clue, but nevertheless missed the criminal. Here he had
grasped the criminal, but still he could not grasp the clue.

The two figures that they followed were crawling like black
flies across the huge green contour of a hill. They were evidently
sunk in conversation, and perhaps did not notice where they
were going; but they were certainly going to the wilder and
more silent heights of the Heath. As their pursuers gained on
them, the latter had to use the undignified attitudes of the deer-
stalker, to crouch behind clumps of trees and even to crawl prostrate in deep grass. By these ungainly ingenuities the hunters
even came close enough to the quarry to hear the murmur of
the discussion, but no word could be distinguished except the
word "reason" recurring frequently in a high and almost childish voice. Once, over an abrupt dip of land and a dense tangle of
thickets, the detectives actually lost the two figures they were
following. They did not find the trail again for an agonising ten
minutes, and then it led round the brow of a great dome of hill
overlooking an amphitheatre of rich and desolate sunset
scenery. Under a tree in this commanding yet neglected spot
was an old ramshackle wooden seat. On this seat sat the two
priests still in serious speech together. The gorgeous green and
gold still clung to the darkening horizon; but the dome above
was turning slowly from peacock-green to peacock-blue, and the
stars detached themselves more and more like solid jewels.

Mutely motioning to his followers, Valentin contrived to creep up behind the big branching tree, and, standing there in deathly silence, heard the words of the strange priests for the first time.

After he had listened for a minute and a half, he was gripped by a devilish doubt. Perhaps he had dragged the two English policemen to the wastes of a nocturnal heath on an errand no saner than seeking figs on thistles. For the two priests were talking exactly like priests, piously, with learning and leisure, about the most aerial enigmas of theology. The little Essex priest spoke the more simply, with his round face turned to the strengthening stars; the other talked with his head bowed, as if he were not even worthy to look at them. But no more innocently clerical conversation could have been heard in any white Italian cloister or black Spanish cathedral.

The first he heard was the tail of one of Father Brown's sentences, which ended: ". . . what they really meant in the Middle Ages by the heavens being incorruptible."

The taller priest nodded his bowed head and said:

"Ah, yes, these modern infidels appeal to their reason; but who can look at those millions of worlds and not feel that there may well be wonderful universes above us where reason is utterly unreasonable?"

"No," said the other priest; "reason is always reasonable, even in the last limbo, in the lost borderland of things. I know that people charge the Church with lowering reason, but it is just the other way. Alone on earth, the Church makes reason really supreme. Alone on earth, the Church affirms that God Himself is bound by reason."

The other priest raised his austere face to the spangled sky and said:

"Yet who knows if in that infinite universe—?"

"Only infinite physically," said the little priest, turning sharply in his seat, "not infinite in the sense of escaping from the laws of truth."

Valentin behind his tree was tearing his finger-nails with silent fury. He seemed almost to hear the sniggers of the English detectives whom he had brought so far on a fantastic guess only to listen to the metaphysical gossip of two mild old parsons. In his impatience he lost the equally elaborate answer of the tall cleric, and when he listened again it was again Father Brown who was speaking:

"Reason and justice grip the remotest and the loneliest star. Look at those stars. Don't they look as if they were single diamonds and sapphires? Well, you can imagine any mad botany or geology you please. Think of forests of adamant with leaves of brilliants. Think the moon is a blue moon, a single elephantine sapphire. But don't fancy that all that frantic astronomy would make the smallest difference to the reason and justice of conduct. On plains of opal, under cliffs cut out of pearl, you would still find a notice-board, 'Thou shalt not steal.'"

Valentin was just in the act of rising from his rigid and crouching attitude and creeping away as softly as might be, felled by the one great folly of his life. But something in the very silence of the tall priest made him stop until the latter spoke. When at last he did speak, he said simply, his head bowed and his hands on his knees:

"Well, I think that other worlds may perhaps rise higher than our reason. The mystery of heaven is unfathomable, and I for one can only bow my head."

Then, with brow yet bent and without changing by the faintest shade his attitude or voice, he added:

"Just hand over that sapphire cross of yours, will you? We're all alone here, and I could pull you to pieces like a straw doll."

The utterly unaltered voice and attitude added a strange violence to that shocking change of speech. But the guarder of the relic only seemed to turn his head by the smallest section of the compass. He seemed still to have a somewhat foolish face turned to the stars. Perhaps he had not understood. Or, perhaps, he had understood and sat rigid with terror.

"Yes," said the tall priest, in the same low voice and in the same still posture, "yes, I am Flambeau."

Then, after a pause, he said:

"Come, will you give me that cross?"

"No," said the other, and the monosyllable had an odd sound.

Flambeau suddenly flung off all his pontifical pretensions. The great robber leaned back in his seat and laughed low but long.

"No," he cried; "you won't give it me, you proud prelate. You won't give it me, you little celibate simpleton. Shall I tell you why you won't give it me? Because I've got it already in my own breast-pocket."

The small man from Essex turned what seemed to be a dazed face in the dusk, and said, with the timid eagerness of "The Private Secretary":

"Are—are you sure?"

Flambeau yelled with delight.

"Really, you're as good as a three-act farce," he cried. "Yes, you turnip, I am quite sure. I had the sense to make a duplicate of the right parcel, and now, my friend, you've got the duplicate and I've got the jewels. An old dodge, Father Brown—a very old dodge."

"Yes," said Father Brown, and passed his hand through his hair with the same strange vagueness of manner. "Yes, I've heard of it before."

The colossus of crime leaned over to the little rustic priest with a sort of sudden interest.

"*You* have heard of it?" he asked. "Where have *you* heard of it?"

"Well, I mustn't tell you his name, of course," said the little man simply. "He was a penitent, you know. He had lived prosperously for about twenty years entirely on duplicate brown-paper parcels. And so, you see, when I began to suspect you, I thought of this poor chap's way of doing it at once."

"Began to suspect me?" repeated the outlaw with increased intensity. "Did you really have the gumption to suspect me just because I brought you up to this bare part of the heath?"

"No, no," said Brown with an air of apology. "You see, I suspected you when we first met. It's that little bulge up the sleeve where you people have the spiked bracelet."

"How in Tartarus," cried Flambeau, "did you ever hear of the spiked bracelet?"

"Oh, one's little flock, you know!" said Father Brown, arching his eyebrows rather blankly. "When I was a curate in Hartlepool, there were three of them with spiked bracelets. So, as I suspected you from the first, don't you see, I made sure that the cross should go safe, anyhow. I'm afraid I watched you, you know. So at last I saw you change the parcels. Then, don't you see, I changed them back again. And then I left the right one behind."

"Left it behind?" repeated Flambeau, and for the first time there was another note in his voice beside his triumph.

"Well, it was like this," said the little priest, speaking in the same unaffected way. "I went back to that sweet-shop and asked if I'd left a parcel, and gave them a particular address if it turned up. Well, I knew I hadn't; but when I went away again I did. So, instead of running after me with that valuable parcel, they have sent it flying to a friend of mine in Westminster." Then he added rather sadly: "I learnt that, too, from a poor fellow in Hartlepool. He used to do it with handbags he stole at railway stations, but he's in a monastery now. Oh, one gets to know, you know," he added, rubbing his head again with the same sort of desperate apology. "We can't help being priests. People come and tell us these things."

Flambeau tore a brown-paper parcel out of his inner pocket and rent it in pieces. There was nothing but paper and sticks of lead inside it. He sprang to his feet with a gigantic gesture, and cried:

"I don't believe you. I don't believe a bumpkin like you could manage all that. I believe you've still got the stuff on you, and if you don't give it up—why, we're all alone, and I'll take it by force!"

"No," said Father Brown simply, and stood up also; "you won't take it by force. First, because I really haven't still got it. And, second, because we are not alone."

Flambeau stopped in his stride forward.

"Behind that tree," said Father Brown, pointing, "are two strong policemen and the greatest detective alive. How did they come here, do you ask? Why, I brought them, of course! How did I do it? Why, I'll tell you if you like! Lord bless you, we have to know twenty such things when we work among the criminal classes! Well, I wasn't sure you were a thief, and it would never do to make a scandal against one of our own clergy. So I just tested you to see if anything would make you show yourself. A man generally makes a small scene if he finds salt in his coffee; if he doesn't, he has some reason for keeping quiet. I changed the salt and sugar, and *you* kept quiet. A man generally objects if his bill is three times too big. If he pays it, he has some motive for passing unnoticed. I altered your bill, and *you* paid it."

The world seemed waiting for Flambeau to leap like a tiger.

But he was held back as by a spell; he was stunned with the utmost curiosity.

"Well," went on Father Brown, with lumbering lucidity, "as you wouldn't leave any tracks for the police, of course somebody had to. At every place we went to, I took care to do something that would get us talked about for the rest of the day. I didn't do much harm—a splashed wall, spilt apples, a broken window; but I saved the cross, as the cross will always be saved. It is at Westminster by now. I rather wonder you didn't stop it with the Donkey's Whistle."

"With the what?" asked Flambeau.

"I'm glad you've never heard of it," said the priest, making a face. "It's a foul thing. I'm sure you're too good a man for a Whistler. I couldn't have countered it even with the Spots myself; I'm not strong enough in the legs."

"What on earth are you talking about?" asked the other.

"Well, I did think you'd know the Spots," said Father Brown, agreeably surprised. "Oh, you can't have gone so very wrong yet!"

"How in blazes do you know all these horrors?" cried Flambeau.

The shadow of a smile crossed the round, simple face of his clerical opponent.

"Oh, by being a celibate simpleton, I suppose," he said. "Has it never struck you that a man who does next to nothing but hear men's real sins is not likely to be wholly unaware of human evil? But, as a matter of fact, another part of my trade, too, made me sure you weren't a priest."

"What?" asked the thief, almost gaping.

"You attacked reason," said Father Brown. "It's bad theology."

And even as he turned away to collect his property, the three policemen came out from under the twilight trees. Flambeau was an artist and a sportsman. He stepped back and swept Valentin a great bow.

"Do not bow to me, *mon ami*," said Valentin, with silver clearness. "Let us both bow to our master."

And they both stood an instant uncovered, while the little Essex priest blinked about for his umbrella.

The Case of Oscar Brodski

(1911)

R. Austin Freeman

Part I

THE MECHANISM OF CRIME

A surprising amount of nonsense has been talked about conscience. On the one hand remorse (or the "again-bite" as certain scholars of ultra-Teutonic leanings would prefer to call it); on the other hand "an easy conscience": these have been accepted as the determining factors of happiness or the reverse.

Of course there is an element of truth in the "easy conscience" view, but it begs the whole question. A particularly hardy conscience may be quite easy under the most unfavorable conditions—conditions in which the more feeble conscience might be severely afflicted with the "again-bite." And, then, it seems to be the fact that some fortunate persons have no conscience at all; a negative gift that raises them above the mental vicissitudes of the common herd of humanity.

Now, Silas Hickler was a case in point. No one, looking into his cheerful, round face, beaming with benevolence and wreathed in perpetual smiles, would have imagined him to be a criminal. Least of all, his worthy, high-church housekeeper, who was a witness to his unvarying amiability, who constantly heard him carolling light-heartedly about the house and noted his appreciative zest at meal-times.

Yet it is a fact that Silas earned his modest, though comfortable, income by the gentle art of burglary. A precarious trade and risky withal, yet not so very hazardous if pursued with judgement and moderation. And Silas was eminently a man of judgement. He worked invariably alone. He kept his own counsel. No confederate had he to turn King's Evidence at a pinch; no one he knew would bounce off in a fit of temper to Scotland Yard. Nor was he greedy and thriftless, as most criminals are. His "scoops" were few and far between, carefully planned, secretly executed, and the proceeds judiciously invested in "weekly property."

In early life Silas had been connected with the diamond industry, and he still did a little rather irregular dealing. In the trade he was suspected of transactions with I.D.B.s, and one or two indiscreet dealers had gone so far as to whisper the ominous word "fence." But Silas smiled a benevolent smile and went his way. He knew what he knew, and his clients in Amsterdam were not inquisitive.

Such was Silas Hickler. As he strolled round his garden in the dusk of an October evening, he seemed the very type of modest, middle-class prosperity. He was dressed in the travelling suit that he wore on his little continental trips; his bag was packed and stood in readiness on the sitting-room sofa. A parcel of diamonds (purchased honestly, though without impertinent questions, at Southampton) was in the inside pocket of his waistcoat, and another more valuable parcel was stowed in a cavity in the heel of his right boot. In an hour and a half it would be time for him to set out to catch the boat train at the junction; meanwhile there was nothing to do but to stroll round the fading garden and consider how he should invest the proceeds of the impending deal. His housekeeper had gone over to Welham for the week's shopping, and would probably not be back until eleven o'clock. He was alone in the premises and just a trifle dull.

He was about to turn into the house when his ear caught the sound of footsteps on the unmade road that passed the end of the garden. He paused and listened. There was no other dwelling near, and the road led nowhere, fading away into the waste land beyond the house. Could this be a visitor? It seemed unlikely, for visitors were few at Silas Hickler's house. Meanwhile the footsteps continued to approach, ringing out with increasing loudness on the hard, stony path.

Silas strolled down to the gate, and, leaning on it, looked out with some curiosity. Presently a glow of light showed him the face of a man, apparently lighting his pipe; then a dim figure detached itself from the enveloping gloom, advanced towards him and halted opposite the garden. The stranger removed a cigarette from his mouth and, blowing out a cloud of smoke, asked—

"Can you tell me if this road will take me to Badsham Junction?"

"No," replied Hickler, "but there is a footpath farther on that leads to the station."

"Footpath!" growled the stranger. "I've had enough of footpaths. I came down from town to Catley intending to walk across to the junction. I started along the road, and then some fool directed me to a short cut, with the result that I have been blundering about in the dark for the last half-hour. My sight isn't very good, you know," he added.

"What train do you want to catch?" asked Hickler.

"Seven fifty-eight," was the reply.

"I am going to catch that train myself," said Silas, "but I shan't be starting for another hour. The station is only three-quarters of a mile from here. If you like to come in and take a rest, we can walk down together and then you'll be sure of not missing your way."

"It's very good of you," said the stranger, peering, with spectacled eyes, at the dark house, "but—I think——"

"Might as well wait here as at the station," said Silas in his genial way, holding the gate open, and the stranger, after a momentary hesitation, entered and, flinging away his cigarette, followed him to the door of the cottage.

The sitting-room was in darkness, save for the dull glow of the expiring fire, but, entering before his guest, Silas applied a match to the lamp that hung from the ceiling. As the flame leaped up, flooding the little interior with light, the two men regarding one another with mutual curiosity.

"Brodski, by Jingo!" was Hickler's silent commentary, as he looked at his guest. "Doesn't know me, evidently—wouldn't, of course, after all these years and with his bad eyesight. Take a seat, sir," he added aloud. "Will you join me in a little refreshment to while away the time?"

Brodski murmured an indistinct acceptance, and, as his host turned to open a cupboard, he deposited his hat (a hard, grey felt) on a chair in a corner, placed his bag on the edge of the table, resting his umbrella against it, and sat down in a small arm-chair.

"Have a biscuit?" said Hickler, as he placed a whisky-bottle on the table together with a couple of his best star-pattern tumblers and a siphon.

"Thanks, I think I will," said Brodski. "The railway journey and all this confounded tramping about, you know——"

"Yes," agreed Silas. "Doesn't do to start with an empty stomach. Hope you don't mind oat-cakes; I see they're the only biscuits I have."

Brodski hastened to assure him that oat-cakes were his special and peculiar fancy; and in confirmation, having mixed himself a stiff jorum, he fell to upon the biscuits with evident gusto.

Brodski was a deliberate feeder, and at present appeared to be somewhat sharp set. His measured munching being unfavorable to conversation, most of the talking fell to Silas; and, for once, that genial transgressor found the task embarrassing. The natural thing would have been to discuss his guest's destination and perhaps the object of his journey; but this was precisely what Hickler avoided doing. For he knew both, and instinct told him to keep his knowledge to himself.

Brodski was a diamond merchant of considerable reputation, and in a large way of business. He bought stones principally in the rough, and of these he was a most excellent judge. His fancy was for stones of somewhat unusual size and value, and it was well known to be his custom, when he had accumulated a sufficient stock, to carry them himself to Amsterdam and supervise the cutting of the rough stones. Of this Hickler was aware, and he had no doubt that Brodski was now starting on one of his periodical excursions; that somewhere in the recesses of his rather shabby clothing was concealed a paper packet possibly worth several thousand pounds.

Brodski sat by the table munching monotonously and talking

little. Hickler sat opposite him, talking nervously and rather wildly at times, and watching his guest with a glowing fascination. Precious stones, and especially diamonds, were Hickler's speciality. "Hard stuff"—silver plate—he avoided entirely; gold, excepting in the form of specie, he seldom touched; but stones, of which he could carry off a whole consignment in the heel of his boot and dispose of with absolute safety, formed the staple of his industry. And here was a man sitting opposite him with a parcel in his pocket containing the equivalent of a dozen of his most successful "scoops"; stones worth perhaps—— Here he pulled himself up short and began to talk rapidly, though without much coherence. For, even as he talked, other words, formed subconsciously, seemed to insinuate themselves into the interstices of the sentences, and to carry on a parallel train of thought.

"Gets chilly in the evenings now, doesn't it?" said Hickler.

"It does indeed," Brodski agreed, and then resumed his slow munching, breathing audibly through his nose.

"Five thousand at least," the subconscious train of thought resumed; "probably six or seven, perhaps ten." Silas fidgeted in his chair and endeavored to concentrate his ideas on some topic of interest. He was growing disagreeably conscious of a new and unfamiliar state of mind.

"Do you take any interest in gardening?" he asked. Next to diamonds and weekly "property," his besetting weakness was fuchsias.

Brodski chuckled sourly. "Hatton Garden is the nearest approach." He broke off suddenly, and then added, "I am a Londoner, you know."

The abrupt break in the sentence was not unnoticed by Silas, nor had he any difficulty in interpreting it. A man who carried untold wealth upon his person must needs be wary in his speech.

"Yes," he answered absently, "it's hardly a Londoner's hobby." And then, half consciously, he began a rapid calculation. Put it at five thousand pounds. What would that represent in weekly property? His last set of houses had cost two hundred and fifty pounds apiece, and he had let them at ten shillings and sixpence a week. At that rate, five thousand pounds represented twenty houses at ten and sixpence a week—say ten pounds a week— one pound eight shillings a day—five hundred and twenty pounds a year—for life. It was a competency. Added to what he already had, it was wealth. With that income he could fling the tools of his trade into the river and live out the remainder of his life in comfort and security.

He glanced furtively at his guest across the table, and then looked away quickly as he felt stirring within him an impulse the nature of which he could not mistake. This must be put an end to. Crimes against the person he had always looked upon as sheer insanity. There was, it is true, that little affair of the Weybridge policeman, but that was unforeseen and unavoidable, and it was the constable's doing after all. And there was the old housekeeper at Epsom, too, but, of course, if the old idiot would shriek in that insane fashion—well, it was an accident, very regrettable, to be sure, and no one could be more sorry for the mishap than himself. But deliberate homicide!—robbery from the person! It was the act of a stark lunatic.

Of course, if he had happened to be that sort of person, here was the opportunity of a lifetime. The immense booty, the empty house, the solitary neighborhood, away from the main road and from other habitations; the time, the darkness—but, of course, there was the body to be thought of; that was always the difficulty. What to do with the body——Here he caught the shriek of the up express, rounding the curve in the line that ran past the waste land at the back of the house. The sound started a new train of thought, and, as he followed it out, his eyes fixed themselves on the unconscious and taciturn Brodski, as he sat thoughtfully sipping his whisky. At length, averting his gaze with an effort, he rose suddenly from his chair and turned to look at the clock on the mantelpiece, spreading out his hands before the dying fire. A tumult of strange sensations warned him to leave the house. He shivered slightly, though he was rather hot than chilly, and, turning his head, looked at the door.

"Seems to be a confounded draught," he said, with another slight shiver; "did I shut the door properly, I wonder?" He strode across the room and, opening the door wide, looked out into the dark garden. A desire, sudden and urgent, had come over him to get out into the open air, to be on the road and have done with this madness that was knocking at the door of his brain.

"I wonder if it is worth while to start yet," he said, with a yearning glance at the murky, starless sky.

Brodski roused himself and looked round. "Is your clock right?" he asked.

Silas reluctantly admitted that it was.

"How long will it take us to walk to the station?" inquired Brodski.

"Oh, about twenty-five minutes to half-an-hour," replied Silas, unconsciously exaggerating the distance.

"Well," said Brodski, "we've got more than an hour yet, and it's more comfortable here than hanging about the station. I don't see the use of starting before we need."

"No; of course not," Silas agreed. A wave of strange emotion, half-regretful, half-triumphant, surged through his brain. For some moments he remained standing on the threshold, looking out dreamily into the night. Then he softly closed the door; and, seemingly without the exercise of his volition, the key turned noiselessly in the lock.

He returned to his chair and tried to open a conversation with the taciturn Brodski, but the words came faltering and disjointed. He felt his face growing hot, his brain full and intense, and there was a faint, high-pitched singing in his ears. He was conscious of watching his guest with a new and fearful interest, and, by sheer force of will, turned away his eyes; only to find them a moment later involuntarily returning to fix the unconscious man with yet more horrible intensity. And ever through his mind walked, like a dreadful procession, the thoughts of what that other man—the man of blood and violence—would do in these circumstances. Detail by detail the hideous synthesis fitted together the parts of the imagined crime, and arranged them in due sequence until they formed a succession of events, rational, connected and coherent.

He rose uneasily from his chair, with his eyes still riveted upon his guest. He could not sit any longer opposite that man with his hidden store of precious gems. The impulse that he recognized with fear and wonder was growing more ungovernable from moment to moment. If he stayed it would presently overpower him, and then—— He shrank with horror from the dreadful thought, but his fingers itched to handle the diamonds. For Silas was, after all, a criminal by nature and habit. He was a beast of prey. His livelihood had never been earned; it had been taken by stealth or, if necessary, by force. His instincts were predacious, and the proximity of unguarded valuables suggested to him, as a logical consequence, their abstraction or seizure. His unwillingness to let these diamonds go away beyond his reach was fast becoming overwhelming.

But he would make one more effort to escape. He would keep out of Brodski's actual presence until the moment for starting came.

"If you'll excuse me," he said, "I will go and put on a thicker pair of boots. After all this dry weather we may get a change, and damp feet are very uncomfortable when you are travelling."

"Yes; dangerous too," agreed Brodski.

Silas walked through into the adjoining kitchen, where, by the light of the little lamp that was burning there, he had seen his stout, country boots placed, cleaned and in readiness, and sat down upon a chair to make the change. He did not, of course, intend to wear the country boots, for the diamonds were concealed in those he had on. But he would make the change and then alter his mind; it would all help to pass the time. He took a deep breath. It was a relief, at any rate, to be out of that room. Perhaps, if he stayed away, the temptation would pass. Brodski would *go* on his way—he wished that he was going alone—and the danger would be over—at least—and the opportunity would have gone—the diamonds——

He looked up as he slowly unlaced his boot. From where he sat he could see Brodski sitting by the table with his back towards the kitchen door. He had finished eating now, and was composedly rolling a cigarette. Silas breathed heavily and, slipping off his boot, sat for a while motionless, gazing steadily at the other man's back. Then he unlaced the other boot, still staring abstractedly at his unconscious guest, drew it off, and laid it very quietly on the floor.

Brodski calmly finished rolling his cigarette, licked the paper, put away his pouch, and, having dusted the crumbs of tobacco from his knees, began to search his pockets for a match. Suddenly, yielding to an uncontrollable impulse, Silas stood up and began stealthily to creep along the passage to the sitting-room. Not a sound came from his stockinged feet. Silently as a cat he stole forward, breathing softly with parted lips, until he stood at the threshold of the room. His face flushed duskily, his eyes, wide and staring, glittered in the lamplight, and the racing blood hummed in his ears.

Brodski struck a match—Silas noted that it was a wooden vesta—lighted his cigarette, blew out the match and flung it into the fender. Then he replaced the box in his pocket and commenced to smoke.

Slowly and without a sound Silas crept forward into the room, step by step, with catlike stealthiness, until he stood close behind Brodski's chair—so close that he had to turn his head that his breath might not stir the hair upon the other man's head. So, for half a minute, he stood motionless, like a symbolical statue of Murder, glaring down with horrible, glittering eyes upon the unconscious diamond merchant, while his quick breath passed without a sound through his open mouth and his fingers writhed slowly like the tentacles of a giant hydra. And then, as noiselessly as ever, he backed away to the door, turned quickly and walked back into the kitchen.

He drew a deep breath. It had been a near thing. Brodski's life had hung upon a thread. For it had been so easy. Indeed, if he had happened, as he stood behind the man's chair, to have a weapon—a hammer, for instance, or even a stone——

He glanced round the kitchen and his eye lighted on a bar that had been left by the workmen who had put up the new greenhouse. It was an odd piece cut off from a square, wrought-iron stanchion, and was about a foot long and perhaps three-quarters of an inch thick. Now, if he had had that in his hand a minute ago——

He picked the bar up, balanced it in his hand and swung it round his head. A formidable weapon this: silent, too. And it fitted the plan that had passed through his brain. Bah! He had better put the thing down.

But he did not. He stepped over to the door and looked again at Brodski, sitting, as before, meditatively smoking, with his back towards the kitchen.

Suddenly a change came over Silas. His face flushed, the veins of his neck stood out and a sullen scowl settled on his face. He drew out his watch, glanced at it earnestly and replaced it. Then he strode swiftly but silently along the passage into the sitting-room.

A pace away from his victim's chair he halted and took deliberate aim. The bar swung aloft, but not without some faint rustle of movement, for Brodski looked round quickly even as the iron whistled through the air. The movement disturbed the murderer's aim, and the bar glanced off his victim's head, making only a trifling wound. Brodski sprang up with a tremulous, bleating cry, and clutched his assailant's arms with the tenacity of mortal terror.

Then began a terrible struggle, as the two men, locked in a deadly embrace, swayed to and fro and trampled backwards and forwards. The chair was overturned, an empty glass swept from the table and, with Brodski's spectacles, crushed beneath stamping feet. And thrice that dreadful, pitiful, bleating cry rang out into the night, filling Silas, despite his murderous frenzy, with terror lest some chance wayfarer should hear it. Gathering his great strength for a final effort, he forced his victim backwards on to the table and, snatching up a corner of the table-cloth, thrust it into his face and crammed it into his mouth as it opened to utter another shriek. And thus they remained for a full two minutes, almost motionless, like some dreadful group of tragic allegory. Then, when the last faint twitchings had died away, Silas relaxed his grasp and let the limp body slip softly on to the floor.

It was over. For good or for evil, the thing was done. Silas stood up, breathing heavily, and, as he wiped the sweat from his face, he looked at the clock. The hands stood at one minute to seven. The whole thing had taken a little over three minutes. He had nearly an hour in which to finish his task. The goods train that entered into his scheme came by at twenty minutes past, and it was only three hundred yards to the line. Still, he must not waste time. He was now quite composed, and only disturbed by the thought that Brodski's cries might have been heard. If no one had heard them it was all plain sailing.

He stooped, and, gently disengaging the tablecloth from the dead man's teeth, began a careful search of his pockets. He was not long in finding what he sought, and, as he pinched the paper packet and felt the little hard bodies grating on one another inside, his faint regrets for what had happened were swallowed up in self-congratulations.

He now set about his task with business-like briskness and an attentive eye on the clock. A few large drops of blood had fallen on the table-cloth, and there was a small bloody smear on the carpet by the dead man's head. Silas fetched from the kitchen some water, a nail-brush and a dry cloth, and, having washed out the stains from the table-cover—not forgetting the deal table-top underneath—and cleaned away the smear from the carpet and rubbed the damp places dry, he slipped a sheet of paper under the head of the corpse to prevent further contamination. Then he set the table-cloth straight, stood the chair upright, laid the broken spectacles on the table and picked up the cigarette, which had been trodden flat in the struggle, and flung it under the grate. Then there was the broken glass, which he swept up into a dustpan. Part of it was the remains of the shattered tumbler, and the rest the fragments of the broken spectacles. He turned it out on to a sheet of paper and looked it over carefully, picking out the larger recognizable pieces of the spectacle-glasses and putting them aside on a separate slip of paper, together with a sprinkling of the minute fragments. The remainder he shot back into the dust-pan and, having hurriedly put on his boots, carried it out to the rubbish-heap at the back of the house.

It was now time to start. Hastily cutting off a length of string from his string-box—for Silas was an orderly man and despised the oddments of string with which many people make shift—he tied it to the dead man's bag and umbrella and slung them from his shoulder. Then he folded up the paper of broken glass, and, slipping it and the spectacles into his pocket, picked up the body and threw it over his shoulder. Brodski was a small, spare man, weighing not more than nine stone; not a very formidable burden for a big, athletic man like Silas.

The night was intensely dark, and, when Silas looked out of the back gate over the waste land that stretched from his house to the railway, he could hardly see twenty yards ahead. After listening cautiously and hearing no sound, he went out, shut the gate softly behind him and set forth at a good pace, though carefully, over the broken ground. His progress was not as silent as he could have wished, for, though the scanty turf that covered the gravelly land was thick enough to deaden his footfalls, the swinging bag and umbrella made an irritating noise; indeed, his movements were more hampered by them than by the weightier burden.

The distance to the line was about three hundred yards. Ordinarily he would have walked it in from three to four minutes, but now, going cautiously with his burden and stopping now and again to listen, it took him just six minutes to reach the three-bar fence that separated the waste land from the railway. Arrived here he halted for a moment and once more listened attentively, peering into the darkness on all sides. Not a living creature was to be seen or heard in this desolate spot, but far away, the shriek of an engine's whistle warned him to listen.

Lifting the corpse easily over the fence, he carried it a few yards farther to a point where the line curved sharply. Here he laid it face downwards, with the neck over the near rail. Drawing out his pocket-knife, he cut through the knot that fastened the umbrella to the string and also secured the bag; and when he had flung the bag and umbrella on the track beside the body, he carefully pocketed the string, excepting the little loop that had fallen to the ground when the knot was cut.

The quick snort and clanking rumble of an approaching goods train began now to be clearly audible. Rapidly, Silas drew from his pockets the battered spectacles and the packet of broken glass. The former he threw down by the dead man's head, and then, emptying the packet into his hand, sprinkled the fragments of glass around the spectacles.

He was none too soon. Already the quick, labored puffing of the engine sounded close at hand. His impulse was to stay and watch; to witness the final catastrophe that should convert the murder into an accident or suicide. But it was hardly safe: it would be better that he should not be near lest he should not be able to get away without being seen. Hastily he climbed back over the fence and strode away across the rough fields, while the train came snorting and clattering towards the curve.

He had nearly reached his back gate when a sound from the line brought him to a sudden halt; it was a prolonged whistle accompanied by the groan of brakes and the loud clank of colliding trucks. The snorting of the engine had ceased and was replaced by the penetrating hiss of escaping steam.

The train had stopped!

For one brief moment Silas stood with bated breath and mouth agape like one petrified; then he strode forward quickly to the gate, and, letting himself in, silently slid the bolt. He was undeniably alarmed. What could have happened on the line? It was practically certain that the body had been seen; but what was happening now? and would they come to the house? He entered the kitchen, and having paused again to listen—for somebody might come and knock at the door at any moment— he walked through the sitting-room and looked round. All seemed in order there. There was the bar, though, lying where he had dropped it in the scuffle. He picked it up and held it under the lamp. There was no blood on it; only one or two hairs. Somewhat absently he wiped it with the table-cover, and then, running out through the kitchen into the back garden, dropped it over the wall into a bed of nettles. Not that there was anything incriminating in the bar, but, since he had used it as a weapon, it had somehow acquired a sinister aspect to his eye.

He now felt that it would be well to start for the station at once. It was not time yet, for it was barely twenty-five minutes past seven; but he did not wish to be found in the house if any one should come. His soft hat was on the sofa with his bag, to which his umbrella was strapped. He put on the hat, caught up the bag and stepped over to the door; then he came back to turn down the lamp. And it was at this moment, when he stood with his hand raised to the burner, that his eye, travelling by chance into the dim corner of the room, lighted on Brodski's grey felt hat, reposing on the chair where the dead man had placed it when he entered the house.

Silas stood for a few moments as if petrified, with the chilly sweat of mortal fear standing in beads upon his forehead. Another instant and he would have turned the lamp down and gone on his way; and then——He strode over to the chair, snatched up the hat and looked inside it. Yes, there was the name, "Oscar Brodski," written plainly on the lining. If he had gone away, leaving it to be discovered, he would have been lost; indeed, even now, if a search-party should come to the house, it was enough to send him to the gallows.

His limbs shook with horror at the thought, but in spite of his panic he did not lose his self-possession. Darting through into the kitchen, he grabbed up a handful of dry brush-wood that was kept for lighting fires and carried it to the sitting-room grate where he thrust it on the extinct, but still hot, embers, and crumpling up the paper that he had placed under Brodski's head—on which paper he now noticed, for the first time, a minute bloody smear—he poked it in under the wood, and, striking a wax match, set light to it. As the wood flared up, he hacked at the hat with his pocket knife and threw the ragged strips into the blaze.

And all the while his heart was thumping and his hands a-tremble with the dread of discovery. The fragments of felt were far from inflammable, tending rather to fuse into cindery masses that smoked and smouldered, than to burn away into actual ash. Moreover, to his dismay, they emitted a powerful resinous stench mixed with the odor of burning hair, so that he had to open the kitchen window (since he dared not unlock the front door) to disperse the reek. And still, as he fed the fire with small cut fragments, he strained his ears to catch, above the crackling of the wood, the sound of the dreaded footsteps, the knock on the door that should be as the summons of Fate.

The time, too, was speeding on. Twenty-one minutes to eight! In a few minutes more he must set out or he would miss the train. He dropped the dismembered hat-brim on the blazing wood and ran upstairs to open a window, since he must close that in the kitchen before he left. When he came back, the brim had already curled up into a black, clinkery mass that bubbled and hissed as the fat, pungent smoke rose from it sluggishly to the chimney.

Nineteen minutes to eight! It was time to start. He took up the poker and carefully beat the cinders into small particles, stirring them into the glowing embers of the wood and coal. There was nothing unusual in the appearance of the grate. It was his constant custom to burn letters and other discarded articles in the sitting-room fire: his housekeeper would notice nothing out of the common. Indeed, the cinders would probably be reduced to ashes before she returned. He had been careful to notice that there were no metallic fittings of any kind in the hat, which might have escaped burning.

Once more he picked up his bag, took a last look round, turned down the lamp and, unlocking the door, held it open for a few moments. Then he went out, locked the door, pocketed the key (of which his housekeeper had a duplicate) and set off at a brisk pace for the station.

He arrived in good time after all, and, having taken his ticket, strolled through on to the platform. The train was not yet signalled, but there seemed to be an unusual stir in the place. The passengers were collected in a group at one end of the platform, and were all looking in one direction down the line; and, even as he walked towards them, with a certain tremulous, nauseating curiosity, two men emerged from the darkness and ascended the slope to the platform, carrying a stretcher covered with a tarpaulin. The passengers parted to let the bearers pass, turning fascinated eyes upon the shape that showed faintly through the rough pall; and, when the stretcher had been borne into the lamp-room, they fixed their attention upon a porter who followed carrying a hand-bag and an umbrella.

Suddenly one of the passengers started forward with an exclamation.

"Is that his umbrella?" he demanded.

"Yes, sir," answered the porter, stopping and holding it out for the speaker's inspection.

"My God!" ejaculated the passenger; then, turning sharply to a tall man who stood close by, he said excitedly: "That's Brodski's umbrella. I could swear to it. You remember Brodski?" The tall man nodded, and the passenger, turning once more to the porter, said: "I identify that umbrella. It belongs to a gentleman named Brodski. If you look in his hat you will see his name written in it. He always writes his name in his hat."

"We haven't found his hat yet," said the porter; "but here is the station-master coming up the line." He awaited the arrival of his superior and then announced: "This gentleman, sir, has identified the umbrella."

"Oh," said the station-master, "you recognize the umbrella, sir, do you? Then perhaps you would step into the lamp-room and see if you can identify the body."

The passenger recoiled with a look of alarm.

"Is it—is he—very much injured?" he asked tremulously.

"Well, yes," was the reply. "You see, the engine and six of the trucks went over him before they could stop the train. Took his head clean off, in fact."

"Shocking! shocking!" gasped the passenger. "I think, if you don't mind—I'd—I'd rather not. You don't think it's necessary, doctor, do you?"

"Yes, I do," replied the tall man. "Early identification may be of the first importance."

"Then I suppose I must," said the passenger.

Very reluctantly he allowed himself to be conducted by the station-master to the lamp-room, as the clang of the bell announced the approaching train. Silas Hickler followed and took his stand with the expectant crowd outside the closed door. In a few moments the passenger burst out, pale and awe-stricken, and rushed up to his tall friend. "It is!" he exclaimed breathlessly, "it's Brodski! Poor old Brodski! Horrible! horrible! He was to have met me here and come on with me to Amsterdam."

"Had he any—merchandize about him?" the tall man asked; and Silas strained his ears to catch the reply.

"He had some stones, no doubt, but I don't know what. His clerk will know, of course. By the way, doctor, could you watch the case for me? Just to be sure it was really an accident or—you know what. We were old friends, you know, fellow townsmen, too; we were both born in Warsaw. I'd like you to give an eye to the case."

"Very well," said the other. "I will satisfy myself that—there is nothing more than appears, and let you have a report. Will that do?"

"Thank you. It's excessively good of you, doctor. Ah! here comes the train. I hope it won't inconvenience you to stay and see to this matter."

"Not in the least," replied the doctor. "We are not due at Warmington until to-morrow afternoon, and I expect we can find out all that is necessary to know and still keep our appointment."

Silas looked long and curiously at the tall, imposing man who was, as it were, taking his seat at the chess-board, to play against him for his life. A formidable antagonist he looked, with his keen, thoughtful face, so resolute and calm. As Silas stepped into his carriage he looked back at his opponent, and thinking with deep discomfort of Brodski's hat, he hoped that he had made no other oversight.

Part II

THE MECHANISM OF DETECTION
(Related by Christopher Jervis, M.D.)

The singular circumstances that attended the death of Mr. Oscar Brodski, the well-known diamond merchant of Hatton Garden, illustrated very forcibly the importance of one or two points in medico-legal practice which Thorndyke was accustomed to insist were not sufficiently appreciated. What those points were, I shall leave my friend and teacher to state at the proper place; and meanwhile, as the case is in the highest degree instructive, I shall record the incidents in the order of their occurrence.

The dusk of an October evening was closing in as Thorndyke and I, the sole occupants of a smoking compartment, found ourselves approaching the little station of Ludham; and, as the train slowed down, we peered out at the knot of country people who were waiting on the platform. Suddenly Thorndyke exclaimed in a tone of surprise: "Why, that is surely Boscovitch!" and almost at the same moment a brisk, excitable little man darted at the door of our compartment and literally tumbled in.

"I hope I don't intrude on this learned conclave," he said, shaking hands genially and banging his Gladstone with impulsive violence into the rack; "but I saw your faces at the window, and naturally jumped at the chance of such pleasant companionship."

"You are very flattering," said Thorndyke; "so flattering that you leave us nothing to say. But what in the name of fortune are you doing at—what's the name of the place—Ludham?"

"My brother has a little place a mile or so from here, and I have been spending a couple of days with him," Mr. Boscovitch explained. "I shall change at Badsham Junction and catch the boat train for Amsterdam. But whither are you two bound? I see you have your mysterious little green box up on the hat-rack, so I infer that you are on some romantic quest, eh? Going to unravel some dark and intricate crime?"

"No," replied Thorndyke. "We are bound for Warmington on

a quite prosaic errand. I am instructed to watch the proceedings at an inquest there to-morrow on behalf of the Griffin Life Insurance Office, and we are travelling down to-night as it is rather a cross-country journey."

"But why the box of magic?" asked Boscovitch, glancing up at the hat-rack.

"I never go away from home without it," answered Thorndyke. "One never knows what may turn up; the trouble of carrying it is small when set off against the comfort of having one's appliances at hand in case of emergency."

Boscovitch continued to stare up at the little square case covered with Willesden canvas. Presently he remarked: "I often used to wonder what you had in it when you were down at Chelmsford in connection with that bank murder—what an amazing case that was, by the way, and didn't your methods of research astonish the police!" As he still looked up wistfully at the case, Thorndyke good-naturedly lifted it down and unlocked it. As a matter of fact he was rather proud of his "portable laboratory," and certainly it was a triumph of condensation, for, small as it was—only a foot square by four inches deep—it contained a fairly complete outfit for a preliminary investigation.

"Wonderful!" exclaimed Boscovitch, when the case lay open before him, displaying its rows of little re-agent bottles, tiny test-tubes, diminutive spirit-lamp, dwarf microscope and assorted instruments on the same Lilliputian scale; "it's like a doll's house—everything looks as if it was seen through the wrong end of a telescope. But are these tiny things really efficient? That microscope now——"

"Perfectly efficient at low and moderate magnifications," said Thorndyke. "It looks like a toy, but it isn't one; the lenses are the best that can be had. Of course, a full-sized instrument would be infinitely more convenient—but I shouldn't have it with me, and should have to make shift with a pocket-lens. And so with the rest of the under-sized appliances; they are the alternative to no appliances."

Boscovitch pored over the case and its contents, fingering the instruments delicately and asking questions innumerable about their uses; indeed, his curiosity was but half appeased when, half an hour later, the train began to slow down.

"By Jove!" he exclaimed, starting up and seizing his bag, "here we are at the junction already. You change here too, don't you?"

"Yes," replied Thorndyke. "We take the branch train on to Warmington."

As we stepped out on to the platform, we became aware that something unusual was happening or had happened. All the passengers and most of the porters and supernumeraries were gathered at one end of the station, and all were looking intently into the darkness down the line.

"Anything wrong?" asked Mr. Boscovitch, addressing the station-inspector.

"Yes, sir," the official replied; "a man has been run over by the goods train about a mile down the line. The station-master has gone down with a stretcher to bring him in, and I expect that is his lantern that you see coming this way."

As we stood watching the dancing light grow momentarily brighter, flashing fitful reflections from the burnished rails, a man came out of the booking-office and joined the group of onlookers. He attracted my attention, as I afterwards remembered, for two reasons: in the first place his round, jolly face was excessively pale and bore a strained and wild expression, and, in the second, though he stared into the darkness with eager curiosity he asked no questions.

The swinging lantern continued to approach, and then suddenly two men came into sight bearing a stretcher covered with a tarpaulin, through which the shape of a human figure was dimly discernible. They ascended the slope to the platform, and proceeded with their burden to the lamp-room, when the inquisitive gaze of the passengers was transferred to a porter who followed carrying a hand-bag and umbrella and to the station-master who brought up the rear with his lantern.

As the porter passed, Mr. Boscovitch started forward with sudden excitement.

"Is that his umbrella?" he asked.

"Yes, sir," answered the porter, stopping and holding it out for the speaker's inspection.

"My God!" ejaculated Boscovitch; then, turning sharply to Thorndyke, he exclaimed: "That's Brodski's umbrella. I could swear to it. You remember Brodski?"

Thorndyke nodded, and Boscovitch, turning once more to the porter, said: "I identify that umbrella. It belongs to a gentleman named Brodski. If you look in his hat, you will see his name written in it. He always writes his name in his hat."

"We haven't found his hat yet," said the porter; "but here is the station-master." He turned to his superior and announced: "This gentleman, sir, has identified the umbrella."

"Oh," said the station-master, "you recognize the umbrella, sir, do you? Then perhaps you would step into the lamp-room and see if you can identify the body."

Mr. Boscovitch recoiled with a look of alarm. "Is it—is he— very much injured?" he asked nervously.

"Well, yes," was the reply. "You see, the engine and six of the trucks went over him before they could stop the train. Took his head clean off, in fact."

"Shocking! shocking!" gasped Boscovitch. "I think—if you don't mind—I'd—I'd rather not. You don't think it necessary, doctor, do you?"

"Yes, I do," replied Thorndyke. "Early identification may be of the first importance."

"Then I suppose I must," said Boscovitch; and, with extreme reluctance, he followed the station-master to the lamp-room, as the loud ringing of the bell announced the approach of the boat train. His inspection must have been of the briefest, for, in a few moments, he burst out, pale and awe-stricken, and rushed up to Thorndyke.

"It is!" he exclaimed breathlessly, "it's Brodski! Poor old Brodski! Horrible! horrible! He was to have met me here and come on with me to Amsterdam."

"Had he any—merchandise about him?" Thorndyke asked; and, as he spoke, the stranger whom I had previously noticed edged up closer as if to catch the reply.

"He had some stones, no doubt," answered Boscovitch, "but I don't know what they were. His clerk will know, of course. By the way, doctor, could you watch the case for me? Just to be sure it was really an accident or—you know what. We were old friends, you know, fellow townsmen, too; we were both born in Warsaw. I'd like you to give an eye to the case."

"Very well," said Thorndyke. "I will satisfy myself that there is nothing more than appears, and let you have a report. Will that do?"

"Thank you," said Boscovitch. "It's excessively good of you, doctor. Ah, here comes the train. I hope it won't inconvenience you to stay and see to the matter."

"Not in the least," replied Thorndyke. "We are not due at Warmington until to-morrow afternoon, and I expect we can find out all that is necessary to know and still keep our appointment."

As Thorndyke spoke, the stranger, who had kept close to us with the evident purpose of hearing what was said, bestowed on him a very curious and attentive look; and it was only when the train had actually come to rest by the platform that he hurried away to find a compartment.

No sooner had the train left the station than Thorndyke sought out the station-master and informed him of the instructions that he had received from Boscovitch. "Of course," he added, in conclusion, "we must not move in the matter until the police arrive. I suppose they have been informed?"

"Yes," replied the station-master; "I sent a message at once to the Chief Constable, and I expect him or an inspector at any moment. In fact, I think I will slip out to the approach and see if he is coming." He evidently wished to have a word in private with the police officer before committing himself to any statement.

As the official departed, Thorndyke and I began to pace the now empty platform, and my friend, as was his wont, when entering on a new inquiry, meditatively reviewed the features of the problem.

"In a case of this kind," he remarked, "we have to decide on one of three possible explanations: accident, suicide, or homicide; and our decision will be determined by inferences from three sets of facts: first, the general facts of the case; second, the special data obtained by examination of the body; and, third, the special data obtained by examining the spot on which the body was found. Now the only general facts at present in our possession are that the deceased was a diamond merchant making a journey for a specific purpose and probably having on his person property of small bulk and great value. These facts are somewhat against the hypothesis of suicide and somewhat favorable to that of homicide. Facts relevant to the question of accident would be the existence or otherwise of a level crossing, a road or path leading to the line, an enclosing fence with or without a gate, and any other facts rendering probable or otherwise the accidental presence of the deceased at the spot where the body was found. As we do not possess these facts, it is desirable that we extend our knowledge."

"Why not put a few discreet questions to the porter who brought in the bag and umbrella?" I suggested. "He is at this moment in earnest conversation with the ticket collector and would, no doubt, be glad of a new listener."

"An excellent suggestion, Jervis," answered Thorndyke. "Let us see what he has to tell us." We approached the porter and found him, as I had anticipated, bursting to unburden himself of the tragic story.

"The way the thing happened, sir, was this," he said, in answer to Thorndyke's question: "There's a sharpish bend in the road just at that place, and the goods train was just rounding the curve when the driver suddenly caught sight of something lying across the rails. As the engine turned, the head-lights shone on it and then he saw it was a man. He shut off steam at once, blew his whistle, and put the brakes down hard, but, as you know, sir, a goods train takes some stopping; before they could bring her up, the engine and half a dozen trucks had gone over the poor beggar."

"Could the driver see how the man was lying?" Thorndyke asked.

"Yes, he could see him quite plain, because the head-lights were full on him. He was lying on his face with his neck over the near rail on the down side. His head was in the four-foot and his body by the side of the truck. It looked as if he had laid himself out a-purpose."

"Is there a level crossing thereabouts?" asked Thorndyke.

"No, sir. No crossing, no road, no path, no nothing," said the porter, ruthlessly sacrificing grammar to emphasis. "He must have come across the fields and climbed over the fence to get on to the permanent way. Deliberate suicide is what it looks like."

"How did you learn all this?" Thorndyke inquired.

"Why, the driver, you see, sir, when him and his mate had lifted the body off the track, went on to the next signal-box and sent in his report by telegram. The station-master told me all about it as we walked down the line."

Thorndyke thanked the man for his information, and, as we strolled back towards the lamp-room, discussed the bearing of these new facts.

"Our friend is unquestionably right in one respect," he said; "this was not an accident. The man might, if he were near-sighted, deaf or stupid, have climbed over the fence and got knocked down by the train. But his position, lying across the rails, can only be explained by one of two hypotheses: either it was, as the porter says, deliberate suicide, or else the man was already dead or insensible. We must leave it at that until we have seen the body, that is, if the police will allow us to see it. But here comes the station-master and an officer with him. Let us hear what they have to say."

The two officials had evidently made up their minds to decline any outside assistance. The divisional surgeon would make the necessary examination, and information could be obtained through the usual channels. The production of Thorndyke's card, however, somewhat altered the situation. The police inspector hummed and hawed irresolutely, with the card in his hand, but finally agreed to allow us to view the body, and we entered the lamp-room together, the station-master leading the way to turn up the gas.

The stretcher stood on the floor by one wall, its grim burden still hidden by the tarpaulin, and the hand-bag and umbrella lay on a large box, together with the battered frame of a pair of spectacles from which the glasses had fallen out.

"Were these spectacles found by the body?" Thorndyke inquired.

"Yes," replied the station-master. "They were close to the head and the glass was scattered about on the ballast."

Thorndyke made a note in his pocket-book, and then, as the inspector removed the tarpaulin, he glanced down on the corpse, lying limply on the stretcher and looking grotesquely horrible with its displaced head and distorted limbs. For fully a minute he remained silently stooping over the uncanny object, on which the inspector was now throwing the light of a large lantern; then he stood up and said quietly to me: "I think we can eliminate two out of three hypotheses."

The inspector looked at him quickly, and was about to ask a

question, when his attention was diverted by the travelling-case which Thorndyke had laid on a shelf and now opened to abstract a couple of pairs of dissecting forceps.

"We've no authority to make a *post mortem*, you know," said the inspector.

"No, of course not," said Thorndyke. "I am merely going to look into the mouth." With one pair of forceps he turned back the lip and, having scrutinized its inner surface, closely examined the teeth.

"May I trouble you for your lens, Jervis?" he said; and, as I handed him my doubtlet ready opened, the inspector brought the lantern close to the dead face and leaned forward eagerly. In his usual systematic fashion, Thorndyke slowly passed the lens along the whole range of sharp, uneven teeth, and then, bringing it back to the centre, examined with more minuteness the upper incisors. At length, very delicately, he picked out with his forceps some minute object from between two of the upper front teeth and held it in the focus of the lens. Anticipating his next move, I took a labelled microscope-slide from the case and handed it to him together with a dissecting needle, and, as he transferred the object to the slide and spread it out with the needle, I set up the little microscope on the shelf.

"A drop of Farrant and a cover-glass, please, Jervis," said Thorndyke.

I handed him the bottle, and, when he had let a drop of the mounting fluid fall gently on the object and put on the cover-slip, he placed the slide on the stage of the microscope and examined it attentively.

Happening to glance at the inspector, I observed on his countenance a faint grin, which he politely strove to suppress when he caught my eye.

"I was thinking, sir," he said apologetically, "that it's a bit off the track to be finding out what he had for dinner. He didn't die of unwholesome feeding."

Thorndyke looked up with a smile. "It doesn't do, inspector, to assume that anything is off the track in an inquiry of this kind. Every fact must have some significance, you know."

"I don't see any significance in the diet of a man who has had his head cut off," the inspector rejoined defiantly.

"Don't you?" said Thorndyke. "Is there no interest attaching to the last meal of a man who has met a violent death? These crumbs, for instance, that are scattered over the dead man's waistcoat. Can we learn nothing from them?"

"I don't see what you can learn," was the dogged rejoinder.

Thorndyke picked off the crumbs, one by one, with his forceps, and, having deposited them on a slide, inspected them, first with the lens and then through the microscope.

"I learn," said he, "that shortly before his death, the deceased partook of some kind of whole-meal biscuits, apparently composed partly of oatmeal."

"I call that nothing," said the inspector. "The question that we have got to settle is not what refreshments had the deceased been taking, but what was the cause of his death: did he commit suicide? was he killed by accident? or was there any foul play?"

"I beg your pardon," said Thorndyke, "the questions that remain to be settled are, who killed the deceased and with what motive? The others are already answered as far as I am concerned."

The inspector stared in sheer amazement not unmixed with incredulity.

"You haven't been long coming to a conclusion, sir," he said.

"No, it was a pretty obvious case of murder," said Thorndyke. "As to the motive, the deceased was a diamond merchant and is believed to have had a quantity of stones about his person. I should suggest that you search the body."

The inspector gave vent to an exclamation of disgust. "I see," he said. "It was just a guess on your part. The dead man was a diamond merchant and had valuable property about him; therefore he was murdered." He drew himself up, and, regarding Thorndyke with stern reproach, added: "But you must understand, sir, that this is a judicial inquiry, not a prize competition in a penny paper. And, as to searching the body, why, that is what I principally came for." He ostentatiously turned his back on us and proceeded systematically to turn out the dead man's pockets, laying the articles, as he removed them, on the box by the side of the hand-bag and umbrella.

While he was thus occupied, Thorndyke looked over the body generally, paying special attention to the soles of the boots,

which, to the inspector's undissembled amusement, he very
thoroughly examined with the lens.

"I should have thought, sir, that his feet were large enough to
be seen with the naked eye," was his comment; "but perhaps,"
he added, with a sly glance at the station-master, "you're a little
near-sighted."

Thorndyke chuckled good-humoredly, and, while the officer
continued his search, he looked over the articles that had
already been laid on the box. The purse and pocket-book he naturally left for the inspector to open, but the reading-glasses,
pocket-knife and card-case, and other small pocket articles were
subjected to a searching scrutiny. The inspector watched him
out of the corner of his eye with furtive amusement; saw him
hold up the glasses to the light to estimate their refractive
power, peer into the tobacco pouch, open the cigarette book
and examine the watermark of the paper, and even inspect the
contents of the silver match-box.

"What might you have expected to find in his tobacco
pouch?" the officer asked, laying down a bunch of keys from the
dead man's pocket.

"Tobacco," Thorndyke replied stolidly; "but I did not expect
to find fine-cut Latakia. I don't remember ever having seen pure
Latakia smoked in cigarettes."

"You do take an interest in things, sir," said the inspector, with
a side glance at the stolid station-master.

"I do," Thorndyke agreed; "and I note that there are no diamonds among this collection."

"No, and we don't know that he had any about him; but
there's a gold watch and chain, a diamond scarf-pin, and a purse
containing"—he opened it and tipped out its contents into his
hand—"twelve pounds in gold. That doesn't look much like robbery, does it? What do you say to the murder theory now?"

"My opinion is unchanged," said Thorndyke, "and I should like
to examine the spot where the body was found. Has the engine
been inspected?" he added, addressing the station-master.

"I telegraphed to Bradfield to have it examined," the official
answered. "The report has probably come in by now. I'd better
see before we start down the line."

We emerged from the lamp-room and, at the door, found the

station-inspector waiting with a telegram. He handed it to the
station-master who read it aloud.

"The engine has been carefully examined by me. I find small
smear of blood on near leading wheel and smaller one on next
wheel following. No other marks." He glanced questioningly at
Thorndyke, who nodded and remarked: "It will be interesting to
see if the line tells the same tale."

The station-master looked puzzled and was apparently about
to ask for an explanation; but the inspector, who had carefully
pocketed the dead man's property, was impatient to start and,
accordingly, when Thorndyke had repacked his case and had, at
his own request, been furnished with a lantern, we set off down
the permanent way, Thorndyke carrying the light and I the
indispensable green case.

"I am a little in the dark about this affair," I said, when we had
allowed the two officials to draw ahead out of earshot; "you came
to a conclusion remarkably quickly. What was it that so immediately determined the opinion of murder as against suicide?"

"It was a small matter but very conclusive," replied
Thorndyke. "You noticed a small scalp-wound above the left
temple? It was a glancing wound, and might easily have been
made by the engine. But—the wound had bled; and it had bled
for an appreciable time. There were two streams of blood from
it, and in both the blood was firmly clotted and partially dried.
But the man had been decapitated; and this wound if inflicted
by the engine, must have been made after the decapitation,
since it was on the side most distant from the engine as it
approached. Now a decapitated head does not bleed. Therefore
this wound was inflicted before the decapitation.

"But not only had the wound bled: the blood had trickled
down in two streams at right angles to one another. First, in the
order of time as shown by the appearance of the stream, it had
trickled down the side of the face and dropped on the collar.
The second stream ran from the wound to the back of the head.
Now, you know, Jervis, there are no exceptions to the law of
gravity. If the blood ran down the face towards the chin, the face
must have been upright at the time; and if the blood trickled
from the front to the back of the head, the head must have been
horizontal and face upwards. But the man when he was seen by

the engine-driver, was lying *face downwards*. The only possible inference is that when the wound was inflicted, the man was in the upright position—standing or sitting; and that subsequently, and while he was still alive, he lay on his back for a sufficiently long time for the blood to have trickled to the back of his head."

"I see. I was a duffer not to have reasoned this out for myself," I remarked contritely.

"Quick observation and rapid inference come by practice," replied Thorndyke. "But, tell me, what did you notice about the face?"

"I thought there was a strong suggestion of asphyxia."

"Undoubtedly," said Thorndyke. "It was the face of a suffocated man. You must have noticed, too, that the tongue was very distinctly swollen and that on the inside of the upper lip were deep indentations made by the teeth, as well as one or two slight wounds, obviously caused by heavy pressure on the mouth. And now observe how completely these facts and inferences agree with those from the scalp wound. If we knew that the deceased had received a blow on the head, had struggled with his assailant and been finally borne down and suffocated, we should look for precisely those signs which we have found."

"By the way, what was it that you found wedged between the teeth? I did not get a chance to look through the microscope."

"Ah!" said Thorndyke, "there we not only get confirmation, but we carry our inferences a stage further. The object was a little tuft of some textile fabric. Under the microscope I found it to consist of several different fibres, differently dyed. The bulk of it consisted of wool fibres dyed crimson, but there were also cotton fibres dyed blue and a few which looked like jute, dyed yellow. It was obviously a parti-colored fabric and might have been part of a woman's dress, though the presence of the jute is much more suggestive of a curtain or rug of inferior quality."

"And its importance?"

"Is that, if it is not part of an article of clothing, then it must have come from an article of furniture, and furniture suggests a habitation."

"That doesn't seem very conclusive," I objected.

"It is not; but it is valuable corroboration."

"Of what?"

"Of the suggestion offered by the soles of the dead man's boots. I examined them most minutely and could find no trace of sand, gravel or earth, in spite of the fact that he must have crossed fields and rough land to reach the place where he was found. What I did find was fine tobacco ash, a charred mark as if a cigar or cigarette had been trodden on, several crumbs of biscuit, and, on a projecting brad, some colored fibres, apparently from a carpet. The manifest suggestion is that the man was killed in a house with a carpeted floor, and carried from thence to the railway."

I was silent for some moments. Well as I knew Thorndyke, I was completely taken by surprise; a sensation, indeed, that I experienced anew every time that I accompanied him on one of his investigations. His marvellous power of co-ordinating apparently insignificant facts, of arranging them into an ordered sequence and making them tell a coherent story, was a phenomenon that I never got used to; every exhibition of it astonished me afresh.

"If your inferences are correct," I said, "the problem is practically solved. There must be abundant traces inside the house. The only question is, which house is it?"

"Quite so," replied Thorndyke; "that is the question, and a very difficult question it is. A glance at that interior would doubtless clear up the whole mystery. But how are we to get that glance? We cannot enter houses speculatively to see if they present traces of murder. At present, our clue breaks off abruptly. The other end of it is in some unknown house, and, if we cannot join up the two ends, our problem remains unsolved. For the question is, you remember, Who killed Oscar Brodski?"

"Then what do you propose to do?" I asked.

"The next stage of the inquiry is to connect some particular house with this crime. To that end, I can only gather up all available facts and consider each in all its possible bearings. If I cannot establish any such connection, then the inquiry will have failed and we shall have to make a fresh start—say, at Amsterdam, if it turns out that Brodski really had diamonds on his person, as I have no doubt he had."

Here our conversation was interrupted by our arrival at the spot where the body had been found. The station-master had halted, and he and the inspector were now examining the near rail by the light of their lanterns.

"There's remarkably little blood about," said the former. "I've seen a good many accidents of this kind and there has always been a lot of blood, both on the engine and on the road. It's very curious."

Thorndyke glanced at the rail with but slight attention: that question had ceased to interest him. But the light of his lantern flashed on to the ground at the side of the track—a loose, gravelly soil mixed with fragments of chalk—and from thence to the soles of the inspector's boots, which were displayed as he knelt by the rail.

"You observe, Jervis?" he said in a low voice, and I nodded. The inspector's boot-soles were covered with adherent particles of gravel and conspicuously marked by the chalk on which he had trodden.

"You haven't found the hat, I suppose?" Thorndyke asked, stooping to pick up a short piece of string that lay on the ground at the side of the track.

"No," replied the inspector, "but it can't be far off. You seem to have found another clue, sir," he added, with a grin, glancing at the piece of string.

"Who knows," said Thorndyke. "A short end of white twine with a green strand in it. It may tell us something later. At any rate we'll keep it," and, taking from his pocket a small tin box containing, among other things, a number of seed envelopes, he slipped the string into one of the latter and scribbled a note in pencil on the outside. The inspector watched his proceedings with an indulgent smile, and then returned to his examination of the track, in which Thorndyke now joined.

"I suppose the poor chap was near-sighted," the officer remarked, indicating the remains of the shattered spectacles; "that might account for his having strayed on to the line."

"Possibly," said Thorndyke. He had already noticed the fragments scattered over a sleeper and the adjacent ballast, and now once more produced his "collecting-box," from which he took another seed envelope. "Would you hand me a pair of forceps,

Jervis," he said; "and perhaps you wouldn't mind taking a pair yourself and helping me to gather up these fragments."

As I complied, the inspector looked up curiously.

"There isn't any doubt that these spectacles belonged to the deceased, is there?" he asked.

"He certainly wore spectacles, for I saw the mark on his nose."

"Still, there is no harm in verifying the fact," said Thorndyke, and he added to me in a lower tone, "Pick up every particle you can find, Jervis. It may be most important."

"I don't quite see how," I said, groping amongst the shingle by the light of the lantern in search of the tiny splinters of glass.

"Don't you?" returned Thorndyke. "Well, look at these fragments; some of them are a fair size, but many of these on the sleeper are mere grains. And consider their number. Obviously, the condition of the glass does not agree with the circumstances in which we find it. These are thick concave spectacle-lenses, broken into a great number of minute fragments. Now how were they broken? Not merely by falling, evidently: such a lens, when it is dropped, breaks into a small number of large pieces. Nor were they broken by the wheel passing over them, for they would then have been reduced to fine powder, and that powder would have been visible on the rail, which it is not. The spectacle-frames, you may remember, presented the same incongruity: they were battered and damaged more than they would have been by falling, but not nearly so much as they would have been if the wheel had passed over them."

"What do you suggest, then?" I asked.

"The appearances suggest that the spectacles had been trodden on. But, if the body was carried here, the probability is that the spectacles were carried here too, and that they were then already broken; for it is more likely that they were trodden on during the struggle than that the murderer trod on them after bringing them here. Hence the importance of picking up every fragment."

"But why?" I inquired, rather foolishly, I must admit.

"Because, if, when we have picked up every fragment that we can find, there still remains missing a larger portion of the lenses than we could reasonably expect, that would tend to support our hypothesis and we might find the missing remainder elsewhere. If, on the other hand, we find as much of the lenses as we could expect to find, we must conclude that they were broken on this spot."

While we were conducting our search, the two officials were circling around with their lanterns in quest of the missing hat; and, when we had at length picked up the last fragment, and a careful search, even aided by a lens, failed to reveal any other, we could see their lanterns moving, like will-o'-the-wisps, some distance down the line.

"We may as well see what we have got before our friends come back," said Thorndyke, glancing at the twinkling lights. "Lay the case down on the grass by the fence; it will serve for a table."

I did so, and Thorndyke, taking a letter from his pocket, opened it, spread it out flat on the case, securing it with a couple of heavy stones, although the night was quite calm. Then he tipped the contents of the seed envelope out on the paper, and, carefully spreading out the pieces of glass, looked at them for some moments in silence. And, as he looked, there stole over his face a very curious expression; with sudden eagerness he began picking out the larger fragments and laying them on two visiting-cards which he had taken from his card-case. Rapidly and with wonderful deftness he fitted the pieces together, and, as the reconstituted lenses began gradually to take shape on their cards I looked on with growing excitement, for something in my colleague's manner told me that we were on the verge of a discovery.

At length the two ovals of glass lay on their respective cards, complete save for one or two small gaps; and the little heap that remained consisted of fragments so minute as to render further reconstruction impossible. Then Thorndyke leaned back and laughed softly.

"This is certainly an unlooked-for result," said he.

"What is?" I asked.

"Don't you see, my dear fellow? *There's too much glass.* We have almost completely built up the broken lenses, and the fragments that are left over are considerably more than are required to fill up the gaps."

I looked at the little heap of small fragments and saw at once that it was as he had said. There was a surplus of small pieces.

"This is very extraordinary," I said. "What do you think can be the explanation?"

"The fragments will probably tell us," he replied, "if we ask them intelligently."

He lifted the paper and the two cards carefully on to the ground, and, opening the case, took out the little microscope, to which he fitted the lowest-power objective and eye-piece—having a combined magnification of only ten diameters. Then he transferred the minute fragments of glass to a slide, and, having arranged the lantern as a microscope-lamp, commenced his examination.

"Ha!" he exclaimed presently. "The plot thickens. There is too much glass and yet too little; that is to say, there are only one or two fragments here that belong to the spectacles; not nearly enough to complete the building up of the lenses. The remainder consists of a soft, uneven, moulded glass, easily distinguished from the clear, hard optical glass. These foreign fragments are all curved, as if they had formed part of a cylinder, and are, I should say, portions of a wine-glass or tumbler." He moved the slide once or twice, and then continued: "We are in luck, Jervis. Here is a fragment with two little diverging lines etched on it, evidently the points of an eight-rayed star—and here is another with three points—the ends of three rays. This enables us to reconstruct the vessel perfectly. It was a clear, thin glass—probably a tumbler—decorated with scattered stars; I dare say you know the pattern. Sometimes there is an ornamented band in addition, but generally the stars are the only decoration. Have a look at the specimen."

I had just applied my eye to the microscope when the station-master and the inspector came up. Our appearance, seated on the ground with the microscope between us, was too much for the police officer's gravity, and he laughed long and joyously.

"You must excuse me, gentlemen," he said apologetically, "but really, you know, to an old hand, like myself, it does look a little—well—you understand—I dare say a microscope is a very interesting and amusing thing, but it doesn't get you much for-rader in a case like this, does it?"

"Perhaps not," replied Thorndyke. "By the way, where did you find the hat, after all?"

"We haven't found it," the inspector replied, a little sheepishly.

"Then we must help you to continue the search," said Thorndyke. "If you will wait a few moments, we will come with you." He poured a few drops of xylol balsam on the cards to fix the reconstituted lenses to their supports and then, packing them and the microscope in the case, announced that he was ready to start.

"Is there any village or hamlet near?" he asked the station-master.

"None nearer than Corfield. That is about half a mile from here."

"And where is the nearest road?"

"There is a half-made road that runs past a house about three hundred yards from here. It belonged to a building estate that was never built. There is a footpath from it to the station."

"Are there any other houses near?"

"No. That is the only house for half a mile round, and there is no other road near here."

"Then the probability is that Brodski approached the railway from that direction, as he was found on that side of the permanent way."

The inspector agreeing with this view, we all set off slowly towards the house, piloted by the station-master and searching the ground as we went. The waste land over which we passed was covered with patches of docks and nettles, through each of which the inspector kicked his way, searching with feet and lantern for the missing hat. A walk of three hundred yards brought us to a low wall enclosing a garden, beyond which we could see a small house; and here we halted while the inspector waded into a large bed of nettles beside the wall and kicked vigorously. Suddenly there came a clinking sound mingled with objurgations, and the inspector hopped out holding one foot and soliloquizing profanely.

"I wonder what sort of a fool put a thing like that into a bed of nettles!" he exclaimed, stroking the injured foot. Thorndyke picked the object up and held it in the light of the lantern, displaying a piece of three-quarter inch rolled iron bar about a foot long. "It doesn't seem to have been there very long," he observed, examining it closely; "there is hardly any rust on it."

"It has been there long enough for me," growled the inspector, "and I'd like to bang it on the head of the blighter that put it there."

Callously indifferent to the inspector's sufferings, Thorndyke continued calmly to examine the bar. At length, resting his lantern on the wall, he produced his pocket-lens, with which he resumed his investigation, a proceeding that so exasperated the inspector that that afflicted official limped off in dudgeon, followed by the station-master, and we heard him, presently, rapping at the front door of the house.

"Give me a slide, Jervis, with a drop of Farrant on it," said Thorndyke. "There are some fibres sticking to this bar."

I prepared the slide, and, having handed it to him together with a cover-glass, a pair of forceps and a needle, set up the microscope on the wall.

"I'm sorry for the inspector," Thorndyke remarked, with his eye applied to the little instrument, "but that was a lucky kick for us. Just take a look at the specimen."

I did so, and, having moved the slide about until I had seen the whole of the object, I gave my opinion. "Red wool fibres, blue cotton fibres, and some yellow, vegetable fibres that look like jute."

"Yes," said Thorndyke; "the same combination of fibres as that which we found on the dead man's teeth and probably from the same source. This bar has probably been wiped on that very curtain or rug with which poor Brodski was stifled. We will place it on the wall for future reference, and meanwhile, by hook or by crook, we must get into that house. This is much too plain a hint to be disregarded."

Hastily repacking the case, we hurried to the front of the house, where we found the two officials looking rather vaguely up the unmade road.

"There's a light in the house," said the inspector, "but there's no one at home. I have knocked a dozen times and got no answer. And I don't see what we are hanging about here for at all. The hat is probably close to where the body was found, and we shall find it in the morning."

Thorndyke made no reply, but, entering the garden, stepped

up the path, and having knocked gently at the door, stooped and listened attentively at the key-hole.

"I tell you there's no one in the house, sir," said the inspector irritably; and, as Thorndyke continued to listen, he walked away, muttering angrily. As soon as he was gone, Thorndyke flashed his lantern over the door, the threshold, the path and the small flower-beds; and, from one of the latter, I presently saw him stoop and pick something up.

"Here is a highly instructive object, Jervis," he said, coming out to the gate, and displaying a cigarette of which only half an inch had been smoked.

"How instructive?" I asked. "What do you learn from it?"

"Many things," he replied. "It has been lit and thrown away unsmoked; that indicates a sudden change of purpose. It was thrown away at the entrance to the house, almost certainly by some one entering it. That person was probably a stranger, or he would have taken it in with him. But he had not expected to enter the house, or he would not have lit it. These are the general suggestions; now as to the particular ones. The paper of the cigarette is of the kind known as the 'Zig-Zag' brand; the very conspicuous water-mark is quite easy to see. Now Brodski's cigarette book was a 'Zig-Zag' book—so called from the way in which the papers pull out. But let us see what the tobacco is like." With a pin from his coat, he hooked out from the unburned end a wisp of dark, dirty brown tobacco, which he held out for my inspection.

"Fine-cut Latakia," I pronounced, without hesitation.

"Very well," said Thorndyke. "Here is a cigarette made of an unusual tobacco similar to that in Brodski's pouch and wrapped in an unusual paper similar to those in Brodski's cigarette book. With due regard to the fourth rule of the syllogism, I suggest that this cigarette was made by Oscar Brodski. But, nevertheless, we will look for corroborative detail."

"What is that?" I asked.

"You may have noticed that Brodski's match-box contained round wooden vestas—which are also rather unusual. As he must have lighted the cigarette within a few steps of the gate, we ought to be able to find the match with which he lighted it. Let us try up the road in the direction from which he would probably have approached."

We walked very slowly up the road, searching the ground with the lantern, and we had hardly gone a dozen paces when I espied a match lying on the rough path and eagerly picked it up. It was a round wooden vesta.

Thorndyke examined it with interest and having deposited it, with the cigarette, in his "collecting-box," turned to retrace his steps. "There is now, Jervis, no reasonable doubt that Brodski was murdered in that house. We have succeeded in connecting that house with the crime, and now we have got to force an entrance and join up the other clues." We walked quickly back to the rear of the premises, where we found the inspector conversing disconsolately with the station-master.

"I think, sir," said the former, "we had better go back now; in fact, I don't see what we came here for, but—here! I say, sir, you mustn't do that!" For Thorndyke, without a word of warning, had sprung up lightly and thrown one of his long legs over the wall.

"I can't allow you to enter private premises, sir," continued the inspector; but Thorndyke quietly dropped down on the inside and turned to face the officer over the wall.

"Now, listen to me, inspector," said he. "I have good reasons for believing that the dead man, Brodski, has been in this house, in fact, I am prepared to swear an information to that effect. But time is precious; we must follow the scent while it is hot. And I am not proposing to break into the house off-hand. I merely wish to examine the dust-bin."

"The dust-bin!" gasped the inspector. "Well, you really are a most extraordinary gentleman! What do you expect to find in the dust-bin?"

"I am looking for a broken tumbler or wine-glass. It is a thin glass vessel decorated with a pattern of small, eight-pointed stars. It may be in the dust-bin or it may be inside the house."

The inspector hesitated, but Thorndyke's confident manner had evidently impressed him.

"We can soon see what is in the dust-bin," he said, "though what in creation a broken tumbler has to do with the case is more than I can understand. However, here goes." He sprang up on to the wall, and, as he dropped down into the garden, the station-master and I followed.

Thorndyke lingered a few moments by the gate examining the

ground, while the two officials hurried up the path. Finding
nothing of interest, however, he walked towards the house, looking keenly about him as he went; but we were hardly half-way
up the path when we heard the voice of the inspector calling
excitedly.

"Here you are, sir, this way," he sang out, and, as we hurried
forward, we suddenly came on the two officials standing over a
small rubbish-heap and looking the picture of astonishment.
The glare of their lanterns illuminated the heap, and showed us
the scattered fragments of a thin glass, star-pattern tumbler.

"I can't imagine how you guessed it was here, sir," said the
inspector, with a new-born respect in his tone, "nor what you're
going to do with it now you have found it."

"It is merely another link in the chain of evidence," said
Thorndyke, taking a pair of forceps from the case and stooping
over the heap. "Perhaps we shall find something else." He picked
up several small fragments of glass, looked at them closely and
dropped them again. Suddenly his eye caught a small splinter at
the base of the heap. Seizing it with the forceps, he held it close
to his eye in the strong lamplight, and, taking out his lens, examined it with minute attention. "Yes," he said at length, "this is what
I was looking for. Let me have those two cards, Jervis."

I produced the two visiting-cards with the reconstructed
lenses stuck to them, and, laying them on the lid of the case,
threw the light of the lantern on them. Thorndyke looked at
them intently for some time, and from them to the fragment
that he held. Then, turning to the inspector, he said: "You saw
me pick up this splinter of glass?"

"Yes, sir," replied the officer.

"And you saw where we found these spectacle-glasses and
know whose they were?"

"Yes, sir. They are the dead man's spectacles, and you found
them where the body had been."

"Very well," said Thorndyke; "now observe"; and, as the two
officials craned forward with parted lips, he laid the little splinter in a gap in one of the lenses and then gave it a gentle push
forward, when it occupied the gap perfectly, joining edge to
edge with the adjacent fragments and rendering that portion of
the lens complete.

"My God!" exclaimed the inspector. "How on earth did you know?"

"I must explain that later," said Thorndyke. "Meanwhile we had better have a look inside the house. I expect to find there a cigarette—or possibly a cigar—which has been trodden on, some whole-meal biscuits, possibly a wooden vesta, and perhaps even the missing hat."

At the mention of the hat, the inspector stepped eagerly to the back door, but, finding it bolted, he tried the window. This also was securely fastened and, on Thorndyke's advice, we went round to the front door.

"This door is locked too," said the inspector. "I'm afraid we shall have to break in. It's a nuisance, though."

"Have a look at the window," suggested Thorndyke.

The officer did so, struggling vainly to undo the patent catch with his pocket-knife.

"It's no go," he said, coming back to the door. "We shall have to——" He broke off with an astonished stare, for the door stood open and Thorndyke was putting something in his pocket.

"Your friend doesn't waste much time—even in picking a lock," he remarked to me, as we followed Thorndyke into the house; but his reflections were soon merged in a new surprise. Thorndyke had preceded us into a small sitting-room dimly lighted by a hanging lamp turned down low.

As we entered he turned up the light and glanced about the room. A whisky-bottle was on the table, with a siphon, a tumbler and a biscuit-box. Pointing to the latter, Thorndyke said to the inspector: "See what is in that box."

The inspector raised the lid and peeped in, the station-master peered over his shoulder, and then both stared at Thorndyke.

"How in the name of goodness did you know that there were whole-meal biscuits in the house, sir?" exclaimed the station-master.

"You'd be disappointed if I told you," replied Thorndyke. "But look at this." He pointed to the hearth, where lay a flattened, half-smoked cigarette and a round wooden vesta. The inspector gazed at these objects in silent wonder, while, as to the station-master, he continued to stare at Thorndyke with what I can only describe as superstitious awe.

"You have the dead man's property with you, I believe?" said my colleague.

"Yes," replied the inspector; "I put the things in my pocket for safety."

"Then," said Thorndyke, picking up the flattened cigarette, "let us have a look at his tobacco-pouch."

As the officer produced and opened the pouch, Thorndyke neatly cut open the cigarette with his sharp pocket-knife. "Now," said he, "what kind of tobacco is in the pouch?"

The inspector took out a pinch, looked at it and smelt it distastefully. "It's one of those stinking tobaccos," he said, "that they put in mixtures—Latakia, I think."

"And what is this?" asked Thorndyke, pointing to the open cigarette.

"Same stuff, undoubtedly," replied the inspector.

"And now let us see his cigarette papers," said Thorndyke.

The little book, or rather packet—for it consisted of separated papers—was produced from the officer's pocket and a sample paper abstracted. Thorndyke laid the half-burnt paper beside it, and the inspector having examined the two, held them up to the light.

"There isn't much chance of mistaking that 'Zig-Zag' watermark," he said. "This cigarette was made by the deceased; there can't be the shadow of a doubt."

"One more point," said Thorndyke, laying the burnt-wooden vesta on the table. "You have his match-box?"

The inspector brought forth the little silver casket, opened it and compared the wooden vestas that it contained with the burnt end. Then he shut the box with a snap.

"You've proved it up to the hilt," said he. "If we could only find the hat, we should have a complete case."

"I'm not sure that we haven't found the hat," said Thorndyke. "You notice that something besides coal has been burned in the grate."

The inspector ran eagerly to the fire-place and began, with feverish hands, to pick out the remains of the extinct fire. "The cinders are still warm," he said, "and they are certainly not all coal cinders. There has been wood burned here on top of the coal; and these little black lumps are neither coal nor wood.

They may quite possibly be the remains of a burnt hat, but, lord! who can tell? You can put together the pieces of broken specta-cle-glasses, but you can't build up a hat out of a few cinders." He held out a handful of little, black, spongy cinders and looked ruefully at Thorndyke, who took them from him and laid them out on a sheet of paper.

"We can't reconstitute the hat, certainly," my friend agreed, "but we may be able to ascertain the origin of these remains. They may not be cinders of a hat, after all." He lit a wax match and, taking up one of the charred fragments, applied the flame to it. The cindery mass fused at once with a crackling, seething sound, emitting a dense smoke, and instantly the air became charged with a pungent, resinous odor mingled with the smell of burning animal matter.

"Smells like varnish," the station-master remarked.

"Yes. Shellac," said Thorndyke; "so the first test gives a posi-tive result. The next test will take more time."

He opened the green case and took from it a little flask, fitted for Marsh's arsenic test, with a safety funnel and escape tube, a small folding tripod, a spirit-lamp and a disc of asbestos to serve as a sand-bath. Dropping into the flask several of the cindery masses, selected after careful inspection, he filled it up with alcohol and placed it on the disc, which he rested on the tripod. Then he lighted the spirit-lamp underneath and sat down to wait for the alcohol to boil.

"There is one little point that we may as well settle," he said presently, as the bubbles began to rise in the flask. "Give me a slide with a drop of Farrant on it, Jervis."

I prepared the slide while Thorndyke, with a pair of forceps, picked out a tiny wisp from the table-cloth. "I fancy we have seen this fabric before," he remarked, as he laid the little pinch of fluff in the mounting fluid and slipped the slide on to the stage of the microscope. "Yes," he continued, looking into the eye-piece, "here are our old acquaintances, the red wool fibres, the blue cotton, and the yellow jute. We must label this at once or we may confuse it with the other specimens."

"Have you any idea how the deceased met his death?" the inspector asked.

"Yes," replied Thorndyke. "I take it that the murderer enticed him into this room and gave him some refreshments. The murderer sat in the chair in which you are sitting, Brodski sat in that small arm-chair. Then I imagine the murderer attacked him with that iron bar that you found among the nettles, failed to kill him at the first stroke, struggled with him and finally suffocated him with the table-cloth. By the way, there is just one more point. You recognize this piece of string?" He took from his "collecting-box" the little end of twine that had been picked up by the line. The inspector nodded. "If you look behind you, you will see where it came from."

The officer turned sharply and his eye lighted on a string-box on the mantelpiece. He lifted it down, and Thorndyke drew out from it a length of white twine with one green strand, which he compared with the piece in his hand. "The green strand in it makes the identification fairly certain," he said. "Of course, the string was used to secure the umbrella and hand-bag. He could not have carried them in his hand, encumbered as he was with the corpse. But I expect our other specimen is ready now." He lifted the flask off the tripod, and, giving it a vigorous shake, examined the contents through his lens. The alcohol had now become dark-brown in color, and was noticeably thicker and more syrupy in consistence.

"I think we have enough here for a rough test," said he, selecting a pipette and a slide from the case. He dipped the former into the flask and, having sucked up a few drops of the alcohol from the bottom, held the pipette over the slide on which he allowed the contained fluid to drop.

Laying a cover-glass on the little pool of alcohol, he put the slide on the microscope stage and examined it attentively, while we watched him in expectant silence.

At length he looked up, and, addressing the inspector, asked: "Do you know what felt hats are made of?"

"I can't say that I do, sir," replied the officer.

"Well, the better quality hats are made off rabbits' and hares' wool—the soft under-fur, you know—cemented together with shellac. Now there is very little doubt that these cinders contain shellac, and with the microscope I find a number of small hairs of a rabbit. I have, therefore, little hesitation in saying that these cinders are the remains of a hard felt hat; and, as the hairs do not appear to be dyed, I should say it was a grey hat."

At this moment our conclave was interrupted by hurried footsteps on the garden path and, as we turned with one accord, an elderly woman burst into the room.

She stood for a moment in mute astonishment, and then, looking from one to the other, demanded: "Who are you? and what are you doing here?"

The inspector rose. "I am a police officer, madam," said he. "I can't give you any further information just now, but, if you will excuse me asking, who are you?"

"I am Mr. Hickler's housekeeper," she replied.

"And Mr. Hickler; are you expecting him home shortly?"

"No, I am not," was the curt reply. "Mr. Hickler is away from home just now. He left this evening by the boat train."

"For Amsterdam?" asked Thorndyke.

"I believe so, though I don't see what business it is of yours," the housekeeper answered.

"I thought he might, perhaps, be a diamond broker or merchant," said Thorndyke. "A good many of them travel by that train."

"So he is," said the woman, "at least, he has something to do with diamonds."

"Ah. Well, we must be going, Jervis," said Thorndyke, "we have finished here, and we have to find an hotel or inn. Can I have a word with you, inspector?"

The officer, now entirely humble and reverent, followed us out into the garden to receive Thorndyke's parting advice.

"You had better take possession of the house at once, and get rid of the housekeeper. Nothing must be removed. Preserve those cinders and see that the rubbish-heap is not disturbed, and, above all, don't have the room swept. The station-master or I will let them know at the police station, so that they can send an officer to relieve you."

With a friendly "good-night" we went on our way, guided by the station-master; and here our connection with the case came to an end. Hickler (whose Christian name turned out to be Silas) was, it was true, arrested as he stepped ashore from the steamer, and a packet of diamonds, subsequently identified as the property of Oscar Brodski, found upon his person. But he was never brought to trial, for on the return voyage he contrived to elude his guards for an instant as the ship was approaching the English coast, and it was not until three days later, when a handcuffed body was cast up on the lonely shore by Orfordness, that the authorities knew the fate of Silas Hickler.

"An appropriate and dramatic end to a singular and yet typical case," said Thorndyke, as he put down the newspaper. "I hope it has enlarged your knowledge, Jervis, and enabled you to form one or two useful corollaries."

"I prefer to hear you sing the medico-legal doxology," I answered, turning upon him like the proverbial worm and grinning derisively (which the worm does not).

"I know you do," he retorted, with mock gravity, "and I lament your lack of mental initiative. However, the points that this case illustrates are these: First, the danger of delay; the vital importance of instant action before that frail and fleeting thing that we call a clue has time to evaporate. A delay of a few hours would have left us with hardly a single datum. Second, the necessity of pursuing the most trivial clue to an absolute finish, as illustrated by the spectacles. Third, the urgent need of a trained scientist to aid the police; and, last," he concluded, with a smile, "we learn never to go abroad without the invaluable green case."

The Gutting of Couffignal
(1924)
Dashiell Hammett

Wedge-shaped Couffignal is not a large island, and not far from the mainland, to which it is linked by a wooden bridge. Its western shore is a high, straight cliff that jumps abruptly up out of San Pablo Bay. From the top of this cliff the island slopes eastward, down to a smooth pebble beach that runs into the water again, where there are piers and a clubhouse and moored pleasure boats.

Couffignal's main street, paralleling the beach, has the usual bank, hotel, moving-picture theater, and stores. But it differs from most main streets of its size in that it is more carefully arranged and preserved. There are trees and hedges and strips of lawn on it, and no glaring signs. The buildings seem to belong beside one another, as if they had been designed by the same architect, and in the stores you will find goods of a quality to match the best city stores.

The intersecting streets—running between rows of neat cottages near the foot of the slope—become winding hedged roads as they climb toward the cliff. The higher these roads get, the farther apart and larger are the houses they lead to. The occupants of these higher houses are the owners and rulers of the island. Most of them are well-fed old gentlemen who, the profits they took from the world with both hands in their younger days now stowed away as safe percentages, have bought into the island colony so they may spend what is left of their lives nursing their livers and improving their golf among their kind. They admit to the island only as many storekeepers, working people, and similar riffraff as are needed to keep them comfortably served.

This is Couffignal.

It was some time after midnight. I was sitting in a second-story room in Couffignal's largest house, surrounded by wedding presents whose value would add up to something between fifty and a hundred thousand dollars.

Of all the work that comes to a private detective (except divorce work, which the Continental Detective Agency doesn't handle) I like weddings as little as any. Usually I manage to avoid them, but this time I hadn't been able to. Dick Foley, who had been slated for the job, had been handed a black eye by an unfriendly pick-pocket the day before. That let Dick out and me in. I had come up to Couffignal—a two-hour ride from San Francisco by ferry and auto stage—that morning, and would return the next.

This had been neither better nor worse than the usual wedding detail. The ceremony had been performed in a little stone church down the hill. Then the house had begun to fill with reception guests. They had kept it filled to overflowing until some time after the bride and groom had sneaked off to their eastern train.

The world had been well represented. There had been an admiral and an earl or two from England; an ex-president of a South American country; a Danish baron; a tall young Russian princess surrounded by lesser titles, including a fat, bald, jovial and black-bearded Russian general, who had talked to me for a solid hour about prizefights, in which he had a lot of interest, but not so much knowledge as was possible; an ambassador from one of the Central European countries; a justice of the Supreme Court; and a mob of people whose prominence and near-prominence didn't carry labels.

In theory, a detective guarding wedding presents is supposed to make himself indistinguishable from the other guests. In practice, it never works out that way. He has to spend most of his time within sight of the booty, so he's easily spotted. Besides that, eight or ten people I recognized among the guests were clients or former clients of the Agency, and so knew me. However, being known doesn't make so much difference as you might think, and everything had gone off smoothly.

A couple of the groom's friends, warmed by wine and the necessity of maintaining their reputations as cutups, had tried to smuggle some of the gifts out of the room where they were displayed and hide them in the piano. But I had been expecting that familiar track, and blocked it before it had gone far enough to embarrass anybody.

Shortly after dark a wind smelling of rain began to pile storm clouds up over the bay. Those guests who lived at a distance, especially those who had water to cross, hurried off for their houses. Those who lived on the island stayed until the first raindrops began to patter down. Then they left.

The Hendrixson house quieted down. Musicians and extra servants left. The weary house servants began to disappear in the direction of their bedrooms. I found some sandwiches, a couple of books and a comfortable armchair, and took them up to the room where the presents were now hidden under gray-white sheeting.

Keith Hendrixson, the bride's grandfather—she was an orphan—put his head in at the door. "Have you everything you need for your comfort?" he asked.

"Yes, thanks."

He said good night and went off to bed—a tall old man, slim as a boy.

The wind and the rain were hard at it when I went downstairs to give the lower windows and doors the up-and-down. Everything on the first floor was tight and secure, everything in the cellar. I went upstairs again.

Pulling my chair over by a floor lamp, I put sandwiches, books, ashtray, gun and flashlight on a small table beside it. Then I switched off the other lights, set fire to a Fatima, sat down, wriggled my spine comfortably into the chair's padding, picked up one of the books, and prepared to make a night of it.

The book was called *The Lord of the Sea,* and had to do with a strong, tough, and violent fellow named Hogarth, whose modest plan was to hold the world in one hand. There were plots and counterplots, kidnappings, murders, prisonbreakings, forgeries and burglaries, diamonds large as hats and floating forts larger than Couffignal. It sounds dizzy here, but in the book it was real as a dime.

Hogarth was still going strong when the lights went out.

In the dark, I got rid of the glowing end of my cigarette by grinding it in one of the sandwiches. Putting the book down, I picked up gun and flashlight, and moved away from the chair.

Listening for noises was no good. The storm was making hundreds of them. What I needed to know was why the lights had gone off. All the other lights in the house had been turned off some time ago. So the darkness of the hall told me nothing.

I waited. My job was to watch the presents. Nobody had touched them yet. There was nothing to get excited about.

Minutes went by, perhaps ten of them.

The floor swayed under my feet. The windows rattled with a violence beyond the strength of the storm. The dull boom of a heavy explosion blotted out the sounds of wind and falling water. The blast was not close at hand, but not far enough away to be off the island.

Crossing to the window, peering through the wet glass, I could see nothing. I should have seen a few misty lights far down the hill. Not being able to see them settled one point. The lights had gone out all over Couffignal, not only in the Hendrixson house.

That was better. The storm could have put the lighting system out of whack, could have been responsible for the explosion— maybe.

Staring through the black window, I had an impression of great excitement down the hill, of movement in the night. But all was too far away for me to have seen or heard even had there been lights, and all too vague to say what was moving. The impression was strong but worthless. It didn't lead anywhere. I told myself I was getting feeble-minded, and turned away from the window.

Another blast spun me back to it. This explosion sounded nearer than the first, maybe because it was stronger. Peering through the glass again, I still saw nothing. And still had the impression of things that were big moving down there.

Bare feet pattered in the hall. A voice was anxiously calling my name. Turning from the window again, I pocketed my gun and snapped on the flashlight. Keith Hendrixson, in pajamas and bathrobe, looking thinner and older than anybody could be, came into the room.

"Is it—"

"I don't think it's an earthquake," I said, since that is the first calamity your Californian thinks of. "The lights went off a little while ago. There have been a couple of explosions down the hill since the—"

I stopped. Three shots, close together, had sounded. Rifle-shots, but of the sort that only the heaviest of rifles could make. Then, sharp and small in the storm, came the report of a far-away pistol.

"What is it?" Hendrixson demanded.

"Shooting."

More feet were pattering in the halls, some bare, some shod. Excited voices whispered questions and exclamations. The but-ler, a solemn, solid block of a man, partly dressed and carrying a lighted five-pronged candlestick, came in.

"Very good, Brophy," Hendrixson said as the butler put the candlestick on the table beside my sandwiches. "Will you try to learn what is the matter?"

"I have tried, sir. The telephone seems to be out of order, sir. Shall I send Oliver down to the village?"

"No-o. I don't suppose it's that serious. Do you think it is any-thing serious?" he asked me.

I said I didn't think so, but I was paying more attention to the outside than to him. I had heard a thin screaming that could have come from a distant woman, and a volley of small-arms shots. The racket of the storm muffled these shots, but when the heavier firing we had heard before broke out again, it was clear enough.

To have opened the window would have been to let in gallons of water without helping us to hear much clearer. I stood with an ear tilted to the pane, trying to arrive at some idea of what was happening outside.

Another sound took my attention from the window—the ring-ing of the bell-pull at the front door. It rang loudly and persistently.

Hendrixson looked at me. I nodded. "See who it is, Brophy," he said.

The butler went solemnly away, and came back even more solemnly. "Princess Zhukovski," he announced.

She came running into the room—the tall Russian girl I had seen at the reception. Her eyes were wide and dark with excitement. Her face was very white and wet. Water ran in streams down her blue waterproof cape, the hood of which covered her dark hair.

"Oh, Mr. Hendrixson!" She had caught one of his hands in both of hers. Her voice, with nothing foreign in its accent, was the voice of one who is excited over a delightful surprise. "The bank is being robbed and the—what do you call him?—marshal of police has been killed!"

"What's that?" the old man exclaimed, jumping awkwardly because water from her cape had dripped down on one of his bare feet. "Weegan killed? And the bank robbed?"

"Yes! Isn't it terrible?" She said it as if she were saying wonderful. "When the first explosion woke us, the general sent Ignati down to find out what was the matter, and he got down just in time to see the bank blow up. Listen!"

We listened, and heard a wild outbreak of mixed gunfire.

"That will be the general arriving!" she said. "He'll enjoy himself most wonderfully. As soon as Ignati returned with the news, the general armed every male in the household from Aleksandr Sergyeevich to Ivan the cook, and led them out happier than he's been since he took his division to East Prussia in 1914."

"And the duchess?" Hendrixson asked.

"He left her at home with me, of course, and I furtively crept out and away from her while she was trying for the first time in her life to put water in a samovar. This is not the night for one to stay at home!"

"H-m-m," Hendrixson said, his mind obviously not on her words. "And the bank!"

He looked at me. I said nothing. The racket of another volley came to us.

"Could you do anything down there?" he asked.

"Maybe, but—" I nodded at the presents under their covers.

"Oh, these!" the old man said. "I'm as much interested in the bank as in them; besides, we will be here."

"All right!" I was willing enough to carry my curiosity down the hill. "I'll go down. You'd better have the butler stay in here, and plant the chauffeur inside the front door. Better give them guns if you have any. Is there a raincoat I can borrow? I brought only a light overcoat with me."

Brophy found a yellow slicker that fit me. I put it on, stowed gun and flashlight conveniently under it, and found my hat while Brophy was getting and loading an automatic pistol for himself and a rifle for Oliver, the mulatto chauffeur.

Hendrixson and the princess followed me downstairs. At the door I found she wasn't exactly following me—she was going with me.

"But, Sonya!" the old man protested.

"I'm not going to be foolish, though I'd like to," she promised him. "But I'm going back to my Irinia Androvna, who will perhaps have the samovar watered by now."

"That's a sensible girl!" Hendrixson said, and let us out into the rain and the wind.

It wasn't weather to talk in. In silence we turned downhill between two rows of hedging, with the storm driving at our backs. At the first break in the hedge I stopped, nodding toward the black blot a house made. "That is your—"

Her laugh cut me short. She caught my arm and began to urge me down the road again. "I only told Mr. Hendrixson that so he would not worry," she explained. "You do not think I am not going down to see the sights."

She was tall, I am short and thick. I had to look up to see her face—to see as much of it as the rain-gray night would let me see. "You'll be soaked to the hide, running around in this rain," I objected.

"What of that? I am dressed for it." She raised a foot to show me a heavy waterproof boot and a woolen-stockinged leg.

"There's no telling what we'll run into down there, and I've got work to do," I insisted. "I can't be looking out for you."

"I can look out for myself." She pushed her cape aside to show me a square automatic pistol in one hand.

"You'll be in my way."

"I will not," she retorted. "You'll probably find I can help you. I'm as strong as you, and quicker, and I can shoot."

The reports of scattered shooting had punctuated our argument, but now the sound of heavier firing silenced the dozen objections to her company that I could still think of. After all, I could slip away from her in the dark if she became too much of a nuisance.

"Have it your own way," I growled, "but don't expect anything from me."

"You're so kind," she murmured as we got under way again, hurrying now, with the wind at our backs speeding us along.

Occasionally dark figures moved on the road ahead of us, but too far away to be recognizable. Presently a man passed us, running uphill—a tall man whose nightshirt hung out of his trousers, down below his coat, identifying him as a resident.

"They've finished the bank and are at Medcraft's!" he yelled as he went by.

"Medcraft is a jeweler," the girl informed me.

The sloping under our feet grew less sharp. The houses— dark but with faces vaguely visible here and there at windows— came closer together. Below, the flash of a gun could be seen now and then—orange streaks in the rain.

Our road put us into the lower end of the main street just as a staccato rat-tat-tat broke out.

I pushed the girl into the nearest doorway, and jumped in after her.

Bullets ripped through walls with the sound of hail tapping on leaves.

That was the thing I had taken for an exceptionally heavy rifle—a machine gun.

The girl had fallen back in a corner, all tangled up with something. I helped her up. The something was a boy of seventeen or so, with one leg and a crutch.

"It's the boy who delivers papers," Princess Zhukovski said, "and you've hurt him with your clumsiness."

The boy shook his head, grinning as he got up. "No'm, I ain't hurt none, but you kind of scared me, jumping on me like that."

She had to stop and explain that she hadn't jumped on him,

that she had been pushed into him by me, and that she was sorry and so was I.

"What's happening?" I asked the newsboy when I could get a word in.

"Everything," he boasted, as if some of the credit were his. "There must be a hundred of them, and they've blowed the bank wide open, and now some of 'em is in Medcraft's, and I guess they'll blow that up, too. And they killed Tom Weegan. They got a machine gun on a car in the middle of the street. That's it shooting now."

"Where's everybody—all the merry villagers?"

"Most of 'em are up behind the Hall. They can't do nothing, though, because the machine gun won't let 'em get near enough to see what they're shooting at, and that smart Bill Vincent told me to clear out, 'cause I've only got one leg, as if I couldn't shoot as good as the next one, if I only had something to shoot with!"

"That wasn't right of them," I sympathized. "But you can do something for me. You can stick here and keep your eye on this end of the street, so I'll know if they leave in this direction."

"You're not just saying that so I'll stay here out of the way, are you?"

"No," I lied. "I need somebody to watch. I was going to leave the princess here, but you'll do better."

"Yes," she backed me up, catching the idea. "This gentleman is a detective, and if you do what he asks you'll be helping more than if you were up with the others."

The machine gun was still firing, but not in our direction now.

"I'm going across the street," I told the girl. "If you—"

"Aren't you going to join the others?"

"No. If I can get around behind the bandits while they're busy with the others, maybe I can turn a trick."

"Watch sharp now!" I ordered the boy, and the princess and I made a dash for the opposite sidewalk.

We reached it without drawing lead, sidled along a building for a few yards, and turned into an alley. From the alley's other end came the smell and wash and the dull blackness of the bay.

While we moved down this alley I composed a scheme by which I hoped to get rid of my companion, sending her off on a safe wild-goose chase. But I didn't get a chance to try it out.

The big figure of a man loomed ahead of us.

Stepping in front of the girl, I went on toward him. Under my slicker I held my gun on the middle of him.

He stood still. He was larger than he had looked at first. A big, slope-shouldered, barrel-bodied husky. His hands were empty. I spotted the flashlight on his face for a split second. A flat-cheeked, thick-featured face, with high cheekbones and a lot of ruggedness in it.

"Ignati!" the girl exclaimed over my shoulder.

He began to talk what I suppose was Russian to the girl. She laughed and replied. He shook his big head stubbornly, insisting on something. She stamped her foot and spoke sharply. He shook his head again and addressed me. "General Pleshskev, he tell me bring Princess Sonya to home."

His English was almost as hard to understand as his Russian. His tone puzzled me. It was as if he was explaining some absolutely necessary thing that he didn't want to be blamed for, but that nevertheless he was going to do.

While the girl was speaking to him again, I guessed the answer. This big Ignati had been sent out by the general to bring the girl home, and he was going to obey his orders if he had to carry her. He was trying to avoid trouble with me by explaining the situation.

"Take her," I said, stepping aside.

The girl scowled at me, laughed. "Very well, Ignati," she said in English, "I shall go home," and she turned on her heel and went back up the alley, the big man close behind her.

Glad to be alone, I wasted no time in moving in the opposite direction until the pebbles of the beach were under my feet. The pebbles ground harshly under my heels. I moved back to more silent ground and began to work my way as swiftly as I could up the shore toward the center of action. The machine gun barked on. Smaller guns snapped. Three concussions, close together— bombs, hand grenades, my ears and my memory told me.

The stormy sky glared pink over a roof ahead of me and to the left. The boom of the blast beat my eardrums. Fragments I couldn't see fell around me. That, I thought, would be the jeweler's safe blowing apart.

I crept on up the shoreline. The machine gun went silent.

Lighter guns snapped, snapped. Another grenade went off. A man's voice shrieked pure terror.

Risking the crunch of pebbles, I turned down to the water's edge again. I had seen no dark shape on the water that could have been a boat. There had been boats moored along this beach in the afternoon. With my feet in the water of the bay I still saw no boat. The storm could have scattered them, but I didn't think it had. The island's western height shielded this shore. The wind was strong here, but not violent.

My feet sometimes on the edge of the pebbles, sometimes in the water, I went on up the shoreline. Now I saw a boat. A gently bobbing black shape ahead. No light on it. Nothing I could see moved on it. It was the only boat on that shore. That made it important.

Foot by foot, I approached.

A shadow moved between me and the dark rear of a building. I froze. The shadow, man-size, moved again, in the direction from which I was coming.

Waiting, I didn't know how nearly visible, or how plain, I might be against my background. I couldn't risk giving myself away by trying to improve my position.

Twenty feet from me the shadow suddenly stopped.

I was seen. My gun was on the shadow.

"Come on," I called softly. "Keep coming. Let's see who you are."

The shadow hesitated, left the shelter of the building, drew nearer. I couldn't risk the flashlight. I made out dimly a handsome face, boyishly reckless, one cheek dark-stained.

"Oh, how d'you do?" the face's owner said in a musical baritone voice. "You were at the reception this afternoon."

"Yes."

"Have you seen Princess Zhukovski? You know her?"

"She went home with Ignati ten minutes ago."

"Excellent!" He wiped his stained cheek with a stained handkerchief, and turned to look at the boat. "That's Hendrixson's boat," he whispered. "They've got it and they've cast the others off."

"That would mean they are going to leave by water."

"Yes," he agreed, "unless— Shall we have a try at it?"

"You mean jump it?"

"Why not?" he asked. "There can't be very many aboard. God knows there are enough of them ashore. You're armed. I've a pistol."

"We'll size it up first," I decided, "so we'll know what we're jumping."

"That is wisdom," he said, and led the way back to the shelter of the buildings.

Hugging the rear walls of the buildings, we stole toward the boat.

The boat grew clearer in the night. A craft perhaps forty-five feet long, its stern to the shore, rising and falling beside a smaller pier. Across the stern something protruded. Something I couldn't quite make out. Leather soles scuffled now and then on the wooden deck. Presently a dark head and shoulders showed over the puzzling thing in the stern.

The Russian lad's eyes were better than mine.

"Masked," he breathed in my ear. "Something like a stocking over his head and face."

The masked man was motionless where he stood. We were motionless where we stood.

"Could you hit him from here?" the lad asked.

"Maybe, but night and rain aren't a good combination for sharpshooting. Our best bet is to sneak as close as we can, and start shooting when he spots us."

"That is wisdom," he agreed.

Discovery came with our first step forward. The man in the boat grunted. The lad at my side jumped forward. I recognized the thing in the boat's stern just in time to throw out a leg and trip the young Russian. He tumbled down, all sprawled out on the pebbles. I dropped behind him.

The machine gun in the boat's stern poured metal over our heads.

"No good rushing that!" I said. "Roll out of it!"

I set the example by revolving toward the back of the building we had just left.

The man at the gun sprinkled the beach, but sprinkled it at random, his eyes no doubt spoiled for night-seeing by the flash of his gun.

Around the corner of the building, we sat up.

"You saved my life by tripping me," the lad said coolly.

"Yes. I wonder if they've moved the machine gun from the street, or if—"

The answer to that came immediately. The machine gun in the street mingled its vicious voice with the drumming of the one in the boat.

"A pair of them!" I complained. "Know anything about the layout?"

"I don't think there are more than ten or twelve of them," he said, "although it is not easy to count in the dark. The few I have seen are completely masked—like the man in the boat. They seem to have disconnected the telephone and light lines first and then to have destroyed the bridge. We attacked them while they were looting the bank, but in front they had a machine gun mounted in an automobile, and we were not equipped to combat on equal terms."

"Where are the islanders now?"

"Scattered, and most of them in hiding, I fancy, unless General Pleshskev has succeeded in rallying them again."

I frowned and beat my brains together. You can't fight machine guns and hand grenades with peaceful villagers and retired capitalists. No matter how well led and armed they are, you can't do anything with them. For that matter, how could anybody do much against a game of that toughness?

"Suppose you stick here and keep your eye on the boat," I suggested. "I'll scout around and see what's doing farther up, and if I can get a few good men together, I'll try to jump the boat again, probably from the other side. But we can't count on that. The getaway will be by boat. We can count on that, and try to block it out. If you lie down you can watch the boat around the corner of the building without making much of a target of yourself. I wouldn't do anything to attract attention until the break for the boat comes. Then you can do all the shooting you want."

"Excellent!" he said. "You'll probably find most of the islanders up behind the church. You can get to it by going straight up the hill until you come to an iron fence, and then follow that to the right."

"Right."

I moved off in the direction he had indicated.

At the main street I stopped to look around before venturing across. Everything was quiet there. The only man I could see was spread out face-down on the sidewalk near me.

On hands and knees I crawled to his side. He was dead. I didn't stop to examine him further, but sprang up and streaked for the other side of the street.

Nothing tried to stop me. In a doorway, flat against a wall, I peeped out. The wind had stopped. The rain was no longer a driving deluge, but a steady down-pouring of small drops. Couffignal's main street, to my senses, was a deserted street.

I wondered if the retreat to the boat had already started. On the sidewalk, walking swiftly toward the bank, I heard the answer to that guess.

High up on the slope, almost up to the edge of the cliff, by the sound, a machine gun began to hurl out its stream of bullets.

Mixed with the racket of the machine gun were the sounds of smaller arms, and a grenade or two.

At the first crossing, I left the main street and began to run up the hill. Men were running toward me. Two of them passed, paying no attention to my shouted, "What's up now?"

The third man stopped because I grabbed him—a fat man whose breath bubbled, and whose face was fish-belly white.

"They've moved the car with the machine gun on it up behind us," he gasped when I shouted my questions into his ear again.

"What are you doing without a gun?" I asked.

"I—I dropped it."

"Where's General Pleshskev?"

"Back there somewhere. He's trying to capture the car, but he'll never do it. It's suicide! Why don't help come?"

Other men had passed us, running downhill, as we talked. I let the white-faced man go, and stopped four men who weren't running so fast as the others.

"What's happening now?" I questioned them.

"They're going through the houses up the hill," a sharp-featured man with a small mustache and a rifle said.

"Has anybody got word off the island yet?" I asked.

"Can't," another informed me. "They blew up the bridge first thing."

"Can't anybody swim?"

"Not in that wind. Young Catlan tried it and was lucky to get out again with a couple of broken ribs."

"The wind's gone down," I pointed out.

The sharp-featured man gave his rifle to one of the others and took off his coat. "I'll try it," he promised.

"Good! Wake up the whole country, and get word through to the San Francisco police boat and to the Mare Island Navy Yard. They'll lend a hand if you tell 'em the bandits have machine guns. Tell 'em the bandits have an armed boat waiting to leave in. It's Hendrixson's."

The volunteer swimmer left.

"A boat?" two of the men asked together.

"Yes. With a machine gun on it. If we're going to do anything, it'll have to be done now, while we're between them and their getaway. Get every man and every gun you can find down there. Tackle the boat from the roofs if you can. When the bandits' car comes down there, pour it into it. You'll do better from the building than from the street."

The three men went on downhill. I went uphill, toward the crackling of firearms ahead. The machine gun was working irregularly. It would pour out its rat-tat-tat for a second or so, and then stop for a couple of seconds. The answering fire was thin, ragged.

I met more men, learned from them the general, with less than a dozen men, was still fighting the car. I repeated the advice I had given the other men. My informants went down to join them. I went on up.

A hundred yards farther along, what was left of the general's dozen broke out of the night, around and past me, flying downhill, with bullets hailing after them.

The road was no place for mortal man. I stumbled over two bodies, scratched myself in a dozen places getting over a hedge. On soft, wet sod I continued my uphill journey.

The machine gun on the hill stopped its clattering. The one in the boat was still at work.

The one ahead opened again, firing too high for anything near at hand to be its target. It was helping its fellow below, spraying the main street.

Before I could get closer it had stopped. I heard the car's motor racing. The car moved toward me.

Rolling into the hedge, I lay there, straining my eyes through the spaces between the stems. I had six bullets in a gun that hadn't yet been fired on this night that had seen tons of powder burned.

When I saw wheels on the lighter face of the road, I emptied my gun, holding it low.

The car went on.

I sprang out of my hiding place.

The car was suddenly gone from the empty road.

There was a grinding sound. A crash. The noise of metal folding on itself. The tinkle of glass.

I raced toward those sounds.

Out of a black pile where an engine sputtered, a black figure leaped—to dash off across the soggy lawn. I cut after it, hoping that the others in the wreck were down for keeps.

I was less than fifteen feet behind the fleeing man when he cleared a hedge. I'm no sprinter, but neither was he. The wet grass made slippery going.

He stumbled while I was vaulting the hedge. When we straightened out again I was not more than ten feet behind him.

Once I clicked my gun at him, forgetting I had emptied it. Six cartridges were wrapped in a piece of paper in my vest pocket, but this was no time for loading.

I was tempted to chuck the empty gun at his head. But that was too chancy.

A building loomed ahead. My fugitive bore off to the right, to clear the corner.

To the left a heavy shotgun went off.

The running man disappeared around the house-corner.

"Sweet God!" General Pleshskev's mellow voice complained. "That with a shotgun I should miss all of a man at the distance!"

"Go around the other way!" I yelled, plunging around the corner after my quarry.

His feet thudded ahead. I could not see him. The general puffed around from the other side of the house.

"You have him?"

"No."

In front of us was a stone-faced bank, on top of which ran a path. On either side of us was a high and solid hedge.

"But my friend," the general protested. "How could he have—?"

A pale triangle showed on the path above—a triangle that could have been a bit of shirt showing above the opening of a vest.

"Stay here and talk!" I whispered to the general, and crept forward.

"It must be that he has gone the other way," the general carried out my instructions, rambling on as if I were standing beside him, "because if he had come my way I should have seen him, and if he had raised himself over either of the hedges or the embankment, one of us would surely have seen him against . . ."

He talked on and on while I gained the shelter of the bank on which the path sat, while I found places for my toes in the rough stone facing.

The man on the road, trying to make himself small with his back in a bush, was looking at the talking general. He saw me when I had my feet on the path.

He jumped, and one hand went up.

I jumped, with both hands out.

A stone, turning under my foot, threw me sidewise, twisting my ankle, but saving my head from the bullet he sent at it.

My outflung left arm caught his legs as I spilled down. He came over on top of me. I kicked him once, caught his gun-arm, and had just decided to bite it when the general puffed up over the edge of the path and prodded the man off me with the muzzle of the shotgun.

When it came to my turn to stand up, I found it not so good. My twisted ankle didn't like to support its share of my hundred-and-eighty-some pounds. Putting most of my weight on the other leg, I turned my flashlight on the prisoner.

"Hello, Flippo!" I exclaimed.

"Hello!" he said without joy in the recognition.

He was a roly-poly Italian youth of twenty-three or -four. I had helped send him to San Quentin four years ago for his part in a payroll stick-up. He had been out on parole for several months now.

"The prison board isn't going to like this," I told him.

"You got me wrong," he pleaded. "I ain't been doing a thing. I was up here to see some friends. And when this thing busted loose I had to hide, because I got a record, and if I'm picked up I'll be railroaded for it. And now you got me, and you think I'm in on it!"

"You're a mind reader," I assured him, and asked the general, "Where can we pack this bird away for a while, under lock and key?"

"In my house there is a lumber-room with a strong door and not a window."

"That'll do it. March, Flippo!"

General Pleshskev collared the youth, while I limped along behind them, examining Flippo's gun, which was loaded, except for the one shot he had fired at me, and reloading my own.

We had caught our prisoner on the Russian's grounds, so we didn't have far to go.

The general knocked on the door and called out something in his language. Bolts clicked and grated, and the door was swung open by a heavily mustached Russian servant. Behind him the princess and a stalwart older woman stood.

We went in while the general was telling his household about the capture, and took the captive up to the lumber-room. I frisked him for his pocketknife and matches—he had nothing else that could help him get out—locked him in and braced the door solidly with a length of board. Then we went downstairs again.

"You are injured!" the princess cried, seeing me limp across the floor.

"Only a twisted ankle," I said. "But it does bother me some. Is there any adhesive tape around?"

"Yes," and she spoke to the mustached servant, who went out of the room and presently returned, carrying rolls of gauze and tape and a basin of steaming water.

"If you'll sit down," the princess said, taking these things from the servant.

But I shook my head and reached for the adhesive tape.

"I want cold water, because I've got to go out in the wet again. If you'll show me the bathroom, I can fix myself up in no time."

We had to argue about that, but I finally got to the bathroom, where I ran cold water on my foot and ankle, and strapped it with adhesive tape, as tight as I could without stopping the circulation altogether. Getting my wet shoe on again was a job, but when I was through I had two firm legs under me, even if one of them did hurt some.

When I rejoined the others I noticed that sounds of firing no longer came up the hill, and that the patter of rain was lighter, and a gray streak of coming daylight showed under a drawn blind.

I was buttoning my slicker when the knocker rang on the front door. Russian words came through, and the young Russian I had met on the beach came in.

"Aleksandr, you're—" The stalwart older woman screamed, when she saw the blood on his cheek, and fainted.

He paid no attention to her at all, as if he was used to having her faint.

"They've gone in the boat," he told me while the girl and two men-servants gathered up the woman and laid her on an ottoman.

"How many?" I asked.

"I counted ten, and I don't think I missed more than one or two, if any."

"The men I sent down there couldn't stop them?"

He shrugged. "What would you do? It takes a strong stomach to face a machine gun. Your men had been cleared out of the building almost before they arrived."

The woman who had fainted had revived by now and was pouring anxious questions in Russian at the lad. The princess was getting into her blue cape. The woman stopped questioning the lad and asked her something.

"It's all over," the princess said. "I am going to view the ruins."

That suggestion appealed to everybody. Five minutes later all of us, including the servants, were on our way downhill. Behind us, around us, in front of us, were other people going downhill, hurrying along in the drizzle that was very gentle now, their faces tired and excited in the bleak morning light.

Halfway down, a woman ran out of a cross-path and began to tell me something. I recognized her as one of Hendrixson's maids.

I caught some of her words.

"Presents gone . . . Mr. Brophy murdered . . . Oliver . . ."

"I'll be down later," I told the others, and set out after the maid.

She was running back to the Hendrixson house. I couldn't run, couldn't even walk fast. She and Hendrixson and more of his servants were standing on the front porch when I arrived.

"They killed Oliver and Brophy," the old man said.

"How?"

"We were in the back of the house, the rear second story, watching the flashes of the shooting down in the village. Oliver was down here, just inside the front door, and Brophy in the room with the presents. We heard a shot in there, and immediately a man appeared in the doorway of our room, threatening us with two pistols, making us stay there for perhaps ten minutes. Then he shut and locked the door and went away. We broke the door down—and found Brophy and Oliver dead."

"Let's look at them."

The chauffeur was just inside the front door. He lay on his back, with his brown throat cut straight across the front, almost back to the vertebrae. His rifle was under him. I pulled it out and examined it. It had not been fired.

Upstairs, the butler Brophy was huddled against a leg of one of the tables on which the presents had been spread. His gun was gone. I turned him over, straightened him out, and found a bullet-hole in his chest. Around the hole his coat was charred in a large area.

Most of the presents were still there. But the most valuable pieces were gone. The others were in disorder, lying around any which way, their covers pulled off.

"What did the one you saw look like?" I asked.

"I didn't see him very well," Hendrixson said. "There was no light in our room. He was simply a dark figure against the candle burning in the hall. A large man in a black rubber raincoat, with some sort of black mask that covered his whole head and face, with small eyeholes."

"No hat?"

"No, just the mask over his entire face and head."

As we went downstairs again I gave Hendrixson a brief account of what I had seen and heard and done since I had left him. There wasn't enough of it to make a long tale.

"Do you think you can get information about the others from the one you caught?" he asked, as I prepared to go out.

"No. But I expect to bag them just the same."

Couffignal's main street was jammed with people when I limped into it again. A detachment of Marines from Mare Island was there, and men from a San Francisco police boat. Excited citizens in all degrees of partial nakedness boiled around them. A hundred voices were talking at once, recounting their personal adventures and braveries and losses and what they had seen. Such words as machine gun, bomb, bandit, car, shot, dynamite, and killed sounded again and again, in every variety and tone.

The bank had been completely wrecked by the charge that had blown the vault. The jewelry store was another ruin. A grocer's across the street was serving as a field hospital. Two doctors were toiling there, patching up damaged villagers.

I recognized a familiar face under a uniform cap—Sergeant Roche of the harbor police—and pushed through the crowd to him.

"Just get here?" he asked as we shook hands. "Or were you in on it?"

"In on it."

"What do you know?"

"Everything."

"Who ever heard of a private detective that didn't," he joshed as I led him out of the mob.

"Did you people run into an empty boat out in the bay?" I asked when we were away from audiences.

"Empty boats have been floating around the bay all night," he said.

I hadn't thought of that.

"Where's your boat now?" I asked him.

"Out trying to pick up the bandits. I stayed with a couple of men to lend a hand here."

"You're in luck," I told him. "Now sneak a look across the

street. See the stout old boy with the black whiskers, standing in front of the druggist's?"

General Pleshskev stood there, with the woman who had fainted, the young Russian whose bloody cheek had made her faint, and a pale, plump, man of forty-something who had been with them at the reception. A little to one side stood big Ignati, the two men-servants I had seen at the house, and another who was obviously one of them. They were chatting together and watching the excited antics of a red-faced property-owner who was telling a curt lieutenant of Marines that it was his own personal private automobile that the bandits had stolen to mount their machine gun on, and what he thought should be done about it.

"Yes," said Roche, "I see your fellow with the whiskers."

"Well, he's your meat. The woman and two men with him are also your meat. And those four Russians standing to the left are some more of it. There's another missing, but I'll take care of that one. Pass the word to the lieutenant, and you can round up those babies without giving them a chance to fight back. They think they're safe as angels."

"Sure, are you?" the sergeant asked.

"Don't be silly!" I growled, as if I had never made a mistake in my life.

I had been standing on my one good prop. When I put my weight on the other to turn away from the sergeant, it stung me all the way to my hip. I pushed my back teeth together and began to work painfully through the crowd to the other side of the street.

The princess didn't seem to be among those present. My idea was that, next to the general, she was the most important member of the push. If she was at their house, and not yet suspicious, I figured I could get close enough to yank her in without a riot.

Walking was hell. My temperature rose. Sweat rolled out of me.

"Mister, they didn't one of 'em come down that way."

The one-legged newsboy was standing at my elbow. I greeted him as if he were my pay-check.

"Come on with me," I said, taking his arm. "You did fine down here, and now I want you to do something else for me."

Half a block from the main street I led him up on the porch

of a small yellow cottage. The front door stood open, left that way when the occupants ran down to welcome police and Marines, no doubt. Just inside the door, beside a hall rack, was a wicker porch chair. I committed unlawful entry to the extent of dragging that chair out on the porch.

"Sit down, son," I urged the boy.

He sat, looking up at me with a puzzled freckled face. I took a firm grip on his crutch and pulled it out of his hand.

"Here's five bucks for rental," I said, "and if I lose it I'll buy you one of ivory and gold."

And I put the crutch under my arm and began to propel myself up the hill.

It was my first experience with a crutch. I didn't break any records. But it was a lot better than tottering along on an unassisted bum ankle.

The hill was longer and steeper than some mountains I've seen, but the gravel walk to the Russians' house was finally under my feet.

I was still some dozen feet from the porch when Princess Zhukovski opened the door.

"Oh!" she exclaimed, and then, recovering from her surprise, "your ankle is worse!" She ran down the steps to help me climb them. As she came I noticed that something heavy was sagging and swinging in the right-hand pocket of her gray flannel jacket.

With one hand under my elbow, the other arm across my back, she helped me up the steps and across the porch. That assured me she didn't think I had tumbled to the game. If she had, she wouldn't have trusted herself within reach of my hands. Why, I wondered, had she come back to the house after starting downhill with the others?

While I was wondering we went into the house, where she planted me in a large and soft leather chair.

"You must certainly be starving after your strenuous night," she said. "I will see if—"

"No, sit down," I nodded at a chair facing mine. "I want to talk to you."

She sat down, clasping her slender white hands in her lap. In neither face nor pose was there any sign of nervousness, not even of curiosity. And that was overdoing it.

"Where have you cached the plunder?" I asked.

The whiteness of her face was nothing to go by. It had been white as marble since I had first seen her. The darkness of her eyes was as natural. Nothing happened to her other features. Her voice was smoothly cool.

"I am sorry," she said. "The question doesn't convey anything to me."

"Here's the point," I explained. "I'm charging you with complicity in the gutting of Couffignal, and in the murders that went with it. And I'm asking you where the loot has been hidden."

Slowly she stood up, raised her chin, and looked at least a mile down at me.

"How dare you? How dare you speak so to me, a Zhukovski!"

"I don't care if you're one of the Smith Brothers!" Leaning forward, I had pushed my twisted ankle against a leg of the chair, and the resulting agony didn't improve my disposition. "For the purpose of this talk you are a thief and a murderer."

Her strong slender body became the body of a lean crouching animal. Her white face became the face of an enraged animal. One hand—claw now—swept to a heavy pocket of her jacket.

Then, before I could have batted an eye—though my life seemed to depend on my not batting it—the wild animal had vanished. Out of it—and now I know where the writers of the old fairy stories get their ideas—rose the princess again, cool and straight and tall.

She sat down, crossed her ankles, put an elbow on an arm of her chair, propped her chin on the back of that hand, and looked curiously into my face.

"How ever," she murmured, "did you chance to arrive at so strange and fanciful a theory?"

"It wasn't chance, and it's neither strange nor fanciful," I said. "Maybe it'll save time and trouble if I show you part of the score against you. Then you'll know how you stand and won't waste your brains pleading innocence."

"I shall be grateful," she smiled, "very!"

I tucked my crutch in between one knee and the arm of my chair, so my hands would be free to check off my points on my fingers.

"First—whoever planned the job knew the island—not fairly

well, but every inch of it. There's no need to argue about that. Second—the car on which the machine gun was mounted was local property, stolen from the owner here. So was the boat in which the bandits were supposed to have escaped. Bandits from the outside would have needed a car or a boat to bring their machine guns, explosives, and grenades here, and there doesn't seem to be any reason why they shouldn't have used that car or boat instead of stealing a fresh one. Third—there wasn't the least hint of the professional bandit touch on this job. If you ask me, it was a military job from beginning to end. And the worst safe-burglar in the world could have got into both the bank vault and the jeweler's safe without wrecking the buildings. Fourth—bandits from the outside wouldn't have destroyed the bridge. They might have blocked it, but they wouldn't have destroyed it. They'd have saved it in case they had to make their getaway in that direction. Fifth—bandits figuring on a getaway by boat would have cut the job short, wouldn't have spread it over the whole night. Enough racket was made here to wake up California all the way from Sacramento to Los Angeles. What you people did was to send one man out in the boat, shooting, and he didn't go far. As soon as he was at a safe distance, he went overboard, and swam back to the island. Big Ignati could have done it without turning a hair."

That exhausted my right hand. I switched over, counting on my left.

"Sixth—I met one of your party, the lad, down on the beach, and he was coming from the boat. He suggested that we jump it. We were shot at, but the man behind the gun was playing with us. He could have wiped us out in a second if he had been in earnest, but he shot over our heads. Seventh—that same lad is the only man on the island, so far as I know, who saw the departing bandits. Eight—all of your people that I ran into were especially nice to me, the general even spending an hour talking to me at the reception this afternoon. That's a distinctive amateur crook trait. Ninth—after the machine gun car had been wrecked I chased its occupant. I lost him around this house. The Italian boy I picked up wasn't him. He couldn't have climbed up on the path without my seeing him. But he could have run around to the general's side of the house and vanished indoors there. The general liked him, and would have helped him. I know that, because the general performed a downright miracle by missing him at some six feet with a shotgun. Tenth—you called at Hendrixson's house for no other purpose than to get me away from there."

That finished the left hand. I went back to the right.

"Eleventh—Hendrixson's two servants were killed by someone they knew and trusted. Both were killed at close quarters and without firing a shot. I'd say you got Oliver to let you into the house, and were talking to him when one of your men cut his throat from behind. Then you went upstairs and probably shot the unsuspecting Brophy yourself. He wouldn't have been on his guard against you. Twelfth—but that ought to be enough, and I'm getting a sore throat from listing them."

She took her chin off her hand, took a fat white cigarette out of a thin black case, and held it in her mouth while I put a match to the end of it. She took a long pull at it—a draw that accounted for a third of its length—and blew the smoke down at her knees.

"That would be enough," she said when all these things had been done, "if it were not that you yourself know it was impossible for us to have been so engaged. Did you not see us—did not everyone see us—time and time again?"

"That's easy!" I argued. "With a couple of machine guns, a trunkful of grenades, knowing the island from top to bottom, in the darkness and in a storm, against bewildered civilians—it was duck soup. There are nine of you that I know of, including two women. Any five of you could have carried on the work, once it was started, while the others took turns appearing here and there, establishing alibis. And that is what you did. You took turns slipping out to alibi yourselves. Everywhere I went I ran into one of you. And the general! That whiskered old joker running around leading the simple citizens to battle! I'll bet he led 'em plenty! They're lucky there are any of 'em alive this morning!"

She finished her cigarette with another inhalation, dropped the stub on the rug, ground out the light with one foot, sighed wearily, put her hands on her hips, and asked, "And now what?"

"Now I want to know where you have stowed the plunder."

The readiness of her answer surprised me.

"Under the garage, in a cellar we secretly dug there some months ago."

I didn't believe that, of course, but it turned out to be the truth.

I didn't have anything else to say. When I fumbled with my borrowed crutch, preparing to get up, she raised a hand and spoke gently. "Wait a moment, please. I have something to suggest."

Half standing, I leaned toward her, stretching out one hand until it was close to her side.

"I want the gun," I said.

She nodded, and sat still while I plucked it from her pocket, put it in one of my own, and sat down again.

"You said a little while ago that you didn't care who I was," she began immediately. "But I want you to know. There are so many Russians who once were somebodies and who now are nobodies that I won't bore you with the repetition of a tale the world has grown tired of hearing. But you must remember that this weary tale is real to us who are its subjects. However, we fled from Russia with what we could carry of our property, which fortunately was enough to keep us in bearable comfort for a few years.

"In London we opened a Russian restaurant, but London was suddenly full of Russian restaurants, and ours became, instead of a means of livelihood, a source of loss. We tried teaching music and languages, and so on. In short, we hit on all the means of earning our living that other Russian exiles hit upon, and so always found ourselves in overcrowded, and thus unprofitable, fields. But what else did we know—could we do?

"I promised not to bore you. Well, always our capital shrank, and always the day approached on which we should be shabby and hungry, the day when we should become familiar to readers of your Sunday papers—charwomen who had been princesses, dukes who now were butlers. There was no place for us in the world. Outcasts easily become outlaws. Why not? Could it be said that we owed the world any fealty? Had not the world sat idly by and seen us despoiled of place and property and country?

"We planned it before we had heard of Couffignal. We could find a small settlement of the wealthy, sufficiently isolated, and, after establishing ourselves there, we would plunder it.

Couffignal, when we found it, seemed to be the ideal place. We leased this house for six months, having just enough capital remaining to do that and to live properly here while our plans matured. Here we spent four months establishing ourselves, collecting our arms and our explosives, mapping our offensive, waiting for a favorable night. Last night seemed to be that night, and we had provided, we thought, against every eventuality. But we had not, of course, provided against your presence and your genius. They were simply others of the unforeseen misfortunes to which we seem eternally condemned."

She stopped, and fell to studying me with mournful large eyes that made me feel like fidgeting.

"It's no good calling me a genius," I objected. "The truth is you people botched your job from beginning to end. Your general would get a big laugh out of a man without any military training who tried to lead an army. But here are you people with absolutely no criminal experience trying to swing a trick that needed the highest sort of criminal skill. Look at how you all played around with me! Amateur stuff! A professional crook with any intelligence would have either let me alone or knocked me off. No wonder you flopped! As for the rest of it—your troubles—I can't do anything about them."

"Why?" very softly. "Why can't you?"

"Why should I?" I made it blunt.

"No one else knows what you know." She bent forward to put a white hand on my knee. "There is wealth in that cellar beneath the garage. You may have whatever you ask."

I shook my head.

"You aren't a fool!" she protested. "You know—"

"Let me straighten this out for you," I interrupted. "We'll disregard whatever honesty I happen to have, sense of loyalty to employers, and so on. You might doubt them, so we'll throw them out. Now I'm a detective because I happen to like the work. It pays me a fair salary, but I could find other jobs that would pay more. Even a hundred dollars more a month would be twelve hundred a year. Say twenty-five or thirty thousand dollars in the years between now and my sixtieth birthday.

"Now I pass up about twenty-five or thirty thousand of honest gain because I like being a detective, like the work. And liking work makes you want to do it as well as you can. Otherwise there'd be no sense to it. That's the fix I am in. I don't know anything else, don't enjoy anything else, don't want to know or enjoy anything else. You can't weigh that against any sum of money. Money is good stuff. I haven't anything against it. But in the past eighteen years I've been getting my fun out of chasing crooks and tackling puzzles, my satisfaction out of catching crooks and solving riddles. It's the only kind of sport I know anything about, and I can't imagine a pleasanter future than twenty-some years more of it. I'm not going to blow that up!"

She shook her head slowly, lowering it, so that now her dark eyes looked up at me under the thin arcs of her brows.

"You speak only of money," she said. "I said you may have whatever you ask."

That was out. I don't know where these women get their ideas.

"You're still all twisted up," I said brusquely, standing now and adjusting my borrowed crutch. "You think I'm a man and you're a woman. That's wrong. I'm a manhunter and you're something that has been running in front of me. There's nothing human about it. You might just as well expect a hound to play tiddly-winks with the fox he's caught. We're wasting time anyway. I've been thinking the police or Marines might come up here and save me a walk. You've been waiting for your mob to come back and grab me. I could have told you they were being arrested when I left them."

That shook her. She had stood up. Now she fell back a step, putting a hand behind her for steadiness, on her chair. An exclamation I didn't understand popped out of her mouth. Russian, I thought, but the next moment I knew it had been Italian.

"Put your hands up." It was Flippo's husky voice. Flippo stood in the doorway, holding an automatic.

I raised my hands as high as I could without dropping my supporting crutch, meanwhile cursing myself for having been too careless, or too vain, to keep a gun in my hand while I talked to the girl.

So this was why she had come back to the house. If she freed the Italian, she had thought, we would have no reason for suspecting that he hadn't been in on the robbery, and so we would look for the bandits among his friends. A prisoner, of course, he might have persuaded us of his innocence. She had given him the gun so he could either shoot his way clear, or, what would help her as much, get himself killed trying.

While I was arranging those thoughts in my head, Flippo had come up behind me. His empty hand passed over my body, taking away my own gun, his, and the one I had taken from the girl.

"A bargain, Flippo," I said when he had moved away from me, a little to one side, where he made one corner of a triangle whose other corners were the girl and I. "You're out on parole, with some years still to be served. I picked you up with a gun on you. That's plenty to send you back to the big house. I know you weren't in on this job. My idea is that you were up here on a smaller one of your own, but I can't prove that and don't want to. Walk out of here, alone and neutral, and I'll forget I saw you."

Little thoughtful lines grooved the boy's round, dark face.

The princess took a step toward him.

"You heard the offer I just now made him?" she asked. "Well, I make that offer to you, if you will kill him."

The thoughtful lines in the boy's face deepened.

"There's your choice, Flippo," I summed up for him. "All I can give you is freedom from San Quentin. The princess can give you a fat cut of the profits in a busted caper, with a good chance to get yourself hanged."

The girl, remembering her advantage over me, went at him hot and heavy in Italian, a language in which I know only four words. Two of them are profane and the other two obscene. I said all four.

The boy was weakening. If he had been ten years older, he'd have taken my offer and thanked me for it. But he was young and she—now that I thought of it—was beautiful. The answer wasn't hard to guess.

"But not to bump him off," he said to her in English, for my benefit. "We'll lock him up in there where I was at."

I suspected Flippo hadn't any prejudice against murder. It was just that he thought this one unnecessary, unless he was kidding me to make the killing easier.

The girl wasn't satisfied with his suggestion. She poured more hot Italian at him. Her game looked surefire, but it had a flaw. She couldn't persuade him that his chances of getting any of the loot away were good. She had to depend on her charms to swing him. And that meant she had to hold his eye.

He wasn't far from me.

She came close to him. She was singing, chanting, crooning Italian syllables into his round face.

She had him.

She shrugged. His whole face said yes. He turned—

I knocked him on the noodle with my borrowed crutch.

The crutch splintered apart. Flippo's knees bent. He stretched up to his full height. He fell on his face on the floor. He lay there, dead-still, except for a thin worm of blood that crawled out of his hair to the rug.

A step, a tumble, a foot or so of hand-and-knee scrambling put me within reach of Flippo's gun.

The girl, jumping out of my path, was halfway to the door when I sat up with the gun in my hand.

"Stop!" I ordered.

"I shan't," she said, but she did, for the time at least. "I am going out."

"You are going out when I take you out."

She laughed, a pleasant laugh, low and confident.

"I'm going out before that," she insisted good-naturedly. I shook my head.

"How do you propose stopping me?" she asked.

"I don't think I'll have to," I told her. "You've got too much sense to try to run while I'm holding a gun on you."

She laughed again, an amused ripple.

"I've got too much sense to stay," she corrected me. "Your crutch is broken, and you're lame. You can't catch me by running after me, then. You pretend you'll shoot me, but I don't believe you. You'd shoot me if I attacked you, of course, but I shan't do that. I shall simply walk out, and you know you won't shoot me for that. You'll wish you could, but you won't. You'll see."

Her face turned over her shoulder, her dark eyes twinkling at me, she took a step toward the door.

"Better not count on that!" I threatened.

For answer to that she gave me a cooing laugh. And took another step.

"Stop, you idiot!" I bawled at her.

Her face laughed over her shoulder at me. She walked without haste to the door, her short skirt of gray flannel shaping itself to the calf of each gray wool-stockinged leg as its mate stepped forward.

Sweat greased the gun in my hand.

When her right foot was on the doorsill, a little chuckling sound came from her throat.

"Adieu!" she said softly.

And I put the bullet in the calf of her left leg.

She sat down—plump! Utter surprise stretched her white face. It was too soon for pain.

I had never shot a woman before. I felt queer about it.

"You ought to have known I'd do it!" My voice sounded harsh and savage and like a stranger's in my ears. "Didn't I steal a crutch from a cripple?"

Pastorale

(1928)

James M. Cain

1

Well, it looks like Burbie is going to get hung. And if he
does, what he can lay it on is, he always figured he was so
damn smart.

You see, Burbie, he left town when he was about sixteen year
old. He run away with one of them travelling shows, "East
Lynne" I think it was, and he stayed away about ten years. And
when he come back he thought he knowed a lot. Burbie, he's got
them watery blue eyes what kind of stick out from his face, and
how he killed the time was to sit around and listen to the boys
talk down at the poolroom or over at the barber shop or a couple other places where he hung out, and then wink at you like
they was all making a fool of theirself or something and nobody
didn't know it but him.

But when you come right down to what Burbie had in his
head, why it wasn't much. 'Course, he generally always had a
job, painting around or maybe helping out on a new house, like
of that, but what he used to do was to play baseball with the high
school team. And they had a big fight over it, 'cause Burbie was
so old nobody wouldn't believe he went to the school, and them
other teams was all the time putting up a squawk. So then he
couldn't play no more. And another thing he liked to do was sing

at the entertainments. I reckon he liked that most of all, 'cause he claimed that a whole lot of the time he was away he was on the stage, and I reckon maybe he was at that, 'cause he was pretty good, 'specially when he dressed hisself up like a old-time Rube and come out and spoke a piece what he knowed.

Well, when he come back to town he seen Lida and it was a natural. 'Cause Lida, she was just about the same kind of a thing for a woman as Burbie was for a man. She used to work in the store, selling dry goods to the men, and kind of making hats on the side. 'Cepting only she didn't stay on the dry goods side no more'n she had to. She was generally over where the boys was drinking Coca-Cola, and all the time carrying on about did they like it with ammonia or lemon, and could she have a swallow outen their glass. And what she had her mind on was the clothes she had on, and was she dated up for Sunday night. Them clothes was pretty snappy, and she made them herself. And I heard some of them say she wasn't hard to date up, and after you done kept your date why maybe you wasn't going to be disappointed. And why Lida married the old man I don't know, lessen she got tired working at the store and tooken a look at the big farm where he lived at, about two mile from town.

By the time Burbie got back she'd been married about a year and she was about due. So her and him commence meeting each other, out in the orchard back of the old man's house. The old man would go to bed right after supper and then she'd sneak out and meet Burbie. And nobody wasn't supposed to know nothing about it. Only everybody did, 'cause Burbie, after he'd get back to town about eleven o'clock at night, he'd kind of slide into the poolroom and set down easy like. And then somebody'd say, "Yay, Burbie, where you been?" And Burbie, he'd kind of look around, and then he'd pick out somebody and wink at him, and that was how Burbie give it some good advertising.

So the way Burbie tells it, and he tells it plenty since he done got religion down to the jailhouse, it wasn't long before him and Lida thought it would be a good idea to kill the old man. They figured he didn't have long to live nohow, so he might as well go now as wait a couple of years. And another thing, the old man had kind of got hep that something was going on, and they figured if he throwed Lida out it wouldn't be no easy job to get his

money even if he died regular. And another thing, by that time
the Klux was kind of talking around, so Burbie figured it would
be better if him and Lida was to get married, else maybe he'd
have to leave town again.

So that was how he got Hutch in it. You see, he was afeared
to kill the old man hisself and he wanted some help. And then
he figured it would be pretty good if Lida wasn't nowheres
around and it would look like robbery. If it would of been me, I
would of left Hutch out of it. 'Cause Hutch, he was mean. He'd
been away for a while too, but him going away, that wasn't the
same as Burbie going away. Hutch was sent. He was sent for rip-
ping a mail sack while he was driving the mail wagon up from
the station, and before he come back he done two years down to
Atlanta.

But what I mean, he wasn't only crooked, he was mean. He
had a ugly look to him, like when he'd order hisself a couple of
fried eggs over to the restaurant, and then set and eat them with
his head humped down low and his arm curled around his plate
like he thought somebody going to steal it off him, and handle his knife with his thumb down near the tip, kind of like a nigger does a razor. Nobody didn't have much to say to Hutch, and
I reckon that's why he ain't heard nothing about Burbie and
Lida, and et it all up what Burbie told him about the old man
having a pot of money hid in the fireplace in the back room.

So one night early in March, Burbie and Hutch went out and
done the job. Burbie he'd already got Lida out of the way. She'd
let on she had to go to the city to buy some things, and she went
away on No. 6, so everybody knowed she was gone. Hutch, he
seen her go, and come running to Burbie saying now was a good
time, which was just what Burbie wanted. 'Cause her and
Burbie had already put the money in the pot, so Hutch wouldn't
think it was no put-up job. Well, anyway, they put $23 in the pot,
all changed into pennies and nickels and dimes so it would look
like a big pile, and that was all the money Burbie had. It was
kind of like you might say the savings of a lifetime.

And then Burbie and Hutch got in the horse and wagon what
Hutch had, 'cause Hutch was in the hauling business again, and
they went out to the old man's place. Only they went around the
back way, and tied the horse back of the house so nobody

couldn't see it from the road, and knocked on the back door and made out like they was just coming through the place on their way back to town and had stopped by to get warmed up, 'cause it was cold as hell. So the old man let them in and give them a drink of some hard cider what he had, and they got canned up a little more. They was already pretty canned, 'cause they both of them had a pint of corn on their hip for to give them some nerve.

And then Hutch he got back of the old man and crowned him with a wrench what he had hid in his coat.

2

Well, next off Hutch gets sore as hell at Burbie 'cause there ain't no more'n $23 in the pot. He didn't do nothing. He just set there, first looking at the money, what he had piled up on a table, and then looking at Burbie.

And then Burbie commences soft-soaping him. He says hope my die he thought there was a thousand dollars anyway in the pot, on account the old man being like he was. And he says hope my die it sure was a big surprise to him how little there was there. And he says hope my die it sure does make him feel bad, on account he's the one had the idea first. And he says hope my die it's all his fault and he's going to let Hutch keep all the money, damn if he ain't. He ain't going to take none of it for hisself at all, on account of how bad he feels. And Hutch, he don't say nothing at all, only look at Burbie and look at the money.

And right in the middle of while Burbie was talking, they heard a whole lot of hollering out in front of the house and somebody blowing a automobile horn. And Hutch jumps up and scoops the money and the wrench off the table in his pockets, and hides the pot back in the fireplace. And then he grabs the old man and him and Burbie carries him out the back door, hists him in the wagon, and drives off. And how they was to drive off without them people seeing them was because they come in the back way and that was the way they went. And them people in the automobile, they was a bunch of old folks from the Methodist church what knowed Lida was away and didn't think so much of Lida nohow and come out to say hello. And when they come in and didn't see nothing, they figured the old man had went in to town and so they went back.

Well, Hutch and Burbie was in a hell of a fix all right. 'Cause there they was, driving along somewheres with the old man in the wagon and they didn't have no more idea than a bald-headed coot where they was going or what they was going to do with him. So Burbie, he commence to whimper. But Hutch kept a-setting there, driving the horse, and he don't say nothing.

So pretty soon they come to a place where they was building a piece of country road, and it was all tore up and a whole lot of toolboxes laying out on the side. So Hutch gets out and twists the lock off one of them with the wrench, and takes out a pick and a shovel and throws them in the wagon. And then he got in again and drove on for a while till he come to the Whooping Nannie woods, what some of them says has got a ghost in it on dark nights, and it's about three miles from the old man's farm. And Hutch turns in there and pretty soon he come to a kind of a clear place and he stopped. And then, first thing he's said to Burbie, he says,

"Dig that grave!"

So Burbie dug the grave. He dug for two hours, until he got so damn tired he couldn't hardly stand up. But he ain't hardly made no hole at all. 'Cause the ground is froze and even with the pick he couldn't hardly make a dent in it scarcely. But any-how Hutch stopped him and they throwed the old man in and covered him up. But after they got him covered up his head was sticking out. So Hutch beat the head down good as he could and piled the dirt up around it and they got in and drove off.

After they went a little ways, Hutch commence to cuss Burbie. Then he said Burbie'd been lying to him. But Burbie, he swears he ain't lying. And then Hutch says he *was* lying and with that he hit Burbie. And after he knocked Burbie down in the bottom of the wagon he kicked him and then pretty soon Burbie up and told him about Lida. And when Burbie got done telling him about Lida, Hutch turned the horse around. Burbie asked then what they was going back for and Hutch says they're going back for to git a present for Lida. So they come back for to git a present for Lida. So they come back to the grave and

Hutch made Burbie cut off the old man's head with the shovel. It made Burbie sick, but Hutch made him stick at it, and after a while Burbie had it off. So Hutch throwed it in the wagon and they get in and start back to town once more.

Well, they wasn't no more'n out of the woods before Hutch takes hisself a slug of corn and commence to holler. He kind of raved to hisself, all about how he was going to make Burbie put the head in a box and tie it up with a string and take it out to Lida for a present, so she'd get a nice surprise when she opened it. Soon as Lida comes back he says Burbie has got to do it, and then he's going to kill Burbie. "I'll kill you!" he says. "I'll kill you, damn you! I'll kill you!" And he says it kind of singsongy, over and over again.

And then he takes hisself another slug of corn and stands up and whoops. Then he beat on the horse with the whip and the horse commence to run. What I mean, he commence to gallop. And then Hutch hit him some more. And then he commence to screech as loud as he could. "Ride him, cowboy!" he hollers. "Going East! Here come old broadcuff down the road! Whe-e-e-e-e!" And sure enough, here they come down the road, the horse a-running hell to split, and Hutch a-hollering, and Burbie a-shivering, and the head a-rolling around in the bottom of the wagon, and bouncing up in the air when they hit a bump, and Burbie damn near dying every time it hit his feet.

3

After a while the horse got tired so it wouldn't run no more, and they had to let him walk and Hutch set down and commence to grunt. So Burbie, he tries to figure out what the hell he's going to do with the head. And pretty soon he remembers a creek what they got to cross, what they ain't crossed on the way out 'cause they come the back way. So he figures he'll throw the head overboard when Hutch ain't looking. So he done it. They come to the creek, and on the way down to the bridge there's a little hill, and when the wagon tilted going down the hill the head rolled up between Burbie's feet, and he held it there, and when they got in the middle of the bridge he reached down and heaved it overboard.

Next off, Hutch give a yell and drop down in the bottom of the wagon. 'Cause what it sounded like was a pistol shot. You see, Burbie done forgot that it was a cold night and the creek done froze over. Not much, just a thin skim about a inch thick, but enough that when that head hit it it cracked pretty loud in different directions. And that was what scared Hutch. So when he got up and seen the head setting out there on the ice in the moonlight, and got it straight what Burbie done, he let on he was going to kill Burbie right there. And he reached for the pick. And Burbie jumped out and run, and he didn't never stop till he got home at the place where he lived at, and locked the door, and climbed in bed and pulled the covers over his head.

Well, the next morning a fellow come running into town and says there's hell to pay down at the bridge. So we all went down there and first thing we seen was that head laying out there on the ice, kind of rolled over on one ear. And next thing we seen was Hutch's horse and wagon tied to the bridge rail, and the horse damn near froze to death. And the next thing we seen was the hole in the ice where Hutch fell through. And the next thing we seen down on the bottom next to one of the bridge pilings, was Hutch.

So the first thing we went to work and done was to get the head. And believe me a head laying out on thin ice is a pretty damn hard thing to get, and what we had to do was to lasso it. And the next thing we done was to get Hutch. And after we fished him out he had the wrench and the $23 in his pockets and the pint of corn on his hip and he was stiff as a board. And near as I can figure out, what happened to him was that after Burbie run away he climbed down on the bridge piling and tried to reach the head and fell in.

But we didn't know nothing about it then, and after we done got the head and the old man was gone and a couple of boys that afternoon found the body and not the head on it, and the pot was found, and them old people from the Methodist church done told their story and one thing and another, we figured out that Hutch done it, 'specially on account he must of been drunk and he done time in the pen and all like of that, and nobody ain't thought nothing about Burbie at all. They had the funeral and Lida cried like hell and everybody tried to figure out what

Hutch wanted with the head and things went along thataway for three weeks.

Then one night down to the poolroom they was having it some more about the head, and one says one thing and one says another, and Benny Heath, what's a kind of a constable around town, he started a long bum argument about how Hutch must of figured if they couldn't find the head to the body they couldn't prove no murder. So right in the middle of it Burbie kind of looked around like he always done and then he winked. And Benny Heath, he kept on a-talking, and after he got done Burbie kind of leaned over and commence to talk to him. And in a couple of minutes you couldn't of heard a man catch his breath in that place, accounten they was all listening at Burbie.

I already told you Burbie was pretty good when it comes to giving a spiel at a entertainment. Well, this here was a kind of a spiel too. Burbie act like he had it all learned by heart. His voice trimmled and ever couple of minutes he'd kind of cry and wipe his eyes and make out like he can't say no more, and then he'd go on.

And the big idea was what a whole lot of hell he done raised in his life. Burbie said it was drink and women what done ruined him. He told about all the women what he knowed, and all the saloons he's been in, and some of it was a lie 'cause if all the saloons was as swell as he said they was they'd of throwed him out. And then he told about how sorry he was about the life he done led, and how hope my die he come home to his old home town just to get out the devilment and settle down. And he told about Lida, and how she wouldn't let him cut it out. And then he told how she done led him on till he got the idea to kill the old man. And then he told about how him and Hutch done it, and all about the money and the head and all the rest of it.

And what it sounded like was a piece what he knowed called "The Face on the Floor," what was about a bum what drawed a picture on the barroom floor of the woman what done ruined him. Only the funny part was that Burbie wasn't ashamed of hisself like he made out he was. You could see he was proud of hisself. He was proud of all them women and all the liquor he'd drunk and he was proud about Lida and he was proud about the

old man and the head and being slick enough not to fall in the
creek with Hutch. And after he got done he give a yelp and
flopped down on the floor and I reckon maybe he thought he
was going to die on the spot like the bum what drawed the face
on the barroom floor, only he didn't. He kind of lain there a couple of minutes till Benny got him up and put him in the car and
tooken him off to jail.

So that's where he's at now, and he's went to work and got religion down there, and all the people what comes to see him, why
he sings hymns to them and then he speaks them his piece. And
I hear tell he knows it pretty good by now and has got the crying down pat. And Lida, they got her down there too, only she
won't say nothing 'cepting she done it same as Hutch and
Burbie. So Burbie, he's going to get hung, sure as hell. And if he
hadn't felt so smart, he would of been a free man yet.

Only I reckon he done been holding it all so long he just had
to spill it.

I'll Be Waiting
(1939)
Raymond Chandler

At one o'clock in the morning, Carl, the night porter, turned down the last of three table lamps in the main lobby of the Windermere Hotel. The blue carpet darkened a shade or two and the walls drew back into remoteness. The chairs filled with shadowy loungers. In the corners were memories like cobwebs.

Tony Reseck yawned. He put his head on one side and listened to the frail, twittery music from the radio room beyond a dim arch at the far side of the lobby. He frowned. That should be his radio room after one A.M. Nobody should be in it. That red-haired girl was spoiling his nights.

The frown passed and a miniature of a smile quirked at the corners of his lips. He sat relaxed, a short, pale, paunchy, middle-aged man with long, delicate fingers clasped on the elk's tooth on his watch chain; the long delicate fingers of a sleight-of-hand artist, fingers with shiny, molded nails and tapering first joints, fingers a little spatulate at the ends. Handsome fingers. Tony Reseck rubbed them gently together and there was peace in his quiet sea-gray eyes.

The frown came back on his face. The music annoyed him. He got up with a curious litheness, all in one piece, without moving his clasped hands from the watch chain. At one moment he was leaning back relaxed, and the next he was standing bal-

242

anced on his feet, perfectly still, so that the movement of rising seemed to be a thing perfectly perceived, an error of vision. . . .

He walked with small, polished shoes delicately across the blue carpet and under the arch. The music was louder. It contained the hot, acid blare, the frenetic, jittering runs of a jam session. It was too loud. The red-haired girl sat there and stared silently at the fretted part of the big radio cabinet as though she could see the band with its fixed professional grin and the sweat running down its back. She was curled up with her feet under her on a davenport which seemed to contain most of the cushions in the room. She was tucked among them carefully, like a corsage in the florist's tissue paper.

She didn't turn her head. She leaned there, one hand in a small fist on her peach-colored knee. She was wearing lounging pajamas of heavy ribbed silk embroidered with black lotus buds.

"You like Goodman, Miss Cressy?" Tony Reseck asked.

The girl moved her eyes slowly. The light in there was dim, but the violet of her eyes almost hurt. They were large, deep eyes without a trace of thought in them. Her face was classical and without expression.

She said nothing.

Tony smiled and moved his fingers at his sides, one by one, feeling them move. "You like Goodman, Miss Cressy?" he repeated gently.

"Not to cry over," the girl said tonelessly.

Tony rocked back on his heels and looked at her eyes. Large, deep, empty eyes. Or were they? He reached down and muted the radio.

"Don't get me wrong," the girl said. "Goodman makes money, and a lad that makes legitimate money these days is a lad you have to respect. But this jitterbug music gives me the backdrop of a beer flat. I like something with roses in it."

"Maybe you like Mozart," Tony said.

"Go on, kid me," the girl said.

"I wasn't kidding you, Miss Cressy. I think Mozart was the greatest man that ever lived—and Toscanini is his prophet."

"I thought you were the house dick." She put her head back on a pillow and stared at him through her lashes.

"Make me some of that Mozart," she added.

"It's too late," Tony sighed. "You can't get it now."

She gave him another long lucid glance. "Got the eye on me, haven't you, flatfoot?" She laughed a little, almost under her breath. "What did I do wrong?"

Tony smiled his toy smile. "Nothing, Miss Cressy. Nothing at all. But you need some fresh air. You've been five days in this hotel and you haven't been outdoors. And you have a tower room."

She laughed again. "Make me a story about it. I'm bored."

"There was a girl here once had your suite. She stayed in the hotel a whole week, like you. Without going out at all, I mean. She didn't speak to anybody hardly. What do you think she did then?"

The girl eyed him gravely. "She jumped her bill."

He put his long delicate hand out and turned it slowly, fluttering the fingers, with an effect almost like a lazy wave breaking. "Unh-uh. She sent down for her bill and paid it. Then she told the hop to be back in half an hour for her suitcases. Then she went out on her balcony."

The girl leaned forward a little, her eyes still grave, one hand capping her peach-colored knee. "What did you say your name was?"

"Tony Reseck."

"Sounds like a hunky."

"Yeah," Tony said. "Polish."

"Go on, Tony."

"All the tower suites have private balconies, Miss Cressy. The walls of them are too low for fourteen stories above the street. It was a dark night, that night, high clouds." He dropped his hand with a final gesture, a farewell gesture. "Nobody saw her jump. But when she hit, it was like a big gun going off."

"You're making it up, Tony." Her voice was a clean dry whisper of sound.

He smiled his toy smile. His quiet sea-gray eyes seemed almost to be smoothing the long waves of her hair. "Eve Cressy," he said musingly. "A name waiting for lights to be in."

"Waiting for a tall dark guy that's no good, Tony. You wouldn't care why. I was married to him once. I might be married to him again. You can make a lot of mistakes in just one lifetime." The hand on her knee opened slowly until the fingers were strained back as far as they could go. Then they closed quickly and tightly, and even in that dim light the knuckles shone like the little polished bones. "I played him a low trick once. I put him in a bad place—without meaning to. You wouldn't care about that either. It's just that I owe him something."

He leaned over softly and turned the knob on the radio. A waltz formed itself dimly on the warm air. A tinsel waltz, but a waltz. He turned the volume up. The music gushed from the loudspeaker in a swirl of shadowed melody. Since Vienna died, all waltzes are shadowed.

The girl put her hand on one side and hummed three or four bars and stopped with a sudden tightening of her mouth.

"Eve Cressy," she said. "It was in lights once. At a bum night club. A dive. They raided it and the lights went out."

He smiled at her almost mockingly. "It was no dive while you were there, Miss Cressy . . . That's the waltz the orchestra always played when the old porter walked up and down in front of the hotel entrance, all swelled up with his medals on his chest. *The Last Laugh*. Emil Jannings. You wouldn't remember that one, Miss Cressy."

"'Spring, Beautiful Spring,'" she said. "No, I never saw it."

He walked three steps away from her and turned. "I have to go upstairs and palm doorknobs. I hope I didn't bother you. You ought to go to bed now. It's pretty late."

The tinsel waltz stopped and a voice began to talk. The girl spoke through the voice. "You really thought something like that—about the balcony?"

He nodded. "I might have," he said softly. "I don't any more."

"No chance, Tony." Her smile was a dim lost leaf. "Come and talk to me some more. Redheads don't jump, Tony. They hang on—and wither."

He looked at her gravely for a moment and then moved away over the carpet. The porter was standing in the archway that led to the main lobby. Tony hadn't looked that way yet, but he knew somebody was there. He always knew if anybody was close to him. He could hear the grass grow, like the donkey in *The Blue Bird*.

The porter jerked his chin at him urgently. His broad face above the uniform collar looked sweaty and excited. Tony stepped up close to him and they went together through the arch and out to the middle of the dim lobby.

"Trouble?" Tony asked wearily.

"There's a guy outside to see you, Tony. He won't come in. I'm doing a wipe-off on the plate glass of the doors and he comes up beside me, a tall guy. 'Get Tony,' he says, out of the side of his mouth."

Tony said: "Uh-huh," and looked at the porter's pale blue eyes. "Who was it?"

"Al, he said to say he was."

Tony's face became as expressionless as dough. "Okay." He started to move off.

The porter caught his sleeve. "Listen, Tony. You got any enemies?"

Tony laughed politely, his face still like dough.

"Listen, Tony." The porter held his sleeve tightly. "There's a big black car down the block, the other way from the hacks. There's a guy standing beside it with his foot on the running board. This guy that spoke to me, he wears a dark-colored, wrap-around overcoat with a high collar turned up against his ears. His hat's way low. You can't hardly see his face. He says, 'Get Tony,' out of the side of his mouth. You ain't got any enemies, have you, Tony?"

"Only the finance company," Tony said. "Beat it."

He walked slowly and a little stiffly across the blue carpet, up the three shallow steps to the entrance lobby with the three elevators on one side and the desk on the other. Only one elevator was working. Beside the open doors, his arms folded, the night operator stood silent in a neat blue uniform with silver facings. A lean, dark Mexican named Gomez. A new boy, breaking in on the night shift.

The other side was the desk, rose marble, with the night clerk leaning on it delicately. A small neat man with a wispy reddish mustache and cheeks so rosy they looked rouged. He stared at Tony and poked a nail at his mustache.

Tony pointed a stiff index finger at him, folded the other

three fingers tight to his palm, and flicked his thumb up and down on the stiff finger. The clerk touched the other side of his mustache and looked bored.

Tony went on past the closed and darkened newsstand and the side entrance to the drugstore, out to the brassbound plate-glass doors. He stopped just inside them and took a deep, hard breath. He squared his shoulders, pushed the doors open and stepped out into the cold damp night air.

The street was dark, silent. The rumble of traffic on Wilshire, two blocks away, had no body, no meaning. To the left were two taxis. Their drivers leaned against a fender, side by side, smoking. Tony walked the other way. The big dark car was a third of a block from the hotel entrance. Its lights were dimmed and it was only when he was almost up to it that he heard the gentle sound of its engine turning over.

A tall figure detached itself from the body of the car and strolled toward him, both hands in the pockets of the dark overcoat with the high collar. From the man's mouth a cigarette tip glowed faintly, a rusty pearl.

They stopped two feet from each other.

The tall man said, "Hi, Tony. Long time no see."

"Hello, Al. How's it going?"

"Can't complain." The tall man started to take his right hand out of his overcoat pocket, then stopped and laughed quietly. "I forgot. Guess you don't want to shake hands."

"That don't mean anything," Tony said. "Shaking hands. Monkeys can shake hands. What's on your mind, Al?"

"Still the funny little fat guy, eh, Tony?"

"I guess." Tony winked his eyes tight. His throat felt tight.

"You like your job back there?"

"It's a job."

Al laughed his quiet laugh again. "You take it slow, Tony. I'll take it fast. So it's a job and you want to hold it. Okay. There's a girl named Eve Cressy flopping in your quiet hotel. Get her out. Fast and right now."

"What's the trouble?"

The tall man looked up and down the street. A man behind in the car coughed lightly. "She's hooked with a wrong number.

Nothing against her personal, but she'll lead trouble to you. Get her out, Tony. You got maybe an hour."

"Sure," Tony said aimlessly, without meaning.

Al took his hand out of his pocket and stretched it against Tony's chest. He gave him a light lazy push. "I wouldn't be telling you just for the hell of it, little fat brother. Get her out of there."

"Okay," Tony said, without any tone in his voice.

The tall man took back his hand and reached for the car door. He opened it and started to slip in like a lean black shadow.

Then he stopped and said something to the men in the car and got out again. He came back to where Tony stood silent, his pale eyes catching a little dim light from the street.

"Listen, Tony. You always kept your nose clean. You're a good brother, Tony."

Tony didn't speak.

Al leaned toward him, a long urgent shadow, the high collar almost touching his ears. "It's trouble business, Tony. The boys won't like it, but I'm telling you just the same. This Cressy was married to a lad named Johnny Ralls. Ralls is out of Quentin two, three days, or a week. He did a three-spot for manslaughter. The girl put him there. He ran down an old man one night when he was drunk, and she was with him. He wouldn't stop. She told him to go in and tell it, or else. He didn't go in. So the Johns come for him."

Tony said, "That's too bad."

"It's kosher, kid. It's my business to know. This Ralls flapped his mouth in stir about how the girl would be waiting for him when he got out, all set to forgive and forget, and he was going straight to her."

Tony said, "What's he to you?" His voice had a dry, stiff crackle, like thick paper.

Al laughed. "The trouble boys want to see him. He ran a table at a spot on the Strip and figured out a scheme. He and another guy took the house for fifty grand. The other lad coughed up, but we still need Johnny's twenty-five. The trouble boys don't get paid to forget."

Tony looked up and down the dark street. One of the taxi

drivers flicked a cigarette stub in a long arc over the top of one of the cabs. Tony watched it fall and spark on the pavement. He listened to the quiet sound of the big car's motor.

"I don't want any part of it," he said. "I'll get her out."

Al backed away from him, nodding. "Wise kid. How's mom these days?"

"Okay," Tony said.

"Tell her I was asking for her."

"Asking for her isn't anything," Tony said.

Al turned quickly and got into the car. The car curved lazily in the middle of the block and drifted back toward the corner. Its lights went up and sprayed on a wall. It turned a corner and was gone. The lingering smell of its exhaust drifted past Tony's nose. He turned and walked back to the hotel and into it. He went along to the radio room.

The radio still muttered, but the girl was gone from the davenport in front of it. The pressed cushions were hollowed out by her body. Tony reached down and touched them. He thought they were still warm. He turned the radio off and stood there, turning a thumb slowly in front of his body, his hand flat against his stomach. Then he went back through the lobby toward the elevator bank and stood beside a majolica jar of white sand. The clerk fussed behind a pebbled-glass screen at one end of the desk. The air was dead.

The elevator bank was dark. Tony looked at the indicator of the middle car and saw that it was at 14.

"Gone to bed," he said under his breath.

The door of the porter's room beside the elevators opened and the little Mexican night operator came out in street clothes. He looked at Tony with a quiet sidewise look out of eyes the color of dried-out chestnuts.

"Good night, boss."

"Yeah," Tony said absently.

He took a thin dappled cigar out of his vest pocket and smelled it. He examined it slowly, turning it around in his neat fingers. There was a small tear along the side. He frowned at that and put the cigar away.

There was a distant sound and the hand on the indicator began to steal around the bronze dial. Light glittered up in the shaft and the straight line of the car floor dissolved the darkness below. The car stopped and the doors opened, and Carl came out of it.

His eyes caught Tony's with a kind of jump and he walked over to him, his head on one side, a thin shine along his pink upper lip.

"Listen, Tony."

Tony took his arm in a hard swift hand and turned him. He pushed him quickly, yet somehow casually, down the steps to the dim main lobby and steered him into a corner. He let go of the arm. His throat tightened again, for no reason he could think of.

"Well?" he said darkly. "Listen to what?"

The porter reached into a pocket and hauled out a dollar bill. "He gimme this," he said loosely. His glittering eyes looked past Tony's shoulder at nothing. They winked rapidly. "Ice and ginger ale."

"Don't stall," Tony growled.

"Guy in Fourteen-B," the porter said.

"Lemme smell your breath."

The porter leaned toward him obediently.

"Liquor," Tony said harshly.

"He gimme a drink."

Tony looked down at the dollar bill. "Nobody's in Fourteen-B. Not on my list," he said.

"Yeah. There is." The porter licked his lips and his eyes opened and shut several times. "Tall dark guy."

"All right," Tony said crossly. "All right. There's a tall dark guy in Fourteen-B and he gave you a buck and a drink. Then what?"

"Gat under his arm," Carl said, and blinked.

Tony smiled, but his eyes had taken on the lifeless glitter of thick ice. "You take Miss Cressy up to her room?"

Carl shook his head. "Gomez. I saw her go up."

"Get away from me," Tony said between his teeth. "And don't accept any more drinks from the guests."

He didn't move until Carl had gone back into his cubby-hole by the elevators and shut the door. Then he moved silently up the three steps and stood in front of the desk, looking at the veined rose marble, the onyx pen set, the fresh registration card in its leather frame. He lifted a hand and smacked it down hard on the marble. The clerk popped out from behind the glass screen like a chipmunk coming out of its hole.

Tony took a flimsy out of his breast pocket and spread it on the desk. "No Fourteen-B on this," he said in a bitter voice.

The clerk wisped politely at his mustache. "So sorry. You must have been out to supper when he checked in."

"Who?"

"Registered as James Watterson, San Diego." The clerk yawned.

"Ask for anybody?"

The clerk stopped in the middle of the yawn and looked at the top of Tony's head. "Why yes. He asked for a swing band. Why?"

"Smart, fast and funny," Tony said. "If you like 'em that way." He wrote on his flimsy and stuffed it back into his pocket. "I'm going upstairs and palm doorknobs. There's four tower rooms you ain't rented yet. Get up on your toes, son. You're slipping."

"I made out," the clerk drawled, and completed his yawn. "Hurry back, pop. I don't know how I'll get through the time."

"You could shave that pink fuzz off your lip," Tony said, and went across to the elevators.

He opened up a dark one and lit the dome light and shot the car up to fourteen. He darkened it again, stepped out and closed the doors. This lobby was smaller than any other, except the one immediately below it. It had a single blue-paneled door in each of the walls other than the elevator wall. On each door was a gold number and letter with a gold wreath around it. Tony walked over to 14A and put his ear to the panel. He heard nothing. Eve Cressy might be in bed asleep, or in the bathroom, or out on the balcony. Or she might be sitting there in the room, a few feet from the door, looking at the wall. Well, he wouldn't expect to be able to hear her sit and look at the wall. He went over to 14B and put his ear to that panel. This was different. There was a sound in there. A man coughed. It sounded like a solitary cough. There were no voices. Tony pressed the small nacre button beside the door.

Steps came without hurry. A thickened voice spoke through the panel. Tony made no answer, no sound. The thickened voice repeated the question. Lightly, maliciously, Tony pressed the bell again.

Mr. James Watterson, of San Diego, should now open the door and give forth noise. He didn't. A silence fell beyond that door that was like the silence of a glacier. Once more Tony put his ear to the wood. Silence utterly.

He got out a master key on a chain and pushed it delicately into the lock of the door. He turned it, pushed the door inward three inches and withdrew the key. Then he waited.

"All right," the voice said harshly. "Come in and get it."

Tony pushed the door wide and stood there, framed against the light from the lobby. The man was tall, black-haired, angular and white-faced. He held a gun. He held it as though he knew about guns.

"Step right in," he drawled.

Tony went in through the door and pushed it shut with his shoulder. He kept his hands a little out from his sides, the clever fingers curled and slacked. He smiled his quiet little smile.

"Mr. Watterson?"

"And after that what?"

"I'm the house detective here."

"It slays me."

The tall, white-faced, somehow handsome and somehow not handsome man backed slowly into the room. It was a large room with a low balcony around two sides of it. French doors opened out on the little private open-air balcony that each of the tower rooms had. There was a grate set for a log fire behind a paneled screen in front of a cheerful davenport. A tall misted glass stood on a hotel tray beside a deep, cozy chair. The man backed toward this and stood in front of it. The large, glistening gun drooped and pointed at the floor.

"It slays me," he said. "I'm in the dump an hour and the house copper gives me the bus. Okay, sweetheart, look in the closet and bathroom. But she just left."

"You didn't see her yet," Tony said.

The man's bleached face filled with unexpected lines. His thickened voice edged toward a snarl. "Yeah? Who didn't I see yet?"

"A girl named Eve Cressy."

The man swallowed. He put his gun down on the table beside the tray. He let himself down into the chair backwards, stiffly, like a man with a touch of lumbago. Then he leaned forward and put his hands on his kneecaps and smiled brightly between his teeth. "So she got here, huh? I didn't ask about her yet. I'm a careful guy. I didn't ask yet."

"She's been here five days," Tony said. "Waiting for you. She hasn't left the hotel a minute."

The man's mouth worked a little. His smile had a knowing tilt to it. "I got delayed a little up north," he said smoothly. "You know how it is. Visiting old friends. You seem to know a lot about my business, copper."

"That's right, Mr. Ralls."

The man lunged to his feet and his hand snapped at the gun. He stood leaning over, holding it on the table, staring. "Dames talk too much," he said with a muffled sound in his voice as though he held something soft between his teeth and talked through it.

"Not dames, Mr. Ralls."

"Huh?" The gun slithered on the hard wood of the table. "Talk it up, copper. My mind reader just quit."

"Not dames, guys. Guys with guns."

The glacier silence fell between them again. The man straightened his body out slowly. His face was washed clean of expression, but his eyes were haunted. Tony leaned in front of him, a shortish plump man with a quiet, pale, friendly face and eyes as simple as forest water.

"They never run out of gas—those boys," Johnny Ralls said, and licked at his lip. "Early and late, they work. The old firm never sleeps."

"You know who they are?" Tony said softly.

"I could maybe give nine guesses. And twelve of them would be right."

"The trouble boys," Tony said, and smiled a brittle smile.

"Where is she?" Johnny Ralls asked harshly.

"Right next door to you."

The man walked to the wall and left his gun lying on the

table. He stood in front of the wall, studying it. He reached up and gripped the grillwork of the balcony railing. When he dropped his hand and turned, his face had lost some of its lines. His eyes had a quieter glint. He moved back to Tony and stood over him.

"I've got a stake," he said. "Eve sent me some dough and I built it up with a touch I made up north. Case dough, what I mean. The trouble boys talk about twenty-five grand." He smiled crookedly. "Five C's I can count. I'd have a lot of fun making them believe that, I would."

"What did you do with it?" Tony asked indifferently.

"I never had it, copper. Leave that lay. I'm the only guy in the world that believes it. It was a little deal that I got suckered on."

"I'll believe it," Tony said.

"They don't kill often. But they can be awful tough."

"Mugs," Tony said with a sudden bitter contempt. "Guys with guns. Just mugs."

Johnny Ralls reached for his glass and drained it empty. The ice cubes tinkled softly as he put it down. He picked his gun up, danced it on his palm, then tucked it, nose down, into an inner breast pocket. He stared at the carpet.

"How come you're telling me this, copper?"

"I thought maybe you'd give her a break."

"And if I wouldn't?"

"I kind of think you will," Tony said.

Johnny Ralls nodded quietly. "Can I get out of here?"

"You could take the service elevator to the garage. You could rent a car. I can give you a card to the garage man."

"You're a funny little guy," Johnny Ralls said.

Tony took out a worn ostrich-skin billfold and scribbled on a printed card. Johnny Ralls read it, and stood holding it, tapping it against a thumbnail.

"I could take her with me," he said, his eyes narrow.

"You could take a ride in a basket too," Tony said. "She's been here five days, I told you. She's been spotted. A guy I know called me up and told me to get her out of here. Told me what it was all about. So I'm getting you out instead."

"They'll love that," Johnny Ralls said. "They'll send you violets."

"I'll weep about it on my day off."

Johnny Ralls turned his hand over and stared at the palm. "I could see her, anyway. Before I blow. Next door to here, you said?"

Tony turned on his heel and started for the door. He said over his shoulder, "Don't waste a lot of time, handsome. I might change my mind."

The man said, almost gently: "You might be spotting me right now, for all I know."

Tony didn't turn his head. "That's a chance you have to take."

He went on to the door and passed out of the room. He shut it carefully, silently, looked once at the door of 14A and got into his dark elevator. He rode it down to the linen-room floor and got out to remove the basket that held the service elevator open on that floor. The door slid quietly shut. He held it so that it made no noise. Down the corridor, light came from the open door of the housekeeper's office. Tony got back into his elevator and went on down to the lobby.

The little clerk was out of sight behind his pebble-glass screen, auditing accounts. Tony went through the main lobby and turned into the radio room. The radio was on again, soft. She was there, curled on the davenport again. The speaker hummed to her, a vague sound so low that what it said was as wordless as the murmur of trees. She turned her head slowly and smiled at him.

"Finished palming doorknobs? I couldn't sleep worth a nickel. So I came down again. Okay?"

He smiled and nodded. He sat down in a green chair and patted the plump brocade arms of it. "Sure, Miss Cressy."

"Waiting is the hardest kind of work, isn't it? I wish you'd talk to that radio. It sounds like a pretzel being bent."

Tony fiddled with it, got nothing he liked, set it back where it had been.

"Beer-parlor drunks are all the customers now."

She smiled at him again.

"I don't bother you being here, Miss Cressy?"

"I like it. You're a sweet little guy, Tony."

He looked stiffly at the floor and a ripple touched his spine.

He waited for it to go away. It went slowly. Then he sat back, relaxed again, his neat fingers clasped on his elk's tooth. He listened. Not to the radio—to far-off, uncertain things, menacing things. And perhaps to just the safe whir of wheels going away into a strange night.

"Nobody's all bad," he said out loud.

The girl looked at him lazily. "I've met two or three I was wrong on, then."

He nodded. "Yeah," he admitted judiciously. "I guess there's some that are."

The girl yawned and her deep violet eyes half closed. She nestled back into the cushions. "Sit there for a while, Tony. Maybe I could nap."

"Sure. Not a thing for me to do. Don't know why they pay me."

She slept quickly and with complete stillness, like a child. Tony hardly breathed for ten minutes. He just watched her, his mouth a little open. There was a quiet fascination in his limpid eyes, as if he was looking at an altar.

Then he stood up with infinite care and padded away under the arch to the entrance lobby and the desk. He stood at the desk listening for a little while. He heard a pen rustling out of sight. He went around the corner to the row of house phones in little glass cubbyholes. He lifted one and asked the night operator for the garage.

It rang three or four times and then a boyish voice answered: "Windermere Hotel. Garage speaking."

"This is Tony Reseck. That guy Watterson I gave a card to. He leave?"

"Sure, Tony. Half an hour almost. Is it your charge?"

"Yeah," Tony said. "My party. Thanks. Be seein' you."

He hung up and scratched his neck. He went back to the desk and slapped a hand on it. The clerk wafted himself around the screen with his greeter's smile in place. It dropped when he saw Tony.

"Can't a guy catch up on his work?" he grumbled.

"What's the professional rate on Fourteen-B?"

The clerk stared morosely. "There's no professional rate in the tower."

"Make one. The fellow left already. Was there only an hour."

"Well, well," the clerk said airily. "So the personality didn't click tonight. We get a skip-out."

"Will five bucks satisfy you?"

"Friend of yours?"

"No. Just a drunk with delusions of grandeur and no dough."

"Guess we'll have to let it ride, Tony. How did he get out?"

"I took him down the service elevator. You was asleep. Will five bucks satisfy you?"

"Why?"

The worn ostrich-skin wallet came out and a weedy five slipped across the marble. "All I could shake him for," Tony said loosely.

The clerk took the five and looked puzzled. "You're the boss," he said, and shrugged. The phone shrilled on the desk and he reached for it. He listened and then pushed it toward Tony. "For you."

Tony took the phone and cuddled it close to his chest. He put his mouth close to the transmitter. The voice was strange to him. It had a metallic sound. Its syllables meticulously anonymous.

"Tony? Tony Reseck?"

"Talking."

"A message from Al. Shoot?"

Tony looked at the clerk. "Be a pal," he said over the mouth-piece. The clerk flicked a narrow smile at him and went away. "Shoot," Tony said into the phone.

"We had a little business with a guy in your place. Picked him up scramming. Al had a hunch you'd run him out. Tailed him and took him to the curb. Not so good. Backfire."

Tony held the phone very tight and his temples chilled with the evaporation of moisture. "Go on," he said. "I guess there's more."

"A little. The guy stopped the big one. Cold. Al—Al said to tell you goodbye."

Tony leaned hard against the desk. His mouth made a sound that was not speech.

"Get it?" The metallic voice sounded impatient, a little bored. "This guy had him a rod. He used it. Al won't be phoning anybody any more."

Tony lurched at the phone, and the base of it shook on the rose marble. His mouth was a hard dry knot.

The voice said: "That's as far as we go, bub. G'night." The phone clicked dryly, like a pebble hitting a wall.

Tony put the phone down in its cradle very carefully, so as not to make any sound. He looked at the clenched palm of his left hand. He took a handkerchief out and rubbed the palm softly and straightened the fingers out with his other hand. Then he wiped his forehead. The clerk came around the screen again and looked at him with glinting eyes.

"I'm off Friday. How about lending me that phone number?"

Tony nodded at the clerk and smiled a minute frail smile. He put his handkerchief away and patted the pocket he had put it in. He turned and walked away from the desk, across the entrance lobby, down the three shallow steps, along the shadowy reaches of the main lobby, and so in through the arch to the radio room once more. He walked softly, like a man moving in a room where somebody is very sick. He reached the chair he had sat in before and lowered himself into it inch by inch. The girl slept on, motionless, in that curled-up looseness achieved by some women and all cats. Her breath made no slightest sound against the vague murmur of the radio.

Tony Reseck leaned back in the chair and clasped his hands on his elk's tooth and quietly closed his eyes.

Slowly, Slowly in the Wind
(1972)
Patricia Highsmith

E dward (Skip) Skipperton spent most of his life in a thunderous rage. It was his nature. He had been full of temper as a boy, and as a man impatient with people's slowness or stupidity or inefficiency. Now Skipperton was fifty-two. His wife had left him two years ago, unable to stand his tantrums any longer. She had met a most tranquil university professor from Boston, had divorced Skipperton on the grounds of incompatibility, and married the professor. Skipperton had been determined to get custody of their daughter, Margaret, then fifteen, and with clever lawyers and on the grounds that his wife had deserted him for another man, Skipperton had succeeded. A few months after the divorce, Skipperton had a heart attack, a real stroke with hemi-paralysis from which he miraculously recovered in six months, but his doctors gave him warning.

"Skip, it's life or death. You quite smoking and drinking and right now, or you're a dead man before your next birthday." That was from his heart specialist.

"You owe it to Margaret," said his GP. "You ought to retire, Skip. You've plenty of money. You're in the wrong profession for your nature—granted you've made a success of it. But what's left of your life is more important, isn't it? Why not become a gentleman farmer, something like that?"

Skipperton was a magnificent adviser. Behind the scenes of

big business, Skipperton was well known. He worked freelance. Companies on the brink sent for him to reorganize, reform, throw out—anything Skip advised went. "I go in and kick the ass off 'em!" was the inelegant way Skip described his work when he was interviewed, which was not often, because he preferred a ghostly role.

Skipperton bought Coldstream Heights in Maine, a seven-acre farm with a modernized farmhouse, and hired a local man called Andy Humbert to live and work on the place. Skipperton also bought some of the machinery the former owner had to sell, but not all of it, because he didn't want to turn himself into a full-time farmer. The doctors had recommended a little exercise and no strain of any kind. They had known that Skip wouldn't and couldn't at once cut all his connections with the businesses he had helped in the past. He might have to make an occasional trip to Chicago or Dallas, but he was officially retired.

Margaret was transferred from her private school in New York to a Swiss boarding school. Skipperton knew and liked Switzerland, and had bank accounts there.

Skipperton did stop drinking and smoking. His doctors were amazed at his willpower—and yet it was just like Skip to stop overnight, like a soldier. Now Skip chewed his pipes, and went through a stem in a week. He went through two lower teeth, but got them capped in steel in Bangor. Skipperton and Andy kept a couple of goats to crop the grass, and one sow who was pregnant when Skip bought her, and who now had twelve piglets. Margaret wrote filial letters saying she liked Switzerland and that her French was improving no end. Skipperton now wore flannel shirts with no tie, low boots that laced, and woodsmen's jackets. His appetite had improved, and he had to admit he felt better.

The only thorn in his side—and Skipperton had to have one to feel normal—was the man who owned some adjacent land, one Peter Frosby, who wouldn't sell a stretch Skipperton offered to buy at three times the normal price. This land sloped down to a little river called the Coldstream, which in fact separated part of Skipperton's property from Frosby's to the north, and Skipperton didn't mind that. He was interested in the part of the river nearest him and in view from Coldstream Heights. Skipperton wanted to be able to fish a little, to be able to say he owned that part of the landscape and had riparian rights. But old Frosby didn't want anybody fishing in his stream, Skipperton had been told by the agents, even though Frosby's house was upstream and out of sight of Skipperton's.

The week after Peter Frosby's rejection, Skipperton invited Frosby to his house. "Just to get acquainted—as neighbors," Skipperton said on the telephone to Frosby. By now Skipperton had been living at Coldstream Heights for four months.

Skipperton had his best whiskey and brandy, cigars and cigarettes—all the things he couldn't enjoy himself—on hand when Frosby arrived in a dusty but new Cadillac, driven by a young man whom Frosby introduced as his son, Peter.

"The Frosbys don't sell their land," Frosby told Skipperton. "We've had the same land for nearly three hundred years, and the river's always been ours." Frosby, a skinny but strong-looking man with cold gray eyes puffed his cigar daintily and after ten minutes hadn't finished his first whiskey. "Can't see why you want it."

"A little fishing," Skipperton said, putting on a pleasant smile. "It's in view of my house. Just to be able to wade, maybe, in the summer." Skipperton looked at Peter Junior, who sat with folded arms beside and behind his father. Skipperton was backed only by shambly Andy, a good enough handyman, but not part of his dynasty. Skipperton would have given anything (except his life) to have been holding a straight whiskey in one hand and a good cigar in the other. "Well, I'm sorry," Skipperton said finally. "But I think you'll agree the price I offer isn't bad— twenty thousand cash for about two hundred yards of riparian rights. Doubt if you'll get it again—in your lifetime."

"Not interested in my lifetime," Frosby said with a faint smile. "I've got a son here."

The son was a handsome boy with dark hair and sturdy shoulders, taller than his father. His arms were still folded across his chest, as if to illustrate his father's negative attitude. He had unbent only briefly to light a cigarette which he had soon put out. Still, Peter Junior smiled as he and his father were leaving, and said:

"Nice job you've done with the Heights, Mr. Skipperton. Looks better than it did before."

"Thank you," Skip said, pleased. He had installed good leather-upholstered furniture, heavy floor-length curtains, and brass fire-dogs and tongs for the fireplace.

"Nice old-fashioned touches," Frosby commented in what seemed to Skipperton a balance between compliment and sneer. "We haven't seen a scarecrow around here in maybe—almost before my time, I think."

"I like old-fashioned things—like fishing," Skipperton said. "I'm trying to grow corn out there. Somebody told me the land was all right for corn. That's where a scarecrow belongs, isn't it? In a cornfield?" He put on as friendly a manner as he could, but his blood was boiling. A mule-stubborn Maine man, Frosby, sitting on several hundred acres that his more forceful ancestors had acquired for him.

Frosby Junior was peering at a photograph of Maggie, which stood in a silver frame on the hall table. She had been only thirteen or fourteen when the picture had been taken, but her slender face framed in long dark hair showed the clean-cut nose and brows, the subtle smile that would turn her into a beauty one day. Maggie was nearly eighteen now, and Skip's expectations were being confirmed.

"Pretty girl," said Frosby Junior, turning towards Skipperton, then glancing at his father, because they were all lingering in the hall.

Skipperton said nothing. The meeting had been a failure. Skipperton wasn't used to failures. He looked into Frosby's greenish-gray eyes and said, "I've one more idea. Suppose we make an arrangement that I rent the land for the duration of my life, and then it goes to you—or your son. I'll give you five thousand a year. Want to think it over?"

Frosby put on another frosty smile. "I think not, Mr. Skipperton. Thanks anyway."

"You might talk to your lawyer about it. No rush on my part."

Frosby now chuckled. "We know as much about law as the lawyers here. We know our boundaries anyway. Nice to meet you, Mr. Skipperton. Thank you for the whiskey and—good-bye."

No one shook hands. The Cadillac moved off.

"Damn the bastard," Skipperton muttered to Andy, but he smiled. Life was a game, after all. You won sometimes, you lost sometimes.

It was early May. The corn was in, and Skipperton had spotted three or four strong green shoots coming through the beige, well-turned earth. That pleased him, made him think of American Indians, the ancient Mayans. Corn! And he had a classic scarecrow that he and Andy had knocked together a couple of weeks ago. They had dressed the crossbars in an old jacket, and the two sticks—nailed to the upright—in brown trousers. Skip had found the old clothes in the attic. A straw hat jammed onto the top and secured with a nail completed the picture.

Skip went off to San Francisco for a five-day operation on an aeronautics firm which was crippled by a lawsuit, scared to death by unions and contract pull-outs. Skip left them with more redundancies, three vice-presidents fired, but he left them in better shape, and collected fifty thousand for his work.

By way of celebrating his achievement and the oncoming summer that would bring Maggie, Skip shot one of Frosby's hunting dogs which had swum the stream onto his property to retrieve a bird. Skipperton had been waiting patiently at his bedroom window upstairs, knowing a shoot was on from the sound of guns. Skip had his binoculars and a rifle of goodly range. Let Frosby complain! Trespassing was trespassing.

Skip was almost pleased when Frosby took him to court over the dog. Andy had buried the dog, on Skipperton's orders, but Skipperton readily admitted the shooting. And the judge ruled in Skipperton's favor.

Frosby went pale with anger. "It may be the law but it's not human. It's not fair."

And a lot of good it did Frosby to say that!

Skipperton's corn grew high as the scarecrow's hips, and higher. Skip spent a lot of time up in his bedroom, binoculars and loaded rifle at hand, in case anything else belonging to Frosby showed itself on his land.

"Don't hit me," Andy said with an uneasy laugh. "You're shooting on the edge of the cornfield there, and now and then I weed it, y'know."

"You think there's something wrong with my eyesight?" Skip replied.

A few days later Skip proved there was nothing wrong with his eyesight, when he plugged a gray cat stalking a bird or a mouse in the high grass this side of the stream. Skip did it with one shot. He wasn't even sure the cat belonged to Frosby.

This shot produced a call in person from Frosby Junior the following day.

"It's just to ask a question, Mr. Skipperton. My father and I heard a shot yesterday, and last night one of our cats didn't come back at night to eat, and not this morning either. Do you know anything about that?" Frosby Junior had declined to take a seat.

"I shot the cat. It was on my property," Skipperton said calmly.

"But the cat—What harm was the cat doing?" The young man looked steadily at Skipperton.

"The law is the law. Property is property."

Frosby Junior shook his head. "You're a hard man, Mr. Skipperton." Then he departed.

Peter Frosby served a summons again, and the same judge ruled that in accordance with old English law and also American law, a cat was a rover by nature, not subject to constraint as was a dog. He gave Skipperton the maximum fine of one hundred dollars, and a warning not to use his rifle so freely in future.

That annoyed Skipperton, though of course he could and did laugh at the smallness of the fine. If he could think of something else annoying, something really *telling*, old Frosby might relent and at least lease some of the stream, Skip thought.

But he forgot the feud when Margaret came. Skip fetched her at the airport in New York, and they drove up to Maine. She looked taller to Skip, more filled out, and there were roses in her cheeks. She was a beauty, all right!

"Got a surprise for you at home," Skip said.

"Um-m—a horse maybe? I told you I learned to jump this year, didn't I?"

Had she? Skip said, "Yes. Not a horse, no."

Skip's surprise was a red Toyota convertible. He had remembered at least that Maggie's school had taught her to drive. She was thrilled, and flung her arms around Skip's neck.

"You're a darling, Daddy! And you know, you're looking *very* fell!"

Margaret had been to Coldstream Heights for two weeks at Easter, but now the place looked more cared for. She and Skip had arrived around midnight, but Andy was still up watching television in his own little house on the grounds, and Maggie insisted on going over to greet him. Skip was gratified to see Andy's eyes widen at the sight of her.

Skip and Maggie tried out the new car the next day. They drove to a town some twenty miles away and had lunch. That afternoon, back at the house, Maggie asked if her father had a fishing rod, just a simple one, so she could try the stream. Skip of course had all kinds of rods, but he had to tell her she couldn't, and he explained why, and explained that he had even tried to rent part of the stream.

"Frosby's a real s.o.b.," Skip said. "Won't give an inch."

"Well, never mind, Daddy. There's lots else to do."

Maggie was the kind of girl who enjoyed taking walks, reading or fussing around in the house rearranging little things so that they looked prettier. She did these things while Skip was on the telephone sometimes for an hour or so with Dallas or Detroit.

Skipperton was a bit surprised one day when Maggie arrived in her Toyota around 7 P.M. with a catch of three trout on a string. She was barefoot, and the cuffs of her blue dungarees were damp. "Where'd you get those?" Skip asked, his first thought being that she'd taken one of his rods and fished the stream against his instructions.

"I met the boy who lives there," Maggie said. "We were both buying gas, and he introduced himself—said he'd seen my photograph in your house. Then we had a coffee in the diner there by the gas station—"

"The Frosby boy?"

"Yes. He's awfully nice, Daddy. Maybe it's only the father who's not nice. Anyway Pete said, 'Come on and fish with me this afternoon,' so I did. He said his father stocks the river farther up."

"I don't—Frankly, Maggie, I *don't* want you associating with the Frosbys!"

"There's only the two." Maggie was puzzled. "I barely met his father. They've got quite a nice house, Daddy."

"I've had unpleasant dealings with old Frosby, I told you, Maggie. It just isn't fitting if you get chummy with the son. Do me this one favor this summer, Maggie doll." That was his name for her in the moments he wanted to feel close to her, wanted her to feel close to him.

The very next day, Maggie was gone from the house for nearly three hours, and Skip noticed it. She had said she wanted to go to the village to buy sneakers, and she was wearing the sneakers when she came home, but Skip wondered why it had taken her three hours to make a five-mile trip. With enormous effort, Skip refrained from asking a question. Then Saturday morning, Maggie said there was a dance in Keensport, and she was going.

"And I have a suspicion who you're going with," Skip said, his heart beginning to thump with adrenaline.

"I'm going alone, I swear it, Daddy. Girls don't have to be escorted any more. I could go in blue jeans, but I'm not. I've got some white slacks."

Skipperton realized that he could hardly forbid her to go to a dance. But he damn well knew the Frosby boy would be there, and would probably meet Maggie at the entrance. "I'll be glad when you go back to Switzerland."

Skip knew what was going to happen. He could see it a mile away. His daughter was "infatuated," and he could only hope that she got over it, that nothing happened before she had to go back to school (another whole month), because he didn't want to keep her a prisoner in the house. He didn't want to look absurd in his own eyes, even in simpleminded Andy's eyes, by laying down the law to her.

Maggie got home evidently very late that night, and so quietly Skip hadn't wakened, though he had stayed up till 2 A.M. and meant to listen for her. At breakfast, Maggie looked fresh and radiant, rather to Skip's surprise.

"I suppose the Frosby boy was at the dance last night?"

Maggie, diving into bacon and eggs, said, "I don't know what you've got against him, Daddy—just because his father didn't want to sell land that's been in their family for ages!"

"I don't want you to fall in love with a country bumpkin! I've sent you to a good school. You've got background—or at least I intend to give you some!"

"Did you know Pete had three years at Harvard—and he's taking a correspondence course in electronic engineering?"

"Oh! I suppose he's learning computer programming? Easier than shorthand!"

Maggie stood up. "I'll be eighteen in another month, Daddy. I don't want to be told whom I can see and can't see."

Skip got up too and roared at her. *"They're not my kind of people or yours!"*

Maggie left the room.

In the next days, Skipperton fumed and went through two or three pipe stems. Andy noticed his unease, Skipperton knew, but Andy made no comment. Andy spent his nonworking hours alone, watching drivel on his television. Skip was rehearsing a speech to Maggie as he paced his land, glancing at the sow and piglets, at Andy's neat kitchen-garden, not seeing anything. Skip was groping for a lever, the kind of weapon he had always been able to find in business affairs that would force things his way. He couldn't send Maggie back to Switzerland, even though her school stayed open in summer for girls whose home was too far away to go back to. If he threatened not to send her back to school, he was afraid Maggie wouldn't mind. Skipperton maintained an apartment in New York, and had two servants who slept in, but he knew Maggie wouldn't agree to go there, and Skip didn't want to go to New York either. He was too interested in the immediate scene in which he sensed a battle coming.

Skipperton had arrived at nothing by the following Saturday, a week after the Keensport dance, and he was exhausted. That Saturday evening, Maggie said she was going to a party at the house of someone called Wilmers, whom she had met at the dance. Skip asked her for the address, and Maggie scribbled it on the hall telephone pad. Skip had reason to have asked for it, because by Sunday morning Maggie hadn't come home. Skip was up at seven, nervous as a cat in a rage still at 9 A.M., which he thought a polite enough hour to telephone on Sunday morning, though it had cost him much to wait that long.

An adolescent boy's voice said that Maggie had been there, yes, but she had left pretty early.

"Was she alone?"

"No, she was with Pete Frosby."

"That's all I wanted to know," said Skip, feeling the blood rush to his face as if he were hemorrhaging. "*Oh!* Wait! Do you know where they went?"

"Sure don't."

"My daughter went in her car?"

"No, Pete's. Maggie's car's still here."

Skip thanked the boy and put the phone down shakily, but he was shaking only from energy that was surging through every nerve and muscle. He picked up the telephone and dialed the Frosby home.

Old Frosby answered.

Skipperton identified himself, and asked if his daughter was possibly there?

"No, she's not, Mr. Skipperton."

"Is your son there? I'd like—"

"No, he doesn't happen to be in just now."

"What do you mean? He was there and went out?"

"Mr. Skipperton, my son has his own ways, his own room, his own key—his own life. I'm not about—"

Skipperton put the telephone down suddenly. He had a bad nosebleed, and it was dripping onto the table edge. He ran to get a wet towel.

Maggie was not home by Sunday evening or Monday morning, and Skipperton was reluctant to notify the police, appalled by the thought that her name might be linked with the Frosbys', if the police found her with the son somewhere. Tuesday morning, Skip was enlightened. He had a letter from Maggie, written from Boston. It said that she and Pete had run away to be married, and to avoid "unpleasant scenes."

> . . . Though you may think this is sudden, we do love each other and are sure of it. I did not really want to go back to school, Daddy. I will be in touch in about a week. Please don't try to find me. I have seen Mommie, but we are not staying with her. I was sorry to leave my nice new car, but the car is all right.
>
> Love always,
> Maggie

For two days Skipperton didn't go out of the house, and hardly ate. He felt three-quarters dead. Andy was very worried about him, and finally persuaded Skipperton to ride to the village with him, because they needed to buy a few things. Skipperton went, sitting like an upright corpse in the passenger seat.

While Andy went to the drugstore and the butcher's, Skipperton sat in the car, his eyes glazed with his own thoughts. Then an approaching figure on the sidewalk made Skipperton's eyes focus. Old Frosby! Frosby walked with a springy tread for his age, Skip thought. He wore a new tweed suit, black felt hat, and he had a cigar in his hand. Skipperton hoped Frosby wouldn't see him in the car, but Frosby did.

Frosby didn't pause in his stride, just smiled his obnoxious, thin-lipped little smile and nodded briefly, as if to say—

Well, Skip *knew* what Frosby might have wanted to say, what he had said with that filthy smile. Skip's blood seethed, and Skip began to feel like his old self again. He was standing on the sidewalk, hands in his pockets and feet apart, when Andy reappeared.

"What's for dinner tonight, Andy? I've got an appetite!"

That evening, Skipperton persuaded Andy to take not only Saturday night off, but to stay overnight somewhere, if he wished. "Give you a couple of hundred bucks for a little spree, boy. You've earned it." Skip forced three hundred dollar bills into Andy's hand. "Take off Monday too, if you feel like it. I'll manage."

Andy left Saturday evening in the pick-up for Bangor.

Skip then telephoned old Frosby. Frosby answered, and Skipperton said, "Mr. Frosby, it's time we made a truce, under the circumstances. Don't you think so?"

Frosby sounded surprised, but he agreed to come Sunday morning around eleven for a talk. Frosby arrived in the same Cadillac, alone.

And Skipperton wasted no time. He let Frosby knock, opened the door for him, and as soon as Frosby was inside, Skip came down on his head with a rifle butt. He dragged Frosby to the hall to make sure the job was finished: the hall was uncarpeted, and Skip wanted no blood on the rugs. Vengeance was sweet to Skip, and he almost smiled. He removed Frosby's clothes, and wrapped his body in three or four burlap sacks which he had ready. Then he burnt Frosby's clothing in the fireplace, where he had a small fire already crackling. Frosby's wristwatch and wallet and two rings Skip put aside in a drawer to deal with later.

He had decided that broad daylight was the best time to carry out his idea, better than night when an oddly playing flashlight that he would have had to use might have caught someone's eye. So Skip put one arm around Frosby's body and dragged him up the field towards his scarecrow. It was a haul of more than half a mile. Skip had some rope and a knife in his back pockets. He cut down the old scarecrow, cut the strings that held the clothing to the cross, dressed Frosby in the old trousers and jacket, tied a burlap bag around his head and face, and jammed the hat on him. The hat wouldn't stay without being tied on, so Skip did this after punching holes in the brim of the hat with his knife point. Then Skip picked up his burlap bags and made his way back towards his house down the slope with many a backward look to admire his work, and many a smile. The scarecrow looked almost the same as before. He had solved a problem a lot of people thought difficult: what to do with the body. Furthermore, he could enjoy looking at it through his binoculars from his upstairs window.

Skip burnt the burlap bags in his fireplace, made sure that even the shoe soles had burnt to soft ash. When the ashes were cooler, he'd look for buttons and the belt buckle and remove them. He took a fork, went out beyond the pig run and buried the wallet (whose papers he had already burnt), the wristwatch and the rings about three feet deep. It was in a patch of stringy grass, unused for anything except the goats, not a place in which anyone would ever likely do any gardening.

Then Skip washed his face and hands, ate a thick slice of roast beef, and put his mind to the car. It was by now half past twelve. Skip didn't know if Frosby had a servant, someone expecting him for lunch or not, but it was safer to assume he had. Skip's aversion to Frosby had kept him from asking Maggie any questions about his household. Skip got into Frosby's car, now with a kitchen towel in his back pocket to wipe off fingerprints, and drove to some woods he knew from having driven past them many times. An unpaved lane went off the main road into woods, and into this Skip turned. Thank God, nobody in sight, not a woodsman, not a picnicker. Skip stopped the car and got out, wiped the steering wheel, even the keys, the door, then walked back towards the road.

He was more than an hour getting home. He had found a long stick, the kind called a stave by the wayfarers of old, Skip thought, and he trudged along with the air of a nature-lover, a bird-watcher, for the benefit of the people in the few cars that passed him. He didn't glance at any of the cars. It was still Sunday dinnertime.

The local police telephoned that evening around seven, and asked if they could come by. Skipperton said of course.

He had removed the buttons and buckle from the fireplace ashes. A woman had telephoned around 1:30, saying she was calling from the Frosby residence (Skip assumed she was a servant) to ask if Mr. Frosby was there. Skipperton told her that Mr. Frosby had left his house a little after noon.

"Mr. Frosby intended to go straight home, do you think?" the plump policeman asked Skipperton. The policeman had some rank like sergeant, Skipperton supposed, and he was accompanied by a younger policeman.

"He didn't say anything about where he was going," Skipperton replied. "And I didn't notice which way his car went."

The policeman nodded, and Skip could see he was on the brink of saying something like, "I understand from Mr. Frosby's housekeeper that you and he weren't on the best of terms," but the cop didn't say anything, just looked around Skip's living room, glanced around his front and back yards in a puzzled way, then both policemen took their leave.

Skip was awakened around midnight by the ring of the telephone at his bedside. It was Maggie calling from Boston. She and Pete had heard about the disappearance of Pete's father.

"Daddy, they said he'd just been to see you this morning. What happened?"

"Nothing happened. I invited him for a friendly talk—and it was friendly. After all we're fathers-in-law now . . . Honey, how do I know where he went?"

Skipperton found it surprisingly easy to lie about Frosby. In a primitive way his emotions had judged, weighed the situation, and told Skip that he was right, that he had exacted a just revenge. Old Frosby might have exerted some control over his son, and he hadn't. It had cost Skip his daughter—because that was the way Skip saw it, Maggie was lost to him. He saw her as a provincial-to-be, mother-to-be of children whose narrow-mindedness, inherited from the Frosby clan, would surely out.

Andy arrived next morning, Monday. He had already heard the story in the village, and also the police had found Mr. Frosby's car not far away in the woods, Andy said. Skip feigned mild surprise on hearing of the car. Andy didn't ask any questions. And suppose he discovered the scarecrow? Skip thought a little money would keep Andy quiet. The corn was all picked up there, only a few inferior ears remained, destined for the pigs. Skipperton picked them himself Monday afternoon, while Andy tended the pigs and goats.

Skipperton's pleasure now was to survey the cornfield from his upstairs bedroom with his 10X binoculars. He loved to see the wind tossing the cornstalk tops around old Frosby's corpse, loved to think of him, shrinking, drying up like a mummy in the wind. Twisting slowly, slowly in the wind, as a Nixon aide used to put it about the president's enemies. Frosby wasn't twisting, but he was hanging, in plain view. No buzzards came. Skip had been a little afraid of buzzards. The only thing that bothered him, once, was seeing one afternoon some schoolboys walking along a road far to the right (under which road the Coldstream flowed), and pointing to the scarecrow. Bracing himself against the window jamb, arms held tightly at his sides so the binoculars would be as steady as possible, Skip saw a couple of the small boys laughing. And had one held his nose? Surely not! They were nearly a mile away from the scarecrow! Still, they had paused, one boy stamped his foot, another shook his head and laughed.

How Skip wished he could hear what they were saying! Ten days had passed since Frosby's death. Rumors were rife, that old Frosby had been murdered for his money by someone he'd picked up to give a lift to, that he had been kidnapped and that a ransom note might still arrive. But suppose one of the schoolkids said to his father—or anyone—that maybe the dead body of Frosby was inside the scarecrow? This was just the kind of thing Skip might have thought of when he had been a small boy. Skip was consequently more afraid of the schoolkids than of the police.

And the police did come back, with a plainclothes detective. They looked over Skipperton's house and land—maybe looking for a recently dug patch, Skip thought. If so, they found none. They looked at Skip's two rifles and took their caliber and serial number.

"Just routine, Mr. Skipperton," said the detective.

"I understand," said Skip.

That same evening Maggie telephoned and said she was at the Frosby house, and could she come over to see him?

"Why not? This is your house!" Skip replied.

"I never know what kind of mood you'll be in—or temper," Maggie said when she arrived.

"I'm in a pretty *good* mood, I think," Skipperton said. "And I hope you're happy, Maggie—since what's done is done."

Maggie was in her blue dungarees, sneakers, a familiar sweater. It was hard for Skip to realize that she was married. She sat with hands folded, looking down at the floor. Then she raised her eyes to him and said:

"Pete's very upset. We never would have stayed a week in Boston unless he'd been sure the police were doing all they could here. Was Mr. Frosby—depressed? Pete didn't think so."

Skip laughed. "No! Best of spirits. Pleased with the marriage and all that." Skip waited, but Maggie was silent. "You're going to live at the Frosby place?"

"Yes." Maggie stood up. "I'd like to collect a few things, Daddy. I brought a suitcase."

His daughter's coolness, her sadness, pained Skip. She had said something about visiting him often, not about his coming to see them—not that Skip would have gone.

"I know what's in that scarecrow," said Andy one day, and Skip turned, binoculars in hand, to see Andy standing in the doorway of his bedroom.

"Do you?—And what're you going to do about it?" Skip asked, braced for anything. He had squared his shoulders.

"Nothin'. Nothin'," Andy replied with a smile.

Skip didn't know how to take that. "I suppose you'd like some money, Andy? A little present—for keeping quiet?"

"No, sir," Andy said quietly, shaking his head. His wind-wrinkled face bore a faint smile. "I ain't that kind."

What was Skip to make of it? He was used to men who liked money, more and more of it. Andy was different, that was true. Well, so much the better, if he didn't want money, Skip thought. It was cheaper. He also felt he could trust Andy. It was strange.

The leaves began to fall in earnest. Halloween was coming, and

Andy removed the driveway gate in advance, just lifted it off its hinges, telling Skip that the kids would steal it if they didn't. Andy knew the district. The kids didn't do much harm, but it was trick or treat at every house. Skip and Andy made sure they had lots of nickels and quarters on hand, corn candy, licorice sticks, even a couple of pumpkins in the windows, faces cut in them by Andy, to show any comers that they were in the right spirit. Then on Halloween night, nobody knocked on Skip's door. There was a party at Coldstream, at the Frosbys', Skip knew because the wind was blowing his way and he could hear the music. He thought of his daughter dancing, having a good time. Maybe people were wearing masks, crazy costumes. There'd be pumpkin pie with whipped cream, guessing games, maybe a treasure hunt. Skip was lonely, for the first time in his life. *Lonely.* He badly wanted a scotch, but decided to keep his oath to himself, and having decided this, asked himself why? He put his hands flat down on his dresser top and gazed at his own face in the mirror. He saw creases running from the flanges of his nose down beside his mouth, wrinkles under his eyes. He tried to smile, and the smile looked phony. He turned away from the mirror.

At that instant, a spot of light caught his eyes. It was out the window, in the upward sloping field. A procession—so it seemed, maybe eight or ten figures—was walking up his field with flashlights or torches or both. Skip opened the window slightly. He was rigid with rage, and fear. They were on his land! They had no right! And they were kids, he realized. Even in the darkness, he could see by the procession's own torches that the figures were a lot shorter than adults' figures would be.

Skip whirled around, about to shout for Andy, and at once decided that he had better not. He ran downstairs and grabbed his own powerful flashlight. He didn't bother grabbing his jacket from a hook, though the night was crisp.

"*Hey!*" Skip yelled, when he had run several yards into the field. "Get off my property! What're you *doing* walking up there!"

The kids were singing some crazy, high-pitched song, nobody singing on key. It was just a wild treble chant. Skip recognized the word "scarecrow."

"*We're going to burn the scarecrow . . .*" something like that.

"Hey, there! Off my land!" Skip fell, banged a knee, and

scrambled up again. The kids had heard him, Skip was pretty sure, but they weren't stopping. Never before had anyone disobeyed Skip—except of course Maggie. *"Off my land!"*

The kids moved on like a black caterpillar with an orange headlight and a couple of other lights in its body. Certainly the last couple of kids had heard Skip, because he had seen them turn, then run to catch up with the others. Skip stopped running. The caterpillar was closer to the scarecrow than he was, and he was not going to be able to get there first.

Even as he thought this, a whoop went up. A scream! Another scream of mingled terror and delight shattered their chant. Hysteria broke out. What surely was a little girl's throat gave a cry as shrill as a dog whistle. Their hands must have touched the corpse, maybe touched bone, Skip thought.

Skip made his way back towards his own house, his flashlight pointed at the ground. It was worse than the police, somehow. Every kid was going to tell his parents what he had found. Skip knew he had come to the end. He had seen businessmen, seen a lot of men come to the end. He had known men who had jumped out of windows, who had taken overdoses.

Skip went at once to his rifle. It was in the living room downstairs. He put the muzzle in his mouth and pulled the trigger.

When the kids streaked down the field, heading for the road a few seconds later, Skip was dead. The kids had heard the shot, and thought someone was trying to shoot at them.

Andy heard the shot. He had also seen the procession marching up the field and heard Skipperton shouting. He understood what had happened. He turned his television set off, and made his way rather slowly towards the main house. He would have to call the police. That was the right thing to do. Andy made up his mind to say to the police that he didn't know a thing about the corpse in the scarecrow's clothes. He had been away some of that weekend after all.

By the Dawn's Early Light
(1994)
Lawrence Block

All this happened a long time ago.

Abe Beame was living in Gracie Mansion, though even he seemed to have trouble believing he was really the mayor of the city of New York. Ali was in his prime, and the Knicks still had a year or so left in Bradley and DeBusschere. I was still drinking in those days, of course, and at the time it seemed to be doing more for me than it was doing to me.

I had already left my wife and kids, my home in Syosset and the NYPD. I was living in the hotel on West Fifty-seventh Street where I still live, and I was doing most of my drinking around the corner in Jimmy Armstrong's saloon. Billie was the nighttime bartender. A Filipino youth named Dennis was behind the stick most days.

And Tommy Tillary was one of the regulars.

He was big, probably 6'2", full in the chest, big in the belly, too. He rarely showed up in a suit but always wore a jacket and tie, usually a navy or burgundy blazer with gray-flannel slacks or white duck pants in warmer weather. He had a loud voice that boomed from his barrel chest and a big, clean-shaven face that was innocent around the pouting mouth and knowing around the eyes. He was somewhere in his late forties and he drank a lot of top-shelf scotch. Chivas, as I remember it, but it could have been Johnnie Black. Whatever it was, his face was beginning to show it, with patches of permanent flush at the cheekbones and a tracery of broken capillaries across the bridge of the nose.

We were saloon friends. We didn't speak every time we ran into each other, but at the least we always acknowledged each other with a nod or a wave. He told a lot of dialect jokes and told them reasonably well, and I laughed at my share of them. Sometimes I was in a mood to reminisce about my days on the force, and when my stories were funny, his laugh was as loud as anyone's.

Sometimes he showed up alone, sometimes with male friends. About a third of the time, he was in the company of a short and curvy blonde named Carolyn. "Carolyn from the Caro-line" was the way he occasionally introduced her, and she did have a faint Southern accent that became more pronounced as the drink got to her.

Then, one morning, I picked up the *Daily News* and read that burglars had broken into a house on Colonial Road, in the Bay Ridge section of Brooklyn. They had stabbed to death the only occupant present, one Margaret Tillary. Her husband, Thomas J. Tillary, a salesman, was not at home at the time.

I hadn't known Tommy was a salesman or that he'd had a wife. He did wear a wide yellow-gold band on the appropriate finger, and it was clear that he wasn't married to Carolyn from the Caroline, and it now looked as though he was a widower. I felt vaguely sorry for him, vaguely sorry for the wife I'd never even known of, but that was the extent of it. I drank enough back then to avoid feeling any emotion very strongly.

And then, two or three nights later, I walked into Armstrong's and there was Carolyn. She didn't appear to be waiting for him or anyone else, nor did she look as though she'd just breezed in a few minutes ago. She had a stool by herself at the bar and she was drinking something dark from a lowball glass.

I took a seat a few stools down from her. I ordered two double shots of bourbon, drank one and poured the other into the black coffee Billie brought me. I was sipping the coffee when a voice with a Piedmont softness said, "I forget your name."

I looked up.

"I believe we were introduced," she said, "but I don't recall your name."

"It's Matt," I said, "and you're right, Tommy introduced us. You're Carolyn."

"Carolyn Cheatham. Have you seen him?"

"Tommy? Not since it happened."

"Neither have I. Were you-all at the funeral?"

"No. When was it?"

"This afternoon. Neither was I. There. Whyn't you come sit next to me so's I don't have to shout. Please?"

She was drinking a sweet almond liqueur that she took on the rocks. It tastes like dessert, but it's as strong as whiskey.

"He told me not to come," she said. "To the funeral. He said it was a matter of respect for the dead." She picked up her glass and stared into it. I've never known what people hope to see there, though it's a gesture I've performed often enough myself.

"Respect," she said. "What's he care about respect? I would have just been part of the office crowd; we both work at Tannahill; far as anyone there knows, we're just friends. And all we ever were is friends, you know."

"Whatever you say."

"Oh, *shit*," she said. "I don't mean I wasn't fucking him, for the Lord's sake. I mean it was just laughs and good times. He was married and he went home to Mama every night and that was jes' fine, because who in her right mind'd want Tommy Tillary around by the dawn's early light? Christ in the foothills, did I spill this or drink it?"

We agreed she was drinking them a little too fast. It was this fancy New York sweet-drink shit, she maintained, not like the bourbon she'd grown up on. You knew where you stood with bourbon.

I told her I was a bourbon drinker myself, and it pleased her to learn this. Alliances have been forged on thinner bonds than that, and ours served to propel us out of Armstrong's, with a stop down the block for a fifth of Marker's Mark—her choice—and a four-block walk to her apartment. There were exposed brick walls, I remember, and candles stuck in straw-wrapped bottles, and several travel posters from Sabena, the Belgian airline.

We did what grown-ups do when they find themselves alone together. We drank our fair share of the Maker's Mark and went to bed. She made a lot of enthusiastic noises and more than a few skillful moves, and afterward she cried some.

A little later, she dropped off to sleep. I was tired myself, but I put on my clothes and sent myself home. Because who in her right mind'd want Matt Scudder around by the dawn's early light?

Over the next couple of days, I wondered every time I entered Armstrong's if I'd run into her, and each time I was more relieved than disappointed when I didn't. I didn't encounter Tommy, either, and that, too, was a relief and in no sense disappointing.

Then, one morning, I picked up the *News* and read that they'd arrested a pair of young Hispanics from Sunset Park for the Tillary burglary and homicide. The paper ran the usual photo—two skinny kids, their hair unruly, one of them trying to hide his face from the camera, the other smirking defiantly, and each of them handcuffed to a broad-shouldered, grim-faced Irishman in a suit. You didn't need the careful caption to tell the good guys from the bad guys.

Sometime in the middle of the afternoon, I went over to Armstrong's for a hamburger and drank a beer with it. The phone behind the bar rang and Dennis put down the glass he was wiping and answered it. "He was here a minute ago," he said. "I'll see if he stepped out." He covered the mouthpiece with his hand and looked quizzically at me. "Are you still here?" he asked. "Or did you slip away while my attention was diverted?"

"Who wants to know?"

"Tommy Tillary."

You never know what a woman will decide to tell a man or how a man will react to it. I didn't want to find out, but I was better off learning over the phone than face-to-face. I nodded and took the phone from Dennis.

I said, "Matt Scudder, Tommy. I was sorry to hear about your wife."

"Thanks, Matt. Jesus, it feels like it happened a year ago. It was what, a week?"

"At least they got the bastards."

There was a pause. Then he said, "Jesus. You haven't seen a paper, huh?"

"That's where I read about it. Two Spanish kids."

"You didn't happen to see this afternoon's *Post*."

"No. Why, what happened? They turn out to be clean?"

"The two spics. Clean? Shit, they're about as clean as the men's room in the Times Square subway station. The cops hit their place and found stuff from my house everywhere they looked. Jewelry they had descriptions of, a stereo that I gave them the serial number, everything. Monogrammed shit. I mean, that's how clean they were, for Christ's sake."

"So?"

"They admitted the burglary but not the murder."

"That's common, Tommy."

"Lemme finish, huh? They admitted the burglary, but according to them it was a put-up job. According to them, I hired them to hit my place. They could keep whatever they got and I'd have everything out and arranged for them, and in return I got to clean up on the insurance by overreporting the loss."

"What did the loss amount to?"

"Shit, *I* don't know. There were twice as many things turned up in their apartment as I ever listed when I made out a report. There's things I missed a few days after I filed the report and others I didn't know were gone until the cops found them. You don't notice everything right away, at least I didn't, and on top of it, how could I think straight with Peg dead? You know?"

"It hardly sounds like an insurance setup."

"No, of course it wasn't. How the hell could it be? All I had was a standard homeowner's policy. It covered maybe a third of what I lost. According to them, the place was empty when they hit it. Peg was out."

"And?"

"And I set them up. They hit the place, they carted everything away, and I came home with Peg and stabbed her six, eight times, whatever it was, and left her there so it'd look like it happened in a burglary."

"How could the burglars testify that you stabbed your wife?"

"They couldn't. All they said was they didn't and she wasn't home when they were there, and that I hired them to do the burglary. The cops pieced the rest of it together."

"What did they do, take you downtown?"

"No. They came over to the house, it was early, I don't know what time. It was the first I knew that the spics were arrested, let alone that they were trying to do a job on me. They just wanted to talk, the cops, and at first I talked to them, and then I started to get the drift of what they were trying to put on to me. So I said I wasn't saying anything more without my lawyer present, and I called him, and he left half his breakfast on the table and came over in a hurry, and he wouldn't let me say a word."

"And the cops didn't take you in or book you?"

"No."

"Did they buy your story?"

"No way. I didn't really tell 'em a story, because Kaplan wouldn't let me say anything. They didn't drag me in, because they don't have a case yet, but Kaplan says they're gonna be building one if they can. They told me not to leave town. You believe it? My wife's dead, the *Post* headline says, 'Quiz Husband in Burglary Murder,' and what the hell do they think I'm gonna do? Am I going fishing for fucking trout in Montana? 'Don't leave town.' You see this shit on television, you think nobody in real life talks this way. Maybe television's where they get it from."

I waited for him to tell me what he wanted from me. I didn't have long to wait.

"Why I called," he said, "is Kaplan wants to hire a detective. He figured maybe these guys talked around the neighborhood, maybe they bragged to their friends, maybe there's a way to prove they did the killing. He says the cops won't concentrate on that end if they're too busy nailing the lid shut on me."

I explained that I didn't have any official standing, that I had no license and filed no reports.

"That's okay," he insisted. "I told Kaplan what I want is somebody I can trust, somebody who'll do the job for me. I don't think they're gonna have any kind of a case at all, Matt, but the longer this drags on, the worse it is for me. I want it cleared up, I want it in the papers that these Spanish assholes did it all and I had nothing to do with anything. You name a fair fee and I'll pay it, me to you, and it can be cash in your hand if you don't like checks. What do you say?"

He wanted somebody he could trust. Had Carolyn from the Caroline told him how trustworthy I was?

What did I say? I said yes.

• • •

I met Tommy Tillary and his lawyer in Drew Kaplan's office on

Court Street, a few blocks from Brooklyn's Borough Hall. There was a Syrian restaurant next door and, at the corner, a grocery store specializing in Middle Eastern imports stood next to an antique shop overflowing with stripped-oak furniture and brass lamps and bedsteads. Kaplan's office ran to wood paneling and leather chairs and oak file cabinets. His name and the names of two partners were painted on the frosted-glass door in old-fashioned gold-and-black lettering. Kaplan himself looked conservatively up to date, with a three-piece striped suit that was better cut than mine. Tommy wore his burgundy blazer and gray-flannel trousers and loafers. Strain showed at the corners of his blue eyes and around his mouth. His complexion was off, too.

"All we want you to do," Kaplan said, "is find a key in one of their pants pockets, Herrera's or Cruz's, and trace it to a locker in Penn Station, and in the locker there's a footlong knife with their prints and her blood on it."

"Is that what it's going to take?"

He smiled. "It wouldn't hurt. No, actually, we're not in such bad shape. They got some shaky testimony from a pair of Latins who've been in and out of trouble since they got weaned to Tropicana. They got what looks to them like a good motive on Tommy's part."

"Which is?"

I was looking at Tommy when I asked. His eyes slipped away from mine. Kaplan said, "A marital triangle, a case of the shorts and a strong money motive. Margaret Tillary inherited a little over a quarter of a million dollars six or eight months ago. An aunt left a million two and it got cut up four ways. What they don't bother to notice is he loved his wife, and how many husbands cheat? What is it they say—ninety percent cheat and ten percent lie?"

"That's good odds."

"One of the killers, Angel Herrera, did some odd jobs at the Tillary house last March or April. Spring cleaning; he hauled stuff out of the basement and attic, a little donkeywork. According to Herrera, that's how Tommy knew him to contact him about the burglary. According to common sense, that's how Herrera and his buddy Cruz knew the house and what was in it and how to gain access."

"The case against Tommy sounds pretty thin."

"It is," Kaplan said. "The thing is, you go to court with something like this and you lose even if you win. For the rest of your life, everybody remembers you stood trial for murdering your wife, never mind that you won an acquittal.

"Besides," he said, "you never know which way a jury's going to jump. Tommy's alibi is he was with another lady at the time of the burglary. The woman's a colleague; they could see it as completely aboveboard, but who says they're going to? What they sometimes do, they decide they don't believe the alibi because it's his girlfriend lying for him, and at the same time they label him a scumbag for screwing around while his wife's getting killed."

"You keep it up," Tommy said, "I'll find myself guilty, the way you make it sound."

"Plus he's hard to get a sympathetic jury for. He's a big handsome guy, a sharp dresser, and you'd love him in a gin joint, but how much do you love him in a courtroom? He's a securities salesman, he's beautiful on the phone, and that means every clown who ever lost a hundred dollars on a stock tip or bought magazines over the phone is going to walk into the courtroom with a hard-on for him. I'm telling you, I want to stay the hell *out* of court. I'll *win* in court, I know that, or the worst that'll happen is I'll win on appeal, but who needs it? This is a case that shouldn't be in the first place, and I'd love to clear it up before they even go so far as presenting a bill to the grand jury."

"So from me you want—"

"Whatever you can find, Matt. Whatever discredits Cruz and Herrera. I don't know what's there to be found, but you were a cop and now you're private, and you can get down in the streets and nose around."

I nodded. I could do that. "One thing," I said. "Wouldn't you be better off with a Spanish-speaking detective? I know enough to buy a beer in a bodega, but I'm a long way from fluent."

Kaplan shook his head. "A personal relationship's worth more than a dime's worth of '*Me llamo Matteo y ¿como está usted?*'"

"That's the truth," Tommy Tillary said. "Matt, I know I can count on you."

I wanted to tell him all he could count on was his fingers. I didn't really see what I could expect to uncover that wouldn't turn up in a regular police investigation. But I'd spent enough time carrying a shield to know not to push away money when somebody wants to give it to you. I felt comfortable taking a fee. The man was inheriting a quarter of a million, plus whatever insurance his wife had carried. If he was willing to spread some of it around, I was willing to take it.

So I went to Sunset Park and spent some time in the streets and some more time in the bars. Sunset Park is in Brooklyn, of course, on the borough's western edge, above Bay Ridge and south and west of Green-Wood Cemetery. These days, there's a lot of brownstoning going on there, with young urban professionals renovating the old houses and gentrifying the neighborhood. Back then, the upwardly mobile young had not yet discovered Sunset Park and the area was a mix of Latins and Scandinavians, most of the former Puerto Ricans, most of the latter Norwegians. The balance was gradually shifting from Europe to the islands, from light to dark, but this was a process that had been going on for ages and there was nothing hurried about it.

I talked to Herrera's landlord and Cruz's former employer and one of his recent girlfriends. I drank beer in bars and the back rooms of bodegas. I went to the local station house, I read the sheets on both of the burglars and drank coffee with the cops and picked up some of the stuff that doesn't get on the yellow sheets.

I found out that Miguelito Cruz had once killed a man in a tavern brawl over a woman. There were no charges pressed; a dozen witnesses reported that the dead man had gone after Cruz first with a broken bottle. Cruz had most likely been carrying the knife, but several witnesses insisted it had been tossed to him by an anonymous benefactor, and there hadn't been enough evidence to make a case of weapons possession, let alone homicide.

I learned that Herrera had three children living with their mother in Puerto Rico. He was divorced but wouldn't marry his current girlfriend because he regarded himself as still married to his ex-wife in the eyes of God. He sent money to his children when he had any to send.

I learned other things. They didn't seem terribly consequential then and they've faded from memory altogether by now, but I wrote them down in my pocket notebook as I learned them, and every day or so I duly reported my findings to Drew Kaplan. He always seemed pleased with what I told him.

I invariably managed to stop at Armstrong's before I called it a night. One night she was there, Carolyn Cheatham, drinking bourbon this time, her face frozen with stubborn old pain. It took her a blink or two to recognize me. Then tears started to form in the corners of her eyes, and she used the back of one hand to wipe them away.

I didn't approach her until she beckoned. She patted the stool beside hers and I eased myself onto it. I had coffee with bourbon in it and bought a refill for her. She was pretty drunk already, but that's never been enough reason to turn down a drink.

She talked about Tommy. He was being nice to her, she said. Calling up, sending flowers. But he wouldn't see her, because it wouldn't look right, not for a new widower, not for a man who'd been publicly accused of murder.

"He sends flowers with no card enclosed," she said. "He calls me from pay phones. The son of a bitch."

Billie called me aside. "I didn't want to put her out," he said, "a nice woman like that, shit-faced as she is. But I thought I was gonna have to. You'll see she gets home?"

I said I would.

I got her out of there and a cab came along and saved us the walk. At her place, I took the keys from her and unlocked the door. She half sat, half sprawled on the couch. I had to use the bathroom, and when I came back, her eyes were closed and she was snoring lightly.

I got her coat and shoes off, put her to bed, loosened her clothing, and covered her with a blanket. I was tired from all that and sat down on the couch for a minute, and I almost dozed off myself. Then I snapped awake and let myself out.

I went back to Sunset Park the next day. I learned that Cruz had been in trouble as a youth. With a gang of neighborhood kids, he used to go into the city and cruise Greenwich Village, looking for homosexuals to beat up. He'd had a dread of homosexuality, probably flowing as it generally does out of a fear of a part of himself, and he stifled that dread by fag-bashing.

"He still doan' like them," a woman told me. She had glossy black hair and opaque eyes, and she was letting me pay for her rum and orange juice. "He's pretty, you know, an' they come on to him, an' he doan' like it."

I called that item in, along with a few others equally earth-shaking. I bought myself a steak dinner at the Slate over on Tenth Avenue, then finished up at Armstrong's, not drinking very hard, just coasting along on bourbon and coffee.

Twice, the phone rang for me. Once, it was Tommy Tillary, telling me how much he appreciated what I was doing for him. It seemed to me that all I was doing was taking his money, but he had me believing that my loyalty and invaluable assistance were all he had to cling to.

The second call was from Carolyn. More praise. I was a gentleman, she assured me, and a hell of a fellow all around. And I should forget that she'd been bad-mouthing Tommy. Everything was going to be fine with them.

I took the next day off. I think I went to a movie, and it may have been *The Sting,* with Newman and Redford achieving vengeance through swindling.

The day after that, I did another tour of duty in Brooklyn. And the day after that, I picked up the *News* first thing in the morning. The headline was nonspecific, something like KILL SUSPECT HANGS SELF IN CELL, but I knew it was my case before I turned to the story on page three.

Miguelito Cruz had torn his clothing into strips, knotted the strips together, stood his iron bedstead on its side, climbed onto it, looped his homemade rope around an overhead pipe, and jumped off the up-ended bedstead and into the next world.

That evening's six o'clock TV news had the rest of the story. Informed of his friend's death, Angel Herrera had recanted his original story and admitted that he and Cruz had conceived and executed the Tillary burglary on their own. It had been Miguelito who had stabbed the Tillary woman when she walked in on them. He'd picked up a kitchen knife while Herrera watched in horror. Miguelito always had a short temper, Herrera said, but they were friends, even cousins, and they had hatched their story to protect Miguelito. But now that he was dead, Herrera could admit what had really happened.

I was in Armstrong's that night, which was not remarkable. I had it in mind to get drunk, though I could not have told you why, and that *was* remarkable, if not unheard of. I got drunk a lot those days, but I rarely set out with that intention. I just wanted to feel a little better, a little more mellow, and somewhere along the way I'd wind up waxed.

I wasn't drinking particularly hard or fast, but I was working at it, and then somewhere around ten or eleven the door opened and I knew who it was before I turned around. Tommy Tillary, well dressed and freshly barbered, making his first appearance in Jimmy's place since his wife was killed.

"Hey, look who's here!" he called out and grinned that big grin. People rushed over to shake his hand. Billie was behind the stick, and he'd no sooner set one up on the house for our hero than Tommy insisted on buying a round for the bar. It was an expensive gesture—there must have been thirty or forty people in there—but I don't think he cared if there were three hundred or four hundred.

I stayed where I was, letting the others mob him, but he worked his way over to me and got an arm around my shoulders. "This is the man," he announced. "Best fucking detective ever wore out a pair of shoes. This man's money," he told Billie, "is no good at all tonight. He can't buy a drink; he can't buy a cup of coffee; if you went and put in pay toilets since I was last here, he can't use his own dime."

"The john's still free," Billie said, "but don't give the boss any ideas."

"Oh, don't tell me he didn't already think of it," Tommy said. "Matt, my boy, I love you. I was in a tight spot, I didn't want to walk out of my house, and you came through for me."

What the hell had I done? I hadn't hanged Miguelito Cruz or coaxed a confession out of Angel Herrera. I hadn't even set eyes on either man. But he was buying the drinks, and I had a thirst, so who was I to argue?

I don't know how long we stayed there. Curiously, my drinking slowed down even as Tommy's picked up speed. Carolyn, I noticed, was not present, nor did her name find its way into the conversation. I wondered if she would walk in—it was, after all, her neighborhood bar, and she was apt to drop in on her own. I wondered what would happen if she did.

I guess there were a lot of things I wondered about, and perhaps that's what put the brakes on my own drinking. I didn't want any gaps in my memory, any gray patches in my awareness.

After a while, Tommy was hustling me out of Armstrong's. "This is celebration time," he told me. "We don't want to sit in one place till we grow roots. We want to bop a little."

He had a car, and I just went along with him without paying too much attention to exactly where we were. We went to a noisy Greek club on the East Side, I think, where the waiters looked like Mob hit men. We went to a couple of trendy singles joints. We wound up somewhere in the Village, in a dark, beery cave.

It was quiet there, and conversation was possible, and I found myself asking him what I'd done that was so praiseworthy. One man had killed himself and another had confessed, and where was my role in either incident?

"The stuff you came up with," he said.

"What stuff? I should have brought back fingernail parings, you could have had someone work voodoo on them."

"About Cruz and the fairies."

"He was up for murder. He didn't kill himself because he was afraid they'd get him for fag-bashing when he was a juvenile offender."

Tommy took a sip of scotch. He said, "Couple days ago, huge black guy comes up to Cruz in the chow line. 'Wait'll you get up to Green Haven,' he tells him. 'Every blood there's gonna have you for a girlfriend. Doctor gonna have to cut you a brand-new asshole, time you get outa there.'"

I didn't say anything.

"Kaplan," he said. "Drew talked to somebody who talked to somebody, and that did it. Cruz took a good look at the idea of playin' drop the soap for half the jigs in captivity, and the next thing you know, the murderous little bastard was dancing on air. And good riddance to him."

I couldn't seem to catch my breath. I worked on it while

Tommy went to the bar for another round. I hadn't touched the drink in front of me, but I let him buy for both of us.

When he got back, I said, "Herrera."

"Changed his story. Made a full confession."

"And pinned the killing on Cruz."

"Why not? Cruz wasn't around to complain. Who knows which one of 'em did it, and for that matter, who cares? The thing is, you gave us the lever."

"For Cruz," I said. "To get him to kill himself."

"And for Herrera. Those kids of his in Santurce. Drew spoke to Herrera's lawyer and Herrera's lawyer spoke to Herrera, and the message was, 'Look, you're going up for burglary whatever you do, and probably for murder; but if you tell the right story, you'll draw shorter time, and on top of that, that nice Mr. Tillary's gonna let bygones be bygones and every month there's a nice check for your wife and kiddies back home in Puerto Rico.'"

At the bar, a couple of old men were reliving the Louis-Schmeling fight, the second one, where Louis punished the German champion. One of the old fellows was throwing round-house punches in the air, demonstrating.

I said, "Who killed your wife?"

"One or the other of them. If I had to bet, I'd say Cruz. He had those little beady eyes; you looked at him up close and you got that he was a killer."

"When did you look at him up close?"

"When they came and cleaned the house, the basement, and the attic. Not when they came and cleaned me out; that was the second time."

He smiled, but I kept looking at him until the smile lost its certainty. "That was Herrera who helped around the house," I said. "You never met Cruz."

"Cruz came along, gave him a hand."

"You never mentioned that before."

"Oh, sure I did, Matt. What difference does it make, anyway?"

"Who killed her, Tommy?"

"Hey, let it alone, huh?"

"Answer the question."

"I already answered it."

"You killed her, didn't you?"

"What are you, crazy? Cruz killed her and Herrera swore to it, isn't that enough for you?"

"Tell me you didn't kill her."

"I didn't kill her."

"Tell me again."

"I didn't fucking kill her. What's the matter with you?"

"I don't believe you."

"Oh, Jesus," he said. He closed his eyes, put his head in his hands. He sighed and looked up and said, "You know, it's a funny thing with me. Over the telephone, I'm the best salesman you could ever imagine. I swear I could sell sand to the Arabs, I could sell ice in the winter, but face-to-face I'm no good at all. Why do you figure that is?"

"You tell me."

"I don't know. I used to think it was my face, the eyes and the mouth; I don't know. It's easy over the phone. I'm talking to a stranger, I don't know who he is or what he looks like, and he's not lookin' at me, and it's a cinch. Face-to-face, especially with someone I know, it's a different story." He looked at me. "If we were doin' this over the phone, you'd buy the whole thing."

"It's possible."

"It's fucking certain. Word for word, you'd buy the package. Suppose I was to tell you I did kill her, Matt. You couldn't prove anything. Look, the both of us walked in there, the place was a mess from the burglary, we got in an argument, tempers flared, something happened."

"You set up the burglary. You planned the whole thing, just the way Cruz and Herrera accused you of doing. And now you wriggled out of it."

"And you helped me—don't forget that part of it."

"I won't."

"And I wouldn't have gone away for it anyway, Matt. Not a chance. I'da beat it in court, only this way I don't have to go to court. Look, this is just the booze talkin', and we can forget it in the morning, right? I didn't kill her, you didn't accuse me, we're still buddies, everything's fine. Right?"

Blackouts are never there when you want them. I woke up next day and remembered all of it, and I found myself wishing I didn't. He'd killed his wife and he was getting away with it. And I'd helped him. I'd taken his money, and in return I'd shown him how to set one man up for suicide and pressure another into making a false confession.

And what was I going to do about it?

I couldn't think of a thing. Any story I carried to the police would be speedily denied by Tommy and his lawyer, and all I had was the thinnest of hearsay evidence, my own client's own words when he and I both had a skinful of booze. I went over it for a few days, looking for ways to shake something loose, and there was nothing. I could maybe interest a newspaper reporter, maybe get Tommy some press coverage that wouldn't make him happy, but why? And to what purpose?

It rankled. But I would just have a couple of drinks, and then it wouldn't rankle so much.

Angel Herrera pleaded guilty to burglary, and in return, the Brooklyn D.A.'s Office dropped all homicide charges. He went Upstate to serve five to ten.

And then I got a call in the middle of the night. I'd been sleeping a couple of hours, but the phone woke me and I groped for it. It took me a minute to recognize the voice on the other end.

It was Carolyn Cheatham.

"I had to call you," she said, "on account of you're a bourbon man and a gentleman. I owed it to you to call you."

"What's the matter?"

"He ditched me," she said, "and he got me fired out of Tannahill and Company so he won't have to look at me around the office. Once he didn't need me to back up his story, he let go of me, and do you know he did it over the phone?"

"Carolyn—"

"It's all in the note," she said. "I'm leaving a note."

"Look, don't do anything yet," I said. I was out of bed, fumbling for my clothes. "I'll be right over. We'll talk about it."

"You can't stop me, Matt."

"I won't try to stop you. We'll talk first, and then you can do anything you want."

The phone clicked in my ear.

I threw my clothes on, rushed over there, hoping it would be pills, something that took its time. I broke a small pane of glass in the downstairs door and let myself in, then used an old credit card to slip the bolt of her spring lock.

The room smelled of cordite. She was on the couch she'd passed out on the last time I saw her. The gun was still in her hand, limp at her side, and there was a black-rimmed hole in her temple.

There was a note, too. An empty bottle of Maker's Mark stood on the coffee table, an empty glass beside it. The booze showed in her handwriting and in the sullen phrasing of the suicide note.

I read the note. I stood there for a few minutes, not for very long, and then I got a dish towel from the Pullman kitchen and wiped the bottle and the glass. I took another matching glass, rinsed it out and wiped it, and put it in the drainboard of the sink.

I stuffed the note in my pocket. I took the gun from her fingers, checked routinely for a pulse, then wrapped a sofa pillow around the gun to muffle its report. I fired one round into her chest, another into her open mouth.

I dropped the gun into a pocket and left.

They found the gun in Tommy Tillary's house, stuffed between the cushions of the living-room sofa, clean of prints inside and out. Ballistics got a perfect match. I'd aimed for soft tissue with the round shot into her chest, because bullets can fragment on impact with bone. That was one reason I'd fired the extra shots. The other was to rule out the possibility of suicide.

After the story made the papers, I picked up the phone and called Drew Kaplan. "I don't understand it," I said. "He was free and clear; why the hell did he kill the girl?"

"Ask him yourself," Kaplan said. He did not sound happy. "You want my opinion, he's a lunatic. I honestly didn't think he was. I figured maybe he killed his wife, maybe he didn't. Not my job to try him. But I didn't figure he was a homicidal maniac."

"It's certain he killed the girl?"

"Not much question. The gun's pretty strong evidence. Talk about finding somebody with the smoking pistol in his hand, here it was in Tommy's couch. The idiot."

"Funny he kept it."

"Maybe he had other people he wanted to shoot. Go figure a crazy man. No, the gun's evidence, and there was a phone tip—a man called in the shooting, reported a man running out of there, and gave a description that fitted Tommy pretty well. Even had him wearing that red blazer he wears, tacky thing makes him look like an usher at the Paramount."

"It sounds tough to square."

"Well, somebody else'll have to try to do it," Kaplan said. "I told him I can't defend him this time. What it amounts to, I wash my hands of him."

I thought of that when I read that Angel Herrera got out just the other day. He served all ten years because he was as good at getting into trouble inside the walls as he'd been on the outside.

Somebody killed Tommy Tillary with a homemade knife after he'd served two years and three months of a manslaughter stretch. I wondered at the time if that was Herrera getting even, and I don't suppose I'll ever know. Maybe the checks stopped going to Santurce and Herrera took it the wrong way. Or maybe Tommy said the wrong thing to somebody else and said it face-to-face instead of over the phone.

I don't think I'd do it that way now. I don't drink anymore, and the impulse to play God seems to have evaporated with the booze.

But then, a lot of things have changed. Billie left Armstrong's not long after that, left New York, too; the last I heard he was off drink himself, living in Sausalito and making candles. I ran into Dennis the other day in a bookstore on lower Fifth Avenue full of odd volumes on yoga and spiritualism and holistic healing. And Armstrong's is scheduled to close the end of next month. The lease is up for renewal, and I suppose the next you know, the old joint'll be another Korean fruit market.

I still light a candle now and then for Carolyn Cheatham and Miguelito Cruz. Not often. Just every once in a while.